FORBIDDEN DESIRE

The space between them grew suddenly sparse, the air nearly too thick to breathe. A need welled up inside him, rising until it broke the threads of restraint he had held over himself. His hands moved to snake out around her body, and he felt the trembling consume her. But still he pulled her closer. A fraction of resistance wavered, then flickered away as she melted against him.

Soft defied hard.

Desire overruled caution . . .

Her skin and body were as perfect as he remembered. Forgetting why they shouldn't be attracted to one another, that they had no future together, he closed his mouth over hers, eliciting a reaction that told him that she, too, had forgotten those reasons . . .

Reckless Hearts

Bonnie K. Winn

J
JOVE BOOKS, NEW YORK

RECKLESS HEARTS

A Jove Book / published by arrangement with
the author

PRINTING HISTORY
Jove edition / May 1995

ISBN: 0-515-11609-2

A JOVE BOOK®
Jove Books are published by The Berkley Publishing Group,
200 Madison Avenue, New York, New York 10016.
JOVE and the "J" design are trademarks
belonging to Jove Publications, Inc.

PRINTED IN THE UNITED STATES OF AMERICA

10 9 8 7 6 5 4 3 2 1

For my son, Brian.
Strength and success
are your watchwords.
I know you will achieve
and use both wisely.

To my agent, Jane Jordan Browne,
and my editor, Judith Stern.
You both know why.

. . . Never till Time is done
will the fire of the heart and the fire
of the mind be one.

Dame Edith Sitwell

Reckless Hearts

Prologue

Wyoming Territory, 1871

Sun, sweat, and screams. The relentless July heat scorched the withering spears of wild grass, dry creeks wound through the dust like barren bowels in a heartless earth, and Abigail Fairchild screamed her pain to the empty skies.

Boyd Harris gripped her hand, ignoring the fingernails that dug into his weather-toughened skin. "Come on. Push."

"I can't," she choked out between pants, cursing the heat, the fates.

"Yes, you can." For a tough man of few words, his voice was surprisingly tender. "For the baby . . ." He paused. "And Michael."

Abigail's eyelids flickered closed, masking weary blue eyes. A mental picture of her late husband formed clearly, and she fought back tears. Boyd was right. She could do this for Michael.

"I wish there was a doctor," she murmured weakly, embarrassed that her foreman was having to birth the baby.

"We're better than ten miles from town," Boyd reminded her, wondering how different a woman's birthing might be from a cow when it calved. Swallowing deeply, he hoped the difference was small. He had been Abigail's foreman for the past five months, long enough to get to know and respect her as his employer, but not long enough to be her midwife.

"I'm glad you're here," she declared with effort as another contraction began. Overwhelmed by the pain, she gripped his hand even more tightly, turning the tanned skin white with pressure.

With his other hand Boyd smoothed the golden hair from her damp forehead, touched by the trust she had placed in him. From the first day, when he had ridden up and offered to be her foreman, she had simply accepted him. The same rustlers who had killed her husband had also killed the foreman of her ranch, the Triple Cross.

Abigail had never mentioned Boyd's past, which no one else could forget. He'd been given full rein over one of the largest ranches in the territory by a simple thank you from Abigail. It had been a long time since anyone had such complete and unquestioning faith in him.

"Boyd, it's worse!" she spit out, panting both from fear and pain. "I thought first babies were always late."

So had he. Not this one. Baby Fairchild was in a hurry. "It seems like a blessing to get it over with early, doesn't it, ma'am?"

Her unexpected smile turned into a grimace before it was complete. Still, a bit of puckish tone remained. "It seems we're beyond 'ma'am' now, don't you think?"

He thought they were galloping past it at far too fast a rate, but he merely nodded as her hand tightened again. Rivulets of perspiration trickled down her temples, and Boyd unfastened his bandanna to wipe them away. "Won't be any time a'tall now, ma'am . . . Abigail."

"How can you tell?" she asked. This was her first birth, one that should have been in the huge canopied bed at the Triple Cross with Michael by her side. A dusty road, unprotected from the scorching sun with only her foreman for help had never been in her plans. But Michael was gone and with him all that had been right.

Boyd cleared his throat, an unaccustomed flush of red staining his neck. "I know. Trust me."

"I do," she answered, more quietly now.

The knowledge stabbed somewhere deep in the heart he kept barred from all entry. If it killed him, this baby would be the healthiest, happiest—

"Aahh!" Her scream echoed around them, astounding

them both. Boyd had unharnessed the horses and tied them to a nearby fir tree. The animals looked up, startled at the sound.

Boyd had made the back of the wagon as comfortable as possible, but it was a hell of a place to have a baby. Earlier, he had emptied some of the flour sacks in order to use the material, but there was no soft feather mattress and down quilt that he was certain she was used to. "You go ahead and holler your head off if you want."

She seemed faintly ashamed. "I'm not one to scream."

"There's a time for everything."

His tall body blocked a good portion of the sun's harsh rays, and he had rolled some of the sacks into a makeshift pillow. What if she had been alone? Terror struck swiftly. She had wanted to ride into town by herself, and Boyd had tried to talk her into staying home. When she refused, he had insisted on accompanying her. Gratitude filled her.

In the few months since Michael's death she had wished to join him, to forget the pain of losing her beloved husband, but never had she wanted to lose their baby. Now her wayward actions had brought her close. She balled one hand into a fist and brought it to her mouth. "Oh, Boyd. Why didn't I listen to you?"

Carefully he dipped the edge of one sack into his canteen and moistened first her forehead and then, ever so carefully, her lips. "If you'd listened, you probably wouldn't be female."

She laughed, a weak pitiful sound, but it was a laugh. "Do you suppose it brought the baby on early?"

Boyd cleared his throat, clearly embarrassed. "I couldn't say. Cows move all the time before their time to drop."

"Nice comparison," she said dryly as another even swifter contraction overtook her.

Soon she could barely grunt, her face and body were wet with perspiration, and her grip on Boyd was deathly. They were close now. He just hoped she would have the strength to keep pushing. The heat had sapped what little energy she had, and her sadness took its toll. How seriously he didn't know. But since Michael's death she had been so incredibly sad it made a body ache to watch her. In her short twenty-four years, Abigail Fairchild had borne more loss and pain than many people twice her age.

"Push, Abigail."

She tried to cooperate as he urged her.

"Don't let up. We're almost there."

"You said that hours ago," she nearly screamed, sounding almost waspish. Definitely not like the gentle woman she was.

Boyd swallowed an unexpected grin. He didn't know for sure but he suspected the change in her attitude meant her time was about here. Gently he examined her once again, then pulled her skirt down over naked legs to rest near her knees, allowing her as much dignity as possible. "This time I want you to *really* push."

"What do you mean *really* push?" Indignation filled her, and she pushed heartily. That was just the result he was hoping for.

"Good. Once more, Abigail."

Exhausted, she leaned back against the flour sacks. "I can't. Not anymore."

"Yes, you can." He pulled her to a sitting position and looked intently into her cornflower-blue eyes. Strands of golden hair that had escaped their pins straggled against her face, but neither that, nor the sweat that glistened against her porcelain skin, diminished her beauty. Boyd deeply pitied Michael for missing this moment. Yet he was equally glad to be the one sharing it.

"I, I—" But the words were cut off as she bent forward.

"Push, Abigail," he urged, both tender and tough, knowing she couldn't let up now.

Her scream was long and lusty, making him wonder again about this woman. She had thrown her head back but suddenly snapped it forward again and met his gaze. "The baby," she whispered.

He checked again. She was right. The head had crowned, and another contraction gripped her. But Abigail shook her head. "I can't do this. I can't."

"Even Solomon wouldn't have been happy with half a baby."

Surprise filled her face, and she stared at him in wonder. "What?"

"You can't go halfway, Abigail." He raised his voice slightly, putting some force into it. "Push!"

And she did. The baby's shoulders passed through, and in moments Boyd held the baby in his hands. Hands that suddenly seemed far too rough and awkward to hold the infant. Somehow he managed the cord, glad for the sharp knife he always carried. Gently he washed the baby's face, cleared its mouth and nostrils, and handed him to his mother. Michael's son, Boyd thought soberly. But the baby clung to Boyd's smallest finger, unwilling to let go—as was the man who held him.

Abigail motioned him closer. "Look what we've done," she said in wonder. Boyd looked. The total dependence of the child took him aback, almost as much as Abigail's trust had. Between them, they were chipping at the granite casing of his heart. Still the baby clenched his finger, content to have his mother and Boyd share his new world.

Within minutes mother and child fell into an exhausted sleep. Boyd watched them in awe. Now that it was over, he could scarcely believe she'd had the baby—and that he had helped. Only now he wasn't certain whether to move them. There had been a great deal of blood, but he didn't know whether that was unusual. He knew riders from the ranch would reach them late in the day or by early evening, once they realized Abigail hadn't returned. His gaze captured mother and child once more. Simply incredible.

Abigail stirred, opening her eyes gradually. Focusing, they came to rest on Boyd. Funny how she'd never noticed how strong he was. If Michael couldn't be with her, she couldn't have asked for a better substitute. Boyd had glanced away, taking the power of his deep blue gaze with him. Those piercing yet surprisingly tender eyes were a memory she would never shake.

While they'd slept, he had fashioned some sort of cover

from the remainder of the sacks and propped it up with
switches from a nearby aspen. She reached out to touch the
precarious awning. A smile escaped as she saw the extent of
the damage. Two months' worth of flour and sugar had been
unceremoniously dumped around the wagon. She imagined
what a sight they made.

The baby nuzzled at her breast, and Abigail felt a fierce
surge of protectiveness. Despite how their lives had gone
astray, she had been blessed. Boyd's tall, broad-shouldered
figure was silhouetted against the sun. What she didn't
know about him was tremendous. What he had done for her,
even more so.

Abigail stroked her son's fine, downy hair as he began an
insistent wail. Instinctively knowing what he sought, she
bared her breast. Boyd chose that moment to rejoin them.
Just as quickly he started to turn away.

"No, it's all right." Surprising herself, Abigail didn't even
blush as she invited Boyd to join them. They had shared too
much to be embarrassed now.

Quietly he sat. The baby suckled noisily, and Abigail
managed to grin. Such a hungry little beast.

"It shouldn't be long now till someone from the ranch
figures out we should be home." Boyd's voice was a cross
somewhere between reverence and embarrassment.

"I think I feel up to traveling now."

Embarrassment won out. "What about . . . ? I
mean . . ."

Abigail knew he referred to her physical state, but she
sensed everything was as it should be. "Let's go home,
Boyd."

He hesitated for a moment and then began to gather their
belongings. Ruefully he gazed at the spilled staples. "Miranda
is gonna have my hide."

"Maybe this little guy will change her mind," Abigail
nearly cooed as she traced one finger over the baby's
miniature features. "Even Miranda is probably partial to
babies."

"I 'spect everyone is, ma'am."

"It's still Abigail," she corrected him, lifting her eyes

from her child. "I haven't even thanked you properly yet. Without you I wouldn't have my baby."

Boyd remained silent, as caught up in the moment as she was. They had crossed boundaries not meant to be breached. But neither of them had any regrets.

"I needed someone to trust. Thanks for being that person," she said softly.

He'd always heard that cowhands grew as crusty and heartless as the land they rode. Now he knew that was a lie concocted to chase away the loneliness when only the stars and a herd of bawling cattle shared their lives.

Closing her waistfront, Abigail kissed her son and then offered him to Boyd. Carefully, as though this time he would surely break him, Boyd accepted the infant, cradling him in his big arms as gently as Abigail had. Unfamiliar feelings hit Boyd with the force of a locomotive.

"Mercy me!" Miranda crowed before catching hold of the babe's tiny fingers. The hard, spare woman thawed, looking much like spring when snow melted on the craggy bursts of the mountain peaks that surrounded them. Her practical no-nonsense voice took on a crooning quality that was foreign to all who knew her. "Would you look at that, Miz Fairchild? A *baby*!"

Abigail caught Boyd's eye, and they shared a look of amusement. But anything they might have said was drowned out amidst the chorus of excited voices. It wasn't every day the mistress went to town for supplies and returned with the new heir.

"Looks just like Michael," one of the cowhands said in awe.

Abigail glanced up just in time to see a rare shaft of inscrutable emotion cross Boyd's face. She shifted the warm, loving bundle, delighted to hear the tiny cooing sound her baby made. "Thank you."

The other cowhands crowded around, each wanting a moment to assess the new discovery. Abigail allowed roughened, work-hardened hands to carefully touch the baby. More than one set of eyes looked suspiciously bright.

Women, and especially children, were too rare in the isolated territory to be taken for granted.

"Now, that's enough. Can't you see Miz Fairchild's about dead on her feet? Out of the way." Miranda had already lost her initial softness. Tall as some men and equally capable, she wasted no time in moving the crowd of well-wishers. Brisk, no-nonsense tones cleared the path as readily as if she possessed broad shoulders capable of pummeling through the crowd.

Abigail was grateful, even though she regretted the disappointment that flashed over several faces. The fact was, Miranda had hit the mark. She was exhausted. Glancing down with a tired smile, she acknowledged it wasn't every day she birthed a baby.

Boyd tightened his grip on Abigail and carried her up the wide staircase that led to the bedrooms. It was a part of the Triple Cross to which he had never ventured. The upstairs looked as elegant as the rest of the house. Rich walnut tables gleamed with polish, and a fine tapestry brocade carpeted the burled wood floor.

Abigail's head drooped wearily against his shoulder, and he felt the indentation against his skin, the flutter of her silky hair as she sighed.

"Now, Miz Fairchild, you'll need a bath, but you can't take one," Miranda ordered as they reached the main bedchamber. "I'll bring a pitcher of water. But first . . ." Her stern voice wavered a moment as the baby's fist waved near her face. "First, we need to get the cradle ready."

"Of course, Miranda." Abigail's face pulled away from Boyd's shoulder, and he forced himself not to tighten his grip. "It's all right, Boyd. You can put me down now."

Reluctantly he did so. Boyd started to turn away, but Abigail swayed unsteadily. Miranda stepped forward, alarm crossing her face.

"The baby, Miz Fairchild."

"Of course, Miranda." Abigail's voice sounded distant, almost detached. "Please take him."

Miranda reached out to take the baby as Abigail swayed again. Boyd reached her before she could pitch forward.

Strong arms slid beneath her back and knees as he picked her up again.

"Thank the Lord," Miranda murmured.

"I'll get her to bed," Boyd replied grimly as he carried Abigail to the four-poster bed and laid her gently on the crocheted lace coverlet. "I didn't expect her to faint."

"It's normal enough."

"Maybe not if we hadn't ridden back so soon."

Miranda's gaze pierced his own intense blue stare. "Would you have waited in that hot sun any longer? And what if the doctor was on the other side of the territory? Would that have helped Miz Fairchild? You think she's weak now? That might have killed her."

Boyd acknowledged her words, but his gaze remained on the paleness of Abigail's skin. She looked fragile and defenseless. Remembering the last hours, he knew she was neither.

But suddenly he felt helpless, clumsy, and oversized in the room filled with fine furniture and flawless Irish linen. At least out on the trail he had been in command of the situation. Here he was worthless.

"I need to bathe Miz Fairchild," Miranda announced. Quickly she closed the space between them and shoved the infant into Boyd's unsuspecting arms. "And I'll need someone to watch him."

"But . . ." Boyd's voice trailed off as the warmth of the tiny body filled his hands.

"Take him to the dressing room," Miranda instructed, her cinnamon-colored eyes snapping, "and don't set foot in here until I tell you to." Her intent was clear as she turned her back on him.

Boyd carefully carried his burden into the next room. A *whoosh* of air slid from his lungs as he successfully maneuvered them both into the cane rocking chair.

"Wasn't sure I could hang onto you and sit down at the same time," Boyd informed his young charge.

Boyd examined the miniature face. He wondered about the boy's eye color, but his eyelids remained scrunched tightly shut. Frowning, Boyd wondered if that was normal. He'd have to speak to Abigail about it.

Meager fists flailed in the air, and Boyd offered his own finger for the child to grab on to. And he did.

A sudden possessiveness filled Boyd. Unexpected, unwanted, but unrelenting. It seemed vastly important that this fatherless child be protected. Without volition his gaze strayed to the room beyond the closed door. He could easily picture Abigail lying on the bed, alone.

She, too, needed protection. It wasn't his job, he reminded himself. He was in charge of land and cattle, not babies or their mothers. With his past, he was hardly a role model for any child and certainly not one born to inherit one of the richest ranches in the Wyoming Territory.

But the infant didn't look like a portion of a dynasty. Boyd drew one finger gingerly across the downy fuzz of hair on the boy's head. No, he looked like a bit of fluff, one who needed shelter from the savage land he had been born upon.

There were men who would kill without a second's hesitation to get control of the Triple Cross. A chill chased through him as Boyd acknowledged even an infant wouldn't lessen that determination. It wasn't his place, but he intended to make it his own. He wasn't going to let anything happen to this baby. As though acknowledging their bond, the young master of the Triple Cross tightened his grip on Boyd's finger.

Setting the rocker in motion, Boyd laid the child against his chest and lulled them both with a steady, soothing motion. Better than an hour must have passed, the precious interval seeming both fleeting yet suspended in time.

The door swung open suddenly and Miranda harrumphed loudly. "Miz Fairchild's asking for you."

Carefully Boyd rose from the chair, still holding the baby securely. Miranda looked as though she might question him on the point, but then let him pass through the doorway.

He wasn't certain what to expect, but it wasn't the radiance he was seeing. Bathed, her hair combed, Abigail sat propped up against a huge stack of pillows. Her smile seemed to light the whole room as he neared. Carefully he offered Abigail her son.

"My beautiful boy," she murmured. She motioned to the chair near the bedside. "Please sit down, Boyd."

"You look right good, ma'am." He couldn't understand it. Except for the bluish circles beneath her eyes, she looked as though she had never endured the long day. He sank down on the velvet-covered chair.

"Abigail," she reminded him. "I just needed a bath and some of Miranda's magic."

Miranda cleared her throat in an embarrassed manner. "I'll be getting you some tea, Miz Fairchild." She glanced at Boyd. It wasn't part of their social structure for her to be serving the foreman, but then this was an exceptional day. "Would you care for some, too?"

Before he could reply, Abigail answered for him. "I believe Boyd would prefer a shot of whiskey."

Miranda's lips thinned a bit in disapproval.

"And, Miranda, make sure it's the best we have."

Boyd wondered if Abigail had read his mind. He could do with a steadying dose. Somehow he didn't expect a lady to understand that sort of thing. Glancing up, he saw the disapproval growing in Miranda's expression.

"Ah, Boyd, can you believe this child?" Abigail lifted huge cornflower-blue eyes and met his gaze. They had shared a miracle, one she didn't seem willing to forget.

His gut tightened. "Perfect, isn't he?"

"I'm inclined to agree." The smile covering her face blossomed even further. "I'm sure every new mother says the same thing, though."

"But you'd be right," he replied gruffly, knowing no child had ever seemed so flawless.

Suddenly Abigail laid her hand over his. Boyd stared in surprise. Delicate, soft, and white, her hand looked out of place on his tanned rough one. "Thank you for making this possible, Boyd. I know that if you hadn't insisted on coming along . . ." Her voice warbled a bit.

"But everything's fine now. That's all that matters."

Her eyelids flickered closed for a moment, and he

realized she was truly weary, despite the good show she was putting on. "You're right."

Miranda entered with a stirring of her skirts. She held a tray containing the two drinks. She placed the footed tray on the bed. "Would you like me to put the baby in the cradle, Miz Fairchild?"

"I think I'd rather hold him and wait to drink my tea, Miranda." She glanced over at Boyd. "But, please, have your drink."

Miranda continued staring and feeling somewhat awkward, Boyd picked up the whiskey. He downed the shot quickly, the pleasure in the fine liquor dissolving under Miranda's continued perusal.

"I've decided what to name him," Abigail announced, her voice soft with pleasure. "Michael Boyd Fairchild."

Two gasps sounded in the room. Boyd could scarcely believe her words, and apparently those same words had shocked Miranda. "I don't think you've thought this through," he protested.

Abigail's eyes were bright and clear. "Oh, but I have. I might not have my son if it weren't for you. I think Michael would be very pleased."

How could he argue? Boyd swallowed suddenly as he stared at his tiny namesake. His sense of duty and responsibility seemed to grow even more.

"Miz Fairchild, you need to be getting your rest," Miranda pointed out.

"But—"

"She's right." Boyd rose. "You both should sleep."

Feeling uncomfortable under Miranda's scrutiny, Boyd tried to move inconspicuously through the room. He almost expected to crash into something before he reached the doorway.

Blessedly he conquered the unfamiliar space and headed downstairs. But before he could escape, Miranda called to him. Stifling the urge to pretend he didn't hear her, he turned back in resignation. "Yes?"

She stepped toward him briskly, but then seemed to hesitate. "Did you need something, Miranda?" He didn't want to sound impatient, but the events of the day were hitting him solidly. He needed a bit of solace to sort them through.

"Boyd, you have to get hold of yourself."

"Ma'am?"

Determination seemed to flicker in her eyes. "You can't keep carrying on like this."

"What are you talking about?"

"Calling Miz Fairchild by her given name, acting as though you're on her same level. It isn't right. Won't ever be right. With all she's been through, she doesn't need the disgrace of gossip."

Of course not. A woman ranch owner didn't fraternize with her foreman. It was a rule of the land as clearly as the sun that dominated it by day and now sank toward the earth.

Boyd met Miranda's gaze, seeing regret touch the woman's eyes. Although she was a stern person, he knew she wasn't unkind. Her devotion to Abigail took priority over all else.

"Don't worry, Miranda. I'd never do anything to hurt Abi—Miz Fairchild."

The distress didn't leave her eyes, and her voice sounded grim. "I hope not."

Boyd entered the bunkhouse and listened to the usual noise and banter that filled the structure. Deliberately he shrugged away the oppression Miranda had stirred.

His assistant foreman, Randy Kreiger, unhitched his suspenders and scratched at his lean stomach. "Can you believe it, Boyd? A baby?" Randy shook his head. "I haven't seen a newborn in . . . Hell, I couldn't say when."

The land, though beautiful and awe-inspiring, was bereft of women and children. Infants were a rarity to be treasured.

"You weren't expecting a heifer, now were you, Randy?"

Tossing a quirt at his friend and boss, Randy managed a sheepish grin. "Hell, you know what I mean."

Boyd grinned as well, remembering the moment. "Yeah."

"You think Miz Fairchild's all right?" Randy asked with concern. They all liked the ranch owner, and something about her delicate nature brought out the protectiveness in all of them.

Thinking of her radiance, it was easy for Boyd to answer. "Yeah. I think she's going to be fine."

"You ever think about getting married, having kids?"

A shadow passed over Boyd's face. "I used to."

"Hell, that stuff's all behind you now. You got a bad deal, but people know the truth now. You never stole that ranch owner's cattle. If they could prove you had, they'd have hanged you." Brutal truth, honest but simple. "Miz Fairchild trusts you." Randy gestured toward the cowhands who were settling in to card games, dominos, and some to their bunks. "There isn't a man here who doesn't know that if you hadn't stepped in when Michael Fairchild died, this ranch might have gone bust. Miz Fairchild's a good woman, but she can't run a ranch. And there's not a man here who doesn't want to ride with you. Past is past, Boyd. You're the only one still holding on to it."

Swallowing, Boyd nodded, acknowledging the other man's words, yet knowing past accusations would be a scar he would always carry. But as he glanced around the room, he was filled with pleasure to know he had the trust of these men, and the woman who employed them all.

It was a trust he couldn't break. Miranda's words rang in his head. Regardless of his feelings, he would stay away from Abigail and the baby. They would get the chance they deserved to be happy. And he wouldn't stand in their way.

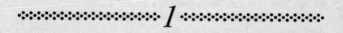

1

One year later

In the past months, despite his best intentions, Boyd had found himself visiting the big house every day. Excuses were easily formulated, reasons conveniently invented. At first he'd told himself he had to be certain Abigail and the baby were both physically healthy and safe.

Abigail had gotten up and around just a few days after the birth, disregarding Miranda's admonitions. For such a soft, fragile thing, Abigail had a lot of pluck. Which had made it easier to cross the lines he'd drawn in his head, and the ones that society had placed between him and Abigail.

Then there was little Michael Boyd. Boyd's heart swelled at the thought. The child had carved a niche in that protected place. Even though logically he knew that he was only in Abigail's employ, Boyd's feelings bordered on the possessive.

The house was in his line of vision now, and Boyd paused as he always did when getting close. The ranch house had been wisely built so that it nestled between the foothills of the great Tetons that towered in awesome splendor over the rugged land. It contained two sprawling stories of well-planned rooms that spelled out comfort and graciousness.

Graciousness instilled by Abigail Fairchild. Boyd's awareness of her increased with each step closer to the house. He wondered if she knew how wide a circle her gentleness touched. Wizened cowhands now visited little Michael

every day when she sat outside with him. Crusty layers fell
away from hardened, cynical men as Abigail shared the joy
of her child with them.

Reaching the front door, Boyd knocked, and Miranda
admitted him with a resigned expression. "What a surprise
to see you this morning, Boyd."

"I have a ranch to run," Boyd pointed out. "And there are
decisions that have to be made."

"Uh-huh." But there was no malice in her words, only
worry. "Well, come on in. You might as well have a cup of
coffee."

Boyd grinned as the woman turned toward the kitchen.
Despite her tough exterior, he suspected she had a heart of
mush lurking inside. To her credit, she'd never repeated her
dire warnings.

Entering the kitchen, Boyd's gaze went to Abigail and
little Michael. Both of them lit up when they spotted him.
Chubby arms stretched toward him as the toddler chortled
and ignored the food his mother tried to spoon into his
mouth.

"I guess you'd rather have Boyd than your oatmeal," she
chided in a soft voice, but a smile laced the words.

Rising from the chair they sat in, Abigail handed her son
to Boyd. Both males seemed happy with the exchange.

"She trying to make you eat that awful stuff?" Boyd
asked the child, running one long finger down Michael's
cheek and eliciting a smile.

"I'm beginning to think you might be a bad influence, Mr.
Harris," Abigail chided him in mock severity.

"Not if I save him from a lifetime of oatmeal."

She laughed, a silvery tinkle that seemed to light up the
room. Trim, soft, and radiant, it seemed impossible to
believe she was the mother of this rambunctious toddler.
She looked like a girl, one who could set hearts racing with
only a smile.

Instead she was a woman who owned one of the most
prosperous ranches in the territory. That thought intruded,
and Boyd remembered the reason for his visit.

"Abigail, we need to talk."

A bit of the pleasure in her smile dimmed. "Sounds serious."

"It is. I think it's time to hire a manager for the ranch."

She continued pouring the coffee, then stared at the filled cup before sliding it to the table in front of Boyd. "Miranda, will you take Michael now and change his clothes?"

The housekeeper's gaze slid between Abigail and Boyd. Without hesitating, she scooped up the child. "Come on, Mikie. Time to get you into some clean britches." Her footsteps and the child's gurgles were the only sounds for a few moments.

"About hiring the manager . . ." Boyd began.

"There won't be a manager," Abigail answered quietly.

Boyd's eyebrows rose. "I know you haven't wanted any major changes since . . . Michael's death. But we have breeding stock to buy, decisions that have to be made that affect the future of the ranch. I've hedged as long as possible, but they can't be put off any longer. You have to think of little Michael's future."

"I am." Abigail's fingers clenched around the top rung of the oak chair opposite Michael. "I've given the matter a lot of thought. Only one person will ever have my son's complete interests at heart."

Boyd wondered suddenly if she intended to have him manage the ranch, putting her money and her trust in him. It was something he'd done in the past. Unfortunately it was the job that also cost his reputation. In essence he'd been running the Triple Cross for almost two years, without the official title and without signing the cheques. He looked at Abigail expectantly.

"And I'm that person," Abigail told him.

The shock made him drop open his jaw. "You?"

"That was said with more than a healthy share of disbelief," she pointed out dryly.

"Begging your pardon, but what do you know about running a ranch?"

"Nothing," she replied calmly. "You're going to teach me. In case you don't realize it, you're the best manager in the territory. I know you don't have the official title, but it's

true." Her voice grew soft. "You've changed since you came
here. You're more like the man I'd heard about, one who
commanded the respect of cowhands and owners alike."

He was pleased, but refused to let her words sway him
from the purpose at hand. "Still, it'd take time to teach you."

"I have time and I want to learn." She leaned forward, her
face puckered with earnest intention.

"But things need to be done immediately, not after you've
had time to do your learning." Boyd wondered suddenly if
childbirth had scrambled Abigail's good sense. Soft, pliable,
she'd listened to his advice ever since he'd become her
foreman. Now she was talking nonsense. Disastrous nonsense.

"We will proceed today," Abigail insisted. "I am not an
unknowledgeable person. I've simply never had a need to
know about the actual functions of the ranch."

Boyd couldn't restrain himself. He gaped at her, wondering if she'd taken leave of her senses. "Abigail, that's plumb
crazy."

"I think not. I'm a fast learner and I have good reason to
succeed." Her gaze strayed toward the doorway and then up
toward the staircase.

Boyd knew she was thinking of her son and admired the
risk she wanted to take, but he knew she had no idea that
what she was trying to tackle was next to impossible.
"Maybe you need to think on this for a while. It's a . . .
uh . . . delicate time for you." He could feel his ears
redden in embarrassment, but he didn't want to throw away
the future of the Triple Cross.

"Men are supposed to be such intelligent, strong creatures. It's amazing how a little thing like childbirth reduces
them to simpering idiocy."

His head snapped up. Had he heard correctly. "Ma'am?"

"I thought we'd gotten past that, too, Boyd."

Although still softly feminine, he sensed a change in her.
It struck him that she no longer resembled a wounded bird.
It was as though she was putting the pain of the past two
years behind her. She was exhibiting a strength he hadn't
seen before in her. He couldn't say she was being aggres-

sive, because she wasn't. Nor was she sounding like a take-charge boss, but he sensed she wasn't backing down, either.

"I think today would be a good time to start my lessons," she continued. "How would an hour from now be?"

Boyd tried to keep the grimness from his voice. "You're the boss."

"I'd rather not have to be treated like some formidable authority figure. Can't we just go on as we have been, Boyd?"

He doubted that, and regretted the loss he sensed was coming, but didn't know a way to win this argument. "An hour, then. I'll be at the corral."

Abigail laid her son down, kissed his downy head, and then took a deep breath. She wondered fleetingly if she was making a huge mistake. Perhaps she should concentrate on doing what she knew best, keeping her home a welcoming place and making her child happy. But her glance drifted over the cradle, and she renewed her determination. A happy home and devoted mother wouldn't insure little Michael's future.

A wave of insecurity assaulted her. She knew so very little about ranching, having always left everything to her husband's able control. But she couldn't let her deficiencies ruin little Michael's future. Despite her brave words to Boyd, Abigail knew it would be difficult to learn something she had no affinity for, something she sensed she wouldn't enjoy.

In the days since her son had been born, she'd done a lot of thinking. True, she could hire a manager. She could even offer Boyd the job. She frowned suddenly. She hoped he didn't think it was a lack of trust that hadn't prompted such an offer.

She pulled the miniature quilt up over little Michael. No, it wasn't any lack of trust. Boyd obviously cared deeply for her child. But she had Michael's entire future to think about. Employees could come and go, but as his mother, she would always be there for him. Having spent many days and long, restless nights thinking of her future, she'd made up her mind. A life without her husband would be rough and lonely, but she could fill that time with something far more useful. She could build a future for her child, and to do so she needed to learn how to run the ranch.

Miranda entered the room, and Abigail reluctantly abandoned the cradle. "I'll leave him in your care now."

The smiles that reached Miranda's eyes these days seemed softer, almost vulnerable. "He and I will be fine."

Seeing the longing on the other woman's face, Abigail wondered why she'd never married. Miranda was a bit on the plain side, but in a territory crying out for women, she could have easily married a dozen times over. Yet she never accepted callers and ignored the cowhands who expressed any interest in her. Miranda had started working at the Triple Cross before Abigail married Michael. The woman's past was still a mystery, one Abigail respected and never pursued. But there were times, like today, that she wondered about her housekeeper.

Abigail started down the stairs, remembered her handkerchief, and headed back toward her bedchamber. An unexpected sound greeted her.

Miranda was singing!

The gentle, lyrical sounds were soothing and delightful. Peeking around the doorway, Abigail watched as Miranda rocked the cradle and sang a beautiful lullaby. After listening for several moments, Abigail drew back out of sight. Shaking her head in disbelief, she wondered again at the seemingly uncompromising woman.

Running down the stairs, Abigail slipped through the door and into the sunshine. Heat filled the air, but a relieving breeze lessened the sensation. One thing had never changed for Abigail—a love of this unconquerable land. It still seemed like a shock at times to wake up to the majesty of the mountains that surrounded the ranch. Like a protective fist, she often thought. Guarding the inhabitants from harm.

Having been raised in the East, she was unprepared for the endless miles of ruggedness. She had met Michael while visiting the Wyoming Territory with her aunt when she was seventeen. It had been the adventure of her lifetime. She had made friends that had endured, and developed a love for a young rancher that didn't lessen when she returned back East. Soon after, he had tracked her down in Boston. A whirlwind courtship and marriage had resulted.

The sun pierced the light cotton she wore, but Abigail disregarded the heat. She had no regrets. Sadness, yes, but no regrets. She wouldn't want to live anywhere else, or have her son grow up without this rich heritage. Admittedly, after Michael's death she had thought of returning back East, and had even decided she would. If she'd had a daughter, their fate might have been different. But Michael's child, his son, deserved the legacy Michael had bequeathed him.

Spotting Boyd at the corral, she raised her hand in greeting. She noticed his expression changing as she walked briskly toward him. Surprise and then a touch of disgust touched his face. Wondering what caused both, she halted a few feet in front of him.

"I'm ready, Boyd."

"Dressed like that?" Midnight-blue eyes narrowed as he drew his glance over her figure.

Self-consciously she clutched the pale yellow material of her full skirt. She'd chosen one of her plainest outfits. She enjoyed beautiful clothes, but this dress was simple, scarcely adorned with anything except a bit of lace around the bodice. She knew better than to show up dressed like she was preparing for a party. "What's wrong with my dress?"

"I'd planned on riding out to the line shacks to get reports on the fence lines."

"Ride? On horseback?" She could hear the echo of her own voice in the breeze. "Couldn't we take a wagon?"

"Are we talking about the same ranch?"

"There's no need to be snippy," she reminded him, wondering how to get control of the situation and not look like a fool.

"I wasn't intending to be. But you can't ride in that dress. You'll just have to change."

"I can't ride at all," she admitted, wishing the incredulous look would disappear from his face.

"And just how did you plan to inspect your ranch?"

Abigail's mouth opened and then closed again without making a sound. She had seen a great deal of the ranch from the roads between here and town. Not having thought the matter through, it hadn't occurred to her that she would need to physically inspect the outlying lands.

"Well, we just figured out lesson number one," Boyd answered for her. "You'll have to learn how to ride a horse."

"But—"

"Unless you've changed your mind and want to hire a manager."

Firming her chin, Abigail met his skeptical gaze. "I'm not that easily put off. I'll go change." She started to turn away, then whirled around. "Change into what?"

His face contorted again, and she wished she wasn't so ignorant of ranching. "Breeches."

"Whatever for?"

"Because you can't ride a ranch sidesaddle and you certainly can't in that . . . dress."

"Very well. I'll be back shortly."

Pivoting around, she walked toward the house, her brows furrowed together in worry. Not being a rider, she didn't own any proper feminine riding habits.

Breeches!

She was no prig, but her mother's breeding was a strong force, one of gentle ways, graciousness, and femininity. Abigail glanced around toward the rugged mountain range that defied subtleties like a buggy and a woman dressed in ladylike fashion. Obviously she would have to give up some of those ways.

Once inside, Abigail rooted through her wardrobe and came up empty. Her gaze riveted on Michael's wardrobe, untouched since his death. No, she wasn't ready to face that, either.

Going back downstairs, she searched for Miranda and found her back in the kitchen. Quickly she outlined the problem. "Do you think there are any breeches on the place that might fit me?"

Miranda looked skeptical. "Maybe. Will Speer's on the

small side. I can have Lucy check the laundry." Lucy, one of the cowhand's wives, washed and mended all of the clothing for the men at the Triple Cross. Along with Rachel, another wife, she sewed their new clothing.

"Would you do that? I'll need a shirt as well."

Miranda laid down the bowl in her hand and rolled her eyes. "If you're sure."

Abigail wished everyone didn't so heartily disbelieve in her abilities. "Yes, I'm sure."

Within a short time Miranda returned with the clothing. It was still too big, but at least she could keep the items on. Staring at her unfamiliar reflection in the mirror, Abigail realized she would need to have some clothing made to fit if she was successful. *When* she was successful, Abigail corrected herself. Too much depended on this for her to fail.

Abigail glanced at her reflection, then tilted her head to look again. She had never dressed in anything but the most feminine garments. It was an unexpected freedom she felt in donning the breeches and shirt. No petticoats, no corset. It was a strange, exhilarating feeling, not one she ever expected to find by donning ugly male clothing.

Realizing Boyd was waiting, Abigail adjusted her belt and then walked down the stairs. She had just pulled open the door when Miranda's voice floated out. "Good luck, Miz Fairchild."

Spoken in a tone that implied she would need the luck, Abigail was hardly reassured by the words. Giving into an unaccustomed urge, she shut the door behind her with more force than absolutely necessary.

A seed of satisfaction sprouted along with the action. Evidently she needed to assert herself more often. Putting some determination in her stride, she headed back to the corral.

Several horses trotted inside the wooden confines. Long, graceful necks were flung back in arrogant fashion as the horses looked down upon their meager human masters. Abigail swallowed, realizing just how large the creatures were. Somehow they seemed more docile when yoked to a wagon. An unhealthy sensation formed in her stomach, and she realized it was fright.

"So you found some clothes."

Abigail whirled around, surprised to find Boyd at her side. "Yes, they're a bit large, but all right for today."

"Good, then we'll get started." He stepped a bit closer, his gaze sweeping her face. "Are you okay? You look kind of pale."

Abigail shook her head, hoping to dispel her fear and send some fortifying blood upward. "I'm fine. It's just a hot day."

"Uh-huh." Boyd gently took her elbow and steered her away from the corral and toward the stables. The stable was refreshingly cool, and she lifted the heavy hair at her neck, grateful for the relief.

"The mare's inside. I'll show you how to saddle her, but next time you should do it yourself so you'll learn how."

Abigail nodded in agreement, glad they were leaving the stirring dust and intimidating horseflesh in the corral. Muffled neighs of greeting came from behind the stall doors as Boyd spoke to the horses and called them by name. Near the end of the row he stopped. "She's in here." He slid the bolt free and unfastened the door. Abigail watched him effortlessly slip the bridle on the horse and then attach the reins.

Catching her gaze as she watched the movement, Boyd smiled. "You'll learn how to do that as well."

Abigail tried to quell the ball of nervousness in her stomach. But then she looked, really looked at the mare. Gleaming chestnut, the horse was a true beauty. Huge eyes flickered in Abigail's direction. Although her fright hadn't disappeared, it had diminished.

Studying the other horses, Abigail could see that Boyd had purposely chosen the smallest, least intimidating of the bunch. She felt a rush of gratitude. They walked to the barn, the mare's tail twitching as she was led. Shadowed, smelling of oats, hay, and the leather of tack and harness, the barn seemed a friendly place.

"We keep saddles in here." He gestured to bits of leather

hanging from pegs. "Most everything you need's in the barn. I'll saddle Dolly for you."

Dolly. That didn't sound so intimidating. Abigail watched as Boyd's competent hands saddled the seemingly gentle animal.

When finished, Boyd turned and pinned Abigail with a piercing gaze. Startled by the intensity of his expression, she nearly stepped back in trepidation.

"Are you sure you're really all healed, Abigail?"

She flushed, knowing what he referred to. Nodding her head, she forced her voice to sound normal. "Yes, I am. It's been a year now." It occurred to her that as a bachelor he wouldn't know how long a woman's confinement took.

His eyes remained locked with hers for another long moment before he released them. "I hope to God you're telling me the truth." His voice flattened with purpose. "You might fall off the horse. I don't want to find you in a pool of blood."

Abigail could feel the heat filling her face. Even with Michael she'd never discussed such delicate matters. But then he hadn't been as earthy as Boyd. "I can assure you that my health has been fully regained. Besides, this lesson is at my request. You won't be held responsible."

"I've been responsible since the day the baby was born."

Abigail dropped her gaze in guilt. Boyd had proved to be more than a loyal friend, more than anything she should have expected. His devotion to herself and little Michael was unquestionable. "Granted. But I promise you I'm fine."

His expression became critical again.

"What is it?" she asked, trying to guess all the possible things she could be doing wrong, unable to think of any.

"Your hair."

She reached up and touched the blond tresses self-consciously. "What's wrong with it?"

He angled his face as he studied her. "Did you bring a ribbon or something to tie it back?"

She shook her head, feeling inordinately foolish.

Boyd pulled the bandanna from his neck. "Turn around and I'll pull it back."

Obediently she turned. Long, strong fingers were gentle as they gathered the waves of her long hair and pulled them back. Stung by unexpected sensations at the touch, her knees wavered a bit. He continued tugging at the locks as she gulped in surprise and more. It occurred to her that he hadn't touched her since he'd brought her home after the baby's birth. Despite the meals and talks they had shared, there had been no physical contact. She could feel her face heat as she realized his touch seemed surprisingly intimate, surprisingly unnerving.

But as he faced her again, he seemed singularly unmoved. His face was set, unwavering as he launched into a litany about riding. Only a muscle that continued to twitch in his cheek seemed amiss. Ignoring her own rapid breathing and alerted senses, she listened as he showed her the basics of mounting the horse.

He held out the stirrup. "It's your turn."

Imitating his movements, she pulled up on to the horse and promptly fell over the other side.

Boyd walked over to where she lay sprawled in the hay, hands on his knees as he bent over to look at her. Apparently satisfied that she wasn't bleeding to death, he offered a hand. "Come on. Up you go." He took her hand and pulled her to a standing position. Abigail wondered which she'd bruised more—her pride or her posterior.

"When you get to the top of the mount, keep your head erect and you won't fall off." He stood close as she started to place her foot in the stirrup. Stopping her, he straightened out the leather that she'd twisted, and then guided her foot in himself. "Helps if you don't start by tripping yourself."

Determinedly she pulled on the pommel, lifted herself up, and pitched clear off the horse.

This time when Boyd reached for her, she could see an impish glow of amusement in his deep blue eyes. While she could appreciate a touch of humor in the situation, she didn't relish the idea of how foolish she must look falling off the horse.

"You know a manager isn't a bad thing," he told her. "A lot of owners who don't live on their ranches have managers. Saves them a lot of time and work. You don't see those Eastern dudes out riding the fences."

"I don't want a manager," she ground out, her patience barely in check.

"You sure you want to try getting on again?"

She gritted her teeth. "Yes, I'm sure."

"Then make sure you hang on tight to the pommel."

Pommel. She closed her eyes briefly. She could do this. If everyone else in the territory could ride a horse, she could, too.

Taking a deep breath, she swung her leg over, crested the top, clutched tightly to the pommel, and continued careening over the side.

"Are you okay?" Boyd squatted down beside her, plucking a few wayward bits of straw from her face as she lay sprawled in an ungainly heap.

Seeing a few stars, she realized maybe she'd put too much strength into that attempt. "I . . . just need to get my equilibrium."

He pushed back his hat, and thick locks of chestnut hair tumbled forward. "Maybe that's all you ought to try for today."

"Did you give up this easily?"

A slow easy grin eased from his mouth. "No. But then I didn't have quite such a hard time of it."

"You've probably been riding since you were born," she muttered, wishing the flash of his smile didn't seem so appealing.

"Close to it. Got on my first horse when I was four, and that was twenty-eight years ago."

"Then you can be patient if I take a few minutes to get the knack of it." His lips twitched, and she frowned. "What's so funny?"

"Just getting on the horse won't make you a rider. That's going to take some time."

"I suppose it will, but first I'm going to learn how to stay on."

With a resigned sigh, he offered his hand and pulled her to her feet. "Then it's going to be a long day."

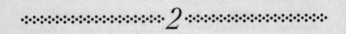

Two weeks of pure torture. Abigail rubbed her protesting muscles. Half of them ached from riding, half from the spills she continued to take. Although she could get seated now, she seldom stayed on long.

Despite Boyd's assurances, she wondered if it was normal to be in such agony simply from riding a horse. For the first two days she had experienced blinding pain. Wondering if she had been premature in determining that she could ride, she had thought her guts would fall out with the pain.

But refusing to give in to what she considered Boyd's expectations, Abigail had forced herself to climb back on the horse day after day. And the pain had receded. Now muscles that had never been exercised so thoroughly protested. But it was a tolerable level of distress, considering the initial onslaught of agony.

Abigail led Dolly from the stables. Young Billy Kendall tipped his hat. "Mornin', ma'am."

"Morning, Billy."

"You want me to saddle Dolly for you?"

The offer was tempting. Then she thought of Boyd's mocking face. He had pounded in the importance of learning to care for one's own mount, which included saddling the beast. "No, thanks, Billy. But I appreciate the offer."

"Sure, Miz Fairchild."

Heading in to the barn, she found her saddle and equipment. She could manage this part of the horse riding. Staring at the saddle, she just wished the darn thing didn't weigh so much. She gazed longingly at the door, wishing she had allowed young Billy to saddle the mare.

In a fairly decent time, however, she had Dolly saddled. Satisfaction filled her. There was something about doing a job herself that far outweighed convenience and a few sore muscles.

Leading Dolly outside, she noticed with trepidation that several men lingered around the corrals. Nervously, she wished they would leave. Not yet a competent rider, she performed even worse with an audience. Glancing up, she saw Billy Kendall flash her a smile of encouragement. Warmed, she swung up on the horse, gratified that she didn't go sailing over.

Keeping the horse to a mild walk, she stepped off the route she had practiced the past two weeks. Determinedly not looking at the men, she completed her path successfully. Pleased, she picked up the pace a notch and started back around the same circuit. As she neared the corral, she made the mistake of looking up. The men watched her with undue interest. John Sims, one of the younger hands, eyed her with special attention. Dolly stepped suddenly and unexpectedly to one side, and to Abigail's mortification, she flew from the saddle.

Ears flaming, she could hear the snickers of amusement. She didn't doubt that they took bets on how long she could stay seated for each ride. Scrambling to her feet, she saw young Billy rush forward. He was one of only a few men not smiling or laughing at her.

He held out his hand. "Let me help you, Miz Fairchild."

"Thank you, Billy." Ignoring the others, she dusted off her pants and picked up Dolly's reins.

"Here's your hat." He held out the dusty Stetson.

"Thanks. I'm all right now."

"Yes, ma'am."

He turned to join his comrades, and Abigail led Dolly away. Too bad she couldn't charge admission for her daily shows. In a way she didn't blame the men. She must look a sight, falling off her horse like a rag doll on a daily basis. Most of these men had been born practically in the saddles of their trusted cow ponies. Dudes were fair game, even female dudes.

She kept on walking, passing the bunkhouse and then venturing farther. Seeing Boyd emerge from his house, she waved. Even though he still discouraged her attempts to run the ranch and insisted that she would be wiser to hire a manager, at least he never openly laughed at her. Watching him step down from his front porch, she wondered about the house he lived in. Although she had seen it from the outside, there had never been any reason to venture inside. And she wasn't even certain why she had suddenly grown so curious about his home.

He walked closer, his eyes roving over her. "Already hit the dirt today?"

Glancing down self-consciously, she could see the evidence of her spill tattooed in the dust that clung to her clothes. "Not too bad a fall," she replied, forcing the cheeriness in her tone. "How're you this morning?"

"Not as energetic as you, it seems. I'm just getting started for the day."

"I kind of wanted to get an early start—thought maybe I wouldn't have such a big audience."

He stuck two fingers through his belt loops. "They still laughing at you?"

"Yes, and I wish you'd ask them not to."

His eyes turned and met hers. "And just how do you suppose I go about doing that?"

She kicked at the dust beneath her feet. "I don't know. I thought you could . . . I don't know, talk to them."

"Or you could take the easy way out."

It was a familiar refrain. "I'm not hiring a manager."

He shrugged. "I'll tell the boys to quit teasing you."

"Don't put it that way!"

"Listen, Abigail. As long as you keep falling off the horse and looking like . . ."

Her interest quickened. "Like what?"

His voice grew gruff, the light in his eyes inscrutable. "Nothing. Just wait to ride until the men head off in the morning before you saddle up."

"Sounds reasonable."

"And Abigail?"

"Yes?"

"Try not to look so . . . so . . ." The light in his eyes shifted again.

"What, Boyd?"

"Hell, just try to stay on your horse." He stalked away and Abigail stared after him, wondering who'd put the burr under his saddle.

In the week that followed, Abigail tried to take Boyd's advice. Still she heard the snickers of men who worked close by. But determinedly ignoring their amusement, she grew a little steadier each day. And yesterday Boyd had told her that they were going to inspect the fences the following day. It was the first excursion out into the real boundaries of the ranch.

Glancing into the mirror, Abigail adjusted the fine linen of her new shirt. Admiring Lucy's handiwork, she preened at her own unlikely reflection. Properly fitting clothes made her new image that much more startling.

Without a backward glance, Abigail discarded the old breeches and shirt that she had been wearing, ones that had belonged to a cowhand. With delight she examined the new garments that Lucy had completed.

Slim, tapered pants eased over her legs, and she examined the entire effect. Twisting her head to see her back in the mirror, she frowned. The pants certainly fit snugly. But otherwise the clothing was to her liking. Even though she was used to the best—her dresses had all been ordered from the finest shops in the East or through *Godey's Lady's Book*—still she was satisfied with the craftsmanship in her new riding outfit.

Peering into the mirror once again, she was almost pleased by what she saw, the freedom of movement in the clothing. Here was a different Abigail Fairchild, with a very different look. Certainly nothing her proper mother would approve of, but Abigail suspected Boyd would hail the clothing as an improvement. Her ill-fitting clothes had already contributed to more than one fall when she had tangled excess yardage from the pants and her feet in the stirrups.

Hearing a knock downstairs, Abigail flinched, knowing she was late. Running to the head of the stairs, she started down. But Miranda had already opened the door. Boyd's deep voice floated up the stairwell along with chortles from little Michael. The two had formed a bond she doubted anyone could break. A niggling bit of worry formed a frown, but she shook away the thought.

By the time she reached the bottom of the stairs, Boyd held Michael, eliciting grins and laughter from the happy child.

"I'm ready," Abigail announced, not wanting Boyd to think she was ill prepared on her first day of actual ranching duties.

"Before your coffee?"

"You're getting to know me too well," she muttered.

He glanced up, shock and something else settling into the lines of his face. She followed as his gaze roved over her figure. His brow drew together as he assessed the form-fitting lines of her pants, the tailored shirt that was a far cry from the loose, oversized clothes she had been wearing. Then his eyes darkened into something she couldn't quite interpret.

"I was up late looking over the books," she continued nervously, filling the sudden silence.

He shuttered his expression. "Good." Then he tickled Michael, who obliged with a huge smile.

"Maybe not." She frowned. "That's one aspect of the ranch I'd rather turn over to a professional. The last accountant left because he couldn't stand it out here in the 'wilderness,' as he called it. Now the books are hopelessly outdated. Nothing balances. And if we're going to be making big purchases, we probably ought to draft the cheques from the proper accounts."

She missed Boyd's muttered reply and decided to ignore it. She doubted it was flattering. From a world that had once offered only comfort and praise, she was now having to prove herself on a daily, almost hourly basis. It was a process that grated on both her nerves and self-confidence.

"How would you go about getting an accountant?" she asked, unconsciously smoothing her hands over her hips.

"By asking for references from people you trust."

Abigail searched through her mind. The person she trusted the most about running a ranch, other than her able foreman, was Jem McIntire, one of the co-owners of the adjoining ranch. Jem, short for Jemima, was the only other female ranch owner in the immediate vicinity. She was also a trusted friend. "Who do you recommend, Boyd?"

"Actually it's been awhile since I managed a spread. Best bet to ask another owner. One you *trust*."

Abigail looked at him in consternation and growing frustration. She knew that her delicate looks were not entirely deceiving, but she was growing tired of being treated as though she were addled-brained. "And I thought I'd run out and find a crook to handle the money."

He flashed a rare smile, and it occurred to Abigail that he usually only smiled when he was with little Michael. She wondered if he ever laughed. And how he would look when doing so.

"I believe I will have that coffee," Abigail said, heading toward the kitchen.

Miranda had already poured a cup to cool. It was just as she liked it, laced with plenty of milk. Boyd placed Michael in his chair and accepted a cup as well. It was black, of course. As uncompromising as the man.

Abigail leaned against the counter, sipping the brew. Although she was looking forward to doing more than simply learning to keep her seat on a horse, today's inspection made her nervous. She wasn't sure how the men would respond to her taking command. Even though her friend Jem took full and unquestioned charge of her ranch, she had been born to the role. Abigail tightened delicate white hands around the coffee cup. It couldn't be any clearer that she hadn't been destined for dirty work.

In the past she had avoided the out-of-doors, except for casual walks or a ride in a protected buggy. While she

admired the ruggedness of her adopted home, it was
something she never dreamed she would have to conquer.
Her talents ran toward fine needlework, music, and maintaining a gracious home. Abigail's gaze slid to her booted
feet. Apparently those talents would have to change.

"Abigail, we should go over what's required today,"
Boyd began.

A flash of defiance flared in deceptively gentle eyes. "I
would appreciate your not treating me as though I'm
completely ignorant."

"I just wanted to make sure you're prepared for today.
You'll need—"

"I am prepared. Please credit me with some sense."
Exasperated, Abigail plunked her coffee cup on the counter
with an unexpected thud and left the kitchen. She could
feel the openmouthed stares that followed her exit. She
shouldn't have spoken so sharply, but she had been laughed
at for weeks, and enough was enough.

Opening the front door, she saw her mare and Boyd's
stallion tied to the hitching rail. He had already saddled both
horses. Not waiting for Boyd's assistance, she placed one
booted foot into the stirrup and swung up on the horse. For
a moment she thought she would go clear over and land on
the other side, but caught herself just in time.

Boyd exited as she straightened in the saddle. She sent
him what she hoped was a confident smile, her balance still
a bit wobbly. His eyebrows rose in acknowledgment of her
accomplishment. Until today, he had always helped her
mount.

"Abigail, are you sure you have—"

"Boyd, please rest assured that I am prepared. Now, shall
we go?"

Resignation colored his expression as he nodded in
agreement. Starting out at a walk and cautiously proceeding
to a canter, Boyd guided them toward the outlying grazing
land. Unfortunately, just as they neared a group of men
working the cattle, Abigail lost her seating. Sliding off the
horse in a tangle of arms and legs, she was dumped almost
in the midst of the group of snickering cowhands.

"That's enough, men," Boyd ordered sharply. The laughter tapered down, but didn't stop completely. "You all like Miz Fairchild. Stop treating her so badly."

The laughter died away completely. She could see dawning looks of comprehension on several faces. Apparently they had thought it was mostly in fun. She wished it didn't hurt to be the butt of everyone's amusement, but it did.

Accepting Boyd's assistance, she remounted her horse. Luckily she kept her seat. Staring at the circle of subdued faces, she managed a smile. "Please go on with what you were doing."

They continued to stare until Boyd nodded at her side. They broke ranks and turned back to the cattle. Glancing sidelong at him, she knew in no uncertain terms who was in charge. It didn't matter that her name was affixed to the title of the ranch; Boyd was their leader. While she didn't want to usurp him, she needed to assert herself into some position of authority.

"You all right?" Boyd asked.

"Actually I'm getting used to it. As long as I don't break anything, I guess I can tumble my way around the entire ranch."

"You're doing better than a week ago."

She regarded him with suspicion, wondering if he was trying to repair her damaged ego. "Really?"

"Yep. Of course, you could save all this grief if you'd just—"

"Hire a manager," she finished for him. "The answer's still no."

"Your call." He shifted in the saddle, the leather creaking under his solid form. His gaze drifted across the cloudless sky. "You ready?"

"Sure." This time when she kicked her horse into a slightly faster pace, she used greater caution and was pleased to keep her seat. Aware that she made a bobbing and weaving motion on the horse when she rode, she wondered how Boyd managed to ride so smoothly and with such ease.

"We'll be climbing a lot today. Keep a tight grip on the reins and remember to use your knees."

"Did you always enjoy riding?" she asked, adjusting her grip and securing her position.

He seemed to consider the question. "I guess so. Never thought about it much. Rode almost as much as I walked growing up. Just part of life." He paused. "What about you? There's got to be something you like to do."

She thought of the dances and parties that had once been so important. "My interests seem insignificant in comparison to running an entire ranch."

"Not if you enjoy them."

Surprised by his insight, she nodded. "I like keeping my home running smoothly, entertaining friends." Her smile deepened. "Reading in front of a fire on a cold winter's night or working on my embroidery. I enjoy parties, but I like quiet companionship as well." Suddenly embarrassed, she halted her spill of words. "I didn't mean to prattle on so."

But there was a strange skirmish of emotions playing about his rugged features. "Don't sell yourself short, Abigail."

Gratified, she rode beside him in silence for a while, finding that her spirits were renewed. She heard the gentle swish of the wind against the aspens competing with the call of songbirds and relaxed, appreciating the beauty of her surroundings.

"This is all second nature to you, isn't it?" she asked after a while. "The land, the challenges."

He considered her words. "It's all I've ever known. Actually, I used to kind of envy some of the dudes."

She glanced at him suspiciously. "Why?"

"Even though they take a ribbin' when they come West, after a while most of them catch on. And they've come from another place, have a whole other set of experiences. Know what it's like to live in a big city. Then they wind up with the best of both places."

"I never thought about it like that," she mused. "I guess I wouldn't trade my beginnings in the East." An unexpected smile flashed. "Even though I wish I could keep a seat on my horse."

"That'll come in time."

"I hope so." Realizing that she had regrouped her enthusiasm for the day's outing, she glanced around in new appreciation of her surroundings. "How far is it to inspect the line fences?"

"Three-, four-hour ride."

"Oh." She could feel a good portion of her newly found enthusiasm drain away. Her muscles still screamed at that sort of abuse, even when all she did was pad around the corral. But she was determined not to let their bad start ruin her first excursion. "But it's a beautiful day to be going somewhere other than the corral."

"Going to be hot."

She might choke him yet. "Boyd, do you think you could be just a bit more positive?"

He chuckled suddenly. "I'm positive it's going to be a long, hot day."

"That wasn't exactly what I had in mind." Sniffing in pretended disdain, she glanced around at the wash of colors that painted the landscape, determined to enjoy herself.

"Just trying to be honest."

"Painfully so, I gather. Have you ever tried looking at only the good side of things?" She angled her head toward him, anticipating his answer.

He didn't reply for a moment. Only the sound of the horses' hooves hitting the ground filled the air. "There was a time when I did." His head turned, and he met her eyes for a moment. "But it seems best when I don't."

Knowing he referred to the past he couldn't quite shake, she eased into a coaxing mode. "I don't see how you can live in such a negative fashion. If I don't believe that everything happens for a reason, that in the end good will win out, I don't think I could function. Otherwise, I wouldn't believe in a future for little Mikie."

"Maybe having kids changes a person," he acknowledged.

"Perhaps," she agreed. "But I believed in good things before he came along."

"Always?" he asked quietly.

A flash of pain accompanied her answer. "Almost always."

Silence grew between them as they continued the long ride. As the incline changed, Abigail nearly lost her seating but managed to hang on. After an hour she began to feel the renewed protest of her muscles. They were climbing upward in the mountains, the uneven foothills difficult for her to manage.

Boyd slowed the pace to accommodate her, but still it was arduous. Glancing over, she saw that Boyd rode with practiced ease, as though they were still on level ground. She had to remind herself with an effort that he'd spent a lifetime in the saddle. Otherwise, she would have screamed in frustration.

After the second hour of riding she felt winded, her energy draining. But, knowing they were near their destination, she eventually gave in to relief. But when he didn't stop after a time, she started to grow frantic. "We must be almost there. Is it much farther?"

He looked at her in surprise. "It's three or four hours each way. We've got a while to go yet."

Shock mingled with the protest she wanted to issue. But she saw the flicker of challenge in his eyes and straightened her spine. "Fine. I just wondered."

"We can turn back if you want to."

And acknowledge that she wasn't learning the ranch, that she would have to hire a manager. "No, I can make it."

She would die before she admitted defeat.

And she almost did.

The incline steepened, and she heard the tumble of rocks beneath the horses' hooves. She wondered briefly where all those stones and pebbles were landing, then decided she didn't want to know in the event that she lost her seating and joined them.

The sun climbed in the sky. With no clouds to block its ascent, the rays were blinding. Swallowing, Abigail wished for a long, cool drink of water, but she was terrified to release her grip to reach for her canteen. Convinced she would have to eat her words and beg Boyd to turn around, she was almost ready to admit defeat.

But Boyd pulled up his reins. "We're here."

She looked up and saw nothing. Blankly she turned to him. "How do you know?" Expecting a structure, something, all she saw was more miles of unrelenting land.

Boyd pointed to a low-flung line of fencing. "That's it."

"What in the world is it supposed to keep in or out?" She couldn't believe it. They had ridden till what seemed to be the end of the earth to look at a scraggly row of wire.

"It's an important division. Keeps our cattle from roaming on to the McIntire spread. About a mile ahead there's a line shack. Harold Ross is the cowhand who lives there. He can tell us the condition of the entire area."

"But what am I learning?" she protested, feeling the pain in her muscles, but little else to tell of anything she had gained from the trip.

"The owner or manager has to know all the men working for him." He met her gaze and corrected himself. "Or her. You've got to know the type of job they're doing. If they're honest. If you can depend on the man to really ride the fences and repair them, or find out that come spring you've lost half your herd because your line shack man's spent the winter nursing whiskey instead of doing his job. The only way that's going to happen is to check up on the men, the area they ride, then decide if what they say matches up to what you've just seen. Running a ranch isn't an armchair job."

Abigail straightened up muscles that were screaming for hot water and a soft bed. "I didn't think it was. I simply wanted to know the purpose of this expedition."

"As we head down, look to the west. See if you can spot any gaps in the fence line. Also, look for any place that's low enough that the cattle could trample it down."

While she was trying to hang on to the horse? He didn't want much. Inclines were both tricky and frightening. But she clutched the reins more tightly and angled her head toward the west occasionally as they descended.

The path narrowed, and Abigail gave up on watching the

fence line. Survival seemed far more important. The crevice
beneath them widened, and she realized with a sickening
feeling that the drop could put her in the bottom of a canyon
if the horse misstepped.

"Beautiful up here, isn't it?"

Abigail jerked her head upward at his words, trying to
keep her concentration on staying alive. "Yes . . . beautiful."

"What do you like best?"

Flat ground. "Uh . . . I'm not sure." She closed her
eyes briefly and uttered a silent prayer. "What's your
favorite part?"

"Being able to see for miles. It's like being on top of the
world."

Her stomach knotted even more. "We won't be on top
very much longer, will we?"

"Why? Heights bother you?"

She glanced at the yawning depth of canyon just to the
side of her. The path continued to narrow, and she realized
they were walking on the brink of the cliff. "It's . . .
different."

"First few times folks come up a mountain, it makes 'em
nervous. But you get used to it."

She glanced at the bottomless cavity that no doubt held
the corpses of other fools who had trod this way. "I'm sure
you must be right."

"It's leveling out straight ahead. Then it's not too far to
the line shack. You seen any bad places in the fences?"

She jerked her head to the west, reminded of the job she
had abandoned. "No . . . that is . . . I don't think so."

"Then you'll be able to talk knowledgeably about the area
with Harold."

"Uh . . . yes. Certainly." She put more force into the
words. How much could she have missed? "I'm looking
forward to meeting him." And getting off this horrible trail.

The path began to widen and, remarkably, to level out.
Now, able to leave the edge that threatened to tumble down
into the canyon, she could breathe a sigh of relief.

"We can pick up the pace now. It'll take some time off the
ride." Boyd kicked his stallion into a canter and shot ahead.

Gritting her teeth against the pain she knew she would feel in her posterior, Abigail kicked her mare as well and then hung on with all her might. Within a short time she spotted the outline of a shack. If she were a more demonstrative person, she would have shouted hallelujah!

Instead she flashed a huge smile at Boyd, registering his surprise. He had probably expected her to give up by now. Narrowing her gaze, she wasn't certain he hadn't purposely chosen their precarious route for her benefit, to convince her to give up and hire a manager.

But she wasn't as weak as everyone imagined. And when it came to her son, she could summon all the strength in the world.

"Ready to start being the boss?" Boyd asked.

Not certain what he meant, she answered cautiously. "I'm sure I'm ready to learn."

"Good. Split-second decisions can make or break the ranch."

She gulped. What kind of decisions? But not wanting to air her ignorance, she held her questions. Questions she realized were growing by the moment.

Slowing as they neared the shack, she watched Boyd for some sort of direction. He swung off his horse, and she followed suit. Before they could knock, the cowhand opened the door. It occurred to her that this must be a very lonely job, living hours away from any other living soul. Her caring nature surfaced immediately.

"Harold," Boyd greeted him.

"This is a surprise," Harold replied. "A good one," he added, glancing at Abigail curiously.

"This is Miz Fairchild."

The man held out his hand. "Harold Ross, ma'am."

"I'm pleased to meet you. Are you new at the Triple Cross?"

He scratched at scraggly, dark hair. "Been better than six months since I signed on."

"He's been out here the entire time," Boyd filled in.

That explained it. She knew most of the hands by name, and this one was a stranger to her.

"Well, it's good to have you as part of the Triple Cross."

"Thank you, ma'am. I'd like to stay here a good long while."

"And we're looking forward to that as well." She glanced at Boyd and saw him frown. Had she said something wrong?

"Let's go over the report, Harold."

"You folks want to come in?"

Abigail thought longingly of a seat not attached to a saddle and started forward.

"No." The solitary word from Boyd stopped the movement.

"Whatever you say," Harold answered.

She listened while Harold detailed his report for Boyd. Trying hard to concentrate, she found it difficult to follow. A person would have to possess a mental picture of the entire ranch to follow all the directions. With a start she realized that's exactly what Boyd had. He knew the ranch as well as she knew the interior of her house. His eyes never missed a detail as Harold told him about the area he was in charge of.

When Harold finished, Abigail glanced between the two men. Boyd hadn't yet spoken. Apparently it was her turn. "Well, continue the good work, Harold. Is that about it, Boyd?"

A muscle jumped in his cheek, and it looked as though he were clenching his jaw. "That's it, all right."

After mounting the horses, they rode away. Having recouped while they stopped, Abigail looked around at the scenery with new appreciation. Sculptured into sheer peaks, razorlike ridges, and perilous canyons, the Tetons rose skyward like a mighty god surveying an endless kingdom. The sun splintered the blue of the water in the stream not too far in the distance, seeming to mingle with the far-reaching expanse of sky.

"I'm beginning to see what you mean about this place," Abigail commented in a gentle tone.

"Really?" Tension laced the words.

She glanced curiously at him. "Something wrong?"

"You just told a man we should have fired that he was doing a good job and you hoped he would be around for a long time."

"Fired?" Her mind scrambled as she tried to sort out his words. "But why?"

"Nothing he said matched up with what we'd just seen."

Guilt nibbled at her conscience. She had given up on assessing the fence line while trying to hang on to the horse. Perhaps she had missed more than she realized. "Was it all that bad?"

"All that bad?" Boyd pushed back his Stetson, revealing a tumble of chestnut hair. "That depends on whether you think a hole in the fence big enough to lose a herd in is worth mentioning."

"But Harold didn't say anything about a hole that large. I was listening to him."

"Precisely."

"Oh." Realization dawned. "You mean he lied about inspecting the fences?"

"What do you think?"

She paused, a fraction of the enormity of the job sinking in. "That I have a lot to learn."

His glance flickered over her, assessing, measuring. "Good. If you didn't know that, we'd be in real trouble. In the future, when a man lies, cheats, or doesn't do his work, he goes." His anger apparently as easily dismissed as it was formed, seemed forgotten as Boyd pointed to the stream ahead, flanked by a grove of aspens. "Let's have our lunch there."

Nodding her agreement, she realized she was in fact very hungry. The morning's exertion was taking its toll. Boyd dismounted first and tied the horse's reins to a tree. She swung her leg over to dismount, but the stress of her muscles showed. Starting to pitch off the horse, she was relieved when Boyd reached up to catch her.

The shock of his hands encircling her arms and shoulders crested through her. It was the same sensation she'd felt when he had tied back her hair. She started to pull back when she noticed an unfamiliar intensity in his sapphire eyes. Shakily, she regarded him.

He stepped away first, turning back to his horse. His voice was muffled as he dug through his saddlebags. "I'll take the horses down to the stream."

"Certainly." Finding that her voice quivered, she forced more strength into it. "I suppose we should let them graze afterward."

His eyes met hers, and she had the definite feeling that he wasn't thinking anymore about the horses than she was.

"Right. Take care of your horse and he'll take care of you," he said aimlessly, as though the words fell from his lips without conscious thought. Almost, she guessed, as though they disguised what he was really thinking.

Suddenly awkward, she stubbed the tip of her boot into the soft grass. "I'll remember that."

His eyes lingered a moment longer, and then he turned toward the stream. She followed the outline of his body, noticing how lean and straight he stood. Tall with broad shoulders, a narrow waist and hips, he made an intriguing silhouette. Realizing the direction of her thoughts, Abigail shook her head to clear it,

Still, the bond she'd developed with Boyd on the day little Michael was born had never diminished. Until now she hadn't thought about any other dimensions. In her mind they shared a fine friendship, a wonderful journey of trust. Not one that should have her staring at the pleasing sight of his body, suddenly unnerved by his closeness.

She had never noticed how overwhelmingly masculine he was. Unlike her late husband, Boyd was tall, muscular, and almost forbidding. She guessed it was this sudden togetherness, time spent learning the ranch, that made her more aware of him. Before, while they had shared little Michael, they had never been alone together for hours at a time.

Still shaken, she turned and surveyed the spot Boyd had chosen. A canopy of leaves provided shade, yet sunlight danced between the branches, creating a latticework design on the grass carpet. It was a perfect place for a picnic.

Immediately she thought of a lovers' retreat and wished the comparison hadn't come to mind.

Lowering herself onto the grass, she tried to arrange her legs in a ladylike position. It was difficult, considering her attire. As Boyd watered the horses, she mused about him, the fact that he was an attractive single man. Her mind took a few leaps of its own, ones she knew should be repressed. Chastising herself, she put the feelings down to her solitary existence. After all it had been over a year and a half since Michael had died. A long time for a woman to be without a man in this lonely and remote territory.

A shadow fell over the space in front of her, and she looked up, surprised she hadn't heard Boyd's return. But her thoughts had been too full. Unable to meet his eyes, she glanced back toward the horses that he had tied to nearby aspen trees. They grazed contentedly under the comforting shade.

Boyd handed her the canteen from her horse's pack. "Fresh water from the stream. It's still cold."

"Thanks. Mine was getting pretty crusty-tasting."

Smiling at the comparison, he sat on the grass. His hands were full of food, and she waited expectantly. Her stomach nearly rumbled in anticipation.

When he didn't offer half, she glanced at the food pointedly. "Looks good."

He took a bite of bread and then swallowed. "It is."

"I don't mean to seem impolite, but aren't you going to share?"

"Didn't you bring a lunch?"

Her mouth fell open. "You didn't tell me to."

"I tried about three times this morning, but you *assured* me that you were completely prepared." He calmly took another bite.

"But you didn't tell me I needed to bring a lunch!"

He swallowed. "You said you were tired of being treated as though you were addle-brained. I did my best to get in a word edgewise, but you wouldn't listen. I even gave it one last try before we left the house."

He was absolutely right. She had been so certain he was

continually underestimating her intelligence that she hadn't allowed him to speak. After staring avidly at the uncommonly delicious-looking food, she disregarded the growling of her stomach and purposely averted her gaze from his lunch. "You're right. It's been said that learning the hard way is the best way. You go ahead and enjoy your lunch." She kept from licking her lips with an effort. "I'm really not hungry."

"Catch." Automatically she reached up as he tossed an apple to her. "Take some bread and jerky, too."

"But it's *your* lunch," she protested without too much conviction.

He picked up a healthy share of the bread, divided the jerky, and handed it to her. "Eat."

Her stomach chose that indelicate moment to growl. She smiled weakly. "Perhaps just a bit."

But her hunger had been unleashed, and she finished every bite of her lunch. Feeling guilty, she wiped her hands on her handkerchief. "You must still be hungry. I ate everything you gave me."

"Oh, I always pack a little extra."

She doubted that, but he had magnanimously refrained from grinding his point home any further. Grateful, she decided that the next time she'd pack a lunch that was far tastier in order to surprise him. "That was good."

"Not what you're used to."

She laughed, the sound mingling with the cry of nearby birds. "I never dreamed when I lived in Boston that I'd be grateful for dried beef."

"Life was different for you then."

She remembered the parties, soirees, and endless activity. "Different, but not better. I'm just beginning to realize how very much more life holds out here. Values are simpler. People, too. Not so much pretension."

"Is that important to you, Abigail?"

She wondered if she imagined that he had lingered overlong when saying her name, giving it almost a magical quality. Feeling a faint buzz in her ears, she recognized it as giddiness, then purposely shook it away. "People are important to me, Boyd."

His eyes seemed to search hers, and her breath caught as he leaned forward. "Good. Then you might make a decent manager, after all."

Disappointment flitted through her along with a feeling of trepidation. She realized suddenly that she'd hoped his remark would be more personal. And she was astute enough to realize that wish signaled disaster. But even as she tried to categorize her feelings, his compelling blue gaze settled on hers, and she felt a stirring deep within.

His face was shadowed by the brim of a wide Stetson while his rugged frame made it seem as though he'd been born to this severe, enduring land. And like the land, he was filled with his own harsh beauty.

His chiseled profile reflected strong, clear features that glowed from the warmth of the sun, his smile a slash of white in that tanned face. And his wide, uncompromising jaw was now only inches from her own.

Despite her wish to bury such feelings, they were alive and growing. And caused by the man who knew her better than any other man alive. One who'd shared the most intimate experience a man and woman could experience. And one with whom she could never share a future.

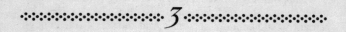

3

Abigail peered at the accountant who had taken over the books, her study, and much of the household in the months since he'd arrived at the Triple Cross. Cameron O'Donnell was a surprise in many ways. If she didn't trust her friend Jem McIntire's recommendation so much, Abigail would have wondered about the man. His appearance and demeanor suggested anything but accountant. Demigod, perhaps. Not accountant. Tall, spare, in his late thirties, with a thick head of coal-black hair and equally dark eyes, he ruled his job and their household with his demands.

Not that he was unkind, but he expected far above the norm. And he spared no leniency when pointing out the weaknesses in the accounting systems or anything else he happened to find lacking. He and Miranda had already locked horns more than once. And although Abigail was supposed to be the boss, she found herself tiptoeing through the house, hoping to avoid the man. Hardly a precipitous start in the business world.

But now she had to confront him. Boyd had informed her it was time to learn about purchasing breeding stock and that it needed to be done immediately. Many things had been pushed aside after Michael's death.

It seemed hard to believe that nearly two years had passed since then. She had been in the first months of her pregnancy when Michael had died. She'd grieved the rest of her term, feeling that emotionally she had been buried alongside him. In the past year she had tried to come to terms with that loss. Now she had a future to build for her son.

First, though, she had to deal with Mr. O'Donnell.

Feeling much like a child going to her father for an allowance, she approached the wide cherrywood desk. Since the accountant had taken up residence, she had scarcely entered the study, and she hadn't dared sit behind the desk.

Before she could speak, his head snapped up, and he pierced her with his strangely dark eyes. "Yes, Mrs. Fairchild?"

"Uh, yes . . . Mr. O'Donnell. I need to discuss a financial matter with you."

"And what would that be?"

She wished he didn't intimidate her so. "The purchase of new breeding stock. Boyd . . . that is . . . Mr. Harris suggested we buy the necessary animals now."

Long, slim fingers tapped on the desk, and Abigail wondered wildly if he was going to refuse, and if he did, how she would explain her failure to Boyd.

"As you know," she continued nervously, "we haven't purchased any breeding stock in far too long. We really can't put it off any longer. It's a necessary expenditure, one that's a vital part of the cattle business. Actually—"

"I assume you will want to extend a line of credit for the expenditures, rather than drawing on your capital."

Relief coursed through her. "Yes, that sounds good." Scrabbling to sound more effective, Abigail amended her words. "I mean, of course." She hesitated, uncertainty creeping into her tone. "This is the proper way to do it?"

His sigh echoed through the room. "Yes, Mrs. Fairchild. Perhaps you could have Mr. Harris provide me with some estimates on the expenditures. That way I can set up a proper amount with the bank." He glanced down at the disorganized ledgers. "And we'll incorporate the expenses in the books."

"Yes, I'll do that." She started to back away.

"Mrs. Fairchild?"

Seeing her escape thwarted, she offered him a smile. "Yes?"

"In the future, large expenditures should be planned in advance so that you can get the best utilization of your money."

She thought quickly. That sounded reasonable. "Certainly. Is that all?"

"For now."

"Thank you, Mr. O'Donnell."

"At your service, ma'am."

Hardly! Pasting a smile on her face, she escaped, feeling as though she had pulled off quite a feat. Boyd didn't understand her reluctance with the man. He had told her bluntly that Mr. O'Donnell was her employee, that she should be giving him the orders. Abigail had been tempted to point out that Boyd, too, was her employee, and she certainly wasn't giving him orders. But she didn't feel quite bold enough to issue such a declaration. It was difficult enough to remind herself that Boyd was an employee.

Nearly skipping out toward the kitchen, Abigail was pleased both with her success and her escape. Nearing the back of the house, she could hear the slamming of pots and pans far before she reached the kitchen. The din increased, and she peeked around the doorway cautiously.

"Miranda?"

The housekeeper whirled around, her composure obviously gone. Even her spare, trim chignon was loose, her auburn hair escaping its normal confines. Pots and pans lay strewn about the kitchen as though thrown there. It dawned on Abigail that they probably had been. Obviously embarrassed, Miranda flushed.

"Is something wrong?"

"Oh, Miz Fairchild!" Miranda twisted her hands in her apron. "I just need to get hold of myself."

Abigail edged closer, trying to be considerate, yet tactful. "Do you want to tell me what brought this on?"

Miranda tried to keep her rigid posture, but failed. "It's that Mr. O'Donnell. Been trotting in here, tellin' me I need to be on a budget. Pushing papers in my face."

"I know what you mean. He scares me, too," Abigail confessed.

"I wish he'd just take care of the books and leave the kitchen alone."

Abigail girded her courage, always more readily gathered for others rather than herself. "Do you want me to talk to him?"

Miranda lifted cinnamon-colored eyes in mortification. "No. That won't be necessary. I'll deal with it."

"I could—"

"No, Miz Fairchild. You got enough to worry about, learnin' the ranch and all. No, it's my problem."

Abigail hesitated and saw that her interference might only worsen matters. "I'll trust it to your good judgment, Miranda. But if he continues to be a problem, come to me."

Leaving the kitchen, Abigail thought she heard a soft cry of distress, but then dismissed the notion. A woman as tough as Miranda wasn't given to such displays, although she softened whenever she spent time with little Michael. Her housekeeper had shown another side of herself since the baby had been born.

Abigail grinned. But then the child could charm a smile from a hardened criminal. The men still showed up when Michael sat outside on his blanket cooing at the sky, trees, and anything else he was just now discovering. Abigail glanced upstairs, glad that Lucy was watching over him. She needed the time to speak with Boyd.

It wouldn't be difficult to find him. He'd either be in the barn or the stables, where he fit in so naturally. His affinity for horses still impressed her. She'd come to the conclusion that even if she developed into a competent rider, she'd never have the grace Boyd possessed. Born to the saddle, he rode like an extension of the animal. Still prone to spills, Abigail spent as much time scrabbling for her balance as she did riding.

She knew she possessed a few talents. She was adept at parties and entertaining; dancing brought out her natural gracefulness. But ranching required a grace of its own, one she saw in Boyd and one she despaired of accomplishing herself.

On a hunch, she entered the barn. Having grown to love the smell of fragrant new hay and pungent, well-worn leather, the barn had indeed turned out to be a friendly place.

The few creatures kept inside greeted her with upturned noses as they sniffed her scent. She had learned so much in a short time. That animals, like people, possessed habits and personalities. Even though she still had problems keeping her seat on the mare, she had grown to learn that Dolly was a gentle beast.

Wandering inside the huge structure, Abigail glanced up at the tall rafters. The last of the day's sunshine poked through the high windows and glinted on stacks of baled hay. Soft sounds of the animals munching on hay and oats filtered through the quiet. A calico cat strolled out of her resting spot, yawned, and then scampered up to the loft. Continuing farther inside, Abigail spotted Boyd.

Squatting down beside one of the horses, he was talking quietly. "Nasty turn on the leg, but we'll get you fixed up." Standing, he patted the horse's flanks.

"They like you."

Boyd whirled around, obviously startled. "Didn't hear you come in."

"Apparently not." Her gaze moved toward the horse. "Is he going to be all right?"

"In a week or so. Got his hoof caught in a prairie dog hole. Lucky the hole wasn't any deeper."

Abigail flinched, knowing the end for the unfortunate animals that actually broke their legs. "I'm glad he'll be okay."

He turned to the horse, squatted down, and rechecked the leg. Abigail's throat grew dry as she watched the denim of his pants cling to long, muscular thighs. Swallowing, her gaze took in his shirt, which was pulled tightly across a well-corded back and impossibly broad shoulders. When he spoke, she nearly jumped in reaction. "I need to be putting on a poultice to keep the swelling down."

"Of course." Gathering her wits, she stepped back, her

skirt and petticoats rustling against the straw that carpeted the floor. "I talked to Mr.. O'Donnell." It was difficult to keep the glee from her voice.

"Oh?"

"We'll have a line of credit for the purchases." She could still feel the satisfaction.

"Good."

Disappointment surfaced. "You don't sound very pleased."

He shrugged. "I didn't think you were out of money."

"Neither did I."

"Then why the fuss?" His eyes lightened suddenly. "You thought the formidable Mr. O'Donnell would say no."

"Of course not," she denied hotly.

"I don't know why you're afraid to tell him what to do."

"Like I tell you what to do?"

He sucked in his breath. "You think I won't listen to you?"

Realizing her blunder, Abigail tried to amend her words. "It's not that. I respect your knowledge about the ranch."

"Uh-huh. Tell you what, *ma'am*. If it's all right with you, I'll get back to tending the horse. Unless you think I should be doing something else."

"Boyd, I—"

"What'll it be, *ma'am*?"

Exasperated, she turned on her heel. "I imagine you'll do as you want."

He didn't answer, and she stalked out of the barn. The sun was sinking in the west as she headed toward the house. But the crimson bath of color was lost on Abigail as she stormed ahead. She'd show him tomorrow who wasn't in control. Thickheaded, obtuse, *infernal man*!

The following morning, determined to be in control of the situation, Abigail waited beside her horse for Boyd to reach the ranch house. She wanted to look professional and prepared. He wasn't going to catch her tardy, in the midst of her breakfast, or without a well-packed lunch. Today she was ready. No more lady playing the rancher. She was going to be efficient and professional if it killed her.

Surprise filtered across his face when he spotted her, and
Abigail relished the satisfaction she felt. The early-morning
sun outlined his rugged form as he approached. He was a
formidable-looking specimen, she admitted. But she was
prepared. Until he spoke.

"Is little Michael still asleep?"

Of course. Boyd started every day playing with her son.
They both looked forward to the exchange. In her plans to
appear businesslike and unflustered, she'd forgotten. "No.
He's in the kitchen with Miranda. I think she's about to give
him his bath and then put him down for a while." Seeing the
disappointment flit over his expression, she added words in
a rush without considering the consequences of seeming
unprofessional. "But I'm sure you can catch them before
they go upstairs. I got out here early to check my saddlebags." She dug purposefully in the leather pouches. "Go on
in."

His face cleared. "I'll just be a minute."

Coward, she chastised herself. So much for being firm
and in control. But the longing on his face was clear. She
knew she should worry about the attachment growing
between Boyd and her son, but she felt only gratitude that
her son had an honest, devoted man like Boyd who cared for
him. Feeling petty for harboring resentment against him, she
knew he was only concerned with their best interests in
trying to instruct her about the ranch. After all, she was the
one who had asked Boyd to teach her.

Rethinking the lunch she had packed, Abigail headed
toward the back door. Slipping inside, she could hear the
sounds of the toddler's laughter and Boyd's deep voice coming
from the front parlor. Opening the larder, she retrieved the
freshly baked chocolate cake that Miranda had worked on
the day before. A thick layer of frosting encased the fragrant
confection. Slicing two generous pieces, she wrapped them
in a linen napkin. She remembered the leftover fried chicken
from dinner and routed around until she found it. Adding the
chicken to her booty, Abigail wrapped it all together in
another napkin and departed again through the back door.

She had time to stuff it all in her saddlebags before Boyd

joined her. Deciding to forget their minor squabble the night
before, she smiled at the pleased look on his face. Obviously
little Michael was as good for Boyd as he was for her son.

"It's a good ride over to the Hodges place," Boyd warned.

"I'm prepared," she announced, glad she'd added a
special lunch for them both.

"Joshua Hodges is willing to sell a couple of bulls, but we
have to look them over before agreeing to buy."

"I will leave that to your expertise."

"That's all right for now, but you'll need to learn how to
judge cattle as well."

"Which is the point for today's trip, isn't it?" she replied,
keeping the patience in her tone with a renewed effort.
While normally never short with anyone, she was finding
that altering her entire lifestyle was more than a little trying.
Having every word and action scrutinized made her nerves
screech.

"You're right. Well, we'd better get a move on."

She blinked in surprise. Just when she thought he would
force a point, he backed off. Darting a look at his face, she
absorbed the quiet strength painted there. His features were
like the rugged landscape, strong but infinitely appealing.

Thick, stubby eyelashes shadowed firm, high cheekbones,
made more pronounced by his jutting jawline. It was not a soft
face, but one that spoke of pain and hard work. He was as
different from her late husband as two men could be. While
Michael had been polished and smooth, Boyd possessed the
rough edges his hard life had carved out for him.

In the past months she'd grown to know that face, and
admire the man behind it. But now it was as though she saw
him for the first time. Her eyes were drawn to the silliest
things. Like the strength of his hands as he easily held the
reins, or the length of his muscled legs as he gripped them
around the proud stallion he rode.

It was absurd.

Boyd was her friend.

A sudden vision of him holding her as she gave birth
surfaced. Swallowing, she knew they'd shared far more than
many husbands and wives.

Still, it didn't explain her sudden obsession with his physical presence. He turned and caught her staring. Forcing her lips into a smile, she searched inanely for something to say. "Beautiful day, isn't it?"

Puzzlement bloomed, but he kindly refrained from saying so. "Uh-huh. You all right?"

Afraid that her thoughts had somehow escaped to reveal themselves on her features, she averted her face. "Perfectly." They rode in silence for some time, and Abigail let the quiet and beauty of her surroundings soothe some of her fractured nerves.

The day beckoned. Early still, the cool morning air blanketed the slopes. Mountain conifers towered above them. Beneath them, tough bear grass provided a cushion for their mounts. Abigail drew in a breath of the sweet-smelling breeze. Lavender buds unfolded into lilac bloom, while here and there grew a patch of the mountain man's true orchid, the Mountain Lady Slipper, gleaming like silken rubies.

The green bulk of Douglas fir and red cedar forests opened before them, and Abigail realized there was a great advantage to riding the land. She had seen far more from her vantage point on a horse in the past months than she had in her years in the West.

"Hodges will carry on like these bulls are priceless," Boyd said into the stillness, his deep voice startling a few of the birds that were perched on the rustling leaves of the alder trees.

"And so negotiation will be important?"

"Yep. Also, not lettin' on if we like the bulls. That'll drive the price up faster than lightning."

"It may surprise you, but I've done my share of bartering. While not for cattle, I have been responsible for purchasing all the household goods. I am aware of how merchants work."

"Yep. But cattle buying's a little different. Hodges isn't a merchant. It'd set his dander back if he thought we were treatin' him like one. No, first he's a cattleman. And he thinks he's doing us a favor by letting us buy the bulls."

"Is he?"

"Pretty much. We need the bulls, and he's got 'em."

"Is this the way business is normally conducted?"

"Nope. There're some local stock fairs in Cheyenne that have decent animals. Then once, twice a year you get on a train and go to a cattle auction. Helps if you know ahead of time what kind of stock you want. Right now we don't have a choice. We need the bulls Hodges has for sale."

Abigail's mind was tripping in frantic haste. "But eventually I'll have to go to the city to make these purchases?"

"Not eventually. In the next couple of months you'll have to make a trip. But this will bridge the gap for now."

Abigail gulped. She was not looking forward to traveling alone, haranguing over cattle whose merits she did not recognize. Her gaze slid sideways. She wondered if this was another tactic to make her abandon her plan and hire a manager.

"But if I had a manager he could do the traveling?"

"'Course. But I thought you were set on running the place yourself."

He had a way of summing things up that made her sound as if she didn't know her mind. "I was just inquiring."

"Uh-huh."

"Are we very far from the Hodges place?"

"No. Just over a few ridges. Haven't you ever been to his place?"

"No. I guess he didn't entertain much, being a bachelor. Actually, I've hardly had any contact with him. When we gave parties, I generally entertained the wives, while Michael talked with the men." A fleeting impression of those happy days stabbed her with a painful intensity. She purposely disregarded the thought. "So I don't really know Mr. Hodges that well."

"He seems to be looking forward to seeing you."

"I can't imagine why . . ." Abigail began. Then it struck her. Surely the man didn't have ideas about their visit other than business. Granted, she was an eligible widow now, one with considerable assets to bring to a marriage, but . . .

"What—" The words stuck in her throat. "What did you tell him?"

"That I'd pass his sentiments on to you."

Abigail noticed the reflexive twitching of a muscle in Boyd's cheek, wondering what caused it. A suspicion touched her thoughts, and she smiled in unexpected satisfaction. "Then I'll make it perfectly clear that I'm only interested in purchasing some breeding stock."

His jaw relaxed a fraction. "There's clear ground ahead, so we can make up some time now."

He kicked his horse into a canter, and she reacted as well. The mare responded to her commands, and soon they were moving quickly. Exhilarated that she didn't fall off, Abigail found herself actually enjoying the ride.

In short time a house came into view. Long, low, and rambling, it bore the appearance of a home needing some attention. The ill-tended vegetable garden cried out for weeding while the unswept yard was little more than a worn place in the dirt. No flowers decorated the untidy porch that needed painting as badly as the railing that struggled to stay upright. Remembering that Hodges had no wife to attend to those details, Abigail felt the stirrings of sympathy, something that came far too easily to her. Purposely she firmed her lips, remembering Boyd's words. If the man thought she was husband hunting, she didn't want to extend sympathy too far.

Hodges waved to them from the corral, and they dismounted. After tying their horses to the hitching rail, Abigail and Boyd joined him.

A bull of a man, Joshua Hodges exuded strength. His blunt features were relieved only with a mustache that shadowed beefy lips. Nondescript brown hair escaped his worn Stetson and matched equally mediocre brown eyes. But enthusiasm lit them as he stared at Abigail. Feeling a twinge of nervousness, she moved closer to Boyd.

"Boyd. Mrs. Fairchild. Good to see you."

"Delighted, Mr. Hodges. It's kind of you to invite us out today," Abigail replied politely.

Joshua flushed in pleasure. "No trouble a'tall. Would you like something to drink?"

"We'd best see to the bulls," Boyd answered for them both.

"Sure. They're in the rear corrals. Come on back."

During the next hour Abigail learned the finer methods of judging a bull, but wisely listened, rather than contributing to the conversation. Boyd negotiated a price on the bulls, having decided to buy them both. Abigail was glad to see the men conclude the deal. The sun had climbed high in the sky, and the temperature was soaring. A trickle of perspiration beaded on her neck beneath her heavy hair.

"I hope to be seeing you again soon, Mrs. Fairchild." Hodges held her hand longer than absolutely necessary as he bid them goodbye.

"I'm glad we could do business, Mr. Hodges. And as you know, a ranch keeps a person very busy."

His smile wavered for a moment, but then returned. "Surely do, ma'am. But I expect you'll find some time now and then for visiting."

Abigail held her smile in place with an effort. She didn't want to offend him, but she certainly didn't want to encourage him, either. "Most of my time is spent with my son, Mr. Hodges. He keeps me very busy."

"Poor fatherless mite," he agreed.

Stiffening, she met Boyd's equally affronted gaze. One thing she never felt about her child was pity. "Well, we'd best be going, Mr. Hodges."

"Certainly." He started forward, but Boyd had already moved closer and gave Abigail a hand up onto the horse.

Boyd mounted, and together they bid Hodges goodbye with combined relief. They rode in silence until his ranch was far behind them. The air seemed somehow sweeter as they left Hodges behind and rode into the virgin forest.

Climbing upward over a rise, Abigail spotted an alpine lake. "Can we stop there?"

"I was thinkin' that it looked like a good spot." He nudged his horse forward, and Abigail followed. They dismounted, and Boyd let the horses graze near the water.

Humor flashed in his eyes. "You remember to bring some lunch this time?"

Thinking of her surprise, she smiled smugly. "I should say so." She retrieved the linen napkins holding the bounty, along with her canteen.

Waiting until Boyd produced fruit and jerky, she unfolded the napkin with a flourish. It was hard to say who was more surprised. They both stared at the globs of chocolate frosting that had melted in the high heat, running down to cover the breaded sides of the chicken. It was, all in all, a hell of a mess.

Gamely she tried to pick one of the pieces of chicken clean, disappointed that it had turned into such a mess. "I can't believe it all melted."

"Good thing I brought lunch for two." Amusement continued to dance in his blue eyes.

Her surprise ruined, Abigail resented looking unprepared once again. Couldn't she do one thing right? It seemed that since she had decided to learn ranching, she had become a complete incompetent. "No, thank you. I'll eat this."

"That?" He pointed to the less-than-appetizing-looking mess.

"Certainly." Bravely she picked up a piece of chicken and felt chocolate run into the palm of her hand. Refusing to be deterred, she lifted the drumstick to her mouth and took a bite. It tasted awful, and, to her mortification, chocolate dripped down her chin.

Laughing outright, Boyd leaned over. "I didn't mean to poke fun at you." He reached out his hand and cupped her chin to wipe the chocolate away.

His touch rocketed through her. She raised startled eyes and met his gaze. Heat stabbed her as she saw the blue of his eyes darken even further. She wondered if his breathing had deepened as much as hers. His hand didn't leave her face; instead he moved it to graze her cheek. His fingers, long, supple, and strong, evoked an emotion she was afraid to give a name to.

He angled his head, and she wondered if he would kiss her. She was scared to find out, yet a not unfamiliar longing gripped her. Thinking such feelings had died, she was amazed to learn that they were alive and soaring. And caused by her foreman.

Studying Boyd's face, she acknowledged the strong, uncompromising jaw, the clean, sturdy lines that spelled out a devastatingly handsome man. Eyes as deeply blue as the ocean were defined by a slash of dark, forbidding brows. Her stomach took a dive to her knees and stayed there. She wondered suddenly what he thought of her.

As though answering her unspoken question, he gently pushed back the heavy length of hair that lay on her shoulders. His fingers then cradled the back of her neck as he pulled her close. Questions fled as she felt the touch of his lips against hers. Not demanding, but giving. A heat-seeking, life-giving sensation. Firm lips molded themselves to hers.

Trembling, she could feel the weakness invade her entire body. He must have felt it because he slowly drew his tongue along the edge of her lips. A soft thrilling dampness stole through her as her body signaled the return of forgotten passion. Leaning into the hard width of his chest, she felt her breasts respond by tightening inside her shirt, the hardened nipples grazing his chest.

Boyd's hands were both strong and gentle as they stroked the length of her back and then settled to rest on her collarbone. One long finger eased to the hollow of her throat and then brushed downward over the soft skin that led to the first button of her shirt. Unfastening it, he boldly reached inside to cup one aching breast.

Bittersweet pleasure shot through her. The dampness between her legs spiraled. The intimate gesture made her acutely aware of desires she had put aside, desires she had no intention of renewing.

Passion flamed like a defiant warning. Shakily she pulled back, uncertain where the embrace could lead. Not certain she could control its destiny, not certain she wanted to.

Rising to her feet, Abigail ducked her face as she walked blindly toward her horse. She might have been raised in the East, but it hadn't taken her long to learn the code of the

West. Her friend Jem's situation had spelled it out clearly. Women ranch owners could never hope to have relationships with their foremen. Ever. It was a dictate of a rigid, uncompromising society and if broken would lead to the blacklisting of her ranch. Pursuing such a relationship had nearly cost Jem her ranch.

Abigail knew that entertaining the notion spelled disaster as surely as the feelings that still tugged her toward Boyd. Reluctantly she met his eyes, knowing there could be nothing else, damnably wishing there could be.

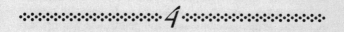 *4*

Boyd inspected the new stock with a vengeance. Cursing himself for being a fool, he took out his frustration on everything around him. Which fortunately, so far, had been only the corral gate that didn't function properly, and an unfortunate cowhand who had greeted him too cheerily.

"You bent on tearing something up?" Randy Kreiger, his assistant foreman, greeted him.

"Don't you have any work to do?" Boyd replied, not bothering to hide his crankiness.

"So, Tom was right. You are meaner'n a bear woke up in the middle of winter."

"I don't know about that. Bears got a little more sense."

"You want to tell me what that means?"

Boyd sighed, remembering the intimate exchange with Abigail. Nope, that was something that had to remain private. If word got out, it would ruin her reputation. A woman ranch owner and her foreman didn't fraternize. Ever. "Hell, no. Just got up on the wrong side of the bed."

"We about ready for the drive?"

"Yep—another week or so. Just got to clear it with Ab—Miz Fairchild. They're her cattle we're taking to market." He needed some time away, to clear his head. The drive would be perfect. A month of dirt and sweat should remind him where he belonged.

"You know, Miz Fairchild's getting along better. Never thought I'd see a delicate lady like her take to learning how a ranch works. She looks like all lace and fluff, but she must have some grit." He grinned suddenly. "Now, if she could just learn how to stay on her horse all the time . . ."

Knowing there was no malice in the other man's words, Boyd didn't take offense. It was true. Abigail had less aptitude for ranching than most anyone he had ever met. Many of the ranch wives, born in the West, rode a horse as easily as a man. But Abigail's Eastern roots were still clearly ingrained. While gracious, soft, and gentle, she was neither a born horsewoman, nor a clear leader.

"Boyd, I'll check on the northern shacks today, unless you need me for something else."

"Sounds good. I'll take the eastern side."

"Miz Fairchild going with you?"

Suspicion flared in Boyd's eyes, and his voice grew taut as he bit out a reply. "Why?"

Taken aback, Randy shrugged and restlessly readjusted his hat. "No reason. Guess you really did get up on the wrong side of the bed."

Boyd ran a weary hand across his face. Too many days of self-recrimination and too many restless nights were catching up to him. "Sorry. Guess I'm acting like a bear, all right."

Awkward now, Randy tried to amend the moment. "It's okay. It's not like you make it a habit. Hell, everybody has a bad day now and then."

"Beers are on me Saturday night."

Randy brightened. "In that case you can be a bear all week!"

Boyd managed a portion of a smile as Randy swaggered away. Yep, getting away was exactly what he needed.

Abigail roamed restlessly through the house. A sense of unexpected agitation filled her. Having spent a sleepless night reliving the moment that Boyd had kissed her had only increased that agitation. Even now she reached up to touch the contours of her lips, remembering the feel of Boyd's mouth against hers. Possessive, promising, dangerous. And what about the reaction he'd awakened in her?

She wondered if she was what her mother had termed a

"loose woman." When Michael died, Abigail thought she'd put all these feelings to rest with him. But she hadn't given her dead husband a moment's thought when in Boyd's arms. Instead she had envisioned a different conclusion to the afternoon, one that would put an end to the aching she had felt all night.

Wandering through the front parlor, she turned and headed toward the kitchen. As she had expected, Miranda was inside. She was seated at the table with a cup of coffee.

She jumped guiltily when Abigail entered. "I was just finishin' up—"

"I wish you weren't. I could use someone to have a cup of coffee with."

"Let me get you some." Miranda rose to pour a cup of coffee, then added a generous dollop of milk. She took it to the table where Abigail had pulled up a chair.

Miranda handed her the coffee, then resumed her seat while Abigail sipped the rich but milk-diluted brew. "Mmm, this is good."

Miranda cautiously sipped her own coffee, unaccustomed to chatting with her employer at the kitchen table. "You plannin' to go riding with Boyd today?"

Startled by the reference to the center of her thoughts, Abigail pushed her cup in a circle, sending a loud scraping sound across the saucer. She winced, ignoring Miranda's question, instead asking one of her own. "Are you happy not being married?"

Miranda choked, sputtering on the coffee and, no doubt, the question.

Abigail jumped up, patting Miranda on the back. "I'm sorry. Please don't pay any mind to what I asked. I realize I was prying."

Regaining her equilibrium, Miranda waved Abigail back to her chair. "No, it's all right, Miz Fairchild. Just no one's asked me that in a spell."

"It's something I've been wondering about. I never expected to think anything of single life after Michael, but now . . ." Restlessness gripped her again as she remembered Boyd's kiss, his warm caresses, her own reawakened desire.

"You're still young," Miranda answered bluntly. "No reason you shouldn't be wondering. And there's a dozen ranch owners who'd probably like to come courting."

Abigail ignored the reference to other owners. Despite the social barriers, she knew her attraction was not to just anyone. No, Boyd had stoked up a response from a deadened fire. One she had purposely banked. "Do you ever wish you'd married, Miranda?"

Indecision flickered across her face. "It's too late for me to be worrying about marriage, Miz Fairchild. My day's past."

Shaken out of her own self-absorption, Abigail looked, really looked, at Miranda. Shining auburn hair topped a face with even features and snapping cinnamon-colored eyes. Although uncommonly tall, she had a fine figure. Abigail imagined how she would look if her hair wasn't crammed into a tight topknot and she was wearing something other than drab, shapeless clothing. If Miranda fixed up more, she could be striking. "Do you want it to be past, Miranda?"

Regret and pain flickered in the older woman's eyes, and Abigail's always sympathetic heart constricted. "Doesn't matter anymore. I never was one to attract the gentlemen."

"I don't know why you say that. You're a lovely woman, Miranda."

The unexpected blush that suffused Miranda's face shocked Abigail. She wondered how long it had been since the woman had received a compliment.

"I'm plain as a vanilla cookie," Miranda protested.

"You just take great pains to make it appear that way," Abigail insisted. "Take your hair, for example. If you'd allow some of the beautiful color to escape that tight little bun, it would frame your face in a most becoming way."

Miranda's hand strayed to the wisps of hair near her topknot, and her voice emerged as little more than a whisper. "You like the color?"

"It's stunning. Far more unusual than plain blond or brown."

A smile grew in the corners of Miranda's mouth, then suffused her face. "Well, I never . . ."

"Maybe it's time you did," Abigail said softly. Although they hadn't discussed her dilemma, Abigail was glad she had stopped to chat with her housekeeper. She wondered suddenly how many of the inhabitants of the Triple Cross were keeping secrets, nursing hidden hopes.

The knocker on the front door rapped suddenly, startling them both. Miranda came back to earth with an almost audible thud. "I'd best see who that is."

In moments she returned, her face wreathed in smiles. "Speak of the devil. It's Joshua Hodges." At Abigail's blank look, she added, "It looks like he's come a-courtin'."

Abigail thought of several unladylike responses, but she managed a smile for Miranda's benefit. "Thank you." She took a few steps toward the door and turned back. "And for the talk as well."

Leaving Miranda with a smile, Abigail clenched her nervous hands together as she entered the parlor. Joshua Hodges sat perched on the edge of a Queen Anne armchair, looking as though he wasn't certain the delicate piece of furniture could hold his weight. She wondered the same thing. Dressed in what must be his Sunday finery, Joshua resembled a bull stuffed into a suit with a boiled collar and a string tie for a noose. If she didn't wish so badly that he hadn't chosen to call on her, she would have laughed at the comparison. "Good afternoon, Mr. Hodges."

He stood up suddenly, the precarious chair tilting as he did. "Mrs. Fairchild." Awkwardly he stuck out a bouquet of handpicked flowers. Apparently they'd wilted somewhat on the journey, much as the man who held them. Carefully slicked-back hair held the impression of his hat, and he looked as though he might burst through the seams of his tight-fitting suit.

"Thank you, they're lovely." Abigail laid them on the marble-topped, walnut table before taking a seat opposite him. Watching her movements, he sat down as well.

"Looks like the bulls I sold you are settlin' in," he offered.

"Oh, if we're going to discuss business, I should call Boyd in. He—"

"No! I mean, I'm not here to talk business. No need to bother Boyd."

She settled back a fraction keeping her smile even, hoping to look interested, but not too interested.

When she didn't speak immediately, Hodges rushed to fill the silence. "But I do think those bulls will do you a good job."

Abigail's eyes widened, wondering if this was the man's awkward attempt at courting. But he seemed to realize his blunder at the same time.

"Not that I'm here to discuss that sort of thing. I know a lady like you doesn't . . . that is . . ." One finger eased under his tight collar, obviously hoping for an escape.

He fumbled so badly, she took pity on him. "The weather's staying quite warm, isn't it?"

Relief flooded his face. Florid cheeks billowed as he responded. "Hotter than a . . . that is, yes, ma'am, it's warm."

Another awkward silence spread between them.

"Would you care for something cool to drink?" she asked, thinking she could flee to the other room. But as she spoke, Miranda entered with a tray.

"Thought you might like some refreshment," Miranda offered as she placed the tray between them.

Abigail eyed the heavily laden tray with dismay. Cookies and slices of cake rested next to a full pot of tea. "Thank you, Miranda. Mr. Hodges, some tea?"

He accepted the tea, a piece of cake, several cookies, and after finishing them, he took a second piece of cake. Despairing of ever getting rid of the man, she ate her own slice of cake so there wouldn't be too much food left, giving him a reason to linger.

"That was right good, Mrs. Fairchild. Don't get sweets like that at home."

"Don't you have a cook?" she asked politely.

"Well, Homer's a good enough cook. But he doesn't have

an inclination for baking cakes and such. Takes a lady's touch for that."

Smiling, she swallowed her amusement. "I must say you're right. I know Miranda provides just that touch."

It was apparent from his expression that he was getting frustrated by his inability to stay on track. He laid his cake plate and cup on the table. "That wasn't exactly what I meant."

"Of course, Miranda is my housekeeper as well." Abigail waved around the serene house. "Perhaps you should consider hiring a woman who can keep your home in order."

His voice was a sputter. "I didn't have a housekeeper in mind."

"Oh?" She smothered the giggle that threatened to erupt. "That's unfortunate. But it's been delightful discussing it with you." She stood, and Joshua followed suit. Outmaneuvered, he followed her to the front door. "It was nice of you to stop by."

"But, I didn't get to—" He pulled up his stocky height and found his voice. "Mrs. Fairchild, I stopped by to see if I could escort you to the dance in town this Saturday."

"That's very kind, Mr. Hodges, but I must decline. You see, I have a child to take care of."

"But what about Miranda?"

Her smile was kind and gentle, as though she spoke to someone of limited intelligence. "But I thought we had that clear. Miranda is my housekeeper and cook."

"So she is, but—"

"You might want to stop by and speak to Boyd before you leave. I'm sure he'd like to thank you again for selling us the new stock." She swung the door another foot toward closing.

"But, I—"

"Oh, and I mustn't forget to thank you for the flowers. That was quite thoughtful. If you'll excuse me now, I must see to little Michael."

"Yes, I know you need to do that, but—"

"Boyd should be over near the corrals. Thank you again for stopping by." Gently she pushed the door closed, slumping against the wooden panel as it clicked into place. Being a widow with a large ranch put her in a precarious, almost vulnerable position. Suddenly she wished she had a place to escape to because she had a sinking feeling this wasn't going to be Joshua Hodges's last visit.

Within the next few days Abigail was bombarded with visitors. All male. And all interested in the widow Fairchild. She had never met a more distasteful bunch of men. One in particular, Edward Peterson, made his intentions clear. He wanted the Triple Cross, and he was willing to wed Abigail to get it. As she closed the door behind him, she suspected that it wouldn't particularly matter if she sprouted two heads or a face full of warts.

All the man wanted was her ranch. Unlike the others, he had made no bones about his intentions. Instead he had outlined why he would be her best choice, stating bluntly that he could make the Triple Cross prosper, insuring a sound future for her and Michael.

She wondered if other women in her position made equally loveless matches, cold-bloodedly considering which man would be the best provider. Remembering the love she had shared with her late husband, the thought chilled her to the bone.

Upstairs she heard the gentle laughter from her son as he played with Miranda. Thinking of the fond devotion Boyd bestowed on little Michael, not for monetary gain, but simply because he cared, she couldn't imagine another man taking his place. It occurred to her suddenly that he had become irreplaceable in many ways. And the realization scared her to death.

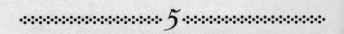

5

"You want to do what?" Boyd asked, disbelief mirrored in both his face and voice.

"I said I want to go on the trail drive," Abigail repeated. "I can't learn unless I'm involved in every aspect of the ranch."

"Excuse me for saying so, but the trail's no place for a woman." He wondered if she'd lost her good sense. Learning the ranch was one thing. Going on a trail drive was another.

"Other owners and managers have no idea of what's involved in a trail drive?" she asked pointedly.

"Well, I didn't say that, but—"

"Then I need to know as well." Her entire stance grew tense as she tapped long, slender fingers against the top of the desk. "It's time I learned everything about running the ranch. I no longer want to be in a vulnerable position." Boyd wondered at the change in her as she paled and then avoided his gaze. "I don't want to depend on anyone else for Michael's future. I have to know every aspect of the ranch."

So when he was gone she wouldn't have to depend on anyone else. The thought was unbidden, but he sensed its accuracy.

"When . . ." She stumbled over the words. "When do you want to leave on this trail drive?"

"Day after tomorrow."

"Then I'll plan on it."

Boyd started to turn away and then heard soft, hesitant tones beckon him.

"Is there anything special I need to bring?"

"A change of clothing." He made his voice purposely blunt. "Although I'm not sure where you'll change in front of a dozen men." He watched her redden in embarrassment, then pale again. "A poncho, duster, and a bedroll."

"No food?"

"The chuck wagon's part of the drive. The cook and biscuit shooter will be in charge of all the grub."

"Biscuit shooter?"

"Cook's helper. They won't fix anything fancy. Beans, stew, hardtack, and coffee that'll burn a hole through your belly."

"See, I need to know these things."

He heard the pleading in her voice and ignored it. She had just told him she didn't expect to have him around much longer. He wondered when she had come to this decision. Had kissing her incited a decision to fire him once she had learned the reins of control?

"If you insist on going, you'll have a reputation one way or another," he continued relentlessly.

She recoiled, but then her strength that was usually disguised beneath lace, ruffles, and softness pushed its way forward. "What about Jem McIntire?"

"She was treated like a man until she married Reese. Is that what you want?"

"I simply want to be treated with respect. I may not be particularly apt, but this is my ranch."

Tension simmered, thick and uncut, between them. The challenge was thrown out. Too late to be redrawn, too potent to go unconfronted.

"And I won't forget it, *ma'am*." Not waiting for her answer, Boyd picked up his hat and strode toward the front door. If she had a reply, he refused to listen to it. But silence swirled in the hall as he left.

Two days. And then one month of pure hell.

Abigail swatted at the mosquitoes hovering near her neck. The sun had climbed high in the sky, bringing bright rays, unrelenting heat, and swarms of insects. Shuddering, she wondered what other kinds of bugs lurked here. They had left early in the morning before daylight and hadn't stopped yet. Six hours in the saddle with no relief. She wondered if Boyd planned to push on without a break simply to see if she would plead for one. Straightening her tired body, she resolved to keep her complaints to herself if it killed her.

Boyd had purposely ignored her since early morning. Although unfailingly polite in front of the men, he had disassociated himself from her as soon as possible, and they hadn't exchanged a word since. She wasn't certain why he had gotten so angry, other than her assertion to come along on the drive. That *had* seemed to set him back. He apparently didn't understand her need to no longer be vulnerable. Which made her wonder suddenly if Joshua Hodges's visit had angered him.

Squirming uncomfortably, she acknowledged that she needed to find a place to stop for some privacy. Not having completely thought things out, she realized that there could be several awkward difficulties on the trail.

Feeling perspiration trickle between her breasts, Abigail wondered how the others appeared so unaffected. Her energy already sapped, she guessed she would be completely drained by the end of the day.

Her stubbornness might be her undoing, but she wasn't going to sit at home and entertain suitors who wanted control of her ranch. Not vain enough to think she would have callers run to her side because of her beauty, she knew her looks and personality were not what interested men now.

No, her primary attraction was owning a ranch that covered a good portion of the territory, one that would prove to be an irresistible lure to most men. A desire to escape Hodges, Peterson, and any other potential suitors had been the driving force behind wanting to go on the trail ride. But she sensed that she had driven a wedge in her relationship with Boyd because of her insistence.

It wasn't in her nature to exhibit such stubbornness, yet she couldn't squelch the need to shape her own destiny. It was glaringly apparent that she wouldn't be in such a tenuous position had she not turned her future over to her deceased husband, content to let him make all their decisions. Now she was paying for that complacency—she was a prime target for the men who saw her as a way to get control of the Triple Cross.

Two more hours passed, and Abigail thought she might scream with the need to stop. Then suddenly as they came down over a rise, a camp appeared in her line of vision. The chuck wagon was unhitched, and a cheery fire blazed. Long-handled pots hung from a frame over the fire, and Abigail could smell food cooking. She sniffed, unable to identify the aroma. But she didn't care what she ate. Anything would taste good. Her stomach rumbled in anticipation.

By the time she reached the camp, Abigail couldn't wait to slide down from her horse. Boyd rode up before she could.

"I'm so glad we stopped," Abigail began, ready to confess both her hunger and weariness.

"Can't run all the fat off the beef," he replied. "They have to stop and graze." He pointed to the west. "There's water close by."

"Oh." So their stop had nothing to do with human comforts, only the cattle. "How'd you get the camp set up so fast?"

He looked at her in a manner that instantly made her feel stupid. "The chuck wagon and scouts go ahead and set up camp, so we don't waste time."

Of course. She could feel the heat of embarrassment color her cheeks. Obviously it took time to set up camp, build a fire. But she tried to sound nonchalant. "That sounds like a good method."

His voice was dry. "It's worked well in the past."

"A routine's good," she acknowledged, wishing she knew more about the whole business. She itched to get her hands on a manual that would outline everything that happened on a trail drive. Unfortunately she knew no such books existed.

"Some of the time the chuck wagon'll ride behind the cattle with the remuda, breathing dust. But we know the route, that water's here. Later on, in unfamiliar territory, we'll just push on until we find water. Otherwise, there's no point in stopping."

"The remuda?" she questioned blankly.

"Remember the eighty extra horses tagging along?" She nodded, and he continued. "The men change mounts two, three times a day. You can only ride a cow pony hard maybe four or five hours at a time."

"What about Dolly?" Abigail asked with a trace of panic. She didn't want to switch her gentle, dependable mount.

His smile contained indulgence and a rare trace of mockery. "I doubt you'll be riding hard enough to need a change of horses."

Stung by the comment, she wished he would go away so she could find some privacy and then fill a plate and eat. But he surprised her again.

"We'd best check out the cattle."

"Excuse me?"

"We need to look over the herd," he repeated.

"But haven't the men been doing that?" Gazing around at the huge, milling mass of cattle, she couldn't imagine what Boyd referred to. With all the dust they kicked up, it was hard to see much other than the animals' heads and flanks as they milled about.

His voice was patient, irritatingly so. "You can't just run 'em all day and hope we're on target. We have to check out the beef, see if we're pacing them right."

She glanced longingly at the campfire and then resolutely disregarded her hunger. "If that's what I need to learn about, let's go."

Boyd introduced her to the point riders, men who rode the front of the herd, keeping the animals headed in the right direction. Then she met the swing riders, flank riders, and finally the dust-covered men who rode drag and kept the lame animals and the stragglers from falling too far behind. Overwhelmed by all the necessary and seemingly flawless precision of the cowhands, Abigail stayed quietly by Boyd's side, trying to absorb just a fraction of the information being thrown at her.

Together they rode through the strung-out line of cows as

Boyd checked on the lead animals who kept abreast of the herd. "The lead animals keep the herd moving," he explained as she watched him. "These steers have a natural instinct to lead, and the others will follow."

"Do they know where they're heading to?" she asked in a horrified whisper, thinking of the slaughtering chutes the beasts were trundling toward.

"I doubt it," Boyd replied dryly. "They are animals, after all."

"But that's terrible," she protested, hating to think that the noble beasts reached such an ignominious end after bravely leading their companions along the trail.

"Would be even more terrible to take all these cows to market and then ask the slaughterhouse not to butcher 'em."

She felt the heat rise in her cheeks. "You needn't be so snippy."

"And you need to know this is a business, Abigail. We're selling meat on the hoof. It's not romantic, it's not noble. It's business, pure and simple."

She snapped her mouth shut, hating his logic, hating that he was also right. For the next hour she rode quietly beside him until he seemed satisfied with his inspection. "We should keep this pace for the next day or so and check again."

"Whatever you say." Coughing, she held her fist to her mouth, overwhelmed by the swirling dust kicked up by the mass of cattle.

"Pull up your bandanna," Boyd instructed.

"What?" She coughed again, harder.

"Your bandanna."

"I don't have one."

She couldn't distinguish his words, but heard the flow of a muttered curse. He pulled his own from his neck. "Tie this on and then pull it up over your face."

Unable to manage the reins and the bandanna, she struggled with both. He issued another muffled curse and led them away from the cattle to the slopes of a gully. Leaning close, he tied on the bandanna, his hands quickly efficient. Still, his touch singed a new path through her, and instantly she remembered his hands on other parts of her anatomy.

Pulling back, he examined her critically. "Now pull it up."

She obeyed, hoping the material would mask her unwanted feelings, the desire that sparked like lightning on a dry prairie.

He nodded. "Keep it up over your mouth and nose and you'll breathe better."

"What about you?" she asked, her voice muffled beneath the cloth.

"I'll scrounge up another one."

She fingered the cotton square. "Thank you."

His voice sounded strained, almost gruff. "It's nothing."

"Would it be all right to get something to eat now?" She needed to get a little distance, put things back into perspective.

"Sure, but don't you think you want to take a break before you head back to camp?"

"Break?" She looked around blankly. All she could see was a lot of scrub and, of course, endless acres of milling cattle.

His eyes met hers. "You might want some privacy."

Her face flushed again. "Yes, thank you. I would."

He pointed up the rise, flanked by scrub and a row of cedars. "No one's riding this part of the herd right now."

Gratefully she kicked her horse forward and headed up the gulch. Knowing that Boyd hoped to make the trip difficult enough to make her quit, she was surprised but pleased that he'd been sensitive to her needs.

When she rejoined him, Boyd simply turned his horse and rode toward the chuck wagon, easing the entire embarrassing moment. The camp, as they approached, issued an aroma that stirred Abigail's hunger even more. She hoped Boyd would eat with her. She found it more than a little disconcerting to be the only woman on the drive.

As Boyd had tried to tell her, she admitted silently. She seemed to be surrounded by masculine walls of flesh. No matter where she looked, there were men. And she couldn't

help but wonder how much more awkward this would grow.
She knew that sleeping, changing clothes, and even more
personal ablutions had to be performed. But back at the
ranch house these things hadn't really occurred to her. Now
they were crowding her thoughts with disturbing intensity.

Glancing up, she saw John Sims's stare fixed upon her,
and she bit back the uncomfortable sensation the man
caused. Certain his glances were harmless, still she didn't
like the way his eyes always seemed to be on her.

To her relief, Boyd fell into step beside her as they
reached the chuck wagon. The stew in the smoke-blackened
dutch oven smelled uncommonly good, and even the dark
coffee looked appealing as they filled plates and cups with
both. She took a sip of the bitter brew and felt it scorch her
mouth. It was as strong as Boyd had promised. Discreetly
she set the cup on the ground, wondering if the coffee was
in fact eating up the lining of her stomach. But the stew was
a different story.

Several bites later, she turned to Boyd with a smile. "I
don't think I'll get tired of this."

"Tell me that in a month."

Her mouth dropped open, and she snapped it shut with an
effort. "A month?"

Angling his head, he carefully watched her expression.
"Sure. How long did you think the drive would take?"

A week or less! Why hadn't she asked? Abigail had never
intended to leave little Michael for so long. Averting her
face, she stared intently at the now unappealing stew. "Oh,
I wasn't positive."

"But not a month," he observed accurately.

She wished for once she could be one step ahead of him.
She hated to appear so inept all the time, as though she
never thought before she acted. "Since I've never been on a
trail ride, I couldn't say."

"We have a lot of ground to cover. And it's not a pleasure
trip."

"I'm aware of that, Boyd." Painfully so. And she didn't
have the work to do that the cowhands did. So far the men
had not only ridden the herd, but she had seen the cook and

the wrangler gathering brush and chopping firewood while other hands had cared for the horses and performed other chores. But maintaining her seat on the horse for hours had been anything but pleasure. Thank goodness they had stopped for the day.

He stood, dumped a bit of uneaten stew in the slop pan, and then added his plate to the wreck pan. "We'll be ready to roll in an hour or so."

"Roll?"

"We ride from sunrise to sunset. We've got a half day yet to put in." With that, he walked away.

This time Abigail didn't bother to close her mouth. Her shock wouldn't allow it.

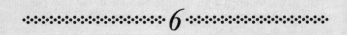

6

By evening Abigail was convinced that she would die in her saddle. She would be buried somewhere in the middle of this desolate land without even a marker. That is, if Boyd stopped long enough to dispose of her body.

By evening, when she nearly stumbled over the already pitched camp, she was too numb to smell the smoke of the fire or the food that was cooking. The sun was still in the sky, but only just barely. Hanging by a thread, daylight was rapidly surrendering to darkness. Every muscle screaming, Abigail managed to dismount, wondering if her legs would support her.

Hanging on to the mare, she swayed for a while before she stood upright. "I don't know how you do it, Dolly. Carrying me, walking all that time." She ran a sympathetic hand over the horse's neck.

Despite the pain it caused, she removed the horse's saddle, knowing from Boyd's relentless lessons that care of the horse came before care of the human. Weighing forty pounds, the saddle nearly dragged her to the ground as she pulled it off.

A young cowhand appeared at her side. "We keep all the horses together in a rope corral at night, ma'am. The nighthawk's in charge of them." He held out his hands for the reins. "I'll take her over, Miz Fairchild."

She focused. Young Billy Kendall. "Thanks, Billy."

He untied her bedroll and handed it to her, along with her saddlebags. Nonchalantly he picked up the saddle she had labored to remove, swung it over one shoulder, and then, tipping his hat, led Dolly away.

Shaking her head at the ease everyone else possessed, she rubbed her aching posterior. Today she had only fallen off three times. She must be improving.

Immensely relieved not to be the one wiping down the horse, she took her bedroll to a nearby tree and slid slowly to the ground, using the tree to support her swaying body. The chores and hard work seemed to have no end. She wondered if she had signed on for a ride to the end of the earth. Closing her eyes in accumulated weariness and pain, she didn't feel herself drift off to sleep. "Abigail!"

She turned away, burrowing into the tree as a hand shook her shoulder.

"Abigail, wake up!"

But she didn't want to. There was blessed escape in sleep.

"Come on. You've got to eat and lay out your bedroll."

Recognizing Boyd's voice, she opened one eye groggily. "I don't have to eat."

"Grumpy?"

If that was laughter she heard in his voice, she was going to kill him. Ignoring muscles that demanded to be left alone, she pulled herself up to a sitting position. "No, I'm just resting."

"You always snore when you're resting?"

"Snore!" She glanced around, saw other men nearby, and lowered her voice. "I do *not* snore!"

"And how would you know that?"

Midnight-blue eyes filled with amusement, and she considered killing him on the spot. Unfortunately she doubted she could lift an arm, much less a weapon. "You are insufferable."

He laid a hand across his chest in mock protest. "You wound me."

"Not yet," she muttered.

"Come on, you need to eat." He reached out a hand to help her up.

"I told you I'm not hungry."

"You think you're tired now? Try the same routine tomorrow on less food and energy, then you'll be tired."

Knowing he was right didn't lessen her resentment. Painfully she pulled herself to her feet, ignoring his outstretched hand. But he didn't seem to take offense. Instead he walked beside her toward the camp, some of his earlier ill humor absent.

Stiff-legged, she knew her walk must resemble a stagger, but she didn't care. She would eat the cursed food and then fall into the oblivion of sleep.

Men relaxed around the fire, eating, smoking, talking, and, remarkably, laughing. She wondered how any of them had the energy. Dully she accepted the plate Henry the cook handed her.

"Hot rocks, Miz Fairchild?" Henry asked.

Squinting, she wondered if she could have heard Henry correctly.

"They're biscuits, ma'am."

She nodded and watched while he plopped the hot biscuits on top of the food. The scraping of forks across tin plates added to the gentle rumble of noise around the chuck wagon. Deciding she needed quiet, she sought a seat farthest away from the others.

She sat cross-legged, tailor fashion, on the unrelenting ground. It occurred to her that there was nothing soft about this land, or the men who rode upon it. Glancing without interest at her food, she recognized the stew from lunch. But for supper Henry had added the biscuits he colorfully referred to as hot rocks. A month of this? She stirred her fork in the chunks of beef, potatoes, and carrots without interest.

Light from the fire was shadowed suddenly, and she glanced up. Boyd stood in front of her. "Mind if I sit here?"

"Suit yourself."

Despite her lack of enthusiasm, he took a seat next to her. "So, what do you think of it?"

"Of what?"

"The trail drive."

She couldn't . . . wouldn't verbalize just what she thought of the torturous day. "How do you like it?"

"Riding all day, biting dust? Trying not to lose your cattle before you get to the railhead? Rain, heat, eatin' beans and hardtack from a chuck wagon? It's a good day's work."

She shouldn't have asked. Stabbing a chunk of potato, she chewed on it instead of answering. Silence drifted between them as she calculated her revenge. A slow death, perhaps. One that made every muscle in his body beg for mercy before the end.

One of the men drew out a harmonica, and sweet notes split the darkness. A haunting melody warbled from the instrument while a few of the men either hummed or sang the words. It was a song of hardship and loneliness.

Unaccountably stirred, Abigail glanced at Boyd. "Why do they sing such sad songs?"

"Just being honest. Songs are like their lives."

Her always sympathetic heart overruled her anger. "Then why do they choose this way of life?"

Boyd swung his gaze toward her, his eyes masked in eloquent shadows. "What makes you think they choose?"

"They're not forced to work at this," she protested.

"Life forces them. There aren't many choices for these men. For any of us."

Startled, she fixed her eyes on him, suddenly curious. "You've never told me about your life. How you came to be a ranch hand."

"It's not important."

The raspiness disappeared from her tone. She replaced it with gentleness. "Tell me."

"Not that much to tell. My father owned a small ranch, but he wanted more. Extended himself to buy more stock. Had a bad winter and lost half the herd. Come spring he couldn't pay off the loans. A bigger ranch gobbled up our place. And I left."

"You were in the army, weren't you?" She remembered that he had served in the war with Reese McIntire, her friend Jem's husband.

He nodded his head. "Rode with Sheridan's troops."

Respect joined already crowded emotions. "One of the most decorated units in the war," she murmured, knowing that he had received a fair share of medals. Jem McIntire had listed that accomplishment along with his many other attributes when Boyd had signed on at the Triple Cross.

Clearly not comfortable being labeled a hero, he swatted at a mosquito. "Good group of men."

It was an understatement, but she didn't push him. "What about your parents?"

"My mother got sick after they lost the ranch. Died the next year. And my father's still drifting."

Saddened by the tale, she laid one hand over his. "Do you ever hear from him?"

"Now and then. It's been about a year since he wrote."

She couldn't imagine such isolation. Even though she was thousands of miles from home, her parents wrote regularly. Each mail packet contained letters. Her family would have come and stayed with her after Michael's death if she had given them permission. Not having such closeness must be incredibly lonely.

"Were you ever close?"

His eyes closed briefly. "Before we lost everything. But when my mother died, it took the heart out of the old man. And he hasn't gotten over it yet."

Having felt the same pain, Abigail swallowed the growing lump in her throat. "I'm sorry."

"No need to be. It's what life dealt." Obviously feeling he had said too much, Boyd stood abruptly. "I've got to check on the men on watch."

She examined the distinctive outline of broad shoulders and lean hips as he strode away. Long legs covered in leather chaps ate up the ground while the distinctive jingle of his spurs matched the beat of his retreating boots.

Gathering her own plate and cup, she deposited them in the wreck pan, noting with surprise that Boyd's aggravation had spurred her to eat almost all the stew. No doubt his plan, she acknowledged.

Fatigued, she gathered the last of her strength and laid out her bedroll in what she hoped was an appropriate place.

Certain that exhaustion would send her immediately to sleep, she was surprised when the cry of an animal reached her ears. Uneasily she listened to the sounds of the night, wondering just what kind of beasties lurked nearby. Remembering tales of wolves, bears, and coyotes, she snuggled deeper into the blanket.

Never having slept on the ground, she imagined the eerie things that could be creeping into her bedroll. Her legs twitched responsively, and she was certain little creatures were already attacking the bedroll. What had possessed her to come along?

The temperature had been dropping steadily along with the sun and she shivered in the coolness. Hot during the days, the mountain air could become equally frigid at night. Madness, she decided. That was what had propelled her into making this trip. She didn't like riding in the hot sun, she didn't like getting dirty, and she especially didn't like sleeping out in the open with only a blanket between her and the predators she was certain were skulking her unprotected form. Yanking her blanket over her face, she tried to shut out the images.

A touch on her shoulder nearly sent her flying.

"Abigail?"

Shakily she lowered the blanket.

Boyd's concerned face stared at her. "You need to be sleeping closer to the fire."

He didn't realize it, but she could have leaped into his arms and stayed there. Instead she tried to shed the fright lodged in her throat. "I didn't know."

"Fire keeps us warm, and the animals away."

Hearing the last part of his statement, she scrabbled to stand, pulling her bedroll along with her. Realizing he could have left her there to freeze or be eaten alive, she sent him a tenuous smile of gratitude.

He seemed taken aback by her wobbly smile and shaken face. He guided her gently toward the fire. She started to lay her blanket down, but he stopped her. "Not there. The ground's uneven." He pointed to some upturned rocks she hadn't noticed. "By morning you'd feel like you slept on a torture rack. Over here."

Following his instructions, she located an even spot. Ignoring propriety, she placed her bedroll fairly close to his, then climbed inside, too grateful to be safe to worry whether she should keep a proper distance from her foreman. With Boyd close by, she closed her eyes and drifted off to sleep.

Deep in slumber, she didn't hear his sigh that echoed over the plain. Nor did she feel the blanket glide over her as he pulled his extra one off, tucked it around her shoulders, and smoothed it over her sleeping body. Sleep enveloped her even as the same misgivings she had felt earlier kept Boyd awake deep into the night.

7

Miranda pounded the dough against the table. Flour rose like dirt during a duststorm. Brushing scraggling wisps of auburn hair away from her face, she sighed aloud in the quiet room. The house, despite baby Michael's presence, was too empty with Miz Fairchild gone.

Fool notion. A fine Eastern-born-and-bred lady like her riding on a trail drive with a dozen grubby men. Miranda winced, thinking of the talk it would cause. Already she had heard murmurs. Nothing substantial yet, but Miz Fairchild's behavior had been bizarre enough to set tongues wagging.

Frowning, Miranda thought of her employer and the ranch's foreman. Despite her affection for Boyd, Miranda knew their growing relationship didn't bode well. Right now it was a special friendship based on the bond of little Michael's birth. Miranda wondered how long it could remain an innocent friendship.

Glancing at the new sheaf of papers on the sideboard, her lips turned downward. In the quiet she imagined she could almost hear the scratch of Cameron O'Donnell's pen as he labored in the study. When he had first arrived at the Triple Cross, she had been stunned by the unexpected wash of feeling he had evoked. Like a schoolgirl caught in the same room with the best-looking boy in class, she had fumbled and stumbled around him. But now . . .

Now she just wanted him to leave. She didn't deny that she was still drawn to those dark eyes and his sculpted face. But he had interfered too much. Putting more force into her movements, she slammed the dough heartily against the table. Air *whooshed* from the flour mixture, and she wished Cameron would disappear as easily. Pain mixed with pleasure at the idea. It had been so long since she had entertained notions about a man that at first she couldn't reconcile her unexpected feelings.

Putting down her reaction to nervousness and adjusting to a stranger in the house, she had finally discarded her excuses and really looked at the accountant. Despite his forbidding ways, when he stepped into a room her heart beat faster. Too old to be acting so foolish, she had told herself to forget such nonsense. But her heart hadn't listened.

At thirty-one, she had been a spinster for almost half her life. As a child she had been adorned with carrot-colored hair that hadn't mellowed into auburn until she was too awkward around men for it to matter. Combined with being far taller than average women, her looks had spelled out a clear road to spinsterhood without detours. It was a destiny she had learned to live with. Until now.

Since the baby had come into the house, she had been feeling differently. Longing attacked her every time she rocked Michael's tiny body, or held his small fingers in her own. Physical waves of what she had missed out on assaulted her on a regular basis. She began to wonder how it would feel to have babies of her own. And then Cameron O'Donnell had joined the household, bringing a male presence she hadn't reckoned on.

Assuming she was past the age to feel such stirrings, she had been shocked to find her eyes lingering on the new accountant. It wasn't as though there was a shortage of men she could have been attracted to. But none of the cowhands she had met had ever stirred her like the tyrant who now commandeered the ledgers of the Triple Cross.

Miranda remembered Miz Fairchild's assertions that she was a lovely woman, and her hands paused for a moment in their assault on the dough. It was almost as though she had encouraged her to believe she could attract the man of her dreams. But then she doubted Miz Fairchild had any inkling that the man concerned was none other than the formidable Cameron O'Donnell. Now that was a notion.

A ridiculous one. She beat harder at the dough. Dipping her hand into the flour jar, Miranda sprinkled some on the breadboard. Fool man came to the ranch intent on changing everybody and everything. Well, she wasn't changing.

"That bread dough do something to anger you?"

Whirling in surprise, she encountered Cameron's steely eyes. Cool, penetrating, they had reached her in a way that friendly, fuzzy glances never could. "Do you always sneak up on a body?"

His eyebrows lifted. "Are you always so cantankerous, or is it me?"

Her glare was pointed. "I'm busy. Did you need something?"

Cameron glanced around the kitchen, his gaze coming to rest on the budget he had prepared. "Are you going to tell me you didn't have time to examine the budget again?"

"Some of us have real work to do." Snatching up the dough, she plopped it in a ceramic bowl where it landed with a thud.

"Which can be hampered if others don't cooperate."

"Do you always talk like that?"

Hawklike eyes sharpened. "Like what?"

"Never mind," she muttered, thinking he ought to take his two-dollar words and march back where he came from.

"You going to tell me what's on your mind?"

She muttered something unintelligible under her breath.

"I wouldn't have thought you were a weak-willed woman, afraid to speak."

Miranda clutched her apron with flour-covered hands. "You come in here, bent on changing everything. Who asked you to?"

"I believe that would be Mrs. Fairchild."

"She never!"

"My plan will profit the ranch, which is what she wants."

"You never give a body time to say what they want. Just orderin' everybody around, making demands. You got Miz Fairchild 'fraid to say boo in her own house."

A mixture of emotions flitted across his normally closed face. Miranda wondered suddenly at the bleakness in his eyes. Guilt stabbed at her, knowing she had attacked him because she was bent on keeping her own secret.

"I won't keep you any longer, Miss Abernathy."

She started to call him back, to recall her ill-spoken words, but shame kept her silent. What excuse did she have to offer, except the truth?

"Come and git it, or I'm throwin' the whole mess in the creek!" Henry hollered. "Bacon, biscuits, and beans. It's all a-goin' in a minute. Move your lazy hides now!"

Abigail bolted upright at the horrendous hollering that broke the silence. For a panicked moment she couldn't remember where she was or what she was doing sleeping on the ground. But as she moved, the screeching pain in her muscles brought everything back into focus.

Stumbling to her feet, she blushed as men crawled out of their bedrolls dressed in little but their longjohns, and some in even less. A glance toward the spot she remembered Boyd sleeping in showed her that it was vacant. Only the imprint against the dirt was proof that he had been there. Following the example of the men, she washed her face with water from the spigot of the barrel attached to the side of the chuck wagon.

She tried to quell her uneasiness at drying on the community towel that was passed to her. Guessing that the situation must be as unique to the men as it was to her proved her only redeeming thought as the men turned to button up wool shirts and then tuck them into their pants. They probably didn't want a woman along on the trail anymore than she wanted to be there at the moment. Only John Sims's eyes lingered on her overly long. Deliberately she turned her back on him, determined to ignore him.

"Morning, Abigail."

She whirled at the familiar voice, inordinately glad to see Boyd right then. "Hello."

His eyes raked over her and then back at her bedroll. "Got to eat fast and make sure to put your bedroll in the wagon. If you leave it on the ground, you won't have one."

Disappointment flooded through her at the impersonal

words, followed by a touch of anger. Did he think she was too stupid to remember her own equipment?

But his next words diffused her reaction. "It's your first drive. A lot of hands forget the first time, then they don't have a bedroll, and that's a lot of nights sleeping out in the cold."

"Oh." So he wasn't purposely being mean. Firming her shoulders, she tried to remember that she had come along to learn. And he was the teacher. "I'll remember."

"Good. We'll be moving out soon."

With that he left. After a rather tasteless breakfast of the promised beans, bacon, and biscuits, Abigail readied for the day. Remembering Boyd's warning, she tossed her billowy bedroll and tarp-enclosed quilts in the bed wagon and found a bit of privacy.

After mounting Dolly, she watched the orchestration and tried to analyze why the men positioned themselves in certain ways around the herd. But even as she tried to figure it out, the men threw the cattle on the trail by closing in on the broad drift of animals and squeezing them into a ragged line of march. Cowhands on the rear and sides held firm, chasing back strays and pressing the rest. The men in the front made an opening up the trail and they were on the way.

As Boyd had explained, the lead steers did in fact move naturally to the head of the herd with the cows falling in behind them. She shook her head in amazement as the column narrowed to a dozen head, then lengthened to stretch into a two-mile line with the cattle four or five abreast. Since she had been assigned to ride a position that basically entailed staying out of the way, she could watch the procedure with almost an overview.

In time she grew used to the sounds the herd made. The muffled *crack-crack* of the cows' ankle joints, the steady thudding of hooves, the random clatter of long horns swung against each other. She watched as an occasional cow, bawling and worried, turned and trotted back against the line of march, looking for her missing calf.

Boyd rode toward her as the herd marched in its own sort of precision drill. Wondering at the quickening of her heart, she put it down to relief at seeing another human to converse with.

"You all right?" he asked as he pulled his horse around to ride next to her.

Ignoring every muscle in her body that declared her a liar, she shrugged nonchalantly. "Fine. Just takes some getting used to."

The look in his eyes told her he wasn't believing her fabrication, but he also wasn't calling her on it. "You've stayed on your horse so far," he said instead.

"Less painful that way," she admitted. Doubting that her body would ever be the same again, she simply hoped she would somehow grow used to the jostling action and the pummeled muscles.

Glancing up, she saw him hide a grin. If she didn't have so much riding on the outcome of her ability to learn the ranching business, she could almost share his amusement. Months ago she would have never considered leaving her pampered existence for a steady diet of heat, dirt, and impossibly hard work.

"It gets better," he said, pushing back his Stetson and revealing thick locks of chestnut hair that dipped over his forehead in a beguiling manner.

She wondered just how it would feel to push her fingers through that rich mane of hair. The wayward thought almost made her blush. Instead she pretended to study her hands as he spoke.

"First few days makes most anybody think he's going to die. But your body gets used to it."

The fascination with her gloved hands was growing thin. Reluctantly she lifted her gaze to meet his. She wished the deep blue of his eyes didn't call to her so. Thinking she needed to find something else to study, she swung her gaze to the trail. But what she saw made her gasp aloud.

Bones, bleached from the sun, winked in the relentless light. To her horror, she felt slightly light-headed as she continued to stare.

Apparently Boyd's gaze had followed hers. "They're cattle bones, Abigail."

"Cattle?" she echoed weakly.

"Yep. Some die on the way."

She felt some of the blood returning to her head. "Do they get sick?"

He shrugged. "That or they go lame, get gored in a stampede, or trampled to death. And calves born on the trail usually can't keep up and have to be shot."

That same blood drained away again. "Isn't that rather cruel?"

"No crueler than seeing the calf starve to death or be left behind to be killed by wolves."

"Oh." She knew her voice was small, but she couldn't suppress the sympathy so easily summoned. Then an encouraging thought surfaced. "At least they're not human bones."

"Nope." He pointed to the side of the trail. "People are buried in the shallow graves."

"People?" She clutched her reins more tightly.

"It's a rough trail. Weather, hardship, disease." She started to nod as he continued. "And then some got killed."

"Killed?" She swallowed, trying to dislodge the fear suddenly trapped in her throat.

"Careless cowhand or a settler who wasn't watching out for Indians."

Her gaze immediately scanned the area around them, imagining skulking red-faced forms poised to ambush them.

Boyd's saddle creaked under his weight as he shifted, pulling up a bit and staring into the distance. "Nothing to worry about, though. Now, I'd best ride ahead."

She barely acknowledged his departure as she continued to search for elusive savages. The hours passed slowly as she searched for imaginary predators, feeling her scalp tingle with the threat of loss. Every hair on her head stood at attention in defense. When the wrangler rode up beside her for a moment, she nearly shrieked aloud before realizing that the sombrero-clad man scarcely resembled an Indian.

"Señora Fairchild?"

She managed to calm her voice. "Yes, Antonio?"

"Señor Harris will be breaking camp soon."

Managing to tear her gaze from the menacing line of junipers, she looked at Antonio. "How do you know?"

He raised an arm toward the west, pointing to Boyd as he rode in a circle and then stopped broadside to the herd.

"Does that mean he's going to stop?" she asked, still confused by this unfamiliar code, the mysteries everyone but her seemed to know so well.

"See how his horse's head is pointed?"

She nodded.

"That's the direction he wants the cattle to turn."

"And everyone knows this?"

"The point men watch him, and then they turn the herd."

Glancing ahead, she could see a curl of smoke that told her the chuck wagon had arrived and the noon meal was being prepared.

"Thanks for telling me, Antonio."

"*De nada,* Señora." He tipped the broad brim of his sombrero and rode away. She'd learned that in addition to caring for the horses in the remuda, Antonio helped the cook. With scarce free time, he had to return to work, and it had been kind of him to take what little time he had to let her know they were breaking for the noon meal.

As she neared the campfire, she slid from the saddle in relief. Knowing the cattle would be grazing or resting, she hoped the men would still be alert and on guard. Feeling the twinge of her unprotected back, she expected to feel the swift pain of an arrow whistling through the air to pierce her unsuspecting skin. It was amazing how calm the others all seemed in the face of imminent danger.

Fretting through lunch, she kept hoping that Boyd would sit down so she could share her concerns with him, but he was kept busy the entire time. Just before the chuck box was repacked, she saw him quickly down a plate of cold beans before changing mounts and heading out.

Taking her courage in hand, Abigail remounted her horse, keeping an eagle eye's watch on her surroundings. When one of the cowhands yelped at the cows to get them moving, she was certain it was an Indian war whoop. Expecting more bloodcurdling yells, she was surprised when their caravan moved on in normal fashion.

The afternoon passed in an agonizingly slow way as her eyes began to sting from the constant vigil, and her neck stiffened in protest. But fear kept her diligent. Suddenly she questioned the wisdom of this trip in earnest. If she died in an Indian raid, little Michael would be an orphan. Her heart squeezed at the thought, but she spared little time or remorse. She needed her energy to watch for marauding Indians.

Glancing up, she saw Boyd wave his hat slowly around his head. Watching the others respond, the side riders spread apart, she guessed they were stopping again. She didn't know whether to be grateful or terrified. They seemed to be an awfully large target.

A huge, defenseless target.

Even though she'd seen the rifles piled in the chuck wagon, she didn't take much comfort in knowing the weapons were stored away, rather than cocked and ready.

"Can I take your horse, Miz Fairchild?"

Abigail jumped, whirled around, and saw the smiling face of Billy Kendall. "That's kind of you, Billy."

"No problem, ma'am." He patiently unfastened her bedroll and saddlebags, handing them both to her. Boyd had explained that men kept their savings in their bedrolls, and anyone caught going through someone else's bedroll was asking for trouble. Consequently bedrolls were handled with care and respect. At the moment Abigail was more concerned with staying alive than keeping her money intact. In fact, she would be willing to trade the profit from the herd for a safe passage home.

Her bedroll and saddlebags in hand, Abigail clutched the somewhat familiar items close. Unable to force herself to accept a plate of beans or even a cup of coffee, she sat close to the campfire, hugging her bedroll and wishing for the thousandth time that she was in the safety of the ranch house.

When Boyd finally entered the campfire area, she was almost past the point of hope. They were all going to die, skewered in the middle of nowhere, like the beef they were taking to market. When he sat down beside her, his long legs stretching out along the ground, she felt an insane urge to tell him they should abandon all caution, and grab a bit of happiness before they all lined similar graves. The consequences be damned. They wouldn't live to hear the tongues wag.

"You already eat?" Boyd asked, his eyes pointedly staring at her hands as she still clutched her bedroll.

Following his gaze, she saw that her fingers were white as she gripped the saddlebags tightly. But it wasn't in her power to release her grip. "I wasn't hungry."

His eyebrows lifted. "I thought we went over that. You eat whether you're hungry or not. Otherwise you won't be able to stay in the saddle all day."

"What's the point?" she asked dully.

His brow puckered into a frown. "I don't understand."

"If we're going to die, why bother staying in the saddle? Why eat? Why do anything?"

"What are you talking about?"

She cradled the bedroll closer. "Indians," she whispered, almost afraid to say the word aloud, afraid she would somehow summon them from the encroaching darkness.

His laugh split the night, and at first she only blinked at him. Then, eyes narrowing, she had the urge to split him.

"Why are you laughing?"

He wiped a tear from the corner of one eye, his entire body shaking with mirth. "'Cause you're so damned serious."

"Death is hardly a laughing matter."

"What makes you think you're goin' to die?"

She gestured to the unending darkness. "Because of the graves on the trail. You said—"

His laughter cut off the rest of her words. "Just because Indians are out there doesn't mean they're stalking *you*."

Suspicion filled her. Had he lied about the contents of those graves? A chilling truth told her he hadn't. Was he just trying to sidestep her fears?

"Look, Abigail. People do foolish or dangerous things on

the trail and they get killed. Indians do some of the killin'. White men some. But we've taken precautions."

She gazed skeptically around the campfire. Men lounged in the darkness, some of the older ones smoking quietly, allowing the younger hands to fill the air with their stories and songs. A few others played cards, and one even read a book. None looked poised for danger. "What kind of precautions?"

"Men are ridin' herd. There's always someone on watch. We'll know if someone approaches."

Dubious, she tried to think over what he had said. On one hand she weighed the fact that between two and four men were on watch. On the other hand she thought of the entire Indian nation poised to attack. No, it wasn't a comparison. It was annihilation. Suicide. Disaster.

And, Boyd, poor fool that he was, sat there smiling encouragement as though she was a child who could be pacified with a sweet.

By the time she laid her bedroll in the darkness, she almost stripped aside the blankets to crawl into Boyd's bedroll with him. After all, if they were going to die, why not at least acknowledge a portion of the desire they felt? It would be a pleasant last feeling to take to the grave.

Long after the cowboys were asleep, she stared, unseeing, into the darkness, a prickle of fear skittering up and down her vulnerable spine, keeping a wary watch.

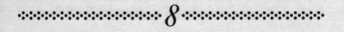 *8*

By morning Abigail's eyes were red rimmed, dry, and blurry. Wide awake, she observed the first movements of the day as the final night-watch riders were relieved. The sun inched upward in the sky as she watched Boyd rise, quietly roll up his night gear, and retrieve his horse. Still no sign of Indians, but it was early yet. Abigail had her things packed and her face washed by the time the cook called out his usual warning.

Despite her trepidation, she was surprised to feel the rumble in her stomach that signaled hunger. Shrugging, she realized the human spirit wasn't easily squashed. She grabbed a plate and dug in the dutch oven, ladling out a healthy scoop of beans. Moving to the next one, she took some fried bacon as well. Washing the entire meal down with a cup of coffee, she felt somewhat fortified for what she planned to do.

During the long, sleepless night she had come to one conclusion. She wasn't going to be without protection any longer. Spotting Boyd, she quickly deposited her plate in the wreck pan and nearly ran to catch up to him. He was fastening his saddlebags in place when she approached.

"You sleep all right?" he asked, studying her face.

Imagining how she must look after a night without sleep, she wished he would remove his intent stare.

"Not especially." She took a deep breath. "I want a gun, Boyd."

Shock nearly made his jaw drop completely open. As it

was, she could see him struggling for control. "What in the hell for?"

"Protection," she answered firmly.

"From what?"

It was her turn for surprise. "How can you ask that? It's a wonder we weren't murdered in our sleep. If the Indians attack, I want to make sure I have my own firearm."

"You know how to shoot?"

She scrabbled for an answer, then realized with a sigh that the truth was necessary. "Not exactly."

"Either you do or you don't." His voice was blunt, leaving no room for argument.

"All right, I don't. But it can't be that difficult."

"You didn't think riding a horse would be difficult, either."

She felt the heat fill her cheeks. "There's no need to be nasty. I'm certain that riding an animal and operating a mechanical weapon are distinctly different."

"Yeah. You fall down with a gun and you'll blow your head off."

Planting her hands on her hips, Abigail met his gaze squarely. "I want a gun."

"Then you'll have to learn to shoot."

"When the time comes—"

"No. I'm not giving you a gun until you know how to shoot."

"Then teach me."

"It could spook the herd."

"I want to learn," she insisted, desperation edging her words. What difference did it make if the whole herd was lost if they were killed by marauding Indians?

"Look, Abigail. You've got more than a dozen men for protection. You don't need to carry a gun."

Firming her chin, she met his gaze. "I hate to be critical, but they hardly inspire confidence." She turned and pointedly stared at the men, relaxed around the campfire as they ate breakfast.

"Just because they aren't swooning like a bunch of women or chomping at the bit like pirates ready to ransack the next prairie schooner doesn't mean they're not prepared."

"I'd rather take my own chances," she replied stiffly.

Muffling a curse, he stalked to the chuck wagon and dug around inside for a moment. He surfaced with a pair of six-shooters. When he returned, she eyed them dubiously.

"Don't you have something a little smaller?"

"In case you haven't noticed, this isn't a general store. And no one with a lick of sense would pull some dinky derringer on an Indian."

She pulled herself up to her full, if not impressive, height. "I'm sure this gun will do fine."

"Good." Without ceremony he dumped the six-shooters in her hands.

Surprised by their weight, she almost swayed as they nearly pulled her down. Straightening up and trying to maintain some dignity, she listened as Boyd explained how the pistols worked. He ended the instruction with a warning. "It would be best if you gave this up. It takes less than a gunshot to stampede the herd."

Stubbornly she refused to yield. "It's my herd, after all. I want to learn how to protect myself."

Short of flinging his arms upward to express his disgust, Boyd's voice and stance were an eloquent expression of his feelings. "Yes, *ma'am!*"

She listened intently as he pointed her in the right direction, then aimed at the tree branch he indicated. Her hand shaking under the weight of the gun, she pulled the trigger. When the shot flew wildly past the target, she lowered the weapon and stared along with the men who had stopped eating breakfast to watch.

Raising the gun, she swung back around toward Boyd and in the direction of the camp. Men dived off tree stumps where they sat eating and hit the ground, raising a cloud of dust as plates and forks flew through the air.

Even Boyd looked a little pale as he pushed the barrel downward. "You don't point a loaded gun, Abigail."

Noticing the strain in his voice, she stared first at him and then the men. "Well, I wasn't planning to shoot anybody!"

"There're a lot of graves lined with people who didn't plan to be shot." He pulled her away from the camp, out of earshot. "You're making the men nervous."

"Me?"

"First, having a woman on the trail . . . well, it's just not done. They're all tiptoeing around, afraid to cuss, be themselves." He adjusted his Stetson, the gesture revealing his own nervousness. "And now giving you a loaded gun . . ." He shook his head slowly.

"When the Indians attack, I plan to be prepared."

"Who said they were going to attack?"

"You did."

He stared at her as though she had lost her mind. "I don't recall sayin' anything of the sort."

"What about those graves?" she retorted. "Full of people the Indians killed."

He laughed, a short barking sound. "Hell, they didn't have good sense. You know when you head through Indian country how to behave. Go and act like a fool and you'll get yourself killed. We don't plan on doing that."

"But I thought—"

"You've read too many dime novels, Abigail. Livin' in the West means havin' the sense not to mess with the people who got here first. If they want a couple head of cattle for passing over their land, you give it to them. If they take a likin' to a horse or two, that's all right. What you don't do is ride through their land and decide you're going to make the rules."

Slightly deflated, she looked down at the heavy piece of metal she still held. "So you don't think I really need this?"

He sighed patiently. "No, I don't. But you keep it, and we'll do some more practicing. For now, you'd better holster it."

Feeling more than a little silly, she slipped the gun back into the leather holster. But she couldn't relinquish her concern as easily. "So you really don't think we have anything to worry about from the Indians?"

"I'm no fool, Abigail. I wouldn't lead us into a massacre. I'd like to keep my own scalp."

She felt her hair prickle at his words. "Oh." Then she brightened. "At least I didn't stampede the herd."

"Thank God for small favors," he muttered with a distinct edge of ingratitude. Then he glanced between her expectant face and the amazed looks of the cowhands who hadn't stopped staring. "What you need is something to keep your mind occupied."

"Such as?" she asked suspiciously.

"How about helping Henry?"

She thought of the cook, who vacillated between friendliness and crusty ill humor. "Is there something I can do on my own that would help him?"

He thought for a moment, his dark brows pulled together. "The only thing I can think of, you won't want to do."

Stubbornly she dug her boots into the ground a bit deeper. "Why don't you let me decide that?"

"We need fuel."

"That doesn't sound so difficult."

"Except for brushwood, about all you're goin' to find is prairie coal."

She stared at him blankly.

"Buffalo or cow chips."

"Oh." It wasn't exactly the job she had in mind, but she also didn't want to appear as though she couldn't dirty her lily white hands, either. She inched her chin upward. "I'm sure I can handle that."

"Uh-huh." He turned toward his horse. "Well, you better use the gloves."

He really did think she had the competence of a total moron. "I'll manage."

They started out after all the dishes had been collected and stowed away. Abigail saw that the calfhide hammock that held the fuel was suspended under the wagon. How hard could this be?

The sun climbed upward, intent on scorching the earth beneath. Grateful for the wide brim of her hat that shaded her face, Abigail rode along for a while before she decided it was time to collect the prairie coal. Looping Dolly's reins to the back of the chuck wagon, she screwed up her courage and tried to ignore her distaste as she looked for dried manure chips. Having decided to dispense with the gloves rather than be thought too delicate, Abigail tried not to flinch as she located the first cow chip and picked it up gingerly.

Shuddering only marginally, she tossed it into the hammock and kept on searching. Dolly plodded along beside her, gentle as always. Abigail's stomach lurched as she continued the unpleasant task, but she refused to admit defeat if it killed her. Glancing around the sun-filled day, it occurred to her that she hadn't given the idea of marauding Indians a thought in hours.

Bending down, she reached for another cow chip.

"What're you doing?"

In the noise of the moving animals, she hadn't heard Boyd's approach. She reached her hand closer to a cow chip and wrapped her fingers around it as he jumped down from his horse and nearly tackled her as he pulled her back. As he slammed into her, she was overpowered not only by his strength, but also the sensation of his touch. She could envision that same strength as they did more than grapple in the daylight.

"I could ask you the same thing," she muttered furiously, wondering who'd witnessed the display. She hated to admit that the majority of her anger stemmed from the reaction she felt. But she didn't have time to vent that anger because Boyd was plucking the cow chip from her hand and hurling it to the ground. At the same time he yanked her backward.

"What was that all about?" she demanded.

He pointed downward, just past their booted feet. A wicked-looking scorpion was scuttling away. She glanced from the poisonous creature back to Boyd's grim face. "They're underneath almost every cow chip on the trail."

"Oh." The blood in her face was definitely draining away this time.

"Why weren't you wearing the gloves?"

"Gloves?" she echoed, hearing a faint tinny sound in the distance, recognizing it as the blood rushing back to her head.

"I know I told you to wear them. They're to protect you against the scorpions."

She didn't dare admit that she had thought she was somehow being tougher by disdaining the gloves. Instead she tried just shrugging.

But this time he didn't accept the casual shrug. "If you're going to learn . . . Dammit, if you're goin' to survive, you've got to listen and follow orders just like any tenderfoot. I'll grant you that the ranch belongs to you, but it won't do you much good if you're six feet under."

Her face blanched, and she couldn't force out a reply.

Disregarding the curious stares of nearby cowhands, he pulled her close again. "And you'd better know I've got an interest in making sure you live."

The hot sun prickled her skin, and her eyes burned with emotion, but she couldn't work past the lump in her throat and the sudden apprehension his words inspired. Despite their best efforts, unexpected, unwanted feelings had erupted between them. And it was time to put a stop to those feelings.

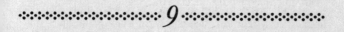

9

Abigail shifted in the saddle, wondering if the past week had toughened her hide or simply dulled all her senses. She scanned the other riders, trying to see if the scouts had located water and grass. She knew when they did they would report to Boyd, and camp would be set up so they could stop.

A week ago she would have looked forward to the evening hour because it meant she could cuddle little Michael in the sanctity of her luxurious bedchamber. Now the prospect of beans and corn bread and a seat that wasn't attached to a horse brought untold anticipation.

Automatically she searched for Boyd's tall silhouette. She had come to recognize the way he sat a horse, able to pick him out from the other men in moments. Even though she studiously tried to appear as though she didn't notice, he hadn't made a move in the past week that she hadn't been acutely aware of.

Also, knowing he had slowed the ride on occasion for her benefit caused mixed emotions. She was glad he was considerate, but she still felt inadequate, knowing others had to be inconvenienced to compensate for her. Despite her best efforts, she was still struggling with the horse, the out-of-doors, and anything connected with the cattle. Not to mention the feelings that Boyd continued to evoke.

Seeing the familiar outline of the chuck wagon ahead, Abigail sighed in relief, unable to keep from wishing it was the ranch she was seeing instead. The trail ride couldn't end soon enough to suit her.

She now recognized Boyd's signal as he waved his hat slowly around his head. The side riders spread apart to give the herd room to turn toward him. Meanwhile Henry was opening the chuck box on the wagon, and she knew that the cook would soon be kindling the fire for supper.

Since daylight still pricked the sky, she was surprised that Boyd had chosen to stop so soon. There were more than two hours of daylight left. But she wasn't complaining.

As though answering her unspoken call, Boyd rode up and reined his horse beside her. "Before you settle in, I want to show you something."

Swallowing her sigh, Abigail followed his lead, kicking her horse cautiously into a canter as they left the fringes of the herd behind and climbed a plateau that led into a line of juniper trees. All she wanted was a solid place to rest.

But as they continued deeper into the forested land, she became intrigued, wondering where Boyd was taking her. The cloak of trees grew denser, and she had the childish feeling they were heading into a magical forest. The ground was carpeted by a profusion of wildflowers. Tall stalks of columbine mingled with the velvety purple of shooting stars and delicate, solitary calypso blooms.

Abigail's breath caught as she spied his destination. Nestled in the secluded grove was a small lake, gleaming like a rare and polished gem.

As they neared, she slowed the horse to a walk and turned to Boyd with a delighted smile. "This is beautiful."

"And practical."

She cocked her head quizzically.

"I thought you might like to bathe. We've been on the trail better than a week."

His thoughtfulness both touched and puzzled her. Lack of bathing facilities was a perfect tool for convincing her this trip was a mistake, but he had ignored that opportunity. She tried to meet his gaze, but saw that he had averted his eyes. A twitch of amusement seized her, knowing he was as uncomfortable as she was about providing her this solitude. "Thank you. I would love a bath." She glanced about nervously. "Are you sure I'll have my privacy here?"

"I'll stand guard."

"What?"

The tips of his ears reddened, but his voice remained even as he pointed to the row of juniper trees that shielded the lake from prying eyes. "Over there. I'll see anyone riding up, and if you need me . . ." He cleared his throat, and her amusement increased. "Just holler."

Glancing around, she saw that he had truly picked a perfect spot. Private, safe. Her skin itched with the thought of shedding the dirty, dust-encrusted clothes and scrubbing until she was clean. She sent him a grateful smile. "I won't be long."

"Take as long as you want."

While he took up watch at the perimeter of the forest, she removed clean clothes and soap from her saddlebags. Just the smell of the fragrant soap picked up her spirits. After laying her fresh clothes on a flat rock that perched near the edge of the water, she peered around self-consciously. Never having removed her clothes in the out-of-doors, she felt absurdly wicked as she unfastened the buttons of her shirt. It occurred to her that she would never have attempted something this bold before.

For a moment she remembered the Indians she had tried desperately to forget the past week. But, remembering Boyd's words, she was certain he wouldn't have brought her here if it wasn't safe. Still, she glanced around and saw nothing moving in the shadows of the trees. After tugging off her boots and then slipping out of her clothes, she stared once again at the still walls of green surrounding her before wading into the water.

Boyd heard tentative ripples of gently parted water, then louder splashing noises. It didn't require a leap of imagination to know that Abigail was buck naked only yards away. Restlessly he dismounted and allowed the horse's reins to trail on the soft grass.

He knew he should have his head examined. A moment of weakness and he was sitting in torture because of it. His mind skipped without hesitation to the memory of her lips yielding softly beneath his, the sweet rush of her breath, the jagged rhythm of her heart next to his. The heaviness of her breast filling his hand.

He glanced down at his big, clumsy hands. Hands that he had used to touch Abigail. Hands that he was certain were far different than what she had experienced in the past. Abigail was used to men of refinement. Her husband had been schooled back East, where she was originally from. Even though Michael Fairchild had been a very capable rancher, he had also been born to money. Just as Abigail had been.

That knowledge didn't reduce his desire, however. Boyd had thought it would pass. Instead it grew daily. Watching her funny, inconceivable approach to everything only worsened matters. When she fell from her horse, as she continued to do, he didn't know whether to laugh, give up on her, or defy convention and scoop her into an embrace.

His gut ached with the knowledge that once he could have approached her on almost her same level. Once he had thought he, too, would own a ranch, rather than run one for others. But the code of the land was rigid, uncompromising. For the hundredth time he reminded himself that foremen didn't fraternize with women ranch owners. And they certainly didn't fantasize about how one particular female owner would look lying in the blue water of a mountain lake, the moisture pooling over milky white skin.

Running a hand across the stubble on his jaw, Boyd resisted the urge to turn and backtrack to the lake. Keeping his gaze turned firmly away from the area from which the intriguing sound of splashing water came, he dug a booted foot into the grass.

The trail ride, despite Abigail's limitations, was proving more difficult for him than her. He had to remind himself that this woman planned to get rid of him, to take him away from the ranch he called home and the child he had grown irretrievably attached to.

Instead she continued to amuse and surprise him. But she was also earning his respect. Not once had she complained about the length of a day's ride, her physical conditions, the hard ground she slept on, or the tasteless food she ate. She never mentioned her aches and pains, and he was certain they were many. Not used to the grueling hours or pace, she had to be suffering, but she had kept her silence about it.

The men were growing to know and like her as well. She asked them all about their families, wives, and sweethearts. And genuinely cared about the answers they provided. More than one cowhand gazed wistfully at her. Like a fairy princess trapped among a score of toads, she shone from the top of her golden hair to the bottom of her generous heart.

And while she radiated, he hid his growing desire under an increasing gruffness. If his curt attitude bothered her, she didn't show it. Instead she seemed to find numerous ways to draw him out, often plying a gentle hand over his in concern. The intensifying ache she caused convinced him her comfort could prove his undoing.

"Boyd?"

Immediately he turned, senses alerted.

She appeared in the glen hesitantly. Her long, golden hair had been pushed back from her face, obviously freshly washed. Shiny and clean, her face radiated from the cool bath. But his gaze was drawn further down. Her white linen shirt clung to her damp skin. Only a thin camisole came between her skin and her shirt.

As she walked closer, he glanced at the damp cloth of her shirt which outlined her breasts. Sucking in his breath, he saw that the moisture had seeped through the shirt to reveal the areolas of her breasts. Dusky pink circles beckoned, and he felt himself harden in response.

He watched her search his face, and knew she recognized his desire. In response, her nipples grew erect. Tasting the dryness of his mouth, Boyd stepped forward. His eyes roved over her like a blind man given a glimpse of light. Even her breeches clung to her skin, emphasizing the slight round-ness of her hips, the perfect lines of her legs.

The late-day sun poked insistent beams through the towering pine trees, rippling over Abigail, illuminating her delicate beauty. Catching his breath, Boyd wondered if he imagined the goddess who stood before him, if in fact the real Abigail still dawdled in the water and this creature lived only in the corridors of his mind.

But her lower lip trembled, and he knew she was real. And frightened. He read her fear in her eyes, recognized the paleness in her cheeks, the agitation in her tightly clenched hands. For a shocked moment he wondered if she thought he would take advantage of their solitary situation.

"Boyd?" Her voice was husky, strained.

"Yes?"

"What are you thinking?"

That I'd like to throw you to the ground, taste your sweet lips, and make endless love to you. "Why?"

She gestured to the canopy of trees encasing them. "Just that it's so secluded here."

Seclusion is what we need, Abigail. "Does that make you nervous?"

Her strained laugh was proof of her anxiety. "Why should it?"

Because it's getting dangerous to be so close to each other. "No reason." He took a step forward, and she edged back.

He watched the movement, the darkening of her eyes. Her voice quivered. "We should probably get back so we won't miss supper."

"Not yet."

"No?" But it wasn't panic or distress he heard in her voice. It was anxiousness, almost wistfulness.

His eyes pinned hers and then traveled over her revealing shirt. Her gaze followed, and her cheeks suddenly pinkened in embarrassment.

"We need to wait awhile," he said quietly.

"I'll put on my duster," she responded, turning to her horse and pulling the coat from near her bedroll. She pulled the coat free and slipped it on. "We can head back."

He wanted to tell her they could run from what was between them, but it couldn't be avoided forever. Eventually they would have to deal with it. Reaching out, he cupped her trembling chin and saw that she waited as anxious as he for his next movement. Passion flared between them. Hot, raw, and unspoken.

The space between them grew suddenly sparse, the air nearly too thick to breathe. A need welled up inside him, rising until it broke the threads of restraint he had held over himself. His hands moved to snake out around her body, and he felt the trembling consume her. But still he pulled her closer. A fraction of resistance wavered, then flickered away as she melted against him.

Soft defied hard.

Desire overruled caution.

Sun-warmed grass met their bodies as they dropped to the natural carpet of the glen. The scent of wild orchids and fairy primrose floated into the air as they crushed the fragile flowers beneath them. His thumbs skimmed over the hollows of her delicate throat and then paused as he reached the revealing bodice of her shirt. His fingers, suddenly feeling too large and clumsy, wrestled with the buttons on her shirt. But he was able to slip them free. Then only the lace ribbons of her camisole stood between his gaze and her flesh. Forcing himself to be gentle, he unfastened those laces. Then sucked in his breath.

Her skin and body were as perfect as he remembered. The rush of cool air puckered her nipples, and he couldn't stop his actions. Forgetting why they shouldn't be attracted to each other, that they had no future together, he closed his mouth over hers, eliciting a reaction that told him that she, too, had forgotten those reasons.

Their sighs mingled in the sweet breath they shared. He skimmed his hands over her throat and down to the breast that puckered in the cool air. One thumb eased over the bud, and he heard her gasp. Attaching his mouth to first one nipple and then the next, he laved them with attention. He continued the suckling motion and, when Abigail moaned in appreciation, he tugged gently with his teeth, feeling her arch off the ground. A fierce wish to have all of her bared before him sent caution flying. He slipped her duster off and pillowed it beneath them.

Molding his supple flesh against hers, he showed her his

arousal. When her movements mimicked his, he searched for and found the warm mound between her legs. Since Abigail wore the form-fitting breeches, she was unencumbered by layers of skirts and petticoats, enabling him to draw his hands between her thighs, feeling her tremble in response.

Quickly unfastening the buttons of her breeches, he pulled them past her thighs, smoothing his hands along the satiny curve of her waist and hips. Then he searched for the golden triangle of curls. His hands found her moist heat with a certainty that made them both gasp. He parted the delicate folds and felt no resistance, only a responding shudder.

Sliding a long finger inside, he found her wet and waiting.

"Yes, Boyd," she whispered as his fingers continued their magic. The sensations were more intense than she could have imagined. All propriety disappeared as his hands roved over her. She guessed she should have protested, but she couldn't have uttered a sound of objection.

Instead she wanted to continue to feel his lips and hands on her. She ached to feel his fullness deep within her as well. She could feel the liquid of her desire drenching her and knew only he could satisfy what she longed for.

Her hips arched against the pressure of his hands as she pushed herself to him. With a sureness that bespoke of his own eagerness, the pad of his thumb circled until he found the vibrating spot of pleasure that made her gasp before moving to accommodate his touch.

His fingers continued plying inside her, moving in and out with a sure promise of what he intended to finish. Feeling the rush of her pleasure, he didn't pull away, instead filling her with his fingers and then probing until she cried aloud.

From a distance, the sound of bawling cows filled the air, mingling with the sound of her passion. Unbidden, the knowledge that the cowhands were camped close by intruded. Regardless of desire or intent, Boyd knew that

acting on either had to be banked. Wanting nothing more
than to fill her, to place his own brand on her flesh, both his
body and soul ached as he knew they must wait. Drawing
away, he saw a flash of light enter Abigail's eyes. He
wondered if it was relief or regret.

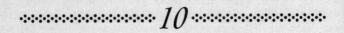

10

Abigail struggled on the difficult terrain. Boyd had warned her that this land would be rougher than anything they had encountered so far.

He was right.

Tall breeches of solid granite rose from the ground, curving upward as far as the peaks of the towering mountains. Canyons hemmed in by pine-covered cliffs fell into seemingly bottomless depths. The wind howled through the deep crevices, combining with the noise from the cattle to create an unearthly symphony.

Boyd whipped close by, slowing his horse to match the gait of hers. His face was grim. "Hang on tight, Abigail. If you fall off while we're going through this pass, it won't be amusing."

Their eyes locked, and she sensed he wanted to say much more. An instant memory of his fingers sliding inside her, bringing her to the brink of ecstasy, flooded her cheeks with heat. Seeing the sapphire of his eyes deepen, she knew he shared the memory. They had left so much unspoken, but she also knew they had shared far more than passion. That was what scared her. They both knew they couldn't share anything more.

His voice tightened, deliberately ignoring what had passed between them. "If you fall, it could be fatal. There's no room to get out of the way of the cattle."

Swallowing a lump of fear, she managed to speak. "I'll be careful." Suddenly she wished for the safety of the ranch house. Boyd had been right all along, she realized, nearly voicing what was fast becoming a litany. As a novice, she had no business on this trip. As a woman, she had less business being in such close proximity to him.

He glanced upward, scanning the sky, purposely keeping his eyes from meeting hers. "Don't like the looks of it."

She tried to follow his gaze, but saw nothing except endless azure. "Do you think it's going to storm?"

Absently he rubbed his thigh. "Just a feeling I get sometimes. Hope to hell I'm wrong."

"What happens if it storms?"

"The cattle can get spooked."

That didn't sound encouraging.

"I'll do my best to stick close, but stay alert." Looking torn, Boyd wheeled back to ride herd.

She stared around at the confusion of cattle. Almost half an hour passed, and still they hadn't moved. Her nerves grew tighter with each passing moment. Unable to still her anxiety, she decided she should ask Boyd what position to take as they rode through the pass. She kicked her horse and cantered up to him. When she reached his side, he was in a deep, heated conversation with one of the hands. After a few minutes it became apparent that the hand was not doing his job properly.

"I won't tell you again, Caruthers. We don't tolerate that kind of behavior at the Triple Cross."

Caruthers remained silent and sulky.

"No slacking off on your shifts. Everyone here pulls the same weight."

Abigail glanced between the two men and instantly made up her mind. She had already failed this test once. "You're fired, Mr. Caruthers."

Both men swung their heads in Abigail's direction in disbelief.

"You can collect your pay from the accountant back at the Triple Cross."

"You'll regret this. Both of you!" Caruthers promised as he jammed his hat farther down on his head and glared between them, before kicking his horse into a gallop and disappearing over the hill.

"What the hell did you do that for?" Boyd demanded.

Her smile slipped a fraction. "I learned back on the ranch. When a hand slacks off, you get rid of him."

"Not when you're in the middle of a trail drive with no extra hands to spare. He would've worked out if I kept an eye on him. One mistake doesn't mean a man gets the sack. Because of that addled-brained decision of yours, we're now one man short just as we're headin' into the most dangerous part of the trail. Between baby-sitting you, which takes one full-time person, and now ridin' another hand short, you've practically sabotaged the entire drive!"

Stung, she wanted to issue a scathing retort, but the enormity of her action was sinking in. "You're exaggerating," she finally managed.

"Are you goin' to do his work?"

"If I could, I would," she retorted.

"But you can't. Which leaves us where?"

"How did I know you weren't testing me?"

He yanked off his Stetson. "This isn't the little red schoolhouse on the hill, Abigail. We fail, no one's goin' to stand us in the corner, then dust us off and tell us to try again. You fail and you lose the ranch, along with the livelihoods of dozens of people who are countin' on you."

Shaken, she simply stared at him. "I didn't realize . . ."

He slapped the discarded Stetson against the leather chaps covering his long legs. "Hell, I know that. But you can't go off half-cocked. It's your ranch, but these men report to me. We discuss actions like firing men before you haul off and let a man go."

She took a deep breath. "In the future I'll remember."

He searched her face, and she met his gaze without flinching, the effort wrung from deep within. "All right. The harm's done, and there's no point grinding it into the dust. Ride your position near the chuck wagon and stay clear of the boulders." He started to turn away and then pulled the horse back, concern written on his face. "For God's sake, Abigail. Be careful." Then he spurred his horse and disappeared into the dusty haze of the herd.

Gripping the pommel with shaking, leather-encased hands,

she concentrated on keeping her footing and her seat, wishing she had kept her mouth shut and not fired Caruthers. Would she ever understand the intricacies of ranch life?

She approached the pass with trepidation. Dolly, steady as always, cooperated with her gentle gait. The next hours passed in excruciating slowness as the cattle moved through the narrow pass. Strung out even more than usual due to the tight confines, the herd seemed to stretch out for miles.

The majority of the cattle had cleared the canyon walls when a low roar of thunder vibrated through the sky and echoed off the mountains. The noise seemed to reverberate like a brass section in a symphony hall as the cattle ran faster, kicking up dirt, hooves pounding in growing terror. Caught on the edge of the flow, she and Dolly fell into the sea of stampeding animals.

Alternately clutching the reins and then the pommel of the saddle, Abigail hung on. Snorting and pawing, the animals ran toward freedom or doom, not particularly choosy about which. White foam frothed from Dolly's mouth as she arched her graceful neck, her eyes rolling as the pandemonium increased. Swirls of dust and dirt filled the air, almost blinding Abigail.

As they cleared the canyon wall, the herd spread out in a wide arc as they continued racing in desperation. Caught in the fringes of the pell-mell, Abigail was finally able to see past the swirling dirt into the distance. As the herd split, she saw a chance to escape. Pulling with all her strength on Dolly's reins, she veered off to one side, away from the stampeding animals.

Riders galloped to the head of the stampede, trying to turn the leaders back. Breathless, Abigail searched frantically for other faces. Men on horseback raced after the disappearing cattle, attempting to slow down their escape. Scattered as though a tornado had picked up their orderly caravan and dumped it askew, the group fanned out, limping for safety. The fastest riders were still galloping forward, trying to turn the herd.

Not seeing Boyd, Abigail was uncertain whether to stay put and out of the way, or try somehow to help. But then she spotted one rider assisting another. Even from a distance, she could see that one of the men was injured. Without further thought, she spurred Dolly toward them. Abigail recognized Billy Kendall and John Sims.

Blood pumped from a raw gash in Billy's leg. Slipping down from her horse, Abigail rushed to his side, giving John orders without a second thought. "Get him on the ground. I need enough material for a tourniquet." She turned to John, ignoring her distaste for him. "Give me your bandanna."

He hesitated for just a moment before slipping it off. "You sure you know what you're doing, ma'am?"

Her normally gentle sky-colored eyes deepened to the shade of honed steel. "I'm sure."

Competently she tied the bandanna into a tourniquet. All her memories of the time she had spent alongside her mother working in hospitals during the war returned in a rush. A shortage of doctors had thrust volunteers into a unique position, one that had taught her far more than basic first aid. "John, hand me the canteen from my horse."

He hesitated, but then reached for the canteen.

"John, I'll need more water, a pan, and bandages." Without flinching, she pushed aside the gaps of torn flesh on Billy's leg and assessed the wound. "Hand me your shirt as well."

"Ma'am?"

"I have to put pressure on the wound and I need a piece of material large enough to wrap around his leg. Your shirt, please."

He hesitated, and her voice sharpened. "I need your shirt, now!"

John turned reluctantly and removed his shirt. Obviously feeling self-conscious, the man handed her his shirt.

"Thank you. Do you have a knife on you?"

He nodded in reply.

"Good, you'll have to build a fire, too. But first go find the chuck wagon and fetch me a needle and thread." John blanched, and she could see his Adam's apple bob visibly. But she turned her attention to wrapping Billy's leg, tying the shirt firmly around the wound to keep it together, to prevent the young man from bleeding to death.

She glanced up and saw John gaping, rather than riding to find what she needed. This time she wouldn't stand for his inaction. She trained her voice into an impressive order. "*Now*, John."

"Yes, ma'am." Shirtless and stumbling, he turned and mounted his horse, kicking it into a fast trot as he went in search of the chuck wagon.

Uncapping the lid of the canteen, she splashed enough water over her hands to rinse the blood away. Patting one hand dry, she laid it on the frightened young man's brow. "You want to tell me what happened?"

His voice was weak, and Abigail realized that he had lost a lot of blood. She just hoped it wasn't too much. "Got between a bull and a boulder. Wasn't anyplace to go. Gored me right good, ma'am."

She continued to stroke his forehead, her voice soothing. "You'll be fine. We'll get you fixed up in no time."

"How bad's it look?" he asked, unable to repress a note of fear.

"Not all that bad," she lied. There was no point in telling him that if it were any worse, he might lose his leg. If she was very careful, she could repair the severed artery and then stitch him so that he wouldn't have to face that agony. No sense in scaring him to death in the process.

"For a while there I didn't think I was gonna get away from that bull," Billy confided, his face now sickly white.

"I'm glad you did." She retied the tourniquet, relieved that it kept the bleeding under control. Leaving Billy for a moment, she dragged her bedroll off the horse and propped it beneath his legs. Billy's eyes were glazed, and she hoped John would hurry.

A flurry of pounding hooves split the already dust-filled air. Glancing up, she saw John returning. Boyd and two other men were with him. Boyd dismounted quickly, rapidly walking to her side. His gaze flickered over the makeshift tourniquet and then to her face. She wondered if he expected her to be pale and near fainting at the sight.

"How bad is it?" Boyd asked, hunkering down beside them.

She glanced meaningfully at Billy. He didn't need to hear this discussion. Starting to rise, she accepted Boyd's outstretched hand as he rose, taking them both to a standing position, and then leading them several feet away.

"The artery is nearly severed. It will have to be mended. Then it all has to be sewn in place."

Boyd took in the information, glancing at young Billy. "And if it's not done properly?"

"He'll lose his leg."

"We don't have a surgeon—"

"I can do it," she offered quietly.

"You?"

She flushed, but held her ground. "There are some things I'm very knowledgeable about. This is one of them."

"But surgery?"

"What other choice do you have?"

"If he's going to lose his leg, it'd be better to only go through the pain once. Out on the trail, men either get better real quick or they die. If we wait too long to take off the leg, he'll get gangrene."

"Billy should have a chance with that leg. I'm not giving up on him, Boyd."

Passing one hand over his face, Boyd straightened and met her stare. "What if you get light-headed and faint?"

"I won't. Trust me, Boyd. I know what I'm doing."

"If you can't go through with it, one of us will be here."

To step in and take over. Refusing to dwell on his lack of confidence, she made her voice purposely brisk. "Did you bring what I need?"

"Chuck wagon should be here in the next couple of minutes. Then if you need anything else, it'll be right there."

Like a saw to sever young Billy's leg. She purposely ignored that thought. "Collect your canteens for now." Turning away from Boyd, she busied herself with her patient.

She could hear the collected mutterings from the cowhands, and she suspected they were voicing doubt over her abilities. Squaring her jaw, she ignored them. Billy was far more important than their collected opinions. In short time the chuck wagon rocked its way over ruts and clumps of Johnsongrass, coming to a quivering standstill.

"Needle, thread, pan, bandages, water, knife, and a hot fire." Abigail ticked the items off on her fingers.

Boyd nodded grimly, ordering John to build a fire. Then Boyd retrieved a bottle of whiskey, uncapped it, and brought it to young Billy.

"No, he can't have that," Abigail ordered.

Boyd lifted his eyes in surprise. "This isn't time for a temperance lecture."

"I'm not giving you one. One of the doctors I worked with believed whiskey thinned the blood, and Billy's lost more than he can afford already."

"But the pain—"

"Will be bearable." She glanced at Billy's still glazed eyes. "But if he bleeds anymore, he won't make it."

Boyd looked undecided, but replaced the cap on the bottle with a strong twist. "If the pain gets bad, I won't promise to keep it from him."

"Let's hope neither of us has to argue that point." Turning, she collected what she needed. "How's that fire?"

"Should be going in a few minutes."

Impatiently she waited as the fire was stoked and then caught, the flames leaping brightly. Her stomach twisted for just a second as she contemplated what was in store. But then it was time to begin.

With Boyd and John holding Billy in place, she began to work. Knowing this was the most difficult part of the surgery, the one that would determine whether she could stop the bleeding and save Billy's leg, Abigail said a little prayer. Then she began to sew the artery closed, taking tiny, almost minuscule stitches. Using the tip of the knife that had been heated in the fire, she cauterized the surrounding wound and repaired what damage she could.

Mercifully, Billy sank into a dead faint when the tip of the hot knife seared him. The smell of burning flesh filled the air. Pushing her heavy blond hair from her face, Abigail met

Boyd's gaze. Obviously he was waiting to see if she could endure the bloody, messy process. If he had any idea of what she had experienced in the war hospitals, he wouldn't be looking so concerned, so sure she would collapse.

With the artery repaired and then cauterized, she uncapped the whiskey and splashed some of the fiery liquid into the wound, hoping to stave off infection. Then she started the painstaking job of sewing the ripped flesh back together. Glancing up, she saw that the men surrounding her were paling, some looking almost green. Taking small, even stitches that gave testimony to her embroidery skills, she patched Billy back together. Feeling a trickle of sweat from between her breasts, she tried to ignore both her nerves and the stares of the men.

Within an hour she had completed the surgery. It was hard to tell who was most relieved: Abigail, Billy, or her audience.

Pushing a hand against the disarrayed hair near her face, Abigail examined the wound before binding it with bandages. She knew Billy faced a battle from loss of blood and the ever-present threat of infection. "You can move him into the chuck wagon now."

Boyd nodded. He and John picked up Billy's limp body and carefully carried him inside the wagon. By the time they emerged, Abigail had cleaned up a big part of the bloody mess.

"We'll camp here," Boyd told her as he approached. "It may take the next day or two to collect the lost cattle."

"Staying in one place will be best for Billy," she agreed. "He'll need rest to build up his strength."

"That was damn fine work, Abigail." Boyd's voice was hesitant, and surprise filtered through his words. "I didn't know you had it in you."

She wiped her hands on a rag that Boyd had fished from inside the wagon. "Sometimes we surprise ourselves—at what we do have deep inside—despite what others think."

He shuffled his feet awkwardly. "I'm sorry if we've poked too much fun at you because of your riding. You know I think more—"

She met his eyes, cutting off his words. "It's not important. Riding's not a true judge of my abilities—anymore
than your past was a fair judge of who you are." Without
waiting for his reply, she turned away.

He was staring. She was certain of it. Maybe she had said
too much, but it was something she had held in too long. His
past was just that. He had to know it was no longer
important.

The cook was banging pans as he began to set up for the
night's supper. Without hesitation she approached him.

"Henry, you'll need to prepare a separate beef broth for
Billy."

"Broth? Sorry, Miz Fairchild, but I ain't got no broth."

"Then you'll have to make some."

"Out of what?"

She wondered if he was being deliberately obtuse, but he
stared at her from open, friendly eyes. His crustiness
seemed to have disappeared once he had seen her surgical
skills. "From beef." She gestured toward the cattle that
milled in the distance. "You may be familiar with them."

"Yes, ma'am. But I ain't got no fresh beef. Only time we
got fresh beef's when a cow goes down."

"Then slaughter one."

"Ma'am?"

From the prickle of hair standing at attention on her neck,
she sensed that all ears and eyes had turned in her direction.
"I said, slaughter one. Billy will have to drink beef broth to
build his blood if he's going to make it. I'm sure you can
cook the extra beef for supper. The men will enjoy the
treat."

The cook glanced uneasily at Boyd for confirmation.

"You heard her," Boyd ordered. "Manuel, look for any
strays that have been injured."

"If we don't find one, Mr. Harris?" Manuel didn't voice
the collective wondering. Slaughtering cattle on a drive,
unless a cow had been injured, wasn't done. They couldn't
eat all the meat before it went bad. Killing cows killed their
profit.

"Then cut out a healthy one." At his words the men's

mouths dropped open perceptibly. "Let's get moving. We've got cattle to round up."

Shaken out of their paralyzed state, the men scattered. Boyd leveled a stare which Abigail found difficult to read. It occurred to her that she'd just issued her first order. While she normally wouldn't have dreamed of usurping Boyd's authority, she hadn't given the command a second thought because it concerned a man's life. From the look in Boyd's eyes, she realized suddenly that she had also just tampered with a man's pride.

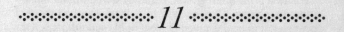

11

Firelight flickered over the chuck wagon, touched the gleaming hides of tethered horses, and illuminated the faces of men intent on eating and relaxing. Purposely Abigail avoided John Sims's gaze. He hadn't stopped staring at her since this afternoon, and his continued perusal was making her even more uncomfortable than it had in the past. Wistfully Abigail gazed across the camp at Boyd, who didn't lift his glance.

She had heard the talk around the campfire. The men were discussing her remarkable surgery, her spunk, and her order that had gone over Boyd's authority. She was sure he had heard those same remarks and felt their sting. While she was pleased by the men's new respect, it wasn't worth damaging Boyd's still-fragile pride.

Despite her attempts the past year to build up his esteem, she knew he suffered from the blows to his reputation in the past. Having been accused of stealing cattle on the ranch he once managed, he had suffered from lack of trust. Even his friends had turned away, willing to blame him without proof.

More than a year ago when he helped save the McIntire ranch and caught the rustler who was raiding all the ranches in the territory, his reputation had been restored. But she knew he was still suffering from a pride that had been beaten down and trampled upon.

Setting her plate down, she swallowed her nervousness, rose, and approached Boyd before she lost her courage. He didn't glance up until her shadow darkened his face. She didn't doubt the delay was deliberate.

"Boyd, would you take a walk with me?"

He looked pointedly at the night surrounding them. "It's dark."

"We don't have to go far." She gestured to the men surrounding them. "Just away a bit." What she had to say wasn't meant to be discussed in front of his subordinates. Or anyone else.

He put his plate and cup down. "Whatever you say, ma'am."

She flinched. Together they walked the path toward the horses. Not certain how to begin, she plunged in. "I know you're upset about today."

"What makes you think that?"

"I'm not stupid, Boyd. You're mad because I gave a direct order to the hands without consulting you first. I know I'm the owner, but it's not my intention to undermine your authority. You're the one who should be giving the men orders." Daring a quick glance at him, she saw the anger still etched in his features. "I respect you too much to diminish that authority," she finished in a rush, silently begging him to understand.

His expression didn't change. "Is that all?"

Exasperated, she stubbed her boot into the grass and caught the leather in a tangle of roots. Struggling to pull it free, she caught Boyd rolling his eyes before he bent down to assist her. "You beat all, you know that?"

She smiled suddenly. "My point exactly. I'm not good at the things you excel in." He straightened up, and she met his skeptical stare. "The only reason I jumped in and gave that order is because Billy's life was at stake. I wasn't thinking about ranching and who should be in charge. If it had been a decision regarding the herd, I would have deferred to your judgment. But this was a man's life, a young man who should have every opportunity to court a sweetheart, take her to dances, and then carry her over the threshold." She met Boyd's eyes, pleading for him to understand. "I couldn't take that away from him without trying."

"Running a ranch isn't a romantic or noble venture, Abigail. Men get hurt. They die." He saw her flinch and knew she was thinking of her husband, who had died protecting the Triple Cross. Boyd wondered if Abigail had given a moment's thought to the others who had died in that same rustling attack. The former foreman of the Triple Cross was one of the casualties. True, Boyd wouldn't be here today otherwise, but Boyd wondered if he, too, would become one of the disposable. One whose life wasn't as important as the owner's interests. Abigail had already dropped the first hint. He wondered if his walking papers were far behind.

Yet, damnably, his reasons for not wanting to leave were far more complex. They were intertwined with the woman who stared at him in a pleading yet beguiling manner. He nearly groaned as he studied her, watching as the distant light from the campfire played over her delicate features, illuminating the glossy, golden hair. His breath accelerated as he spotted the ragged beat of her pulse at the hollow of her throat. Shadows played over the curve of her cheek, past the full richness of her lips. He barely heard her words as she moved those lips.

"I know only too well that people die, Boyd. But there's no reason to sacrifice Billy." She turned away, hiding her expression.

He felt a moment's shame at reminding Abigail of her loss. "I want the boy to heal as well. I'm only tryin' to prepare you for the reality of this kind of life."

"I think I'm all too aware of the pitfalls, Boyd." Her voice, while soft, held an underlying awareness.

He searched her expression, wondering if she, too, was thinking of the danger of their attraction. The sudden darkening of her eyes, the flush he saw in her cheeks, convinced him she shared his thoughts. His eyes grazed past the graceful slope of her neck, downward, focusing on the shirt that had clung so provocatively on her at the lake. The matching heat in her eyes convinced him that she, too, shared the memory of that moment. Glancing into the obsidian shadows of the moonless night, Boyd saw that the campfire and men were far away, the darkness shrouded and complete.

But even in that dim light he searched out the light that always glowed in her eyes, the pale porcelain of her skin that gleamed like alabaster. Perhaps she was a goddess, after all, one who floated in and out of his life with disturbing regularity.

Almost to assure himself of her reality, he reached out to touch the velvet of her cheek. The touch singed them both. He felt the path of white-hot fire race from his fingertips through his body. It was difficult to determine if her nearness caused pain or pleasure. Slowly his thumb eased over her lips, massaging them in an imitation of what his body beckoned to complete.

Abigail's eyelids drifted closed, her long lashes casting shadows over her pale skin, even in the darkness. He could see the throb of her pulse at the hollow of her throat, leaping in tune with the acceleration of her breathing. Delight pierced him at the thought of causing such desire.

The unevenness of his thoughts tripped with alarm. One moment he was deciding exactly how to walk away from this impossible situation. The next he was envisioning lying down with this beautiful lady and making her his own.

But for now he reached out with his other hand and cradled the back of her neck. When she leaned willingly against him, he knew he was lost. Had she ever pointed out the vast differences in their positions, the hopelessness of a shared future, he might have been able to label her a snob and turn his back on that disdain. Instead she offered gentleness, trust, and friendship. Her lack of guile cut through his carefully constructed defenses like a whip of steel.

With agonizing gentleness he pulled her close, dipping his head to taste her lips. The soft rush of her breath caressed him like a velvet fist, drawing him close, tantalizing and provocative. Probing deeply, he reveled in the taste and texture as she met the dip of his parrying thrusts with growing boldness, her hands roving over his shoulders and chest.

It was the boldness that surprised him. Despite his feelings for her, he didn't expect a genteel lady like her to have the same wants, the same desires as a toughened cowhand. But the ragged beat of her heart against his was proof that she did. Knowing he couldn't be the refined gentleman she was used to, he gave up trying to be. It would be her decision to accept or reject the man he was, but he wouldn't pretend to be something else.

Lightning zigzagged through the sky, followed by the low rumble of thunder. Fat drops of rain sliced through the air, plopping on the ground with loud smacking sounds. The storm Boyd had sensed beforehand arrived in all its fury. Earlier thunder that had prompted the stampede hadn't been a false messenger. Hoping this thunder wasn't the harbinger of even more trouble, Boyd reluctantly released Abigail's lips as the rain sluiced over their faces. With a groan of exasperation, he pulled her along with him toward the campfire.

Cowhands who had hunkered down to go to sleep were up and running toward the jury-rigged rope corral. The ropers were heading to the remuda to get fresh mounts. With the storm brewing, it was even more important that only the best roper try to lasso the horses in the remuda since a badly thrown rope spooked the horses. No one wanted another stampede, especially in the middle of the dark, murky night. As Boyd had told her, cattle were more prone to stampede at night.

"Take cover in the chuck wagon," Boyd ordered Abigail.

"But maybe I can help—"

"You can help the most by staying where I know you're safe." Mindful of the men swarming around them, he resisted the temptation to pull her close and reassure her with the imprint of his kiss. Instead he guided her toward the chuck wagon. "You can keep an eye on Billy."

"But—"

"Can't you please do as I ask, just this once?" he asked impatiently. The stubborn set of her face dredged up an unwanted premonition. All of her pliable, gentle qualities seemed to have disappeared along with the onset of more unpredictable characteristics once she had decided to be a working ranch owner. Now she was more intractable and stubborn, not at all like the woman he had grown to know in the past two years. But he couldn't waste more time worrying, nor could he tie her to the chuck wagon, though the idea tempted him mightily.

"I'll get back here as soon as I can and let you know if the herd's all right."

Her nod was barely perceptible. Rain poured from the sky in a nearly solid sheet of ebony and gray. Like the sharp stab of dagger points, the rain assaulted everything in its path. Ignoring the storm, Boyd retrieved his stallion. Rearing as a bolt of lightning punctured the sky, the horse calmed under the reassuring strength of Boyd's authority. Together man and beast whirled around and disappeared into a sheet of watery darkness. The driving rain obliterated even the roar of the horse's hooves as they pounded into the gloom.

Abigail paced the narrow confines of the wagon. Billy slept quietly, despite the constant splatter of rain against the wagon's covering and the blasts of deafening thunder. Although pleased that her patient was faring so well, she resented being cooped up in the wagon with him.

With a shiver Abigail acknowledged that she didn't relish being soaked to the skin, but she also didn't like being shoved aside while important work was being done. Although in years past she had patiently waited at home during events like this, now she found that same patience sadly lacking. She wanted to be part of what was happening, rather than keeping the home fires burning, waiting to hear what had happened instead of experiencing it.

Donning her poncho, Abigail pushed open the canvas flaps at the end of the wagon and peered into the blinding rain. Securing the hood over her head, she climbed outside. It took a few moments to adjust to the water dashing over her face and into her eyes. She pulled the hood up farther and searched for Henry, the cook. He should be able to tell her what really needed to be done.

Searching around the outside perimeters of the wagon,

she didn't see him. Puzzled, she stared in all directions. Where could the man have gone? Setting off, she decided to search in a wider circle.

Abigail discovered that trundling through the rain was more difficult than she had imagined. Glancing back over her shoulder, she found that she couldn't distinguish the wagon amidst the blur of the rain. A trace of panic touched her, but then she shook away the fear. As soon as the rain cleared, she was certain she would be able to see the wagon clearly.

The remuda! That was where Henry must be. He and the tail riders were no doubt attending the horses. Initially she had been amazed to learn that they had brought over eighty extra horses to provide fresh mounts for the riders. But seeing the men stay in the saddle nearly around the clock demonstrated the wisdom in having a well-stocked remuda. Those horses required care, however, especially during flashes of lightning and the deafening roar of the accompanying thunder. And that was one place she could help. She didn't ride or rope well enough to help with the herd, but she could deal with horses in a corral.

Head bent down, she carved a path through the storm, trying to navigate in the right direction. It was disconcerting to discover that every turn seemed the same in the unending darkness. Still she pressed on, the muck from the dry dust mingling with the rain to form a mud that threatened to pull the boots from her feet.

As she forged ahead, she couldn't see anything but more sheets of unrelenting rain and darkness. She wondered suddenly if she had wandered off on the wrong course. Stopping stock-still, she peered all around, slowly making a circle. No matter where she looked, everything seemed the same.

The chuck wagon was completely indistinguishable. Despite the rain soaking the land, her mouth felt suddenly dry. Trying to remain calm, she calculated how far she must have walked. The rain washed away any trace of her footsteps, making it impossible to retrace her path.

Hearing a low roar nearby, she tried to focus on the

source, realizing that it sounded different from the thunder. Cocking her head, she could only distinguish a wild rush of noise. It seemed to come from below. Leaning over to investigate, she realized she was standing above the source of the sound. Lightning pierced the sky, and Abigail sucked in her breath in horror.

Rushing, raging water! She remembered hearing dire stories around the campfire of rivers with headwaters in the mountains. Unseen storms could, without warning, send floods surging across the trail fords. Staring downward she could see evidence of just such a flood. The arroyo beneath her was filling with a gigantic torrent of water. Stumbling, she scrabbled backward. But as she moved she struck something firm. She started to turn when an abrupt push sent her tumbling forward.

Disbelief filled her as she fell into the abyss that stretched out before her. The cold shock of the water terrified her while the current sucked at her body, threatening to pull her beneath the murkiness. Flailing wildly, she fought the tentacles of certain death. Raw pain creased through her lungs as she struggled, her breath coming in short excruciating gasps, her arms and legs burning with the effort of staying afloat. The banks of the ground flew by as water pushed her along the newly formed canal.

Striking out with her hands, she closed them over a protruding tree trunk. Hope burst and then slid away as the tree branch snapped under the strength of the water, propelling her along with it. Her limbs, nearly frozen by the cold water, flexed as she fought to find something sturdier to grab on to.

When the course of the arroyo turned and threw her toward the middle of the water, she almost gave up. A sudden picture of her child, orphaned and alone, shot a new burst of strength into her battered body. Seeing a tree branch within a few feet of her, she flung herself forward, arms outstretched, each finger straining to reach as far as possible.

Tree bark scraped the skin from her hands, but she held on. This branch, thicker and sturdier, held her weight.

Frantically peering upward, she didn't know how she would climb the distance between the branch and the ledge above. Drawing hot, ragged draughts of air into her starved lungs, she knew she couldn't cling indefinitely to the log. Her hands, numb with cold, were losing their grip.

She tried to drag herself upward on the log, but the combination of the tearing current and her weakened, shaking muscles prevented her from moving more than a few inches. Frustration filled her. She couldn't fail now.

Digging her fingers into the log, she felt splinters gouge her now broken nails, impaling themselves into the tender flesh beneath. But she ignored the pain. A shout cut through the noise of the rushing water. She wondered briefly if she had imagined it. A rope plopped into the water beside her, and she knew the sound was no figment of her imagination.

"Grab on, Abigail!" Boyd's hoarse shout reached her.

Too paralyzed with fear to release her grip on the log, she stared at the rope, transfixed.

"Now, Abigail! The water's rising!"

Panicked, she looked behind her. The water was higher. Soon the log she clung to would be beneath the surface. Her fear of drowning outweighed her fear of losing a grip on her lifeline. Obeying blindly, she closed her eyes for a brief moment before releasing the log and clutching the rope.

"Put it around your waist!"

Responding to his hoarse shouts, Abigail fastened the rope securely around her waist, feeling the tug as Boyd started hauling her up out of the water. As she hung, suspended in midair, she flailed against the muddy bank when it seemed that the rope had stopped moving. But she felt it tugging again, and once again she was ascending the slippery bank.

Mud and rain battled to drench her as she neared the top. Scrabbling against the eroding handholds, she contacted with Boyd as he pulled her up and over the fast collapsing side. Relief mingled with fear as she fell into his comforting embrace. He held her close for several long moments, imprinting his body on hers as though assuring himself that she was really safe. Then he set her away from him, shaking her lightly.

"What came over you? Takin' off on your own like that?"

Her mouth opened, but all she could think about was the push that landed her in the middle of what had nearly proved to be her end.

"Come on, let's get you back to camp." Not giving her time to answer or protest, he swung her up on his horse. In a moment she was shielded by his large body. His warmth seeped through her soaked clothes. He seemed solid as an unyielding rock as he buffeted the elements, quickly covering the distance back to camp. She saw that the bed wagon had been unhitched next to the chuck wagon.

Boyd slid to the ground, reaching up and helping her down. She hated to be treated like an invalid, but her teeth rattled, and her body was caught in a spasm of shivering. Boyd guided her to the bed wagon.

"It's not as cozy as the chuck wagon, but it's dry inside, and you can have some privacy. Get out of those clothes. I'll bring your saddlebags so you can change."

Stumbling up and inside the wagon, she stared around blankly.

"Abigail, there should be some blankets inside, too."

When she didn't answer, he stepped up and peered inside. "Abigail? You all right?"

"Sure." With a conscious effort, she tried to control her shaking limbs. "Or I will be as soon as I'm dry."

"Get stripped down and wrap up in the blankets. I'll be right back." With that he disappeared, his eyes filled with concern and what looked like anger.

Trembling with cold, shock, and fear, she managed to sink to a crate, huddling in the inadequate warmth of the wagon. Numbly she tried to still the shivering that started somewhere deep within her soul.

When Boyd pushed open the flaps of the wagon, she started violently.

"Abigail! You haven't gotten out of those wet clothes!"

In a distracted, almost distanced fashion, she glanced down at her soggy attire.

Stifling a curse, he climbed inside and grabbed a stack of scratchy woolen blankets. His eyes scanned her face, seeming to measure the blueness of her lips and the shock that consumed her eyes. He dragged the heavy poncho off and wrapped one of the thick, voluminous blankets around her.

Then he squatted down and tugged at her boots. They fell to the floor of the wagon with a thud, accompanied by a hiss of the water they contained. Pushing the boots out of the way, Boyd matter-of-factly stripped off her hose. Reaching for another blanket, he dried her feet. Then without ceremony he removed the blanket, pulled her denims off, and then stripped off her shirt and camisole. Her teeth chattered with the chill as he picked up another dry blanket and wrapped her securely.

Gently he cupped her chin and tipped it upward. "Abigail, I'm going to get some hot coffee. Will you be all right for a few minutes?"

She nodded numbly, afraid to tell him what had really happened. More terrified not to tell him.

"I'll be right outside." His voice deepened, a warning note entering his gentle tone. "I'll give you time to dress and I'll check on you in a few minutes."

He left and shut the wagon flap behind him. Despite her lethargy, she let the blanket slip off her shoulders, then stared at the shirt and breeches that Boyd had thoughtfully brought to her. She intended to don her clothes, but couldn't force herself to move.

A few minutes later, when Boyd discreetly cleared his throat and then entered, she was still garbed in only a blanket. Strong but gentle hands wrapped the blanket more securely around her. "You feeling better?"

Unable to speak, she nodded her bent head.

Using great caution, Boyd picked up another blanket and used it to dry her hair. Feeling the sensitive movements of his hands as they massaged her head and then gently fingercombed her hair, she felt her guard slipping. Hot tears of fear pooled in her eyes. Only her pride kept her whimpers silent.

Lowering the blanket he had used to dry her hair, Boyd turned to her. Shock suffused his features as he spotted her tears, but his expression quickly turned to one of understanding. "It's probably best to let it out, Abigail. Hell, I didn't mean to yell at you out there. I was just worried and I couldn't believe you'd wandered off by yourself. Guess I didn't realize just how stubborn you've gotten."

Abigail ducked her head, trying to hide the welling tears.

"I understand if you're angry," he said in a soft, crooning voice.

"It's not that," she finally blurted out.

He reached out and pushed away the hair that fell from her forehead to hide her eyes. "What then, Abigail?"

"I'm scared!"

"That's understandable. You nearly drowned out there."

She swallowed, feeling the fear close in. "That's . . . not why I'm scared."

. Puzzled, he stared at her.

"Someone pushed me into the water," she finally admitted, her voice somewhere between a whisper and a croak.

Disbelief warred in his eyes. "Pushed you?"

"Yes. I couldn't see . . . and then I realized that all this water was rushing practically underneath my feet, and I started to back up. I ran into something . . . and then I was pushed."

Boyd remained maddeningly calm. "You say you couldn't see anything?"

"Well . . . no."

"Could you have backed into a tree?"

She tried to remember. It had seemed as though she had run into a solid wall. "I . . . don't know."

"It was dark, the rain was blinding, you couldn't see what you ran into, but you're sure you were pushed?"

Abigail slowly shook her head. Weariness and fear had taken their toll. Had she imagined the feeling of being pushed headlong into the rushing waters? It had been dark, and she had been confused. "I thought someone pushed me." Even now the feeling returned, the sickening lurch, the shock of the icy water as she plunged beneath the surface. Shuddering, she hid her head.

Immediately Boyd encircled her in a warm embrace. Pulling the blanket more securely around her, he scooped her up and walked them both to an empty space at the end of the wagon. Crouching down, he settled her on his lap as he stretched his long legs out through the length of the wagon's floor.

Abigail kept her face turned to the solid, reassuring warmth of his chest as he continued to cradle her close. Not caring what anyone would think if they were discovered, she craved the strength he represented. Had she only imagined that someone had such an evil intent? It was easy to blame her overactive imagination now that she was safe and dry.

The rain continued to splatter the canvas covering of the wagon, and thunder growled in the murky darkness. The only illumination in the wagon was the occasional flare of lightning as it pierced the sky. Abigail could feel the steady beat of Boyd's heart as he continued to hold her. The scratchy wool of the blanket even seemed comforting as Boyd held it in place. The thick smell of rain continued to scent the air. Abigail found herself drifting toward sleep where tendrils of fear reached through her dreams, beckoning, tormenting. And she wondered which was real—the terror or the safety.

12

Boyd felt the dead weight of his own limbs as they lay twisted beneath Abigail's sleeping form. Daylight would be peeking over the camp soon. He should have checked on the men and the cattle hours earlier, but he had done neither. Instead he had watched over Abigail, fear and suspicion waging their own wars through the night.

Remembering his worries about little Michael when he was born, Boyd wondered if his concern had been misplaced. It didn't take too much figuring to know that with Abigail out of the way, the Triple Cross would be up for grabs. In the wild, lawless territory, men made their own rules. That included grabbing the land of those who employed less hands to fight for their ranches, the weak and the vulnerable.

Gazing down at her heart-shaped face, troubled even in sleep, there was no doubt that Abigail was vulnerable. Boyd's gut twisted, wondering who among them had so little compunction he would kill a defenseless woman. Careful not to disturb her, he picked up her hands, turning them over to see the raw, scraped palms. He traced a path around each jagged nail, imagining her terror as she held on to the log in the rushing water.

She sighed, a defeated, fearful sound that tore at him. Her long lashes draped the velvet of her cheeks, still pale after her ordeal. Her brow was furrowed even in sleep. He knew that he not only had to protect her, he also had to convince her that she was wrong about the attempt on her life. She didn't have the fortitude to withstand the knowledge that one of her own people might be planning her demise. Then he would have to make sure he was with her every step of the way, to protect her.

She shifted suddenly, a movement that caused the blanket to slip from her shoulders. With a dryness in his throat, he acknowledged what he had been trying to forget all night. Beneath the blanket Abigail was all satiny skin. And nothing else.

The peach blush of her skin seemed all that much more pronounced against the drab, gray wool blanket. The delicate curves and hollows of her throat and shoulders were revealed as the blanket slipped away. Even the gentle slope of her breasts threatened to spill into sight. His conscience battled with his desire as he reached toward the material.

Boyd damned his moral upbringing as he pulled the blanket upward, settling it over her shoulders. Now wasn't the time to take advantage of the situation. Still she shifted in his arms, her hips and legs rubbing against his under the blanket. It was a delicious torment.

One he knew he had to end. It wouldn't do to be caught crawling out of the bed wagon that Abigail was sleeping in. His men were loyal, but the ranch was a lonely place, and gossip filled those empty hours. Allowing himself the luxury of smoothing back her golden hair, feeling it ripple like silk beneath his fingers, he pressed one kiss to her temple. Then, putting purpose ahead of regret, he shook her shoulder gently, calling her name in a soft voice.

Like the evening primrose that dotted the countryside, she unfolded as she awoke. Dark lashes fluttered open to reveal eyes as clear and blue as the sky. Her pink mouth formed an "O" of surprise as she met his eyes and realized she still laid in his arms.

"Morning, Abby."

It was the first time he had used the affectionate nickname, and he saw that she registered the term with surprise. At the same time he could feel the shuffling of her limbs against him, and then their sudden dead stillness. Apparently she hadn't remembered going to sleep unclothed. It was no doubt a shock to awake and find herself clad only in a blanket.

She struggled to somewhat of a sitting position, which was an awkward feat given the small confines of the wagon and their own nearness. "Hi."

Her voice was small and uncertain. It made Boyd want to pull her close, reassure her, and then spend the rest of the day sliding that blanket off and rediscovering what was underneath.

"You sleep all right?"

Nodding her head, she tried to look everywhere but at him, which wasn't easy considering he filled up most of the available space. "Is it morning?"

"Not quite. But I'd like to check on the men and the herd before daylight strikes." He left the obvious unspoken, that he needed to leave the wagon unseen, but she caught his message nonetheless. He saw it in the flush of her cheeks, the darkening of her eyes.

She cleared her throat, her voice rich with embarrassment. "Would you know where my clothes are?"

He reached up and plucked the neat pile of her dry clothes from the top of a barrel. "You didn't feel quite up to dressin' last night."

Her glance traveled down the length of the blanket. Although her body was well covered, he guessed she must be wondering if it had stayed that way throughout the night. "I don't remember a lot of what happened."

He felt a burst of relief. "That's probably for the best. Rain's ended now. A flood on your first drive's a lot to go through." He resisted the urge to smooth the worry from her brow, to kiss the frown from her lips.

Putting all of his strained but considerable restraint into action, Boyd pulled away. As she secured the blanket in place, he watched the flutter of her hands, pale and delicate, as out of place in the incongruous surroundings as he was in her life. The sobering reminder propelled him to cover the distance to the rear of the wagon. Climbing outside, he turned to secure the flap. Abigail's face was a mixture of relief and entreaty. Wishing to give in to the latter, he yanked the canvas shut instead, wishing it were as easy to close his heart.

In the bright heat and light of the day, Abigail's fear began to recede and finally disappear. In retrospect she wondered if the elements had bewitched her senses, making the gloom and eeriness of the night into something more terrifying than had actually happened.

Fortunately they hadn't lost many head of cattle. Considering both the stampede and then the subsequent storm, it was a miracle they had much of a herd left. Glancing down the line at Boyd's tall, straight figure, she knew who was responsible for that accomplishment. She realized it wasn't just the ability to ride a horse and judge stock that made him so successful. It was his natural leadership. It was clear to Abigail these men would do anything for Boyd. But then he had earned that confidence.

She wondered if, despite her good intentions, she would ever win that same loyalty. Knowing that Boyd intended to set the herd moving again soon, she climbed into the chuck wagon to check on young Billy Kendall. His unnaturally pale skin was evidence that he was still in pain. But his eyes were wide open, and he watched as she climbed inside.

His voice was weak. "Mornin', Miz Fairchild."

"Good morning, Billy. How are you feeling?" Taking care not to alarm him, she checked his temperature, laying her hand against his brow. Fortunately the skin was cool to the touch. She was glad to see that he wasn't developing a fever, which usually signaled infection and dreaded gangrene.

"My leg's still hurtin', but I'm all right." Despite his words, she could see the fear he was trying to hide. Fear that he might lose his leg after all.

She gentled her voice. "I need to rebandage your wound, Billy." Pulling off the bandage, she knew they both held bated breath at what she would find. While still ugly, the incision didn't show any fiery signs of infection, no shooting splotches of violent color, no warning marks tattooing his skin. Wiping the area clean with salt water, she took care not to embarrass him as she carefully rebound the wound. "It looks very good. If you continue healing at this rate, you'll be up and around soon."

All the doubt and uncertainty of his youth crept into his tone. "You really think so?"

Despite the ravages of the previous evening, she made her smile bright. "Yes, I do. You'll need to keep drinking all the beef broth that Henry makes you, and for the next few days you have to stay off the leg, but I think you're on the mend."

His eyelids flickered shut, and she saw his Adam's apple bob. She felt the sting of her own tears, knowing how she would react if this were her son, afraid for his own future, determined not to show that fear. "Thank you, ma'am. I know if it weren't for you I wouldn't have my leg. . . ." His voice began to wobble, and Abigail took his hand in hers.

"I'm just glad I was here, Billy. And I have to thank you, too. Until you needed me to perform that surgery, I was pretty useless on this trail drive." She saw him start to protest and waved off his words. "No, I know the truth. I've been in the way, caused more work and trouble than I should have. Boyd warned me that I wasn't ready to come along, but I insisted. I'm sorry you were hurt and I'd change that if I could, but I'm glad you made me feel useful again."

A shy touch of color stained his cheeks. "I never thought of it that way, ma'am. But I know I'm the one who comes out ahead here." He glanced down at his leg, which she had carefully covered with a blanket. "I don't know how I'd have gone on if—"

"Fortunately you won't have to find out." She turned purposely brisk. "Now, I want you to eat that broth." Slipping her hand from his, she turned and retrieved the bowl she had brought in.

He hitched himself up on the pallet until he was in a sitting position. Taking the bowl, he drank from it slowly. She didn't remind him that there was a spoon nearby. Such niceties didn't seem quite as important as they once had.

Sitting with him while he finished the soup, she thought of the evening before and wondered if she had exaggerated the significance of what happened. Danger was all around them. Billy Kendall was proof of that. Perhaps she had only stumbled. Still, the memory of a firm touch against her back was difficult to wish away.

"We lose many cattle, ma'am?"

Abigail brought herself back to the present with an effort. "Not too many—some died in the flood. Boyd says we were lucky."

"He'd know. Mr. Harris is the best man I've ridden for. But I guess you know that, ma'am."

Yes, she did. In more ways than young Billy could know. "Well, you'd better get your rest. We'll be moving out soon. I'll check on you when we stop."

"Thanks, Miz Fairchild. For everything."

She resisted the urge to ruffle his hair and then smooth his brow. At his tender age, that transitional stage of young manhood, the gesture would probably embarrass him.

She started to step down when she found herself face to face with John Sims. The uncomfortable feeling he always evoked was even stronger this morning.

He gulped and removed his hat. "I just came to check on Billy."

Abigail kept her voice even. "He's doing well. But feel free to visit him. I'm sure he'll enjoy the company."

"Yes, ma'am."

She stepped out and started to walk away. Feeling the hair prickle on the back of her neck, she turned back and saw him still staring. But when she discovered him looking at her, he ducked inside the wagon.

Trying to dispel the uneasiness he caused, she took a deep breath of the rain-washed air. The sky, a cloudless canopy of robin's-egg blue, held no hint of further storms. Abigail turned and surveyed the milling mass of cattle and men. Since the first day on the trail when it had all seemed like an unorganized mess, she had come to learn just what a precisely tuned orchestration the trail drive really was. Someone was always working the cattle, chopping wood for fires, caring for the remuda of horses.

The staggering amount of work required had taught her a

new respect for the entire business. Before it had almost seemed as though the ranch had run itself. She was beginning to realize what a fallacy that notion was. And she suspected she had seen only a fraction of the complexity involved.

Heading over to the campfire, she sniffed appreciatively at the aroma scenting the air. It was a different odor than she had grown used to. In an instant she remembered the slaughtered beef. Apparently there would be a change in the diet. Grinning with satisfaction, she approached Antonio who was dishing up breakfast.

"No beans this morning, Antonio?"

"No, Señora, we're having . . ." His voice trailed off, and he turned an unpleasant shade of red.

"What?" she encouraged him.

"Sonofabitch stew," Henry supplied for him, hauling up a full pot from the rack.

"Oh," she answered. Then, not wanting to sound put off, she asked brightly, "And what does that contain?"

"Cut up heart, tongue, liver, marrow gut, testicles—"

"That'll be enough, Henry." Boyd walked up next to her, filling his coffee cup. "Miz Fairchild's not plannin' to cook some when she gets home."

Taking her elbow, Boyd guided her away from the cook and wrangler, leaning close to speak quietly. "Close your mouth, Abigail."

She did so, unaware that her jaw was flapping in the wind. "Is this some joke I'm not supposed to catch on to?" she whispered.

"Nope, the stew's considered a delicacy. Besides, we had a whole cow to get rid of. But if you're not up to eatin' it . . ." He made a move as though to take away the plate. Stubbornly she hung on to it.

"I didn't say I wouldn't eat it." She stared at the stew, wondering just what was what. "What . . ." She cleared her throat. "What exactly is marrow gut?"

"Lining of the stomach."

Now, didn't that sound appetizing. Nearly as much as the other ingredients Henry had listed. Stabbing her fork aimlessly around her plate, she wondered how much she would have to eat not to appear to be a weakling. A delicate female among all these big, brave men. Glancing at Boyd, she saw that he wasn't going to be a lot of help.

"Ground's real soft from the rain," he said as he sipped his coffee.

"Uh-huh." She stared again at the seemingly huge plate of stew.

"A person could dig a hole in the dirt with the heel of a boot," he continued.

"I suppose so." What if she ate it and then threw it up in front of everyone?

"A hole that size would hold a plate of stew."

She blinked and then turned to him in surprise.

"And I got some hardtack in my saddlebags that'd last a body till we stop again," he said in that same quiet, reasonable tone.

She glanced from him to the ground and saw that he had already dug a respectable hole with his boot. Cautiously peering around, she saw no one looking and slid the contents of the plate into the hole. She scraped loose dirt over the hole quickly, covering the evidence in seconds.

Gratefully she shared a conspiratorial smile with Boyd and saw him drop a provocative wink. Her heart beat faster, and a sudden image of how they had lain together the night before made the heat in her cheeks rise.

Apparently he shared the sensation because he rose abruptly. "I'll get that hardtack." He disappeared without saying more, and she sensed he needed to get away, to cool the sudden heat that had flared between them.

She made a good show of sitting with her empty plate for a respectable length of time, slowly sipping her coffee. When it seemed as though enough time would have passed to have eaten, she returned her plate to the wreck pan and gave the worried-looking Antonio a smile. Facing the crusty Henry, she fixed him with a particularly bright smile, savoring the surprise on his face.

Flexing her sore hands and arms, Abigail went to the remuda to fetch her mare. Kyle, the roper who could lasso on one attempt, expertly threw the rope. Once Dolly was separated from the other horses, Kyle saddled the horse without asking Abigail. He then handed her a good portion of hardtack and a sack of dried apples. Surprised, she stared at the man.

He shrugged self-consciously as he motioned toward her scraped hands. "Boyd said you might need some help for a few days."

"Oh. Well, thank you." Even more surprised, she led Dolly away from the remuda, looking back in time to see Kyle tip his hat in her direction.

She wondered just what else Boyd had been up to. Seeing that they were about ready to ride out, Abigail took her position near the chuck wagon. Since she wasn't experienced enough to be a swing rider, one of the cowhands who rode in pairs to keep the cattle from breaking into groups or leading the herd in the wrong direction, she rode close to the chuck wagon and bed wagon. At times, when she grew tired of breathing the dust of the cattle, she rode to the side of the herd along with the remuda.

The cattle started moving, their bawling cries and snorts echoing in the canyon. Dust rose like a vaporous cloud beneath their pawing hooves. Cowboys rode alongside, their shouts and whistles piercing the air in competition with the beasts they sought to control. Pulling her bandanna up over her face, Abigail nudged her horse and joined the moving caravan.

It occurred to her that not too many months ago, she would never have dreamed that sitting in the saddle, knowing her place in the works of the cattle drive, would begin to seem almost second nature. She had grown used to having the afternoon pass almost hypnotically as the prairie unfolded, carrying them closer to the railhead.

The hours passed as the days had. Long, hot, and tiring. Since they had gotten a late start, she knew there would be no noontime stop. Instead, Boyd had warned her, they would push on until they could go no farther.

The rain had washed the air clean, but left its mark on the dusty ground. Great puddles of mud littered the dirt, places that had no grass to provide a soft cushion for the moisture. The bawling of cows caught in bog holes rendered the air. Abigail watched as the cowhands came to retrieve fresh mounts after riding for hours, then pulling the cows from repeated mishaps, horses and men both exhausted.

More than one mud-spattered cowhand looked ready to call it a day, give in to the exhaustion claiming them, but still they pushed on. When the sun finally appeared ready to release its hold on the day, Abigail saw Boyd for the first time in hours. Drenched in mud, he rode near the chuck wagon, and Abigail suspected he was giving the order to make camp.

She saw his eyes flicker her way, wearily acknowledge her presence, and then move on. Feeling a moment of disappointment, she wished he would have spared her a word. Because of her status as ranch owner, the men were respectful, but they didn't say much to her. None of the overworked hands had the time for idle conversation, but still she felt isolated. She had begun to look forward to the evenings, time she could share with Boyd.

On an impulse, she decided to follow him. Dolly couldn't keep up the same pace as Boyd's stallion, and Abigail lagged behind, able to follow his silhouette as he rode far ahead. The path he took was a semicircle from the camp. Then he cut through a stand of aspen. She almost turned back but, ignoring that impulse, continued on. Entering the grove of trees, she wondered for a brief moment if he had disappeared into the greenery. Uneasily she glanced around at the growing dusk.

Then she heard unexpected sounds: humming and splashing. Curious, she dismounted and tied Dolly's reins to a sapling. Taking care to be quiet, she walked cautiously on a bed of pine needles and wild grass. Bending back the branches of a protruding bush, she stopped suddenly.

Her throat growing dry, she stood as though paralyzed. Eyes widening, she stared at Boyd as he bathed in the fresh water of the lake that wound in a curve from camp to the secluded portion that Boyd had sought out. Her gaze fastened on the sun-gilded planes of his chest and abdomen.

Sculpted muscles that she had only guessed at bulged from the width of his well-defined chest. Arms of steel soaped his equally muscled back. All muscle and sinew—he was a magnificent specimen of smooth golden skin and hard, taut flesh.

He stood hip deep in the water. Despite the lengthening shadows, Abigail could see the tapering of his perfectly proportioned body from the broad shoulders to his lean waist. Unable to pull her eyes away, she stared at the fascinating swirl of hair that beguiled, hinting at the manhood hidden by the deep water.

One thought stood out with clarity. Boyd was very different from her late husband. While Michael had been a handsome man, he hadn't possessed the raw power, the overwhelming masculinity that made her want to flee in terror and at the same time melt closer. Boyd wouldn't command a level of high-dealing bank officials, but there was no doubt he was master of this raw land.

Warmth curled in Abigail's belly as she continued to stare, transfixed. She could imagine the unleashed power at his disposal. Remembering his touch against her skin, she shivered, wondering how it would feel to have his entire magnificent body next to hers, his skin abrading hers, his . . .

Unbidden, a memory of his hands on her sent the heat rushing through her lower regions, and she realized she ached for his touch again. The magic he had created had been nearly unbearable in its pleasure.

With a start Abigail drew back as Boyd turned to stride toward shore. She was afforded a view of the rippling muscles of his back as they flowed down over tight buttocks and then poured into endlessly long legs. Staring far longer than she should have, Abigail felt the dampness pool between her legs, the fire that singed a path through each aching spot in her body. Never had she been held in such rapt delight.

For an insane moment she considered walking forward, confronting Boyd and finding out the extent of that delight. She could almost feel his hands as they touched her, the magic his adroit fingers could work. Somehow she guessed he could bring even greater pleasure than he had hinted at that day. But even as she thought of walking toward him, doubts assailed her. What could they hope to share except passion and the scorching tongues of anyone who found out? Her heart heavy, she drank in the strength of his face, his body, his undeniably gentle soul, knowing they couldn't belong to her.

Realizing suddenly that she was in danger of being discovered, Abigail tore her gaze from the body that beckoned. She didn't dare start a relationship that threatened to consume them both. It wouldn't be fair to either of them. Both of them had too much to lose. And, God help her, she didn't want Boyd to be forced to leave because of her weakness.

She backtracked quickly and, disregarding caution, leaped on Dolly, hoping the fast action wouldn't unseat her. Blessedly, she hung on and kicked Dolly into an unexpected canter. The mare reacted, sending them flying out of the aspen grove and back on the path toward camp.

Abigail hoped the cool breeze of approaching evening would still the heat she felt in her cheeks. Daring one glance backward, she doubted anything could douse the fire Boyd had ignited.

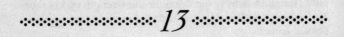
Tired, but refreshed, Boyd returned from his quick bath in the lake. Grateful that they hadn't lost more of the herd, he had spent the day troubleshooting. He had a good crew of men who cared about the ranch and the kind of job they performed. But right now, all of them, himself included, were dead tired.

Accepting a plate from the cook, he stopped to gaze around the campfire, wondering how Abigail was faring. It took him a few moments to locate her. Seated far away from the main group, almost hidden in the shadows, she kept her face downward. He hoped she wasn't having a delayed reaction to what had happened during the flood. It had been his experience in the past that men faced danger, even death, fearlessly, but afterward were haunted by their close encounters.

Temporarily forgetting his own weariness, Boyd summoned a smile as he approached. "Got room for a tired cowhand?"

She jumped, nearly dropping her plate. If his hands hadn't been full, he would have caught it for her. But she scrabbled to regain her balance. "Yes, certainly."

Puzzled, he glanced at her. Her voice was unnaturally high, as was the color in her cheeks. Still agitated, she clutched her dinner plate as though a high tide might wash it away. "Long day, wasn't it?"

"Uh, yes . . . it was."

"Never seen so many stupid cows in all my days," Boyd lamented. "It's like they were trying to fall into the bogs."

"Oh?"

He slanted a glance at her. It was rare for her to be so quiet. He had come to look forward to their conversations each evening. She was not only good company, but also amusing and full of interesting talk. "Yeah, they're obstinate, dumb, troublesome creatures, intent on making life miserable."

"I see."

Watching closely, Boyd saw her knot her bandanna into an unrecognizable lump with one hand, before lowering it to her lap and then picking up her tin cup of coffee. Something was definitely on her mind. "Got myself covered in mud right good. Had to wash off before I was decent company."

Sputtering, she nearly spit out her coffee. Concerned, Boyd laid down his plate and patted her on the back as she continued to cough and choke. "Hell, I guess I should know better than to bring up bathtime in front of a lady."

Abigail coughed even harder. Her face took on the hue of a ripe tomato. Pulling her arm up over her head to free her diaphragm, Boyd stared at the mixed emotions swarming across her face. If he didn't know better, he would think she was ready to explode. "You all right, Abby?"

She cleared her throat finally. "Yes, I just got some coffee caught the wrong way." She attempted a smile, but it looked more like a plea. "You're right, it has been a long day."

Boyd felt certain there was something she was leaving unsaid, but he didn't know how to find out what it was. And if it centered around her scare, he didn't need to be reminding her of her suspicions. The sooner she forgot about it, the better.

He thought of something that would cheer her. Pointing toward the west where the lake wound around the area they had camped in, he caught her attention. "You can't see it in the dark, but there's a lake just past here. We could delay starting in the morning, give you enough time to take a quick dip."

"No!" Her tone resembled a shriek, and she lowered it consciously. "I mean . . . that's not necessary. Really."

"If you're worried about the men coming around, I can stand watch again."

Her voice grew frantic. "No!" She picked at the cloth of her breeches, her cheeks stained bright red again. "That's not a good idea."

Boyd chuckled, his teeth a slash of white in his tanned face. "Hell, you can trust me, Abigail. Much as I might like to, I won't peek."

She jumped up suddenly, desperation edging her words. "I'd better go check on Dolly."

Boyd tried to balance the plate and cup in his lap as he watched her unexpected movement. "There's no need. The tail rider has her in the rope corral."

"Still, she's had a long day." Abigail's voice rose until it was a querulous waver. "You're the one who told me that it's more important to take care of the horse than the person."

"Well, yeah, but—"

"You can't bend the rules just for me, you know."

"But—"

"It doesn't do any good to teach me one thing and then ignore what I'm supposed to be doing."

Not waiting for his reply, she fled into the night. Boyd shook his head as he watched her disappear. Something was wrong with her. She was itchier than a polecat trapped in a grizzly's cave. After he ate, he would make sure she was all right before bedtime.

Glancing up, Boyd saw John Sims following the same path Abigail had. Briefly he wondered what the man was doing. Then he shook his head, realizing he was growing too suspicious. John was no doubt headed toward the remuda.

Finishing his meal, Boyd knew he had one more thing to do before he could consider getting some sleep. He dumped his plate in the wreck pan, refilled his coffee cup, and grabbed another. Making his way to the chuck wagon, Boyd set the cups down as he pushed the flaps open. He could see that Billy was still awake. Picking up the coffee, he stepped inside.

"Hey there, Billy."

Billy sat up a bit more. "Hey, Mr. Harris."

"Thought you might like a cup of this day-old mud."

Billy accepted the mug gratefully. "I could stand some."

They both sipped the familiar, bitter brew. It was a staple that represented a semblance of security for otherwise unanchored souls.

Boyd scrutinized Billy's face as he held the steaming cup close. His color was good. As Abigail had reported, he definitely seemed on the mend. Grateful for her talents, Boyd acknowledged that he would have hated to see the young man lose his leg. As she had pointed out, Billy had a full life ahead of him, one that required all of his limbs.

"You feeling better?"

Billy's smile was genuine. "Yep. Miz Fairchild says I'm mending right good." His gaze traveled down his bandaged leg. "She's something, ain't she?"

That she was. More and more, when Boyd thought of Abigail, he felt the gusts of warmth touch his carefully protected heart. "Yeah, she's determined, all right."

"You know, I never thought Miz Fairchild was so strong." Billy stumbled over the words. "I mean, being such a proper lady and all. Who'd have thought she could make it on a trail ride?"

He hadn't, Boyd acknowledged silently. Sure that she would crack and fail immediately, he had hoped she would so she would return to the ranch where she belonged.

"She's a surprising lady," Boyd admitted out loud.

"I know if it wasn't for her I probably wouldn't have my leg." Billy colored, as though remembering Boyd would have been responsible for that other decision. "I don't mean anything by it—"

"It's all right, Billy." Boyd took a deep breath. "You're right. None of us would have known how to perform surgery on your leg. You've got Miz Fairchild to thank."

Billy took a big swallow of the coffee. "When her husband died, I figured she'd head back East. I'm sure glad she didn't."

Boyd tipped his own coffee to his mouth, savoring the acrid taste before answering. "Me, too, Billy." *Me, too.*

The night riders were on duty, keeping watch over the herd. Calm now that the storm had traveled past, the cattle slept as darkness filled the night. Boyd searched for Abigail, feeling a touch of concern. Lately she had taken to placing her bedroll not far from his. Every evening before he drifted off to sleep, his last thought was an image of her face, her lips curved in sleep, dark eyelashes fanning over her cheeks, golden hair pillowing her head. He frowned, wondering where she could have gone.

Remembering her words about being pushed into the rushing water, he felt a twinge of fear. What if she had been right? What if someone was stalking her and he had let her wander off into the darkness alone? Adrenaline pumping through his veins, Boyd increased his pace, his weariness forgotten.

He had already looked at the rope corral, where she said she was going, but the cowhand manning the corral had only scratched his head and reported that she hadn't been there since she had left the mount at the end of the day. Boyd had detoured to the remuda, then searched the campfire area, thinking she might have decided to rejoin the cowhands for their company. But she hadn't been in either place.

His eyes scanned the unending darkness. She was such a small person, and this was a huge land to get lost in. Increasing his pace, he tried to keep a check on his fear, reminding himself that she wasn't stupid enough to wander off alone. But the reality that she didn't fully appreciate the dangers of the land intruded.

Deciding that if he didn't find her in the next ten minutes he would gather the men and search for her, Boyd continued checking the immediate area. His gaze skipped over the obvious places, seeing the campfire, chuck wagon, bed wagon, and corral.

He turned his head, his gaze backtracking over those same places. He had checked all of them except the bed wagon. His eyes narrowed as he stared at the inconspicuous bunting of the canvas-covered vehicle. Striding forward, he started to push open the flaps when his gaze was caught by a small flash of color beneath the wooden frame of the wagon.

Stooping downward, he peered underneath. Abigail's eyes met his, looking much like a trapped deer caught in the sights of a shotgun. A quick perusal told him that she had laid out her bedroll beneath the wagon. A spear of unexpected disappointment darted through him. He had grown used to having her close by each evening.

"Abigail," he greeted her.

"Boyd," she responded.

Silence loomed between them.

He decided to break it. "What are you doing over here?"

Her eyes widened even farther before she dropped them, plucking at the blanket of her bedroll. "I thought it might rain."

Immediate understanding filled him. Apparently her fear had taken forefront. She must be afraid that it would storm and she might be trapped again in a flood. "There's no need to be frightened, Abby."

Once again, a blending of mixed emotions crowded her expression. He guessed she was trying to hide her fear, to convince him that she was as capable as a male owner would be in the same situation. Her bravery touched him, and her words convinced him that he was right. "Oh, I'm not scared. I just want to stay dry."

Smiling, he backed away and then stood up. "I'd best check on the men on this shift."

Her voice quivered. "Good idea."

After checking who was riding herd, making sure everything was as it should be, Boyd collected his own bedroll and returned to the bed wagon. Trying not to make too much noise as he plopped the blankets on the ground, he was surprised when she bolted upright as though he had set off a cannon next to her ear.

"What are you doing?" she demanded.

He pushed his Stetson back, trying to appear appropriately casual. "Decided you were right." He made a pretense of studying the sky off to the side of the wagon. "It could rain, and I'd like to stay dry."

"But . . ." Her voice trailed off, and he felt the pull of her gaze as she stared at him. "Do you think it's proper to sleep under the same wagon?"

Fresh amusement assailed him. "Considering our bedrolls have been this close for weeks, I don't see that it matters that we're underneath the wagon together."

"But yesterday you said we shouldn't be seen inside the wagon together." Panic edged her words.

He was tempted to reach out to touch the earnest-looking face. Her delicate chin was firmed in a most intriguing manner, and her bravery was far more appealing than the sulks and faints of most women. "I said 'inside' the wagon." With intentionally great care, he placed his bedroll a respectable distance away from hers. "No harm in sharing a roof." He reached up to touch the wooden underside of the wagon. "Shabby as it might be."

"Well, pardon me. I don't know all the rules of trail-ride etiquette."

Boyd lifted his eyebrows in surprise. She sounded downright snippy, not at all the tone he had grown used to hearing from her. He guessed she was reacting more to the fear than he had expected. Turning to face her, he felt an unexpected stab of pain in his thigh. He flinched, unable to hide the reaction.

"Boyd, what is it?"

Absently he rubbed his leg. "Nothing."

"Nothing?" She turned on her side, her anger seeming to seep away. "You looked as if someone had stabbed you."

He sucked in his breath, silently watching her gaze travel down the length of his thigh.

"What's wrong? Did you hurt yourself today?"

He grimaced as the ache continued to grind inside his leg. "Not today. Long time ago."

She wouldn't let go of the subject. "When?"

Concealing his exasperation, Boyd tried to remember that this might be a good diversion for her fear. "In the war. Took a minié ball in my thigh."

He could read sympathy in her expression and was glad
to see it didn't contain pity as well. That was an emotion he
didn't tolerate well.

"Does it bother you often?"

"Only when the weather changes, or if I've been hauling
too many ornery cows out of a bog."

"That's how you knew it was going to storm," she said
with sudden insight. "Even though the sky was clear, you
knew we were in for a drenching."

"The ache in my leg's generally accurate," he admitted.

"Between the storm and the work today, you must be in
a lot of pain!" she exclaimed.

He wondered at the remorse he saw written on her face.
But her expression cleared as she became briskly efficient.
Even though he tried to demur, to insist he wasn't in that
much pain, she was unstoppable.

Plumping one of her own blankets into a roll, she slid it
beneath his leg. "This will relieve some of the pressure."

"It's really not necessary," he protested, knowing that in
the past he had always taken a slug of whiskey to dull the
pain and called it even.

Unexpected fire lit her eyes. "I want to do this."

Realizing that he'd taken her mind off her fear, Boyd
decided to lean back and enjoy her ministrations. He
wondered, though, what she was thinking as she nibbled on
her bottom lip, obviously torn about something.

"Have you ever tried massage?" she finally asked in a
hesitant tone.

A sudden image of her hands touching him in such an
intimate manner shot an immediate response to his groin.
His voice was suddenly deep, almost gruff. "Nope." His
mouth went dry, and he hoped she couldn't detect any sign
of his desire.

Two spots of color dotted her cheeks, and he guessed she
was trying to maintain a sense of detachment. "Then we'll
try it."

Hesitantly her delicate hands hovered above his thigh.
The anticipation was nearly as mesmerizing as the touch of
her hands as they finally reached his denim-clad leg. Roving

over the length of his thigh, her fingers were like a magical lute, singing an age-old tune. He could feel the beads of sweat dot his forehead as he strove to maintain control. The bulge of his response filled the limited space in his denims as she gently continued to knead his thigh. The pain of his old wound was forgotten as she performed the sweet torture.

When her hands moved upward, he sucked in his breath, wondering that she didn't stumble across his engorged flesh.

Her head was bent, her voice conscientious as she determinedly worked on his leg. "Is this close to the source of the pain?"

Any closer and she would be draped across his fullness, and he would be pulling her into his arms. His voice was strangled as he answered, "Yes, it's very close."

"Up higher?" she asked innocently, fervently massaging his now flaming leg.

He forced some control into his tone. "Maybe just a little."

Her hands were close to the juncture of his thighs and he nearly moaned as she ran her fingers over the pressurized space that had swelled to fill his denims. "I'm sorry you're in such pain."

She didn't know the beginning of it. "You're making it much better."

Abigail lifted luminescent blue eyes. "I'm sorry I was so short with you earlier. I didn't realize you had a war wound that required attention."

Any more attention and he'd be pulling her to the ground, tasting the sweet honey of her lips, and then taking his time to discover other equally honeyed places. "Abigail, if you continue the massage, I'm not sure where it's going to lead."

Confusion filled her face, followed by sudden and obviously embarrassing understanding. Her hands froze. Seeing the mortification chase across her features, he gave into the impulse to pull her close.

"Don't be embarrassed, Abby." He stroked the tendrils of golden hair away from her face. "I'd like nothing better than to feel your touch." He hesitated, wishing he could put his complex feelings into words, knowing to do so would only damage this woman he had grown to care for too much. "But we both know it isn't wise."

She looked as though she, too, had a confession, but instead she simply nodded in agreement. He wondered suddenly what she was hiding. "No, I guess it isn't, Boyd." Her gaze drifted downward, her words a mere whisper on the wind. "Despite how we feel."

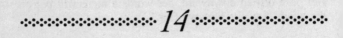

14

In an unexpected fit of restlessness, Miranda had abandoned the list of chores that needed to be done and now
wandered toward the meadow that sloped downward behind
the ranch house. Breathing in the sweet perfumed air, she
tried to focus on the cause of her anxiety.

All week chores had been started, then abandoned. Today
she had begun baking a cake and found herself daydreaming
while adding in the ingredients. Unable to recall whether
she had added the baking powder or salt, she found that she
had to discard the batter. But she had no wish to attempt a
second cake. Her energy seemed to be sapped along with the
onset of her restlessness.

All day she had found herself lost in her thoughts,
thoughts she didn't want to pursue, but ones that refused to
leave her alone.

Relentlessly she tried to turn her attention away from the
man who toiled in the study near the kitchen. She had hoped
her fascination with Cameron O'Donnell would dissipate.
But now her preoccupation with the man seemed to inten-
sify. Thinking that her interest in him was perhaps a fleeting
fancy, for the first time in years she had carefully studied
other men on the ranch, even those in town when she had gone
shopping. But none of them caused the fluttering and
anticipation that Cameron did by simply entering the same
room.

Cursing her ill-fated choice, Miranda had decided to
ignore men altogether, including Cameron O'Donnell. That
attempt appeared to be equally unsuccessful. Feeling like a

fool, one who was old enough to know better, she purposely altered her behavior toward Cameron. Instead of arguing each time they met, she treated him with cool politeness. But after each encounter, she had grown more frustrated.

Glad that Lucy was watching little Michael, Miranda strolled through the grass and wildflowers, content to listen to the songbirds that filled the air with their tunes. Colorful butterflies fluttered casually amidst the tall stalks of columbine and tansybush. A poignant ache rocked through her body, gripping Miranda with unwanted intensity.

Suddenly the life she had been content with no longer held any peace. She wanted something more, something she couldn't even define. Feeling the sting of tears beneath her eyelids, Miranda shook them away, afraid to give in to the weakness.

"So here you are."

Startled by the unexpected voice, Miranda spun around to face the man who plagued her thoughts and, damnably, her dreams. "What are you doing here?"

"Still as friendly as ever, I see," Cameron noted dryly.

Miranda schooled her voice to be calm and distantly polite. "You startled me. Is there something I can do for you?"

His dark eyes narrowed, the light in their fathomless depths sending a shiver through her. "I like you better when you're biting my head off."

Her eyebrows shot up in surprise, but he spoke before she could.

"It's better than the cold freeze."

She turned away abruptly. "I don't know what you're talking about."

"Somehow I doubt that, Miss Abernathy."

"Miranda," she blurted out before she could stop the wayward words.

It was his turn to be surprised. "Miranda?" The name lingered as he drew it out slowly. It didn't sound as prim and spinsterish when he said it.

Embarrassed, she turned away again, staring into the undulating foothills. Somewhere she registered the beauty of the purple and tangerine blush that marked the beginning of sunset. Feeling incredibly awkward, she wished simultaneously that Cameron would leave and that he would stay and ease the restlessness she couldn't suppress.

He stepped beside her, his gaze following hers. "It's beautiful out here, isn't it?"

Throat dry, a lump threatening to choke her, Miranda nodded. "I've always liked it."

"Are you from around here?"

Miranda continued to avoid his gaze. "From Texas originally. My parents wanted to homestead, so we came out this way."

"And did they?" He paused. "Homestead, that is?"

"No, they died on the way here. Influenza."

"Brothers and sisters?"

She shook her head. "None of them made it." Her voice turned bitter. "I was the only lucky one."

"That some time ago?"

Laughing unexpectedly, she angled her head, unaware of the flirtatious tilt. "Is that your way of saying I'm old?"

He didn't rise to the jibe. "Not at all." His gaze swept the length of her burnished copper hair and then down her still-trim figure. "No man in his right man would think you're past your prime."

Flustered, she swung her head, intent on escaping his far-seeing gaze. But he moved faster, blocking her way. "Running away, Miranda? I wouldn't think it of you."

She pulled herself back with an effort. "You don't know me well enough to judge that."

"Not because I haven't tried." He extended a long slim hand and cupped her chin. "You have walls around you higher than the mountains."

She wanted to protest, to tell him that he was wrong, but his touch paralyzed her. When he lifted that same hand to caress her cheek, she felt the weakness invade her body. Unexpected, unwanted, undeniable.

"Why is that, Miranda?"

Her head swam with his words, the sound of her name on his lips, the sensation of his potent touch. But she swallowed the lump of fear, wishing she could dissolve the desire as easily. Knowing it was best to be on the offense, rather than the defense, she turned the tables. "What about you, Cameron O'Donnell? I've never met a more forbidding man."

The deep slash of his brows quirked. "An admirable admission, Miranda."

"Admission?" Warily, she watched him.

"Until now you've pretended that I didn't exist." He stepped a fraction closer. "I prefer you more like this."

Afraid of what he thought she might have revealed, Miranda took an ever stronger defensive stance. "I don't know what you mean."

"That's where you're wrong. And that's what scares you."

"You have a head full of nonsense," she scoffed, hoping she could pull off the charade. Unaccustomed to flirtations, she didn't know how to fence verbally with a man. She was plain-spoken and blunt, unaware of the nuances most men and women used during their interchanges.

"Is that what you'd call it?" he asked, his voice as tempting as his touch.

She stared at him, reminded of a hawk. He had intense eyes and features not in the least bit softened by his dark brows and black hair, and a spare, tall body that spoke of caged energy. She tried to remember what he was asking, but her mind was muddled. "Stuff and nonsense." She had intended to sound gruff and uncaring, instead to her horror she sounded nearly breathless.

When his head angled, she wondered for a frenzied moment if he was going to kiss her. Instead one hand reached up to sift through the few loose hairs not secured in her tidy bun. "It's a shame."

"What is?" She tried to suppress her sudden rapid breathing, wondering if she was about to have a heart attack. That would explain why she was close to having a fit of the vapors.

"Keeping all this hair tied up in a knot."

Her hand strayed involuntarily to the neat bun she was accustomed to wearing. Memories of merciless teasing about her red hair assaulted her. She wondered if he would stoop so low as to insult her as well. Even though logically she knew her hair had changed to a more muted color, still the thought stung. "I'll thank you not to be talking about my hair."

If possible, those nearly black eyes darkened further. "It's like a beacon. Rich, luxurious, and tempting."

Miranda did something she couldn't remember doing in years. She blushed. From the top of her red hair to the hollows of her throat. Feeling the heat, she willed the tell-tale color to disappear, but judging by Cameron's chuckle, she must still be blazing.

"Enchanting," he said, surprising her again. "Not many women I know can still blush."

"You think I'm a foolish old maid," she bit out hotly.

"Not at all, Miranda." His voice was suddenly gentle. "I simply didn't know anyone other than eighteen-year-old virgins still blushed."

The reference to virgins scorched her already prickly sensibilities. "Now I guess you know better."

"Yes, I guess I do. Miss Miranda, would you walk with me awhile?"

She couldn't still the suspicion. "Where to?"

"Everywhere. Nowhere." He smiled at the confusion on her face and held out his hand. "Just through the meadow. I don't believe I've seen more than the house since I arrived."

Miranda hesitated, remembering times when she had gazed longingly at blond, petite women as they were swept off on the arms of beaus. Considering she was as tall or taller than most of those men, it had never been a dream within her reach. But as she tilted her head back to meet Cameron's gaze she realized that next to his superior height she didn't feel quite so awkward. "If you really want to see the place, I can walk with you."

"Ah, yes. That's what I want, Miss Miranda."

Despite her inexperience, she wondered at the sudden inflection in his tone that signaled something other than the casual innocence of his words. But even as she tried to guess at his meaning, his gaze met hers, bland and unthreatening.

Uncertain what else to do, Miranda started to move forward. Cameron's light touch on her elbow shot through her as though a bolt of harnessed lightning had found its way through her unsuspecting body. Trying to still the trembling he caused, she walked forward blindly, not seeing anything in her path.

The remaining rays of the sun slanted against them as they traveled the distance of the meadow. The journey for Miranda's heart was far greater as she took the first step and feared the next.

After the initial stampede, the herd had stampeded again that same night in fits and starts from midnight until dawn with every cowhand in the saddle and thoroughly exhausted by morning.

But now the animals were calm again. A herd could begin a drive by stampeding and fall into a pattern that was difficult to break. On the other hand, the cattle could stampede, recover from the experience, and remain calm the rest of the journey. Since the animals hadn't given them any more trouble the last few days, it looked as if they had the luck of a calm herd.

Abigail was exhausted. Ever since she had seen Boyd's magnificent, naked body, she had been obsessed by thoughts of him. When he had crawled beneath the wagon cover next to her that same night, she had lain awake all night simply imagining what would have happened if she hadn't cowardly fled the lake. Combined with the remembered feel of his hands on her, she had slept the tortured sleep of the damned.

The fact that he didn't know that she had brazenly spied on him touched her conscience as well. When he had innocently confessed that he wouldn't stoop to such measures, she felt an immense sense of guilt. What kind of person was she that she would not only invade his privacy, but also enjoy it? Her frustration was so great, she gave long, agonizing thought to the consequences if she and

Boyd were to pursue a relationship. But no matter what angle she examined their problem from, no solution emerged.

She sighed as she swatted the flies from her neck and urged Dolly forward with a motion of her knees. They were riding over a rise, and from her vantage point Abigail could see the long string of the herd down below, stretched out far ahead. Like great brown rivers, the cattle continued on the move. Remembering Boyd's words about the beauty of the land, the satisfaction he felt in his work, she could see a glimpse of his sentiments.

Despite dust, thirst, blisters, cold, and danger, these men who rode the land brought more than just talent to their jobs. Even though Boyd had pointed out that many of them had no other choices in life, they exhibited a fierce loyalty that stirred her heart. It was also another sobering thought. They all depended on the Triple Cross for their livelihood. True, there were other ranches they could go to work for, but many had been part of the ranch for the greater part of their lives. Her indiscretion could change a lot of lives.

Glancing up, she saw Randy Kreiger ride close. The assistant foreman, Boyd's right-hand man and friend, had kept a respectful distance during the trail drive. In some ways she suspected he was somewhat intimidated by having the ranch owner, a female one at that, along on the drive. He acted reserved, almost shy.

"Miz Fairchild." He tipped his hat respectfully.

"Hello, Randy."

"Right nice day, isn't it?"

Somehow she doubted that he had come by to discuss the weather. "Yes, it is, Randy. Aren't you riding point today?"

"John relieved me. I have to change mounts. Just thought I'd see if you were doing all right."

Abigail wasn't sure what to make of this overture. While she appreciated his concern, she didn't want to be treated like some sort of invalid just because she had taken a tumble in the river. "I'm perfectly fine, Randy. It's really not necessary to check up on me."

Randy tipped back his hat and scratched at the lank

brown hair he revealed. "Gosh, ma'am, I didn't mean any offense."

"None taken, but the men need to know exactly what type of owner I am."

"Beggin' your pardon, ma'am, but I think they got that message when you patched up young Billy. Lot of owners think if a hand gets hurt, it's his own trouble. Not many of them would care if he got put back together. They sure wouldn't bother to do it themselves."

The men of the Triple Cross were making it extremely difficult for her to maintain any professional distance. Somehow she was beginning to feel as though she had acquired a ragtag bunch of friends and relatives instead of employees. But it wasn't a displeasing notion. "Well, thank you, Randy. I only did what any compassionate person would."

"Mebbe so." He shrugged. "But it's not what I'm used to seein'."

"Oh." Disconcerted, she stared past him at the line of moving cattle, pretending absorption in the same sight she stared at day after day. "I'm glad what I did was appreciated." Her voice was soft even to her own ears.

He smiled suddenly, taking years off his worn face. "Yes'm. It was." But almost as suddenly, his smile disappeared, his whole face pulled into a frown.

"What's wrong, Randy?"

She turned in the saddle and twisted to see what he was staring at. This time she couldn't prevent her mouth from falling open in shock. She didn't particularly care if every fly in the territory landed inside. Because riding in at full charge were the Indians she had dreaded encountering, then dismissed because of Boyd's reassuring words.

With headdresses, full war paint, and dressed in buckskins, what appeared to be a hundred Indians were galloping toward them. No doubt with murder and mayhem in mind. Behind their gruesome painted masks, she could see no trace of friendliness.

The savages quickly formed a circle around them, and Abigail tensed even more, wondering if they would kill her outright or keep her alive for even worse things. . . . She wished suddenly and violently for the gun she had replaced in the chuck wagon so meekly at Boyd's request. In a fit of sudden unreason, she vowed to kill Boyd herself if they survived.

But now her throat closed up, and her mouth dried into cotton as she watched the band narrow. Boyd, she saw, sat calmly in his saddle, not lifting his rifle from its scabbard. Cautiously peering around, she saw that none of the men were drawing their arms. Panic was choking her as she realized they were truly helpless.

Fine thing, she fumed silently. The men had the weapons and they weren't using them!

She sucked in her breath as the apparent leader of the band approached Boyd. Despite the man's savagery, he exuded dignity as well. In the stillness she strained to hear the Indian's words, his exchange with Boyd, but she couldn't make out what either man said. Boyd's right arm shot up suddenly. Abigail waited with bated breath to see if the Indian would retaliate, but everyone remained still as Boyd made a sign with his upraised arms.

"What's he doing?" Abigail whispered, unable to keep her silence any longer.

"His arm is raised in the cattle sign. It means the brave can take an animal to eat in exchange for allowing us to cross their land."

"Then they'll leave?"

Randy shrugged. "Mebbe."

Hardly comforted, she watched as the swing riders cut out a head of beef. The Indian leader pointed his gun at the steer, a single pistol shot to the head killing it.

"Why—" she started to ask, wondering why they were killing the beef here instead of taking it with them.

But as she watched, the Indians fell upon the animal. Having killed it, they skinned it at once. All of the braves crowded round, jostling each other for position. They ate the steer while the flesh was still twitching, the warm blood running down their chins. The stench in the heat was overpowering.

Abigail clutched her stomach, fearing she would be sick and draw their attention to her. Boyd and the other cowhands, she noticed, didn't even flinch. Instead they all sat their horses, barely moving a muscle while the gruesome feast continued. Only the swishing of the horses' tails and the pawing of the cattle could be heard alongside the grunts and greedy chewing.

Eventually sated, the leader turned again to Boyd, who then made another sign with his arms. A second steer was cut out from the herd. Abigail waited with her eyes closed to hear the report of another pistol shot, then knives slicing through the hide. Instead she heard the scrabble of the braves mounting their ponies. Forcing one eye open, she saw them depart with the steer in tow.

Weakness and aftershock set in. Forcing herself not to sway in the saddle, she watched as Boyd approached. She had been right all along, and he had foolishly ridden into a trap. And because of his obviously incorrect assumptions, she hadn't kept a proper watch, either. She waited regally for his heartfelt apology in not acknowledging the reality of her fears.

"See, I told you there was nothing to worry about," Boyd offered as he reined his horse in beside her.

The only retort she could manage was an incomprehensible croaking sound.

Randy cleared his throat and kicked his horse into a canter, leaving them alone.

"How can you say that?" she hissed in fury. The fool man had nearly gotten them killed with his casual attitude.

"Easy. You still got your hair attached to your head. No one's dead, and we're moving the herd."

She stilled the automatic reflex to touch her hair and reassure herself it was intact. "Not one of you was prepared to defend us!"

"Would you have pitted a dozen hands against more than forty braves?" he asked in a voice suddenly too casual, deceptively free of emotion.

"Yes! No . . . I don't know. But you all just sat there, waiting!"

"And how many Indians have you dealt with?"

She stuttered for a moment, then her eyes narrowed in remembered fury. "You're the one who told me not to worry about them!"

"Was I wrong?"

Sputtering, she nearly spit out the words. "Wrong? We're just lucky we're not all dead!"

His casual expression quickly turned to steel, and she flinched at the hardness in his eyes. "Luck has nothing to do with it. We're alive because I know how to deal with hungry braves. If we'd pulled our guns, we'd all be laying face-down in the dirt." His voice purposely slowed. "Except for you. They'd keep you alive a long time, enjoying you even as you prayed for death. With your snow-white skin and blond hair you'd have been a prize to be passed around the entire tribe, and then possibly traded to the next tribe for at least a pony or two."

The blood drained from her head at the graphic picture he painted. "Then why didn't you let me keep my gun?"

"Because I know how to deal with these Indians. When are you goin' to learn, Abigail? This is my land. I understand it. Puttin' on a pair of pants, learnin' to ride a horse, and even goin' along on one trail ride doesn't prepare you. It takes time and respect. Respect for the land, the men who ride it, and the people it really belongs to. Remember that, Abigail. This isn't a game where we can put the pieces back in the box if you drop them. You lose them, you lose your life."

Whirling his stallion around, Boyd headed toward the front of the herd, waving his hat to start them up again. The lead steers pawed anxiously to reach the next watering hole, and the cows fell in behind them. It took longer for Abigail to start again, even longer to realize the truth in Boyd's words.

15

Boyd rode restlessly at the head of the herd, tempted several times to turn back and seek out Abigail. Two days had passed since what she referred to as the Indian attack, but her attitude hadn't warmed a fraction. Maybe he had been too hard on her, but dammit, she had to learn that the stakes were high.

Since she refused to speak to him, it was difficult to get any message across to her. If she hadn't riled him and gotten so mad herself in the process, he could have enjoyed her initial reaction. It was as though every bogeyman in every dream she had ever had suddenly sprang to life in the form of forty hungry Indians. A reluctant grin creased Boyd's face even now at the thought. If Longknife and his friends hadn't been so hungry, they would never have provided quite the show they had.

And what a willing audience they had found in Abigail. It was clear from the terror on her face that she thought she would be next on the menu. If she hadn't given in to her anger, he guessed she might have leaped into his arms instead. He would have far preferred the latter action.

Even now, as he angled to get a better view of her, Boyd could see the defiant tilt to her head that signaled she was still mad. Despite recognizing the anger, his gaze moved hungrily over her.

Full, lush breasts strained against the linen fabric of her shirt. The breeches that now fit like a second skin encased her shapely legs like the finest calfskin gloves, revealing the curve of her hips, the trim span of her waist. In an instant he

remembered the hot, slick feel of her on his fingers when
they were at the lake a few days ago. His body tightened at
the memory, reminding him uncomfortably of the fulfillment they had been denied.

As he watched her, she removed her hat and shook her
heavy mane of hair back from her face, lifting it to reveal
the soft curve of her neck. He swallowed, his throat dry, as
he watched the play of sun on her golden tresses.

She turned suddenly and met his gaze. He could tell from
the sudden flush on her face that she could read his desire.
For a long moment her eyes held his, and he wished they
were closer so he could read if they spelled out an
answering need or continued rejection. Then she hastily
pulled on her hat, stuffing her hair up beneath it. Turning her
back on him, he was afforded a view of her less telling side.

He sighed as Randy rode up beside him. "Any sign of
water yet, Boyd?"

Boyd tore his gaze away from Abigail. "No. And it's
gettin' bad." He knew it was never good to have a dry run.
The cattle suffered, lost weight, and ultimately it could
mean a big cut in the profits.

"I'll go up ahead with you a few miles," Randy offered.
"The river must've changed course. Maybe between us we
can spot it."

Making up his mind, Boyd nodded. He needed some
distance between himself and Abigail. Maybe it was good
that she was so mad. Like a cold dash of water, it reminded
him that they had taken their friendship too far already. He
didn't want her to lose the Triple Cross because she got
blacklisted. Enough vicious gossip could ensure that fate.
Even though the people in the territory were basically good,
none of them would consider going against the code of the
land. Like righteous vigilantes, they would swoop down and
censure their own.

The fact was the ranch was too important to her and to
little Michael. She couldn't lose her child's legacy. More
important, he couldn't be the cause of that loss.

His mind churned as they rode for hours. The land sloped
upward, the gullies deeper, the terrain rougher. And al-

though the sky remained cloudless, Boyd almost imagined he smelled the ripe scent of rain.

"You been thinkin' about Johnson's offer?" Randy asked.

Boyd lifted his head in surprise. He didn't know that his job proposal had become public knowledge. It was the first manager's position he'd been offered since his reputation had been stained. While being foreman of the Triple Cross commanded respect, being manager meant total control of the ranch and its finances. With Johnson as an absentee owner, he'd have unlimited power. Even though he knew he had been innocent of the charges and there had been no proof of his guilt, it had been difficult to shed the effects of the gossip. "How'd you find out about that?"

Randy shrugged. "Lot of men are hankerin' for that job. It's a big spread. And to be manager—hell, that's the next step to ownin' your own ranch."

It was a definite step up from being foreman, and if he had a lick of sense he would have jumped at the opportunity. Having been part of a family that had owned a ranch, then having managed even bigger spreads, Boyd had never dreamed he would be reduced to being a cowhand. Only his job as foreman of the Triple Cross had restored some of that lost pride. He should have jumped at the chance to manage Johnson's ranch, but he had declined, knowing he couldn't leave Abigail. It was a fool choice, he realized, since he couldn't stay with her forever. But even if it was stolen time, it was time he wouldn't sacrifice.

"That's a pretty big jump from being manager to owning your own place," Boyd answered.

"In time you could be lookin' at havin' enough to make a go of it." Randy spoke with enthusiasm, a bright light engulfing his features.

"Sounds like something you want."

"Hell, who wouldn't? Do you really want to ride herd till you're so old your bones ache just with the thought of it?"

Boyd shook his head. His own dreams had always been wrapped up in recovering his father's ranch, restoring his family and the pride in their name. "Can't say as I do. How about you?"

Randy expelled a loud sigh. "Hell, I'm just dreamin'. But it keeps me from gettin' too thirsty."

"You had to mention water."

"We're bound to find the river soon," Randy answered, wiping his forehead against the sweat gathered there.

"Hell, I'm beginning to think the whole thing dried up."

But Randy strained forward in his saddle. "There, up past that gully." Bright sunlight glinted off a blessed patch of blue.

Spurring their horses on, they lost no time reaching the river. But after dismounting they bent to taste the water and immediately spit it out. An enormous deposit of alkali had fouled the water.

"Cows take a long drink of that, and we'll lose 'em," Randy said grimly.

Since he had voiced what they both knew, Boyd merely nodded in agreement. And there was no way around the river that wound for miles in each direction. No detouring to avoid the trap. Even now the animals marched closer.

"What're you goin' to do, Boyd?"

He made up his mind instantly, despite the danger he knew it presented. "Stampede 'em across."

"Hell, what if we can't keep 'em turned around? And what if after we cross, we don't find water for a while? They'll turn right back around and head for here."

"That's a chance we'll have to take," Boyd replied. He knew, too, that if cattle didn't reach water in a certain amount of time, they would turn back to the last watering hole. Conversely, if the herd stayed straight on course, and too many days had passed by the time they reached water again, they could stampede and kill themselves as they plowed into the water.

Resolutely he remounted and turned back toward the drive to tell the men of his plan. And for once Abigail was going to have to listen to him, or she could break her pretty neck.

The men were prepared, the herd was approaching the river, and Abigail was sulking. Boyd shot a final warning glance at her as they approached. She sniffed and turned away. He wondered if she thought this, too, was a trial run.

Knowing how hard it would be to prevent the herd, thirsty from the dry run, from stopping to drink while fording the river, Boyd had instructed the men well. Now he just hoped to hell his plan worked.

The men kept the cattle under tight rein as they reached the riverbank. Fortunately the water was low and fordable, but as always a river was ready to mete out its share of trouble. As treacherous as a spurned woman, a river crossing could prove unpredictable and greedy for misery. It was often difficult to get the cows to cross if the water was high. The cowboys weren't any more eager to cross than the animals, since many of them couldn't swim. Fortunately, however, this water wasn't too high and could be waded.

Boyd leaned forward in his saddle and waved his hat vigorously. At the prearranged signal, the men waved and rattled their ponchos and slickers. Spooked, the leaders of the herd took off on a splashing run right through the river and out on the other side. More cows fell in behind them, thrashing their way through the water.

As Boyd had predicted, once across, the cattle tried to double back. Dust rose in choking clouds as cowhands whistled, threw stinging ropes, and kneed their horses in front of the belligerent cattle.

As the herd continued pouring across the river, the men were able to lead the thirsty beasts away from the fouled water and up to high ground, far from the luring smell of water. Boyd paused long enough to see that Abigail remained seated at Henry's side in the chuck wagon, grateful for once to see that she had the sense to do as he had asked.

When the last of the cattle were contained on the other side of the river, the remuda, bed wagon, and chuck wagon started to cross. In midcrossing, after the bed wagon driven by Antonio had made it to shore, with the horses moving along well, Boyd could see that Abigail and Henry were apparently arguing.

Trying to disregard a sudden feeling of foreboding, Boyd watched in amazement as Henry reined in the horses and stopped the wagon. Abigail was just starting to fill the extra water barrel when the entire wagon promptly sank to its axles in quicksand.

Unable to squelch the string of curses that started as soon as he realized what Abigail had talked Henry into doing, Boyd kicked his horse and headed back to the riverbank. He could almost feel sorry for Henry, who looked as if he knew that Boyd wanted to take off at least one layer of his hide.

"What the hell did you think you were doin'?" Boyd yelled to them both, directing the brunt of his anger at the responsible party.

"Don't just stand there. Get us out!" Abigail demanded, looking for all she was worth like a royal monarch whose throne had just collapsed.

As Boyd watched, the draft oxen, straining and twisting, ripped off the wagon tongue. "Now, I'd say that presents a problem, *ma'am*." He didn't bother to hide his disgust.

Deflated, Abigail sat back down on the wagon seat.

Boyd stayed on horseback, wading into the river. "You couldn't drink the water. What the hell did you want it for?"

"Washing," she replied stubbornly.

"Hell's bells!" But then he turned to the cook. "Henry, you'd better get on to the other side. We'll have to rig up a new part for the wagon."

"What about me?" Abigail asked.

"Don't worry. You'll get down," Boyd promised grimly. Riding up next to the wagon, he reached out his arms and picked her up, setting her promptly into the low water of the river. Since the water only came up to her thighs, she was in no danger, but she looked suddenly like a cat thrown into bathwater. Every claw drawn, she was ready for battle.

"How dare you?" she asked, her voice low, her fury clear.

"Funny thing for you to be askin' now that you've ruined the tongue of the wagon. Didn't happen to pack a spare in your saddlebags, did you?"

"How as I supposed to know that it would sink?"

"Because maybe if you'd listened to Henry when he told you that he couldn't stop, you'd have figured out there was a reason for what he was sayin'."

"How do you know what Henry said?" Immediately she snapped her lips shut, obviously realizing what she had revealed.

"'Cause he knows better. And I know you."

"You don't have to be such an infernal, pious . . ." she began.

He enjoyed the look of shock in her eyes as Dolly came up behind her and nudged her. It was a gentle push, but enough to send Abigail to her knees in the water. Dunked and properly soaked, it was hard to tell whether she resembled a spitting cat or a wet, ruffled hen.

Dripping, bedraggled, she jammed her waterlogged hat back on her head before she marched, somewhat droopily, toward shore. What she lacked in dignity, she made up for in defiance. Reaching land, her boots squished as she walked toward the line of trees nearby.

She seemed to be marching in an almost lopsided manner as she tried to maintain her dignity despite the sodden clothes that weighed her down, the boots that lurched from the water they still held.

Boyd could almost laugh at the sight if their chuck wagon wasn't still stuck in the river. Henry unhitched the oxen and led them to shore. Boyd nearly swore, knowing he would have to spare a detachment of hands from the already overtaxed men who were trying to keep the cattle from doubling back to the water. Glancing around, he spied a grove of cottonwood and knew they could fashion a pole that would work as a substitute tongue for the wagon.

But it meant splitting the men at a crucial time. If he let too many of them work on the wagon, the others might not be able to contain the herd. Yet, if they stayed too long where the herd was bedded for the night, the cattle could break loose and return to the water.

Boyd directed John Sims to help Henry and Antonio chop the cottonwood and carve out the pole. Fortunately Billy Kendall had been transferred to the bed wagon a few days earlier as his wound healed, and he rested there on the other side of the shore. Boyd hated to think of subjecting Billy to fording a river with his painful leg.

As he approached Abigail, Boyd thought of a million things he wanted to say and knew he wouldn't utter any of them. For all her foolheaded antics, she did own the blessed herd. Instead he watched as she squeezed out her hat and then emptied the water from her boots.

"Henry and Antonio are busy chopping down a tree so they can fix the wagon. That means I don't have a cook or a cook's helper. Which leaves you to fix supper."

"Me?" she croaked.

"You know your way around a kitchen," he answered evenly, remembering the pleasant sun-filled mornings he had spent in her home the past year, sharing coffee and the sweets she often baked. She had been amiable, good-natured, willing to listen to his suggestions, in fact had agreed to them all. Now she was an intractable minx. He sometimes wondered if he had dreamed that entire pleasant time. Looking at the disheveled mess she made as she sat on the ground, he was convinced of it.

"But the food and pans are out there in the wagon," she protested.

"I'll get Antonio to carry in the chuck box and the ovens, but it'll be up to you to build the fire and cook supper. I haven't got any men to spare." He captured her sulky glare and held it. "Either we lose the herd or we lose the wagon. And if we lose that wagon, we're in big trouble, Abigail. Now, do you think you're up to it?"

Determination flared in her sky-colored eyes. "Maybe I shouldn't have told Henry to stop the wagon, but I'll certainly do my part to rectify the mistake."

Boyd wanted to reach out and pull her close, capture that blaze of anger that he knew could turn as easily to passion, but instead made his voice gruff. "See that you do."

He mounted his horse and started to spur the animal forward when he felt a hard thud in the middle of his back. Turning the horse around, he stared first at the ground and then at Abigail. Her wet boot lay next to his horse, covered in a rising cloud of dust where she had apparently thrown it.

"Sorry," she said with a deceptive smile. He started to

shrug it off, chalking it up to her anger, when she added sweetly, "I meant to hit you in the head."

The smoke-blackened ovens were heavy, Abigail discovered, as she tried to shift them into position. Her arms ached from chopping wood for a fire, then getting the blasted thing started. Kindling had been difficult to scrounge up, and the fire had ignited in fits and starts, much like an old maid at a stag dance. She had finally added some prairie coal and ignited it with bacon rind.

Grinding enough coffee for more than a dozen men was a chore as well, but she knew how the men needed their coffee, and would want it long before the supper was completed. If it ever was, that is. Frying the bacon hadn't been terribly difficult. Time-consuming, but not difficult.

The biscuits, however, were another story. Unlike at home, these were not coming out as she expected them to. She was used to whipping up biscuits that were feather light and melted in your mouth. Dropping one of the heavy biscuits on the ground, she heard its distinctive thud, knowing the only thing that would melt it would be a blacksmith's forge. Deciding that corn bread might be the answer, she started the laborious chore of mixing enough cornmeal and flour to fill a dozen hungry men.

An hour later she could hear the men still chopping on the cottonwood tree. Staring down at the dinner she had cooked, Abigail had to admit it looked less than appetizing. The corn bread was more brown than yellow, misshapen, and nearly flat. Proud of her skill as a cook, she was dismayed by the mess she had produced. She doubted the men would be pleased, either.

Apparently there was a knack to baking in these Dutch ovens, a skill she didn't possess. Feeling her pride suffer yet another blow, she was convinced that if they had an embroidery contest, at this point she would manage to lose that as well.

Even though she hadn't liked Boyd's high-handed method of ordering her to cook dinner, she had planned to outdo Henry and present a dinner that had the men begging for more. As she stared at the lumpy, congealed mess of bacon, the hard, tasteless biscuits, and even flatter cornbread, she somehow doubted that would come to pass.

Ever since she had thrown Boyd's expertise about the Indians in his face, things hadn't been going well. She should have listened to Henry, and then she wouldn't be laboring over the hot ovens now. And, damnably, she realized that Boyd had been right about the Indians as well, but somehow she had lost much of her amiability on the trip.

It was as though after a lifetime of being agreeable, the person who always tried to set things right for others, smoothing over situations and hurt feelings, she had balked. Something had snapped inside—the person always responsible for peacemaking no longer wanted to be the negotiator.

At least the coffee should be good, she thought as she poured a cup to taste the brew. After it cooled a bit, she swallowed and nearly spit it back out again. Henry's coffee was bad, but hers was even worse. Cooking without a proper stove and oven was far more difficult than she had ever imagined, and it wasn't a skill that came without practice. Discouraged, she watched as the first line of riders approached. Seeing Boyd close behind them, she was tempted to turn tail and run, not claiming credit for the disaster. But pride asserted itself, and she plastered on a semblance of a smile as the men dismounted and quickly grabbed plates and cups.

She watched nervously as they took their first tastes, expecting a chorus of outrage. But, although she saw more than one grimace, a few screwed-up expressions, and even a flinch or two, no one verbalized their complaints.

The very fact that no one said anything almost made her cry. She didn't deserve their kindness. If not for her foolish stubbornness, they would be eating a meal prepared by an experienced trail cook. A lump stuck in her throat as she realized the quiet generosity of these loyal cowboys.

As Boyd loaded his own plate and stopped to speak to her, she raised eyes swimming in tears. She lifted a hand to dash them away, but Boyd's fingers were there first, gently brushing the moisture from her cheeks. Certain that if they weren't surrounded by the men he would have cradled her close in comfort, she was moved even further.

She had made Boyd's life a living hell since the trip started, and if she was completely honest, she would admit that he had bent over backward to accommodate her, to relieve the anxieties he could have easily taunted her with. He had provided privacy when she needed it, comfort without being asked. Withholding any or all of those things could have changed her mind about hiring a manager. It had occurred to her during the past weeks that Boyd might have misinterpreted her insistence to be the one in control. Perhaps he thought she didn't trust him enough to be the manager.

As he placed his plate down, he walked around the campfire, past the ovens. Suddenly it was very important to prove that she did trust him. But he seemed to have something different in mind as he pulled her away, toward the line of junipers near the edge of where they had made camp.

"Are you all right?" he asked, not releasing her hands, his fingers absently massaging hers.

"Sure. Dinner was more difficult to prepare than I thought."

"It's different than a kitchen with a woodstove and oven," he admitted, his concerned gaze still not leaving her face. "Is this too much for you?"

She pulled her hands away, facing the woods, while struggling to push back the hair that had fallen into her face. "I wish you wouldn't persist in thinking I'm totally inept," she said, her newfound resolutions falling away. But she immediately regretted the rush of words as she saw his face suddenly close, his lips compressed in a tight line.

"Sorry to have troubled you." His voice was equally stiff.

He started to turn away when she reached a hand out to stop him. "I'm sorry, Boyd. I'm hot, I'm tired, and the truth is, I am inept. I haven't done one thing right since we came on this drive."

"No need to be that hard on yourself," he replied. His eyes softened. "There's not a man here who didn't learn the hard way. 'Course, most of them signed on as green hands, ridin' drag, or being the biscuit shooter's helper."

"Instead of planning to run the whole show?" she asked wryly.

"Something like that."

A noise vibrated from the camp and she could see men running to leap on their horses.

"Hell!" Boyd muttered, releasing her hands.

"What is it?" she asked, panicked by the look on his face.

"Cattle are turnin' back. Get what you can packed in the chuck box and take the wagon up on high ground. Move fast or leave the stuff behind. It's not worth gettin' killed over." Indecision flashed over his face, but then he pulled her close, kissing her hard. "I mean it this time, Abigail. Don't go wanderin' into the way."

He didn't wait for her answer as he ran toward his horse. She watched him, worry and something else crowding her emotions as she rubbed her fingers across her lips, feeling his imprint still. Her throat crowded with unnamed feelings as she prayed he would be safe.

The night sky was crowded with stars, deep and brilliant as only the rugged land would allow. The quarter moon hid behind the cover of high clouds, and a gentle breeze caressed the aspen leaves, sending them into passionless trembling.

Abigail looked down on the herd from her vantage point on top of a hill, far from the water. Carrying Boyd's suggestion a step farther, after quickly repacking the bed wagon and dousing the fire she had driven away from the water and toward high ground. While Boyd and the cowhands worked to get the herd under control, Henry and his helpers had carved a new tongue for the wagon and hoped to pull the chuck wagon out of the river in the morning.

But now Abigail sat in the quiet of the beautiful night and watched. The men, exhausted by running the obstinate cattle all day, had eaten briefly and then resumed their positions. Two late riders wouldn't be nearly enough tonight as the breeze carried the sweet aroma of the water to the thirsty cattle. If the night wasn't so full of hazards, she knew that Boyd would have driven the herd farther ahead to escape the luring smells. But he couldn't take the chance of losing cattle, horses, or men.

Even though the herd was officially bedded, she could hear the plaintive bawling of the cows. Although the animals normally only rose as the watch changed, the restless beasts had gotten to their feet several times so far. She heard the strains of men singing to calm them down. Recognizing the tune to "Dinah Had a Wooden Leg" and the "Unfortunate Pup," she smiled, hoping the music would work. Abigail knew that Boyd feared another stampede. And unfortunately nighttime was the prime time for stampedes.

But it seemed difficult to reconcile that possibility with the calm, enchanting evening. When she saw a rider approach, Abigail recognized the tall silhouette even in the darkness. Although he had to be weary, Boyd moved with purpose as he strode toward her. She headed toward the pots of still warm food, but he waved her away.

"Just coffee, Abigail."

She poured him a cup, and he pulled his hat off, wiping his brow with a muscular forearm. The distinctly male action was one she might have frowned upon in the past, as it didn't portray the best of manners. Somehow the gesture seemed clean and forthright when Boyd did it.

"Is the herd settling in?" she asked, offering him the cup.

"Pretty much," he replied, accepting the coffee, then taking a long drink without allowing the liquid to cool. She grimaced at the action, guessing he must be bone-tired to drink the scalding liquid without even flinching. Even as she completed the thought, he sank to the ground at a nearby tree, resting his back against the bark. "Want to sit with me for a few minutes?"

She complied, glad to rest herself. Her shoulders twisted, the muscles sore from hefting the heavy ovens, not twice, but four times that day, after moving the wagon up the hill. A grimace crossed her face as the pain rocketed unexpectedly.

"Move over in front of me," he ordered.

"Why?"

"Don't question everything, woman." His voice was a counterfeit grumble, and she smiled suddenly, glad he had taken a few moments to be with her.

Scooting in front of him, she nearly gasped aloud as he began to massage her aching shoulder muscles. It felt so good, she could have purred. As it was, she leaned back, sinking her hands down on his outstretched legs. They both knew they were taking a dangerous chance. Anyone could happen along and discover them. But care was abandoned, as it had been when Boyd had kissed her that afternoon.

Smelling the fresh scent of her river-cleansed hair, he forgot his exhaustion. Every tired muscle relaxed as she trailed her hands on his legs.

"How's that?" he asked, his hands moving up to massage her neck and then caressing her back.

"Wonderful," she replied in a husky voice.

"Your muscles have had quite a workout today."

She twisted around suddenly. "I'm sorry, Boyd. I didn't know the wagon would sink. It's like this entire trail drive. I never dreamed that I'd cause so much trouble. If I'd known, I'd have listened to you and stayed home!"

"Now you tell me," he answered with a mock growl, pulling her more securely to him.

She resisted for a second, then sank back against him. "I'm getting far too used to this," she warned.

Again the scent of her river-washed hair rose to assail his nostrils. As always, she was a breath of fresh air, surprising, elusive, tantalizing. And equally dangerous.

But they both put caution aside as he continued his gentle assault on her body. If she didn't respond, or if she held back, he could exercise more control. She should be the one pointing out the differences between them, telling him that any future for them was impossible. It was a feeble excuse, but the only one he could cling to in his weaker moments.

Moments like now. The memory of their time by the lake seemed to assail them both. Like a blind man, he could see her naked body simply by touch. Closing his eyes, he could let her scent be his guide. And like a starving man, he hungered for the love he knew she could bestow. His wounded heart told him to ignore that hunger, deny that thirst. Love required trust, and trust brought only hurt.

Her small hands touched him gently, and he strove to remember that he shouldn't trust her, either. She had interests to protect. Interests that couldn't include him.

But then her eyes turned toward him, half invitation, half unquestioning trust. He felt the rigid armor surrounding his fragile heart slip yet another notch.

Neither noticed the shadow that slipped unobtrusively through the trees, the eyes that watched, noted, and then disappeared, leaving nothing but the trembling leaves of the aspen in its wake.

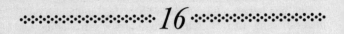

16

Miranda did something she said she never would. She sought out Cameron O'Donnell. Busy at work, his head bent over the desk, he looked up in surprise as she entered the study. The room was his domain, one she didn't disturb. But then, normally she didn't have a problem this severe.

"Miranda? This is a surprise."

She twisted her hands nervously, wishing for the bravado she usually possessed, but it wasn't forthcoming. "There's trouble," she blurted out.

He stood up instantly, walking from behind the desk. He stopped only inches away from her, his dark eyes glittering dangerously. "What kind of trouble?"

Nervously she paced a few steps away from him, her shoes soft against the rich Aubusson rug. "I went to town," she began and then stopped, wondering how to form the words.

"Did someone accost you?" he asked, the ominous tone sending shivers up her spine.

She shook her head. "Nothing like that."

He closed the space between them and gripped her arms. Stunned by the contact, she lifted surprised eyes to meet his. If her mind wasn't consumed with worry, she could have forgotten her problems and concentrated on the sensations of his touch. But the worry won out.

"One of our hands, Daniel Caruthers, just got back in town. He was on the trail drive with Miz Fairchild, and she up and fired him."

"So?"

"So he's telling everybody she fired him 'cause he knew too much."

The perplexed look on Cameron's face was genuine. "About what?"

She returned to twisting her hands in the material of her apron. "He says Miz Fairchild and Boyd are carrying on something fierce." Her voice warbled in combined fury and loyalty as she met his gaze intensely. "I don't believe it!"

"What makes you think anyone else will, then?"

"'Cause they already do. Caruthers signed on at the Johnson place, but tongues are wagging all over town."

"Only till something more interesting comes along," he soothed, not removing his hands from her arms, instead caressing them in a comforting motion.

But Miranda couldn't keep the grimness from her voice. "I don't think so. Gossip is spreading like wildfire. People know she's a widow—a young one."

"An eligible one who owns a valuable ranch," Cameron observed.

"She's had callers already," Miranda confided. "Joshua Hodges came a-callin' before she left. Then half a dozen others since then who hadn't heard she went on the trail drive."

"She's a lovely young widow. Unfortunately her situation is one that's ripe for gossip."

"Bunch of nosy busybodies." Miranda sniffed. But then she turned toward the window, unable to keep her voice from quivering. "They'll cause trouble."

"But we can't act any differently. To do so would court suspicion. If anyone has the nerve to approach you on the subject, act as though it's laughable. Respond that Caruthers was always trouble and the Triple Cross is well rid of him. Offer your pity to Johnson, who's now saddled with him."

A light dawned in Miranda's troubled eyes as she lifted them to meet his. "Do you think that'll really work?"

He shrugged. "The best defense is to do nothing at all. Acknowledging a problem is close to admitting it's true."

"I'm glad you're here," she blurted out suddenly, realizing it was true.

"It's turned out to be a job with many duties," he responded, trying to keep his tone light.

Averting her eyes, she decided it was time to confess the truth. "I never should have told you that you made Miz Fairchild uncomfortable. Truth is, you made *me* feel that way. She was glad you came here and straightened things out."

"And why is it I made you uncomfortable, Miranda?" His voice lowered, compelling her to lift her head.

Her heart constricted suddenly, its runaway beat threatening to burst from her chest. Her feelings were simple and yet at the same time so complex. Which of her shortcomings and secrets should she admit to? That she was a loveless spinster who now found herself breathless when she was near him? She considered telling him how he affected her, creeping into her dreams, possessing her thoughts. But as his gaze continued to pierce her, she knew the cost of that confession. Instead she opted for a truth that while painful didn't lay her entire soul bare.

"You know how I've told you that I didn't have time to work on the budgets you draw up?"

Obviously disconcerted, he nodded.

"It's not the time." She paused, willing the heaviness in her chest to subside. "I was ashamed to tell you, but that's not why I didn't work on them."

"Why, then?"

She pulled her gaze away from the endless vista she could see from the window and forced herself to meet his eyes, willing her pride to carry her through. "Because I can't read."

The words rang between them, and she felt the sudden shame the admission had always cost her. The oldest in the family, her parents had never been able to spare her to attend school. Instead she had cared for her younger siblings until the time had passed for lessons.

"Why didn't you just tell me?" he asked gently.

Two spots of color dotted her cheeks. "I was ashamed."

"There's no need to be. There are far more important abilities."

She laughed bitterly. "How can you say that? Your life's full of books and learnin'."

"An empty life it is," he admitted, the quiet confession obviously troubling him.

She gestured toward the walls lined with fine leather-bound books. "When you're hankerin' for something, you can read any of these books."

"Books make fine companions," he acknowledged. "But on a cold, lonely night a man desires more than a book to keep him company." His hand reached out to touch the curve of her cheek. "He wants warmth and beauty."

Breathless, she stared at him. Convinced that the beating of her heart must certainly be audible, she wondered that it didn't deafen them both. When his other hand reached to cradle the back of her neck and pull her close, she didn't even consider resisting. Swallowing a sob of pent-up desire, she went willingly into his embrace. The first pressure of his lips against hers was like an awakening she had dreamed of, longed for, yet didn't know existed.

When his tongue slid around the outer edges of her lips, seeking entrance, she felt an unexpected thrill that washed through her body with an alarming speed. His hands moved down the soft curves of her hips, making her open her mouth to gasp. Stealing the opportunity, he pressed his tongue inside. As he explored, tantalized, she couldn't begin to acknowledge the spectrum of feelings he ignited.

Holding her body close, he pressed intimately against her. His hard chest met her breasts, his thighs touched hers. She knew she should pull back before they crossed all boundaries of propriety, but she had a greater desire to discover the sensations he caused than a desire to protect her moral standards.

When his fingers reached to unpin her hair, she heard a matching gasp from him as the full, unbound length of auburn hair fell into his outstretched hands. He plied the silken strands away from her face before returning his attention to her mouth. As she tried to recover from that assault, he boldly cupped one breast, and she felt her immediate response as the nipple hardened.

Were she a woman who swooned, this would have been the moment. Instead she closed her eyes and savored the wash of excitement that moved through her like a runaway train. When she felt him finally pull away, disappointment pierced her, a sudden aching, overwhelming loss.

But when she could finally meet his eyes, she saw that they had darkened with the seeds of passion. Lowering her gaze, she saw that his ragged breathing matched her own rapid, tortured gasps. It occurred to her in a glorious and blinding revelation that Cameron O'Donnell was as affected as she. For the first time in her life, her feminine awareness asserted itself. And she knew what joy must surely be.

"So, Billy, are you ready to try out the crutch that Henry carved for you?" Abigail asked as she held the piece of wood up for his inspection. She had wrapped the top of the crutch with a thick pad of material so that his underarm wouldn't blister.

He eyed the crude crutch with a mixture of optimism and healthy doubt. "I sure want to get around again."

"This is the first step," she answered, glad that she had thought to ask Henry to cut enough extra wood for the crutch while they were making the new tongue for the chuck wagon.

"Is it true we're almost to town?" he asked hopefully.

"It's still a few days away."

"That's close," he responded with youthful enthusiasm, already practicing with his new crutch. His leg was mending well. Only healthy flesh surrounded the wound, no putrid signs of infection. He would limp for a good long while, but he would be walking.

"When we get to town, I want the doctor to check the wound thoroughly."

"No doctor could have done a finer job, ma'am."

She rose to leave when he stopped her.

"Miz Fairchild?"

"Yes, Billy?"

"Thanks again for saving my leg. If ever you need anything, I'll be there."

Her face softened at the fervent appreciation in the young man's eyes. "That's good to know, Billy. I might need to call on you sometime."

Feeling immeasurably uplifted, she left the wagon. Since her debacle with sinking the wagon, she had been hard put to find a valid reason for her presence on the trail drive, or for that matter, the ranch itself. But Billy's words gave her hope. She could only wish that young Michael would grow to be such a fine man.

As the days had turned to weeks, she had missed her child fiercely. Even though she knew he was in Miranda's capable hands, Abigail worried about him constantly. But, knowing her housekeeper loved the child as well, Abigail took comfort in the excellent care she was sure Michael was receiving.

She could picture her son's chubby legs pumping as he earnestly pursued his newest adventure, his arms flailing for her attention, his bright, toothless grin. She had never been away from him before and had never dreamed it would be so difficult.

Even though she'd resolutely pushed away thoughts of leaving her child, he had never been far from her mind. Along with her worry of being able to cope on the trail had been the reminder that little Michael's future was the reason for her insistence to come along. Survival had dominated her thoughts, but it was in the quiet times that she missed the baby most.

Glancing up the trail, she admitted to herself that she hadn't counted on other difficulties as well. Physical hardships aside, she knew the lasting trouble would be in her altered relationship with Boyd.

And, if she were to be totally honest, she would acknowledge a certain wicked freedom her new lifestyle afforded her. The abandon and wildness was something no one had brought out in her other than Boyd. She wondered if she should feel guilt or remorse over the fact. But it felt too good to be sorry for. And she also knew it would be equally difficult to return to her old ways.

Her smile faded as she considered how her relationship

with Boyd would have to change when they returned to the ranch. Even though she didn't want to admit it, her feelings for him had somehow passed simple desire. While Abigail had entertained wild notions that they could defy the code of the land, she knew she couldn't endanger her son's legacy. She felt enough guilt at being able to thaw her frozen heart and allow another man entry. She couldn't betray her husband's memory by losing the ranch.

Yet even as she lectured herself soundly, her gaze traveled the length of the trail drive, hungrily seeking out Boyd's outline as he rode in front of the point. She had only to close her eyes to picture his face, weathered from the sun, the laugh lines that fanned out next to his eyes, the long, measuring looks from eyes that were impossibly blue.

But when she stopped daydreaming, there was no smile on her face. She realized suddenly that too much of her time was spent thinking about Boyd, dwelling on what he said, or how his touch made her feel.

It was time to put a halt to those feelings. A deep and sudden ache filled her at the thought. A looming emptiness eroded the good intentions and made her want to run to Boyd's arms for solace. But that was the one place she couldn't turn to. Ever again.

Days passed, and water was still difficult to find. Although the herd hadn't stampeded again, the search was always on, and rain had been scarce. Boyd felt a familiar twinge in his thigh, and he scanned the sky. Puffy, innocent-looking clouds drifted in the pale blue, almost milky-white sky. But Boyd knew how deceptive the sky could be— promising sunshine one moment, delivering punishing hailstones the next.

Call it old cowhand intuition, but he sensed the weather would change. And he believed it would bring trouble. Having already encountered one sudden flood this trip, his expression tightened. Grimly he considered the impact of another bad storm on the already spooked cattle and knew he would be glad to get this herd to the railhead.

His eyes fastened on Randy Kreiger, who rode along the

other side. The man was unusually quiet. One of the things
he had always admired about his assistant was his steady
good humor. But it was not apparent today.

"Something on your mind, Randy?"

"You ever think about the land? Owning some, I mean.'

Boyd paused. It was a subject never far from his mind or
heart. "Guess every old cowhand does."

"But your family owned a ranch once."

A familiar shaft of pain hit him. Despite shrugging off the
importance of that time, the agony of losing both family and
future had never left him. "That they did."

"Do you miss it?"

Boyd's eyes clouded over. "Yep."

"You ever think about gettin' another ranch?"

Gut tightening, Boyd nodded. "It's not that easy, though.'

"On what we make, you mean?"

"Something like that. It's hard to save enough to amount
to a hill of beans."

"Try it on less than a third of your salary." Randy's words
were edged with bitterness.

Boyd looked at him with concern. "You got your eye on
someplace special?"

"Nah. Just dreamin'. No way I'll ever have a nest egg that
big."

"You could sign on as a drover, make a lot more money
than you are now. Or see if Johnson still needs a manager."

"You trying to get rid of me?"

"Why would I do that? You're the best assistant I could
ask for, but if you're hankerin' for a ranch—"

"I might as well be hankerin' for the moon."

"You could sign on to one of the spreads that'll give you
a percentage of the cattle for your pay."

"And graze them where?" Randy shook his head. "I have
to eat my own words, Boyd. That won't work. Wish I knew
some lonely widow who'd take a shine to me."

Boyd eyed him sharply. "What do you mean?"

"Oh, some lady with a tiny spread nobody else wants
Just enough to get me started."

Boyd's expression cleared. "Think that's likely?"

"Hell, no. Don't pay me no never mind, Boyd. Must be that chili Henry made last night that's got me dreamin'. Indigestion does strange things to a body." Randy laughed, trying to sound carefree, but Boyd recognized the disappointment and frustration behind the sound.

They were the same feelings he had. If life had treated him differently, he might have a chance with Abigail. He knew better than to brood over things he couldn't change, but there were moments . . . times when he knew, if given the chance, that he could make a ranch like the Triple Cross grow and prosper beyond Abigail's wildest dreams. He could give little Michael a future beyond compare. But then he glanced at his friend, saw the discouragement on Randy's face, and knew he wasn't in a position to offer anything to anyone. That was a bitter pill, but one he needed to acknowledge.

Even as the thoughts took form, so did the storm he had predicted. The sky opened up with a cannonade of hailstones as big as quail's eggs. The sheet of flying fury quickly pelted birds and rabbits to death while the cattle bawled their disapproval, milling in circles as they grew more restless.

Even though the hailstones were raising welts on the men, they kept their positions, trying to ensure that the herd didn't stampede. Boyd searched quickly for Abigail and saw that she was nearly drowning beneath the assault. He galloped quickly toward her.

"Get off your horse and pull your saddle over your head!" he yelled over the storm.

"What about you?"

"Just do it, Abigail! It's going to get worse."

As he spoke, an enormous flash of lightning hit the side of the hill, gouging out a huge hole. Another bolt flashed almost immediately. In rapid succession the lightning forked, followed by chain lightning. Then the peculiar blue lightning that was so rare and unusual that it scarcely seemed real suddenly lit the air. It rapidly developed into ball lightning, which rolled along the ground, then settled down like a fog.

Boyd sucked in his breath, aware that the air smelled of burning sulphur from the huge lightning display. He could see that the acrid substance had settled on the horns of the cattle, the ears of the horses, and the brims of the men's hats.

The storm was like a live, tangible force, growing and leaping out of control as a driving rain added to the other elements. They would be lucky if they weren't all killed. He tore his gaze from Abigail, who, for once, had obeyed promptly. He had to keep the herd under control. They might not survive another stampede.

Signaling to Randy to go with him, he galloped to the head of the herd, turning the lead steers back so that the herd took the shape of a rotating wheel. Muscles straining, ignoring the hail that continued to pelt them, the men gradually slowed the cattle. Even as the thunder rolled over the land like the strident voice of a vengeful God, the cattle drew to a shuddering standstill. Once stopped, it was as though all the men took a collective breath and held it, hoping against hope that the herd wouldn't stampede.

They didn't.

But the storm caused the herd to drift off the trail and scatter. Ignoring the painful welter of daggerlike rain and continued hail, the whole crew rode in front of the drift to press the animals back in line.

Bruised and battered, men and cattle alike limped into position. Boyd stared at this near disaster while a grim thought struck him. Perhaps this drive was as cursed as he was.

17

The river was high. Water from the storm filled the raging banks. Underlaid with quicksand, the streamside trees bore tangles of driftwood in their tall branches, marking the high water of past floods. A rude scattering of graves nearby attested to those who had foolishly tried to cross during similar circumstances.

Abigail gulped as she saw this evidence. Her foolish mistake in getting the chuck wagon stuck in the quicksand of the river now seemed like a minor prank in comparison. She watched the torrents of angry, rushing water and wished Boyd could find a way around the river. But he had already told her that they had no choice. That the river stretched for miles in either direction. If they didn't go forward, they couldn't reach the railhead.

The first cattle started across. Hope beat in her breast as she saw them move smoothly across. But then that hope fluttered and died. Halfway across, once in deep water, they began to panic and started to mill, swimming in circles, turning into a turbulent confusion of horns, heads and bodies pushed under the surface.

"They're going to drown!" Randy yelled at the point riders, jumping off his own horse.

To Abigail's horror, the men started stripping down to their longjohns to jump in and aid the crossing. A movement from the bank caught her eyes as Boyd, stripped down, was the first to reach the bank. He plunged into the water.

"Hell, Boyd. Don't get underneath 'em!" Randy yelled,

leaving the obvious unspoken. If he did, Boyd would be trampled to death.

Of course Boyd had to be the leader, Abigail fumed, holding her breath as she watched him successfully navigate through the bawling mess of cattle. They were so jammed together that he pulled himself up and started walking across their broad backs as though the animals were a raft. She saw him grab the horns of one of the large steers she recognized as a leader.

Then, to her amazement, Boyd mounted the huge beast. Muscles strained, rippling over his broad shoulders, corded back, and sculptured arms, as he held on as the steer pulled for shore. The herd followed, unblocking the jam they had created. Despite the fear still lodged in her throat, Abigail recognized this for what it was—a magnificent sight. Man conquering beast, every raw element exposed.

The warmth that suddenly curled in her belly wasn't simply desire for a powerful and handsome man, she realized. It was pride. Although everything between them had been forced to remain hidden, she suddenly wanted to shout to the skies. This strong, intelligent, magnificent man belonged to her.

She smiled as she saw Boyd jump from the steer once they were on the other side. Waving wildly, she made a cheering sign toward him. At first he looked surprised, then a grin split his features, and her heart melted. His eyes held hers, then he turned to the task at hand, but she saw the appreciation that shone there.

What would she ever do once they returned to the ranch and they could no longer be together? What if he decided to leave rather than compromise her position? Her life would be empty without him. The realization ricocheted through her like a terrible bolt of lightning, making the previous day's storm pale in comparison. Her feelings were not simply a reawakening of passion.

Boyd meant far more to her than that. He had stolen the place in her heart that she had planned to keep empty until she died. After the sweet, gentle love she had shared with Michael, she had never expected to discover a new and different sort of love. One that made her soar and reach for the stars as Boyd did.

Glancing at her surroundings, she realized that she couldn't be here in this time, or this place, with anyone else. Michael would have patted her on the head and told her gently that she couldn't conquer the impossible. Boyd had told her bluntly what to expect, and had taught her what she needed to know to survive. Though she had exasperated him beyond belief, he had never told her it was impossible.

Instead they had journeyed together through this adventure, as they had through young Michael's birth. While she would never resent the protective cloak that her late husband had always drawn around her, she knew she could never be that same innocent person again. Instead, that same cloak would suffocate her today.

It occurred to Abigail that she now knew Boyd far better than any other living human being. They had shared and triumphed over more than she would have dreamed possible. The bond between them had started when she offered him trust. It had cemented when he had delivered her baby. The past year had reinforced that bond.

A sudden memory surfaced of the mornings they had shared her son during leisurely breakfasts. They had been more than simple repasts. Each meal, treated like a normal family moment, had been the road to her healing process. With his straightforward manner, Boyd had helped her put the past behind her. Those first weeks had been painful, but between Boyd and her son, she hadn't been allowed time to wallow in self-pity. Instead Boyd had always made her concentrate on the future of the ranch, and ultimately her own future.

Dumbstruck, she sat on her horse and watched the cattle cross. She had never before realized how carefully he had navigated the process of her recovery. Feeling like a sleepwalker awakening from a deep and perilous sleep, she opened her eyes for the first time. She didn't know whether to be delighted or terrified.

Searching deep into her soul, she acknowledged that her life had never required a great deal of sacrifice. Pampered as a girl, then married to an affluent man, she had never known anything but happiness until Michael's untimely death. But a relationship with Boyd would require sacrifice. Her breath stilled as she wondered if she was prepared to make all kinds of adjustments. Unbidden, the thought of her child intruded. Did she have any right to make a choice that affected his future so sorely, no matter how the outcome determined her own happiness?

"Miz Fairchild?"

Startled, she turned and stared into John Sims's eyes. As always, a bit of unease gripped her when she caught him watching her.

"Yes?" Her voice was sharper than she intended, and purposely she gentled it. "Did you need something?"

"It's about time for you to be crossin', ma'am."

Her unease multiplied. Somehow she didn't want to trust her fate in crossing to this man. "Will Boyd be coming back to this side of the river?"

John shrugged nervously, his eyes darting away, not quite meeting hers. "I can help you cross."

Gut instinct gripped her. "I believe I'll wait."

Randy Kreiger rode up. "Something wrong?"

John blanched. "No, sir. I was just tellin' Miz Fairchild to get ready to cross."

"He's right. You need to be in the next group."

Swallowing, she nodded her head, then looked pointedly at John Sims.

"I'll ride across with you, ma'am," Randy offered. "John needs to get back to the herd."

"Well, if that's what you think is best." She offered John a smile to show her appreciation, then turned her attention to Randy.

Looking as though he wished he could say something, Sims wheeled his horse around instead and rode toward his position.

Randy aligned his horse with hers, and she took a deep breath as she stared at the raging water. A memory of her spill into the arroyo surfaced. As though sensing her distress, Dolly pawed the ground and snorted.

"Only a few miles past that river is the town we're headin' to, ma'am." Randy's encouragement was thinly disguised, but she managed a partial smile. Boyd had given her the same hopeful news when he had told her they had no choice but to cross. Even the prospect of a bath and a real bed were meager inducements to risk her life in the river.

But then she glanced up and met Boyd's worried gaze. It was clear he was ready to ford the river again to fetch her. She straightened up in the saddle. The river still looked frightening, but she wasn't willing to have Boyd risk crossing twice simply because she couldn't overcome her fear.

"I'm ready, Randy."

"Yes, ma'am."

Together they plowed into the churning water. Abigail held her breath, but Dolly was unflappable as usual. When they reached the deepest part of the water, a litter of heavy brush and broken trees swept by, looking as though everything that grew from the shore had been plucked out by the roots and sent swirling and bobbing across the currents. But Dolly, bless her gentle nature, only rolled her eyes and kept a steady course. In short time they reached the opposite shore.

"Good job, Abby," Boyd greeted her. "You didn't even look scared."

She doubted that. If there was a mirror handy, she suspected she would look like a pale imitation of a ghost. "Is town really close?" She couldn't express the longing in her voice.

"We'll be there by evening."

"A real bed . . ." she murmured.

"And food."

"A bathtub . . ." she continued.

"And whiskey."

Registering what he had said, she glanced at him quizzically. "We going to the same town?"

But he only laughed.

As they rode toward town, she could see that the men shared Boyd's boisterous mood. Jokes flew like swiftly

drawn arrows, and laughter replaced the intensity of the la
few days. As they grew closer, she could see a sudde
huddling of the men who rode near the point.

Curiously she watched as the herd progressed down tl
road leading to town. Stephen, one of the point men, ro
out toward the front, the position Boyd normally assume
Wondering why, she spotted a man from town standing ne
the side of the road, waving toward Stephen.

"Who's that?" she asked.

"Drummer," Boyd replied briefly. "From one of tl
outfitting stores, no doubt." Catching her quizzical stare, I
elaborated. "Probably wants to sell us chuck wagon gr
ceries."

"What's Stephen doing?"

Boyd swallowed a growing smile. "I got a good idea.'

As they watched, Stephen stopped, spoke to the drumme
and accepted generous blandishments of cigars and whi
key.

"What's that for?" Abigail asked.

"Drummers usually give the boss something extra so he'
buy from them."

"But Stephen's not the boss."

"Exactly."

Confused, she stared at him.

"Just watch."

Within a few minutes Randy galloped up to the drumme
and Stephen, yelling as he approached. "Stephen, the bo
says you better move it, you lazy cuss, or he'll turn you o
soon as we get to town."

"The boss?" the drummer echoed, stupefied, his face
comical mix of realization, anger, and embarrassment.

Stephen tipped his hat to the errant salesman, cigars an
whiskey in hand, then doubled back, a grin splitting his fac
as he waved to his comrades.

The drummer threw the rest of his wares on the ground i
disgust, glaring at Stephen and Randy as they gallope
away.

All the other cowhands immediately yelped with glee
this rare and precious success of buncoing a dude.

Abigail turned to Boyd in dawning understanding. "They had that set up all along!"

Boyd's sheepish grin emerged, full-fledged. "Afraid so. Don't worry. I'll pick up an order from the drummer while I'm in town."

Abigail found herself reluctantly smiling. "I guess it is pretty funny." Hearing the snickers of the men still relaying up and down the herd, she couldn't restrain a giggle. "Is this a preview of what's to come while we're in town?"

Boyd shoved his hat back and let his grin crease the edges of his face. "Only worse. By the time we're ready to head home, you'll think the stampeding cattle were easier to round up."

She kept his words in mind as the town came into view. It wasn't much as towns went. Of course its primary attraction was the railhead which brought in cattle, and subsequently business for the saloons, dance halls, gambling palaces, and hotels that lined the main street. The horses and cattle kicked up dust in the dirt-paved thoroughfare, but no one seemed to mind.

A general store sported a sign bragging that it offered butter, eggs, produce, and goods. But the sign drawing the most attention was one advertising baths. Men caked in dust and grime, having had only one another for companionship, were anxious to wash away all evidence of the trail.

"Will everyone be able to wash up soon?" Abigail asked, her own anxiousness seeping through.

"Don't worry. The hotel will bring up a tub for a price. You don't have to use the public bathhouse. The men'll get a turn as soon as their shift's up."

"But I thought they'd have free time once they reached town!"

"They will, but not all at once. Someone still has to watch the herd till we get them all into boxcars."

"Oh."

"But there are holding pens in town. It's not like ridin' watch out on the trail."

She breathed a sigh of relief. "Good. They all look tired and in need of rest."

"Hell, the worst part isn't wantin' rest."

"No?"

"Nope. Hardest part is to sit in the saddle, still grimy, starin' at the lights of town, knowin' you're close enough to Sodom to be pleasured, but stuck out on watch, envyin' everyone else who gets to go to town."

She stared at him. It was quite a speech for Boyd. Instantly she wondered just how often he'd been "pleasured" in Sodom. Accompanying the thought was an equally large spurt of jealousy. She couldn't keep the stiffness from her tone. "I see."

"We'll check into the hotel, and then I'll head over to the stockyards."

"You needn't go with me. I'm sure I can check into a hotel."

He stared at her, scandalized. "Abigail, you can't check into a hotel alone. What would people think?"

Since she'd never checked into a hotel alone, Abigail had never considered the consequences. But then, that, too, was something Michael had always handled. "Very well. Whatever you think."

He slanted a glance at her, and she realized he had no inkling of why she was irritated. Sighing, she stayed quiet as they neared the hotel. As they split off, Randy led the group toward the railhead holding pens.

Having seen no other people other than Indians for quite some time, Abigail was somewhat overwhelmed by the bustle of town. Men swaggered down the crude boardwalk, and she watched them discreetly.

As she tied Dolly's reins to the hitching rack, Abigail stared at Boyd as he stepped up on the wooden platform. Incredibly long legs, encased in denims and leather chaps, stood out in the crowd, his height making him tower over the men nearby. She heard the distinctive clank of his spurs as he turned, his broad shoulders and tapering hips an impressive sight. Sucking in her breath, Abigail realized that he was even more extraordinary than she had realized.

"You comin'?" he asked.

Distracted, she nodded, giving Dolly a reassuring pat,

realizing she needed the encouragement more than the horse did.

Once inside, Boyd handled the registration, asking for single rooms for himself and Abigail, and enough rooms for the other men to double up and stay in. Although other trail bosses let the men pay for their own rooms, Boyd had explained that if you wanted to keep good hands, you treated them decently. Abigail agreed completely. Their bonus for the drive was hardly much inducement if they spent it all on hotel rooms.

The balding hotel proprietor handed them each keys. "You're in number ten, ma'am. And number nine for you, sir."

Boyd cleared his throat. "Don't you have two singles that aren't next to each other?"

"Nope. You got the last ones. Actually it's a suite, but it divides into two singles. There are two other drives in town. You're lucky to get these rooms."

"Maybe another hotel," Abigail murmured.

"Full up," the proprietor announced. "Only reason I got any rooms is 'cause another drive checked out this afternoon."

Abigail and Boyd stared at each other. His voice sounded unnaturally gruff as he signed the register. "These rooms will do fine."

Silently they climbed the stairs. Boyd walked Abigail to her room, all politeness as she turned the key in the lock.

"I'll be down at the loading pens," he informed her, not meeting her eyes. "I'll be back around seven o'clock."

"And I'll go find the doctor to check on Billy," she added, afraid also to meet his gaze.

"They're just rooms," he said, not sounding convinced.

Connecting ones, she wanted to shout. Instead she forced a smile. "Of course."

Silence loomed between them.

"Would you—"

"I thought—"

Self-consciously they both stopped. But Boyd shoved back his hat and found the words at the same time. "Would

you like to have dinner tonight in the dining room dow
stairs?"

"That would be nice." Hating the formality that wa
growing between them, she impulsively reached out an
took his hand. "No one knows us here, Boyd. There's n
need to change how we behave until we get back to th
ranch."

Seeing the dart of pain that flickered across his face, sh
wished she could recall the errant words. "I didn't mean tha
the way it came out," she tried to explain.

"Guess no matter how you say it, it all boils down to th
same thing. When we get back to the Triple Cross, it a
ends."

Watching him walk away, she felt a corner of her hea
crumble and wondered if she could let him keep walkin
away.

The afternoon passed quickly. It hadn't taken long t
locate the doctor. Billy passed his examination with flyin
colors. The grizzled-looking doctor had taken on a look c
respect when Billy detailed Abigail's surgical procedure. H
had then pronounced Billy fit and damned lucky to still hav
his leg.

Stopping by the general store, Abigail had picked out
simple dress, petticoats, and new undergarments. Althoug
she knew she could only wear them one evening or so, sh
felt them far worth the money. Then she picked up sham
poo, rosewater soap, and some sweet-smelling lotion. On a
impulse, she also selected a new shirt for Boyd along wit
a bandanna to replace the one he had loaned her.

As she was about to pay for her purchases, her eyes fell o
a pocket watch. Gold, carved with a picture of a wild stallion
she knew in a glance that it suited Boyd perfectly. No
allowing herself to give the purchase any more thought, sh
added it to her collection and quickly paid for everything.

On the way back she chastised herself for being a fool
She could hardly give him such a significant gift. Yet, sh
felt inordinately pleased to know it rested in her parcels
Returning to the hotel, she ordered a hot bath and soake

until her skin wrinkled, lathering herself in the delicious aroma of the rosewater soap. She allowed her hair, washed with fragrant shampoo, to dry in the last rays of the afternoon sun that shone through the lace curtain of the window.

As evening approached, she drew a match from the box near the door and lit the oil lamps, even though a few latent sunbeams lingered. She enjoyed the play of the lamplight combined with the dying sunshine. The pungent smell of sulphur mixed with the feminine smells of her soap and lotion. Dressed in her new undergarments and petticoats, anointed with lotion, she luxuriated in the feel of civilization. Still, she realized she was waiting, impatience tingeing her comfort.

And she knew for whom she waited. She reached for her dress, deciding it was time to ready for the evening. Her glance fell on the new shirt she had bought for Boyd. Lifting her eyes to the door connecting the two rooms, she wondered if it was locked. She hadn't bothered to check it earlier in the day. It would be a wonderful surprise to lay the new shirt on his bed for Boyd to find when he returned. Glancing at the pocket watch, which she had set in the store, she knew it would be a good hour before he was back.

Impulsively she rose from her spot near the window, grabbed the shirt, turned the doorknob, and strode into the adjoining room. Halting, she stared in confusion. Instead of the empty room she had expected to find, his bedroom was filled with a tub, much as hers had been earlier. There the semblance ended, for his tub was still full.

Of him.

Swallowing, she stared at the massive expanse of muscled chest that greeted her, the lean tapering torso, the water that hinted at what it hid. But even as she wondered about that, her eyes traveled upward to meet his and read the intent painted there. No excuses, no embarrassment, only long-denied fulfillment.

She could have turned and fled. Uttered an excuse, an apology, and secured herself in the safety of her own room. But she did neither.

Instead the heat she saw in his eyes transferred itself to her. Warmth curled like a beguiling seducer, making her breasts tingle from his glance alone, the dampness between her legs run hot and wild.

As she watched him, she saw the answering need on his face as he rose from the tub. Like a great beast he shook the water from his muscled frame. Perfectly proportioned, the muscles of his broad shoulders rippled with the movement. He lifted heavy, tapered thighs from the tub, landing on well-shaped calves as he stepped on the rug.

Beads of moisture sluiced over him, clinging to the thatch of dark hair on his chest, the swirling pattern of fine hairs that led to the arousal her eyes now fixed upon.

He approached, no timidity in his manner, rather like the commanding man she knew he was. And Abigail stood her ground. She didn't want to run away from his formidable approach. Instead she stepped closer, the shirt in her hands forgotten as it fell to the floor.

There was no future with him, an inner voice mockingly reminded her.

But there was today.

No one knew them in this town. She could have the fulfillment she had craved since his first touch.

Then he stood within inches of her. She lifted her eyes and was lost. His powerful arms pulled her close, the moisture from his bath soaking through the layers of her clothes. The dampened material abraded her already sensitized nipples.

"Ah, Abby," he groaned, burying his lips against her throat. Melting against him, she felt her knees buckle as his hard body leaned against hers.

With little effort, he scooped her up, his lips traveling to capture hers. With three great strides, he took them to the bed. She scarcely realized the motion as her back met the mattress. But then his weight was against her—chest to chest, hipbone to hipbone.

Even the meager petticoats and undergarments seemed like far too much compared to the tantalizing length of bare flesh stretched out on top of her. But Boyd's hands were quickly dispatching the impediments. His strong hands, no longer clumsy, confidently pulled off her petticoats and tossed them to the floor. Long fingers toyed briefly with the ribbons lacing her camisole. But in moments they, too, were unfastened. She sucked in her breath as he pulled the fabric free, exposing her breasts.

Hearing a matching groan from him, she eased her eyelids closed as pleasure rocketed through her. For Boyd was tasting each breast, suckling first one and then the other. He drew his tongue slowly over each peak, teasing her with gentle nibbles. The fire shot straight through her.

But he didn't give her time to examine the feelings as he untied the fastening to her pantalets and tugged them free. Dispatching the final garment, he then cradled her face in his hands, compelling her to meet his eyes.

What she saw there melted her heart further. Amid the blaze of passion, she saw the love they had yet to voice.

"Be sure, Abby. Because we can't go back."

Her eyelids drifted shut briefly, but when they reopened they blazed with a matching fierceness. "I'm very sure."

He kissed her then, not the hard, demanding kiss she might have expected, but one of such great tenderness, she felt the walls protecting her fragile heart collapse. He lengthened the kiss, exploring her lips, her face, while his hands began their magic.

His scent filled her nose, his heat brushed her arms and breasts. She luxuriated in the sheen and texture of his skin, the symmetry of his body, the velvety feel of him in her hands. She heard his gasp, and an unexpected smile of pure feminine pleasure curved her lips.

But then he slanted over her, his hands moving over the curves of her body. His fingers danced with a rhythm that made her want to beg for more and at the same time almost shout for him to stop, for the pleasure was so great. He skimmed past her rib cage and the curving valley of her waist. His fingers lingered on the curve of her hips and then plied over her shaking legs. He danced around the center of her pleasure, not yet touching her there, prolonging the anticipation.

His strong hands cupped her calves and then slid up the length of her thighs, finally trailing on the tender inside curve of her leg. So very near. Yet still he heightened the expectation, and her entire body trembled with the wanting. He shifted, his mouth capturing hers as his fingers brushed the golden curls at the apex of her thighs.

Jolting with the movement, she bit back a groan as one strong finger slipped inside, finding the waiting warmth, the telling wetness that signaled her readiness. But his mouth continued its journey down the tender hollows of her throat as his fingers continued to fill her, the pad of his thumb circling the rosy peak that make her jerk and arch nearly off the bed. His fingers coaxed a swelling pressure from the folds of her womanhood that seemed as though she might burst from it.

He continued the dual assault, and she thought she would die of the sensations. When she felt the hard evidence of his arousal nudge her belly, she grew desperate, wanting to feel him inside of her.

"Please, Boyd. Please . . ."

"I want to be inside of you, too, Abby. To fill you and never let you go." He withdrew his fingers and poised over her.

The thrust was as wild and strong as she had expected. Still the shock of his fullness made her dig her fingers into his shoulders as her legs wrapped around his. All of him was big, she realized as he filled her completely. Each powerful stroke was sending her higher. Instinctively she rose to meet each thrust, reveling in the feel of him. His supple flesh moved over hers, bringing her to a brink she had only wondered about.

Her fingers roamed over his back, down his hips, and then settled on his buttocks. She felt him clench in response as her fingers continued their play.

Sheathing him in warmth, she felt the power of each thrust grow stronger, even as a building sensation threatened to rock her apart. Unable to still the cry, she tried to bury her mouth against his chest as the sound echoed around them.

But before her cry could end, he spilled his seed, drenching her womb, anchoring her soul.

His movements stilled, but his lips captured hers. Intense, unrelenting as though trying to stamp his own brand upon her. Her fingers lifted to sift through his thick hair, and then when he released her, she kissed each hand in turn. The lamplight flickered over the planes of his commanding face. His eyes brightened, and she suspected the emotion that hid behind that sudden sheen and the bobbing of his Adam's apple. But then he shifted to his side, pulling her with him, hiding her in his embrace. She recognized the effort for what it was. He hoped to keep the world at bay.

Knowing it was futile, she willingly accepted his touch anyway. For tonight at least, he had succeeded. Desperation drove them, but passion incited the fire. Then she forgot to think as his lips captured hers and his fingers danced over her once again.

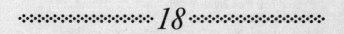

18

The last of the sunshine had disappeared behind the flutter of the curtains. Shades now drawn, only the golden glow from the oil lamps lit the two exhausted, but hardly satisfied bodies. Boyd drew his fingers gently in a line from Abigail's flushed breasts, over her rib cage, to tease the concave flatness of her stomach.

As her huge, lapis-colored eyes focused on him, he could still scarcely believe he held her in his arms. Every fantasy had come to fruition, each desire a reality. She was a beguiling mixture of innocent and temptress. Even now her thighs moved sinuously against his heated flesh, while her rosy lips curved in invitation, and he felt himself tighten in response.

Answering that invitation, he let his mouth trail down the path his fingers had carved. His mouth fastened on her breast, sliding his tongue over the hardening peak, moistening the dusky areola. Traveling down the velvety length of her skin, he reveled in its satiny texture. He tasted the bow of her hips, the hollow of her navel. The lamplight flickered over their bodies. Unable to resist the lure of her golden curls that beckoned between her thighs, his mouth continued downward. He tasted the tangled warmth of her damp curls and heard her squeak of surprise.

Gently he parted her legs, pushing her knees upward, bracing them on his shoulders so that his mouth could continue its journey. At his first taste of her warm heat, she stiffened.

"Boyd!" Shock colored her embarrassed cry.

But he didn't stop his exploration, his tongue flicking into the soft folds, tasting both their flavors. Masterfully he lavished his attention on her, concentrating his attention at the juncture of her milky thighs.

Her voice sounded strangled. "I can't . . ." But a shudder raked her, then another. "We can't . . . shouldn't . . ."

He continued tasting her sweet honey. Another shudder rocked through her, and he exulted at her reaction.

As he lowered her legs, she met his eyes shyly. "It's just that I've never . . ."

"Neither have I. I never wanted to. Until you." He hadn't expected to make the confession, but nothing about Abigail had gone according to plan.

She used her hands and mouth to show him how that admission made her feel. A delighted shiver danced across his skin as she stroked, nibbled, and kissed him. Her soft lips took the turgid bud of his nipple into her mouth. A groan escaped him as her fingers shyly at first and then with growing boldness plied across his skin. Muscles he controlled without thought now trembled under her delicate touch. But it was the emotion in her eyes that devastated him. Eyes that told of the feelings they had yet to speak aloud.

Years of keeping his heart protected fell away under her ministrations and the pull of her cornflower-blue eyes. Feeling helpless to stop the rush and tumble of their love, he chose instead to dive into the raging current she had created. If he drowned, he would die a happy man after his time with this incredible woman.

She sought out the nerve-filled skin of his inner thighs, her touch tantalizing him as she inched closer to the heavy, pulsing weight at its center. He felt her stop as she discovered the scar of his wound, then the flutter of her lips as she kissed that same spot. The simple gesture was the final fissure in his cracking heart. He could no longer defend it from the love that had grown there despite his efforts to keep it at bay.

He didn't know how, but if it killed him, he wasn't going

to lose this woman. It was as though he had known from that first moment when he had brought her child into the world.

They had come full circle, adding dimension to that course on the way. But he couldn't give her up, any more than he could give up his relationship with her son. While the love had taken root, budded, and flowered, he had denied the feelings, but as he gazed at the trusting face turned toward his, he knew he could deny it no longer.

Raising over her, he searched for regret and saw none. Instead he saw both anticipation and love. Reaching with one hand to brush the strands of silken hair back from her cheeks and forehead, he vowed to cherish and protect her.

"Abigail . . ."

"I know, Boyd." Her soft hand stroked his cheek and then rested on his lips. "I know."

And with her words, he took her again, knowing that if they repeated the act a million times, he would never grow tired of her.

The sudden rap on the door wakened them both. Startled, they sat up, took a moment to stare at each other in the early-morning sunshine before Boyd dragged the sheet around his lean hips and walked to the door.

"Who is it?" he asked without turning the lock.

"Telegram for you, Mr. Harris."

Raking a hand through tousled hair, he turned to stare at Abigail. "Shove it under the door," he instructed in an even tone.

The crackle of paper filled the quiet in the room. He stared at the missive, sensing it was ominous. He picked up the paper, almost afraid to read its contents.

"Boyd?"

Ignoring the premonition, he ripped open the envelope. Silently he read it, his jaw firming, his lips thinning into a grim line.

Fear threaded Abigail's words. "What is it? It's not Michael . . ."

"No!" He pushed the hair back from his forehead and

reluctantly crossed to her side, offering her the paper he wished he could destroy, along with its message.

Her eyes widened as she digested the contents.

Trouble. Come home immediately. Takeover.

It was signed by Cameron O'Donnell.

"The Triple Cross?" she whispered.

"Someone's probably been plottin' ever since we left," he replied grimly. "Just waitin' for his chance to jump in when the place wasn't protected."

"But who?"

"That's what we've got to find out." He stared out at the breaking dawn. "Better get dressed fast. We're takin' the train home."

"What about the herd and our horses?"

"I'll leave a couple of men to make sure the cows get in the boxcars. We'll take the horses back with us on the train. That's why they've got cattle cars." He tried to cheer her up. "Don't worry. We won't leave Dolly behind." But the effort failed. He could see the worry clouding her expression.

"Do you think we're already too late?"

"I vowed I'd keep the Triple Cross safe for you and Michael the day he was born. I'm not givin' up now." Pulling on his denims, he stared out the window for a moment. "Hell, I knew we wouldn't have much time here, but I never dreamed . . ."

"I wouldn't have changed a thing," she replied, meeting his gaze without flinching. "Now we just have to go home and take care of the problem."

Tenderness welled up inside him, along with a burgeoning sense of responsibility. As she reached for her camisole, his hand snagged hers, and he brought it to his lips. "Trust me, Abigail. That's all I ask."

"That was never a question. It won't ever be."

Drawing a fortifying breath, he hoped she was right. But with the arrival of the telegram, foreboding hadn't been far behind.

Tickets in hand, they boarded the train as soon as it pulled into the small station. The rattling single train ran only once a day, and they were lucky to have secured seats for themselves as well as the men. Boyd had left Randy Kreiger and a few men behind to make sure the cattle were loaded and on their way to the agent who would sell the herd.

Taking a seat opposite Boyd, Abigail smoothed the fabric of her skirt, glad she had bought the dress the day before. So much had happened in the last twenty-four hours, it was boggling to imagine that only a day had passed. Boyd had briefed the men as to the possible situation at the Triple Cross. Without exception, every man had agreed without question to return and defend the ranch.

For most of them, the return trip on the train was a rare treat. Not that anyone wanted to ride back into a battle, but their energy would be high from the rest they would get on the train. Since they only covered about ten miles a day on horseback while moving the herd, the train ride would be swift in comparison.

Black smoke billowed from the locomotive, and the whistle blew as they pulled out of the station. In short time ashes from the engine car drifted back and into the open windows of the passenger cars. The soot settled on their clothes and dusted their faces.

Boyd leaned forward, placing a possessive hand over Abigail's, damning any curious glances. "No matter who's behind the takeover, he won't get the Triple Cross."

Staring into the chiseled strength of his face, she didn't doubt him. He could command an army, and had in the past. "I trust you, Boyd."

Emotions skittered over his face, each more telling than the last. "I wanted to give you more than one night in a hotel," he finally answered, his voice too low to carry to anyone else.

She glanced at the passengers across the aisle, then disregarded them, realizing they couldn't hear over the noise of the chugging train. "I feel as though we've stolen that time." Her fingers closed around his. "But no matter what happens, it will be a special time."

His fingers clenched in response, no doubt wondering if

he was being relegated merely to a memory. "A special time," he echoed, unable to keep the bitterness from his voice.

"We have to concentrate on the Triple Cross," she said, hoping to ease that suspicion. "I think it's our first priority."

She felt his clasp on her hands relax a fraction. "You're right, of course."

"I'm not dismissing what we shared," she added, trying to still the sudden catch in her throat. "But right now we need to be worrying about the ranch, not ourselves." A smile softened her face, taking the sting from her words. "There'll be plenty of time for that in the future."

His body tensed, and she met his eyes across the space of the closely packed seats. It was a blithe assumption. One neither could be sure of. One neither really believed.

"Do you have a plan?" Abigail asked as the silence stretched between them.

"I want to arrive quietly, find out what's goin' on."

"We're not going to burst on the scene like avenging angels?"

"Not this time. I want to know who's behind this. How they knew this was the time to strike."

"I'm certainly glad for Cameron O'Donnell," she replied, unable to keep the wonder from her voice.

"Not scared of him anymore?" Boyd asked with a ghost of a smile.

"I never . . ." She fiddled with the loose folds of her skirt. "All right, so he intimidated me. You didn't have to deal with him, treating me as though he was my father doling out an allowance."

"I did deal with him," he reminded her gently. "But I never got that feeling."

"Of course not. You're a man!"

His face creased into lines of satisfaction. "It can be an advantage."

She leaned forward earnestly. "But that's not all of it. I've seen Jem McIntire order men around, and they jumped to obey. The way the men do with you. But I've seen other foremen try to lead a group, and no one even listens to them. It's all in the person who's in charge."

One dark eyebrow lifted in wry acknowledgment.

"Do you want a heartfelt apology? Okay. You were right. I was wrong. You're a leader, and I'm not. The men respect you. If you led them into quicksand, they'd follow."

"I hope not."

She sniffed and turned to the window. "You know what I mean. Something about you commands loyalty and respect. Heaven knows you have mine. Along with everything else."

"Do I, Abigail?"

She turned away from her view of the miles of landscape that bumped past as they wound around the countryside. "I'm afraid so, Boyd . . . even though I know it's probably not wise."

"No, it's not. And if it means losing the Triple Cross to be linked up with me, I'll walk away." His voice was blunt, his eyes sober and unrelenting.

Abigail felt her heart catch and knew he spoke the truth. Boyd was a man of integrity and principle. He would leave rather than risk her son's legacy. "But I don't want you to go," she whispered.

"It's not what I want, either. But I'll do what I have to."

Abigail controlled the quick sting of tears that threatened. "We need you, Boyd. Michael and I both do."

A shaft of pain pierced his expression, and Abigail's heart constricted even further, knowing she had caused it.

"Michael needs the legacy his father died for." Blunt, uncompromising, the words rang between them.

Abigail lifted her eyes to his, knowing there was no rebuttal to the truth. Still she reached into her reticule and pulled out the pocket watch she had purchased the day before and pressed it into his hands.

"I want you to have this."

"But—"

"I didn't realize when I bought it . . . but it will be a token of our time together. When you wear it, you can think of me." Something to remember me by.

"I didn't give you anything." And I don't want you to forget.

Her lips trembled as they formed a smile. "Oh, but you did, Boyd. And it will always be in my heart."

19

The quiet *clip-clop* of horses' hooves split the silent night as the group passed under the arches that proclaimed they were entering the Triple Cross. A short distance away, the ranch and bunkhouse loomed in the darkness. No one spoke as they crossed that last space.

"Hold it right there!" The clear voice rang out of the darkness, simultaneously with the snapping sound of a trigger being cocked. A flash of metal gleamed obscenely in the moonlight, evidence of the rifle aimed at them.

"Is that you, O'Donnell?" Boyd asked in amazement.

The dark-haired, hawklike man seemed part of the shadows even as he stepped forward. Obsidian eyes viewed them all suspiciously before he lowered the weapon. "Welcome home." His voice was dry, controlled.

Other cowhands emerged from the shadows as well, lowering their weapons as they recognized Abigail and Boyd.

"So it's bad enough that you've had to take up arms," Boyd stated grimly.

"We've lost better than a dozen hands," Cameron reported. "Some were run off, some lured away."

"Who's left?" Boyd asked.

The men came forward one at a time, showing themselves.

Boyd silently gauged each face, noted who was missing, and then addressed them. "I won't dance around the truth. We're in for a fight. We need you in order to keep the Triple

Cross, but I don't want anyone stayin' who isn't here for the long run. Some of you have families."

His gaze touched them, each in turn. "No one will think any less of you if you leave. But if you stay, it'll be rough. People will get hurt, some will die." Their expressions didn't change, except to gain more determination. He nodded, satisfied. "We'll hire more men if we can get them. Looks like Mr. O'Donnell already has a watch set up. The men from the drive will relieve you at midnight."

Taking his words as a dismissal, the cowhands melted back into the shadows. The others, fresh from the drive, dismounted and led their horses to the corral. There was little talk. The air was filled with grim purpose.

"Good to see you, Mrs. Fairchild," O'Donnell greeted Abigail.

Feeling as though she had been forgotten until that moment, she cleared her throat, trying to hide her nervousness. She had never been greeted with a loaded gun before. "Hello, Mr. O'Donnell. We're grateful for your prompt action."

Boyd dismounted, holding the reins loosely in his hands. "We need to talk," he said briefly, addressing the other man.

O'Donnell's flintlike eyes glinted in the darkness. "I'll be in my study, now that you're back."

Abigail joined Boyd as the other man disappeared into the house. "You don't sound very pleased with him."

"I need to know what's been going on around here. He's the best man to tell me."

"Are you sure that's all? I mean, you don't suspect him, do you? After all, he sent us the telegram warning us of the trouble."

"So he did."

She laid a restraining hand on his arm. "Is there something you're not telling me?"

Sapphire eyes deepened to ebony. "I play my cards close to my chest, Abigail. But I'll tell you anything you need to know."

"Before or after it happens?" she questioned dryly.

"When the time's right."

"Are you going to speak to him now?"

His eyes cut toward the house. "The sooner the better."

She hesitated. "I don't know why, but I trust him. I know he intimidated me, but I don't believe he's dishonest."

"I hope you're right."

Abigail and Boyd entered the big house, both of them headed for the same destination. Even though it was late, they wanted to see little Michael. Abigail didn't even question Boyd's assumption that he, too, needed to see her child.

Walking down the hall, they could see the flicker from an oil lamp left lit in his room, and the gurgle of soft cries that signaled he was still awake. Quietly they entered. The surprise wasn't lost on Michael.

Expectantly he glanced up at them, a child showered with love, accustomed to kindness from all. His face crinkled in babyish joy.

"Ma-ma!" Standing up, Michael reached his arms toward Abigail, who immediately scooped him up and held him close, breathing in the fresh baby scent of him.

"Hello, Michael Boyd," she murmured to him.

"Hi, pal," Boyd crooned to him, taking one of his flailing hands.

"Ba-ba," Michael responded.

Abigail and Boyd's eyes met. It was Michael's attempt at Boyd's name, but it came out sounding more like da-da. The figure Boyd had become.

"You been a good boy?" Abigail asked as she nestled her cheek against Michael's face.

"Nope, he's been out chasin' the girls, haven't you?" Boyd asked, the special twinkle he reserved for the baby lighting up, engulfing his face. "Miranda, Lucy, and Rachel can probably tell some tall tales by now."

"Don't you listen to him," Abigail responded as she continued to hug her son. But he wriggled away after a moment, demanding to be set down.

Placing him on the rug, Abigail watched as Michael pulled at Boyd's pant leg, commanding his attention. Boyd reached for the child, lifting him high in the air, eliciting whoops of delight.

Seeing them together, Abigail wondered how she could ever consider separating them. Boyd walked with Michael to the window, pointing out the constellations, telling him that he would soon learn to tell time by the position of the Big Dipper.

It mattered not that Michael didn't understand the words. Boyd's love filtered through clearly.

Abigail joined them at the window. Boyd held Michael while she leaned her head against his sturdy shoulder. Even though she knew the interval would have to end, for just this moment, this stolen time, she clung to what they shared.

Boyd strode through the house, putting aside his thoughts of little Michael. Miranda had come to put the toddler to bed for the evening, and their homecoming had been prematurely aborted.

Boyd paused at the entrance to the study, respecting Cameron O'Donnell's domain. The lamps were turned up high, reflecting their light on the leather-bound volumes that lined the bookshelves. The room smelled of leather, fragrant tobacco, and the woody smell of the oak walls. Cameron sat at the desk, but he wasn't absorbed in his ledgers. They were neatly closed, the quill pen resting in its holder, the ink capped.

He was waiting.

Cameron held a long, slim cigar in his hand and gestured to the chair in front of the desk. Boyd sat down heavily, the weight of the past few days catching up with him.

"Cigar?" Cameron asked.

Boyd accepted the cheroot, rolling it between his fingers and thumb, then sliding the fine cigar beneath his nose to inhale the aroma.

The scratch of the match and the quick spurt of sulphur filled the air. Boyd drew in the tobacco and then exhaled. Cameron uncorked a decanter of whiskey, poured them both stiff shots, and shoved one tumbler over on the desk toward Boyd.

"What do you want to know?" Cameron asked.

Boyd's eyebrows lifted. So the other man wanted to take the offense. Silently he admired the tactic. "What's been goin' on?"

"Gossip," Cameron answered flatly.

It wasn't the response Boyd expected, and he automatically straightened in the chair.

"Caruthers came back to town after Mrs. Fairchild fired him. Had a lot to say about what was going on out on the trail drive between you and Mrs. Fairchild."

Gut tightening, Boyd stared at Cameron. "And?"

"Some people chose to believe his stories. Andrew Johnson hired Caruthers, lending credence to his tales. Then Mr. Peterson told others that he'd spoken for Mrs. Fairchild's hand, but that if the ranch was going to be compromised, he was going to step in before it fell into ruin."

"And take it for himself," Boyd finished.

Cameron took a long swallow of his drink. "So it seems."

"What's he done so far?"

"He rode in, made his demands, gave us a deadline, and left. When he returned, I greeted him with a loaded Winchester. The men were lacking leadership with both you and your assistant gone. I did what I thought was best."

"You're pretty handy with a gun for an accountant."

"You're pretty handy with figures for a foreman."

Boyd took a swallow of his own drink, silently acknowledging Cameron's words. "So when's this deadline?"

"Tomorrow." Cameron met Boyd's eyes steadily. "When you returned, I thought he'd decided to set his watch ahead."

"Your telegram made it sound urgent, so we came back by train."

Cameron's eyes darkened and shadowed, seeming to be as black and emotionless as the granite cliffs that rose from the mountain crags. "Peterson won't back down easily."

Boyd lowered his tumbler of whiskey. "I won't, either."

Their eyes met. "Good. I'd hate to see Mrs. Fairchild lose her ranch."

"Then you're with us?" Boyd stated as much as asked.

A light flickered in the fathomless depths of Cameron's dark eyes. "I have my own interests to protect."

Boyd's eyebrows drew together in a question.

"Nothing as dramatic as taking over a ranch," Cameron assured him. "But the women here deserve our protection and loyalty."

Boyd stared at the other man, an even greater question forming in his mind. The only other unattached woman at the ranch was Miranda Abernathy.

Surely not.

But then he met the other man's steady regard. Knowing the news of his association with Abigail would be greeted with equal disbelief, Boyd didn't form the question. Instead he read the answer in Cameron's silence.

"I can't tell you how good it is to have you back, Miz Fairchild!" Miranda bustled about the room, fluffing pillows, turning down the bed, arranging the water pitcher and bowl, laying out a frilly nightgown and wrapper.

Abigail hid her impatience with the fussing. She had expected to look forward to this special treatment. Instead she found herself resenting what seemed to be wasteful niceties.

"Miranda, stop!"

The older woman did, with a look of surprise and disappointment.

Abigail closed the space between them. "I appreciate everything, but I'm sure you'd like to take some time for yourself, or to do something more important."

Miranda's hands stilled. "Are you upset with me?"

"Of course not!" Abigail ran a hand over her face, instantly regretting her words. "But it's not necessary to fuss over me."

"I just thought—"

"Of course you did. The room looks wonderful." Abigail plumped down on the bed with forced enthusiasm. "It'll be wonderful to sleep in a real bed again." Alone, a mocking thought reminded her.

"You must have fared pretty well out there," Miranda said slowly.

"Actually I surprised myself." Abigail chuckled, a spontaneous sound. "Not that I didn't cause more trouble than Boyd's worst nightmares could have predicted. But I got to understand what the men go through, some of the complexities of this ranch business. I still have so much to learn, but it was a beginning."

Miranda sat down heavily on the chair opposite Abigail. "So, you intend to keep on with this ranch business. I mean, tryin' to run it yourself."

"Why, yes." Abigail's tone was brisk and strong. Despite any setbacks, that goal hadn't changed.

Miranda lifted her cinnamon-colored eyes, and Abigail was shocked to see the anxiety troubling them. "I'm worried, Miz Fairchild."

Abigail rose from the bed and crossed to Miranda's side. "What is it? I know about the takeover attempts—"

"Not everything," Miranda blurted out, then bit her lower lip.

A sense of dread settled in Abigail's chest. "What should I know?"

"That there's been gossip." Miranda reached out and clasped Abigail's hands. "I want you to know I don't believe any of it, but there's other people . . ." She shook her head. "Well, not everybody knows you like I do."

"What kind of gossip?" Abigail asked flatly.

"About you and Boyd," Miranda blurted out, then rushed on to cover the words. "You don't have to explain. I know that you're close friends. With what you shared with the baby's birth and all—"

"It's more than that," Abigail interrupted quietly. Withdrawing her hands, she turned to the window, seeing only darkness. "You might as well know the truth. I don't want you defending something without good cause."

"But Caruthers—"

"Lied." Abigail turned back to face Miranda. "At that time he made up everything he's apparently been spreading around." She ran her hands over the back of the curved

Queen Anne chair, her head still bent. Raising her face, she met Miranda's gaze. "But after he left, things changed. I won't tell you less than the truth. If you're shocked, I'm sorry. If you can't abide working here and knowing this, I'll understand."

Miranda stood up in a rush, and Abigail swore she could see a sheen of tears in the other woman's eyes. "If the Lord doesn't see fit to judge, I don't think I should, either. Besides, a body's entitled to some happiness in this lifetime. If yours is with Boyd, then I'll stand beside you. It won't be easy for either of you."

"No, it won't. Thank you, Miranda. I know you're a God-fearing woman, and this goes against your principles—"

"Principles have a way of sticking in your throat on a cold, lonely night, Miz Fairchild. They can't hold you close and they can't love you."

Abigail wondered at both the words and the new expression on Miranda's face. Angling her head, she noticed the new hairstyle Miranda was sporting and the bright yellow blouse she wore—such a distinct change from her normal gray. And the look on her face. If she didn't know any better, Abigail would almost think it was a lovesick look that consumed Miranda's features.

She shook her head, dispelling the fancy. Miranda was the practical one, she reminded herself. She, on the other hand, was the one who had become involved in an impossible, dangerous attraction.

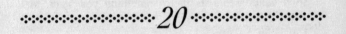

20

The line of armed men, their rifles propped in strategic, conspicuous places, looked vastly out of place in the clear, sun-filled day. Indecent, offensive, and threatening.

Protective, formidable, and watchful as well.

Abigail slanted a glance at Boyd, seeing his determination, feeling his purpose. They stood side by side, leading their men. The sun glinted on the row of rifles and the holstered revolvers the men had strapped on. A month ago she couldn't have imagined the scene. Now she couldn't imagine standing on the sidelines while it was played out.

The horizon remained changeless for hours, seeming to glaze over and blur as the sun inched upward. Then a speck appeared, quickly growing larger. The shape of a horse and rider appeared. The man wasn't alone. Flanked on either side by half a dozen men, he rode closer. His face came into relief, and Abigail recognized Peterson. Interesting way to come courting, she thought wryly, fear traveling its insistent way forward. Licking her lips, she purposely swallowed that fear.

Peterson pulled up his horse, the dust swirling around the pounding hooves. A broad-shouldered, intimidating man, his face was all angles and jutting bones, sharp features and thin lips. Abigail had a sudden image of him as her husband and nearly recoiled.

Collecting herself, she watched as he approached with no timidity in his manner, rather like a warlord coming to collect his bounty. Gathering courage from Boyd's calm countenance, she stood her ground.

"Mrs. Fairchild." Peterson spoke forcefully, showing no surprise at her appearance.

"Mr. Peterson," she answered evenly, watching Boyd's rifle shift upward a fraction.

"You're back."

"So it would seem. Is there something you want, Mr. Peterson?"

"The Triple Cross."

Abigail sucked in her breath and heard the hiss of Boyd's as well. The man was still gallingly blunt.

"That won't happen," Boyd replied flatly.

"Unless I'm mistaken, you're only the foreman, Harris. My business is with the owner."

"He speaks for me," Abigail asserted.

Peterson's snakelike glance flickered between them. "So, what I heard is true."

"Since I don't know what you've heard, that would be hard to answer, Mr. Peterson. I made my position clear a month ago, however. Should you wish to press your suit, I must tell you I'm still not receiving callers." Abigail spoke firmly, hiding the shaking she felt inside.

"Callers," he barked out. The tall stallion beneath him snorted at the sudden sound. "Compromised women seldom have callers."

Boyd stepped forward, shielding Abigail. "That'll be enough, Peterson. Get off the Triple Cross."

"It won't matter if you defend her honor, Harris. There's none left to protect." His glance shifted to pin Abigail in his compelling gaze. "But the offer's still good, Mrs. Fairchild. Either I'll marry you or I'll take the Triple Cross. It's up to you. Once you're blacklisted, it won't matter one way or the other."

Boyd pulled the trigger on the rifle and pointed it at Peterson's heart. "I won't tell you again. Get off the Triple Cross. And don't come back."

Wheeling around, Peterson galloped away, followed by his grim and silent comrades.

"That isn't the end of it," Boyd announced flatly. Turning to the men, he issued orders for continued watches.

"Do you really think he'll be back?" Abigail stared at Boyd in concern before her eyes cut to the retreating riders.

"Yep. Right now I'm goin' to try to hire some more hands."

"Will that be enough to stop him?"

"Unless you want to marry him," Boyd answered grimly.

Her head jerked up in shock. "You sound half serious."

"Every owner in the territory's goin' to be at your front door with more marriage proposals than you can shake a stick at. And Peterson's right. If you don't want to be blacklisted, you'll have to take one of them." His boots stomped a path to the corral where he retrieved his horse.

Staring after him, Abigail felt her heart shatter as she realized he spoke the truth.

Abigail slowed Dolly as she approached Jem McIntire's ranch. She hoped her friend was home. A tomboy who was happier on horseback running down a wayward steer, dressed in men's clothing, Jem was as different from Abigail as two women could be. It was that very difference that had cemented their deep friendship. Each brought out the best qualities in the other.

Knowing how difficult Jem's beginning with her husband, Reese, had been, Abigail hoped her friend could offer some guidance. Nearing the yard, she scanned the corral but didn't see Jem outside. Jem's ranch was one of the largest in the area. She and Reese ran it together like a well-oiled clock. Looping the reins over the hitching rack, Abigail rapped the door knocker.

When Jem pulled open the door herself, Abigail could have shouted in relief.

"Abigail! I didn't know you were back. I'm so glad to see you. You'll never know what I've thought since I heard about you and . . . Come in, and we'll get something cool to drink." She stopped her own barreling monologue to stare at Abigail. "Why are you dressed like that?"

Abigail stared down at the breeches she had grown accustomed to wearing. "It's easier when I want to ride."

"But you've never been on a horse!" Disbelief warred with admiration. "Have you?"

Her face sheepish, Abigail merely nodded.

"Sounds like you've got a lot to tell me, Abby. I just assumed you were riding next to Henry in the chuck wagon on the trail drive. Lordy, you take off for a month and come back a different person." She led the way into the study, raising her voice to an impressive holler. "Could we have some lemonade, Della?"

A muffled reply came back through the hallway, and Abigail guessed it was an affirmative reply.

"So, tell me. Who got you on a horse and why?"

Abigail briefly detailed her insistence to learn the ranching business and Boyd's part in teaching her.

"Whew," Jem replied, a mix of emotions scattering across her face. "You know how I feel about Boyd. You couldn't ask for a better man to run the Triple Cross, or to teach you. But are you taking on too much?"

Hurt, Abigail stared at her friend. "I thought you, of all people, would understand and support me."

"You know I'm behind you. I just meant with little Michael to raise, this is a lot to take on, especially alone."

"Maybe I won't be alone."

Jem sucked in her breath. The rumors had reached her, but she hadn't been certain what to believe.

"So you've heard," Abigail stated.

There was no point in pretending. "There've been some stories going 'round, but I wanted to talk to you first."

"It's pretty hopeless," Abigail replied dismally. "After Michael died, I never expected to feel anything for another man. Certainly not for someone who was as much a friend as a foreman."

Jem knew the story of little Michael's birth. But she also knew the detailed history that lay among all of them. When Jem's former fiancé, Charles, had rustled the cattle on both ranches, Michael Fairchild had been killed defending them. He had been killed in Reese's place, by the man Jem had thought she loved, something none of them could ever forget.

And Boyd had once been in Jem's employ. She had refused to trust him, listening instead to ill-based gossip about his past rather than judging the merit of the man. Then Boyd had risked his life to save Reese from being killed. Jem had much to be grateful to Boyd for, and much bad judgment to regret. Guilt and gratitude laced her feelings, a stranglehold of debt and a desire to mend her past actions.

Jem chose her words carefully. "Do you love him?"

The glow that suffused Abigail's face told the entire story. "Oh, Jem . . . At first I thought it was simply passion."

Jem's eyebrows quirked. "That sounds terribly familiar. But, if I remember correctly, you were the one who told me passion was wrapped up in love."

"So, my sage advice comes back to haunt me."

"Then it is love." Jem stared intently at her friend.

"I never planned this."

"People seldom do. How many times did you try to point out what I should have known about Reese? I tried awfully hard to believe that I was in love with the wrong man until it was almost too late."

Abigail leaned forward earnestly. "But would you have endangered your ranch for him?"

"Knowing what I do now, absolutely." Past guilt stabbed at Jem again. "But your situation is more complicated. I know you want to keep the ranch for little Michael. I didn't have an obligation like that. And I can't honestly say what I'd choose if I were you. You have an obligation to Michael, what he left for your son, but you have a duty to yourself and to Boyd."

"I can't hurt Boyd again, Jem. You know the past he's battled to be free of, the unjustified accusations. He's rebuilt his reputation, but now it's in danger of being ruined again."

"You're both in danger, Abby. I wish I could say that it doesn't matter what others think, but I've had my ranch blacklisted, and it strangles the life out of a place."

"I know," Abigail answered dully.

"If you decide to make your life with Boyd, I'll stand by you." She paused, her voice growing unusually soft. "Because you were right. You can't marry for any reason except love."

"Oh, Jem! You don't have to align yourself with us, to risk the consequences again."

"It's the least I can do. Boyd was accused of the same things my father was. And instead of believing Boyd because I know how it feels to be falsely accused, I was worse than the others. I judged Boyd and found him guilty without evidence. Of all the people involved, I should have given him the benefit of the doubt. But even though I didn't, he never held it against me." Jem's voice trembled a moment, something that was rare in the tough woman. "Despite the way I treated him, he never hesitated in saving Reese." Strength returned, and she gazed fiercely at Abigail. "I'll stand beside you two, and so will Reese. He's always believed in Boyd."

"You're a good friend, Jem."

"A little late, perhaps."

"No. Your heart's big, and that's what counts. I just hope it will be enough to have you two on my side."

"Is there something else you're not telling me?"

Abigail hesitated. "Marriage offers. From Joshua Hodges and Edward Peterson. Joshua has been easy to fend off, but Peterson has made it clear he wants the Triple Cross—either by marrying me or taking over the ranch."

"A land grab," Jem stated grimly.

"Exactly."

Both of them thought of all the smaller ranchers who had been run off by bigger, more powerful owners who had the men, money, and guns to steal their land. The ranchers' deeds of title meant little against someone determined to take what he wanted. With the law hundreds of miles away, there was no one to stop the takeovers, and a piece of paper was little defense against armed mercenaries. If a rancher didn't give up, he was killed, and then his land was up for the taking.

Occasionally neighboring ranchers stood up for the ones being threatened, but most often it was a battle between a heavily armed troop and an obvious underdog. Quite often the underdog simply took his family and left. That was how many of the biggest ranchers had enlarged their holdings. While unscrupulous, it was part of the rawness of the land they lived in.

Jem's brows drew together. "I was afraid of a takeover attempt. Most people know that you'll eventually control the Cushman spread as well. His ranch combined with the Triple Cross will make you the wealthiest owner in the territory."

Randolph Cushman's illegitimate son, Charles, had killed Michael Fairchild. Because of his guilt, Cushman had promised to will his ranch to Abigail and her child. It was a consideration Abigail had forgotten until that moment. Suddenly she felt like the golden goose. No wonder its neck had felt precarious.

Abigail sank back in her chair. A whirring sound grew louder. Della, Jem's housekeeper, wheeled into the room. As adept in her wheelchair as many people with the use of their legs, she had a tray across her lap that contained tea and dessert cakes.

"Howdy, Miz Fairchild. You're lookin' good."

"Thank you, Della. So are you."

Della placed the tray efficiently on the table between the two women. "I'll leave you to your visit."

"Thank you, Della," Jem called after her as she wheeled away.

"Do you think we can defend against a takeover?" Abigail asked after Della had left.

"I'll lend you as many men as you need," Jem offered instantly.

"Is this something you need to discuss with Reese?"

"He'd say the same thing. I'm offering you more than empty assurances when I say that we'll stand beside you. Anything in our power to give you is yours."

For the first time since the telegram had delivered its terrible message, Abigail felt like crying. But Jem's practical nature took hold.

"Reese will come and talk to Boyd, see what you need."

Abigail shoved the hint of tears away. "Boyd's trying to hire more hands now. Some of ours left."

"If they weren't loyal, you're better off without them. You don't need to be worrying about your back."

A sudden image of being pushed into the river on the trail drive flashed in Abigail's memory. Had that somehow been connected to the present trouble?

Jem was pressing a cup of tea in her hands. "Drink this. Della's always saying it'll make you feel better. Personally I think a shot of whiskey does the trick, but I'm trying my damnedest to be a lady." Dressed in denims, her mud-encrusted boots thrust out in front of her, Jem didn't look as though she had stepped from the pages of *Godey's*.

Abigail managed an unexpected smile. "Thanks for being you, Jem. I don't think I could bear it if you'd changed, too."

"Not likely, I'm afraid." Her gaze swept over Abigail's unlikely ensemble. "But I'm not sure I can say the same for you."

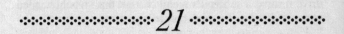

21

Abigail contained her frustration with a concerted effort. Joshua Hodges sloshed the remainder of his coffee into the delicate saucer as he spoke. The man couldn't seem to talk without gesturing, and he didn't have the good sense to replace the cup and saucer on the table while he waved his beefy arms about like two unwieldy, overstuffed sausages.

"Now, Abigail, we're two adults. No need to act as if what I'm suggesting is a surprise. I don't care about gossip. I'd be proud to have you as my wife." His stout face perspired earnestly as he leaned forward. "I'll take good care of you and the poor fatherless little mite."

Abigail flinched, despite herself. She still didn't like his negative references to her son. "I'm honored by your offer, but I'm sorry, the answer's still no."

A frown puckered his forehead, sending his blunt features into a scowl. "If you don't want to lose your ranch, you're going to have to get married."

"I don't believe that, Mr. Hodges." A thread of steel laced her words. She didn't like anyone telling her what she had to do. Especially in light of her feelings for Boyd. "I intend to keep running the Triple Cross, and I'll fight any takeover attempts."

"That probably isn't wise, Abigail. A woman alone . . . This is dangerous, lonely country."

A shiver of fear skittered up her spine. It was the second such reminder in two days. Not that she really wanted to believe anyone would take steps that drastic. Still . . .

"Instead of taking your answer, why don't I give you

some more time to think on it? Once you've mulled it around, you'll see that I'm right." Hodges pushed the words past his puffy lips while twisting his hat between sweaty palms. Abigail felt a momentary pang of sympathy for him. He really didn't do this well.

"I'm sorry. The answer won't change, but I would be glad to count you as a friend." Abigail's gentleness surfaced. She had no desire to hurt this man.

Joshua Hodges checked a growing scowl, then turned to the door. "We'll see."

She laid a restraining hand on his burly arm. "I'm both flattered and honored by your offer, but I'm truly not taking callers at this time. I'm sure I'll be seeing you at functions in town—the cattlemen's association, or at church. I'd hate to think that our conversation today will make that awkward."

He cleared his throat. "Just give it some more thought, Abigail. You can't have any future with that foreman of yours." Jamming his hat on his head, he left.

She shook her head, realizing the man simply couldn't take no for an answer. At least he wasn't threatening like Peterson, but still it didn't bode well to live among her rejected suitors.

Miranda stepped into the room, accompanied by the rattle of glasses on a tray. Abigail turned around and greeted her housekeeper with a weary smile. "He's the third one today."

"What did you tell him?"

"The same as the others." Abigail accepted the glass of tea that Miranda offered and drank the liquid gratefully. Turning down prospective husbands had worked up her thirst.

"What if the ranch does get blacklisted?"

Abigail lowered the glass. "Are you worried about your job? I know that everyone's concerned, but I have no intention of losing the ranch."

"What if you don't have a choice?"

Abigail's heart thudded painfully against her chest. "I don't believe it's that bad yet."

Miranda ran anxious fingers over the side table. "I been talkin' to Cameron."

Abigail lifted her eyebrows in surprise.

Miranda blushed, a mottled red covering her face. "I've been getting along better with him this last month."

Staring in surprise, Abigail tried to assess this new change, choosing her words carefully, wondering if Miranda's transformed appearance had something to do with her altered relationship with Cameron O'Donnell. "I'm glad to hear it."

"He's pretty worried," Miranda confided. "He thinks the ranch is vulnerable, what with not havin' a full crew and Peterson set on takin' over."

"And do you think that will happen?" Abigail asked quietly.

"Well . . . no. Neither does Cameron, really. Just that it could happen if you don't marry someone."

"It's not that simple." Abigail didn't want to remind Miranda that her heart belonged to someone already. Someone she couldn't marry.

"That's why I'm worried, Miz Fairchild. I know how you feel about Boyd, and I know what it's like to want love and not have it. But I also know how you feel about little Michael, about havin' him inherit the ranch some day, keeping alive what his daddy died for."

Abigail's eyelids drifted closed for a moment. Miranda had just verbalized her worst fears. A sickening lurch of uncertainty shot through her. What was she going to do?

"I just want you to know that I'll stand by you no matter what happens. I don't want to leave the Triple Cross, but wherever you go, I'll go."

Tears stung anew. The support from friends and loyal employees was ripping her apart. Because all it would take was a simple yes to one of her marriage proposals to keep the ranch together without a battle that could cost injuries, even lives, most certainly their jobs.

Remembering her husband's brutal murder, Abigail wondered if she could be responsible for anyone's death while defending the ranch. Could she inflict that kind of pain on their loved ones? Her voice was ragged as she answered. "I have more to consider than I realized, Miranda. The enormity of this entire ordeal is beginning to sink in."

"Maybe I shouldn't have said anything, Miz Fairchild. I don't want to make things worse."

"Offering your loyalty could hardly make it worse. I wasn't considering everything involved. I've been selfish, thinking only of what *I* wanted."

"I don't believe that," Miranda protested. "You're always thinkin' of others. There's not a selfish bone in your body."

Abigail's laugh was caustic. "I'm willing to exchange the happiness of everyone on this ranch for my own."

"Not only your own," Miranda reminded her soberly.

The pain in Abigail's heart intensified. Was she willing to wound Boyd in exchange for the security and happiness of everyone else?

Days passed as Abigail studiously avoided Boyd. She saw the hurt in his eyes as she purposely stayed hidden in the ranch house, sometimes peeking down the stairwell at him as he asked Miranda about her. The conflict on Miranda's face as she lied to Boyd about imagined headaches and other vagaries. The concern in Boyd's face as he worried about her health. The dawning awareness and deeper hurt when he realized she was avoiding him.

Abigail suffered as well, both from the pain she caused Boyd and from being cooped up inside the house all the time. She didn't realize how much she had changed in a month. Now she longed for the tang of fresh air whipping against her face as she rode unfettered across the countryside, the stretching of her muscles that no longer wanted to be confined.

Depressed, she stared out the window one afternoon. Michael was napping in the next room, and she watched the men as they rode the cattle, envying them their freedom. It was absurd, she realized. She was a prisoner of her own fears and indecision. Her face fell into a frown as she watched Boyd cross the yard. He shouldn't be here, she thought as longing pierced a path through her.

He strode up to the front door, and she heard him knock. Miranda answered, and their voices drifted upward to her open window. She couldn't make out the words, but assumed they were part of the same routine that had been played out the past few days. Expecting to see him walking away, she was surprised when she didn't see him back away from the front door and retreat from the ranch house.

She was even more surprised to hear the pounding noise of his boots on the stairs. Panicked, she stared around the room, realizing in an instant that she couldn't hide, that to even think so was a foolish notion.

Boyd stormed into the bedroom. The grim determination on his face caused her to take an unconscious step backward.

"Don't bother," he barked out. "There's no place to go unless you plan to hurl yourself out the window to avoid me."

Guessing at the pain that prompted his remark, she stayed her ground, keeping her voice even. "I don't want to avoid you."

"You could have fooled me." Bitterly he stared at her, hurt and anger warring for dominance. "But that's not what I came to talk about."

Feeling her hands tremble with nervousness, wishing she could fling herself in his arms and seek the comfort she knew he could provide, instead she shoved her hands behind her back to hide them. "What did you want to discuss?"

"The cattle," he bit out. "We're missin' better than a hundred head."

She couldn't contain the gasp that seemed to fill the sudden silence. It was all happening again, the same circumstances that had led to Michael's death. The cattle had started disappearing, and he had stubbornly believed he could catch the rustlers without getting hurt himself. Now he was lying in a pine box, six feet under the ground, proving just how wrong he had been.

"We've searched the whole spread. They haven't wandered off. They've been stolen," Boyd continued, his voice and expression flat, only his snapping eyes betraying his feelings.

"But who—"

"Don't you think I've asked myself that a hundred times already? And it's certainly not the same person who rustled the last cattle from the Triple Cross."

No, Cushman's son had been hanged for his crimes. This was a new threat, unknown and that much more frightening.

"Why now?" Abigail whispered, unable to mask her despair.

"That's pretty clear." Boyd met her eyes, forcing her to read the truth. "Someone wants the Triple Cross. And if framin' me for the disappearance of your cattle will make me leave, then the ranch will be easy pickins."

Fear chased cold currents of disbelief through her blood. "But I don't believe you're responsible. No one could ever make me believe that."

Gratitude fleetingly chased across his face before his expression sobered. "But the rustlin' makes your situation that much more vulnerable."

Fear was slaking its relentless way to her heart, and she felt it clutch without mercy. "What do you mean?"

"You're close to being blacklisted," he said, his voice flat. "You could lose your army contracts for the horses. And now anyone who's waverin' about whether to stick with you will know that your cattle are disappearing. Along with your choices."

"What do you mean?" she whispered, unable to tear her gaze from the frightening countenance of his face.

"You're going to have to choose one of your suitors and agree to marry him." The words were wrung out of him, like blood from a stone, the pain of them etched across his features.

"But I don't want to marry anyone else!" she cried, ready to admit her love for him.

He met her gaze steadily. "Are you ready to throw away your son's legacy? With the cloud that'll be hangin' over me from the cattle that are stolen, I won't even be able to help you defend the ranch. It's time I walked away, Abigail. You

owe it to yourself, your son, and all the people who count on
you."

His integrity stabbed her. So sharp and clear. No murky
edges.

But her heart was breaking as well. The tears pooled in
her eyes and spilled over her cheeks. "Don't make me do
this, Boyd."

He kept his hands at his sides with an effort, refusing to
reach out and give her the comfort she needed. "No one can
decide except you, Abigail."

"Promise you won't leave," she begged.

Indecision etched his face.

"I'll make a decision, but only if you'll stay," she
pledged, brushing away the tears that threatened to blind
her.

"I won't leave right away," he finally agreed. "But once
you decide, you know I can't stay." The full enormity of his
pain flashed in his eyes, and Abigail wanted desperately to
reach out to him, to pull him close and assure him that no
one would ever take his place.

But it was a promise she couldn't make.

And he saw that in her eyes. Turning away, he left as he
came, the clinking of his spurs the only sound in the
tension-filled silence.

Then he was gone.

Swallowing the bitter lump in her throat, Abigail stared
unseeing into the horizon, knowing he had taken her heart
with him.

 *22*

The birds sang, but Abigail heard only muted dullness. The sun pushed insistent beams through a latticework of tree branches and leaves, but she saw only bleak gray. Wildflowers swayed in the gentle breeze, releasing their pungent fragrance, but she didn't smell the lavender loveliness.

It simply wasn't fair. She had suffered the largest loss she had ever expected in her life when her husband had been murdered, and now she was facing another loss—one she suspected might kill her. For the first time in her life, Abigail couldn't fathom the cruel twists that fate dealt her.

Because in the past weeks Boyd had kept his promise. He had stayed, but he had also kept his distance. The agony of that distance had only intensified, especially as Edward Peterson and Joshua Hodges renewed their courting.

It was an odd combination of suitors. Peterson threatened more than he cajoled. Hodges continued his bumbling calls that made Abigail want to scream. Remembering the heat of Boyd's kisses, the passion she had discovered in his arms, she knew that she could not willingly go to another man.

When two other bachelor ranchers, one old enough to be her father, the other an ill-tempered curmudgeon, also extended proposals, Abigail knew she couldn't delay the decision much longer. Peterson had told her bluntly that he would not wait much longer to take what he wanted, whether she agreed to marriage or not.

The threat of blacklisting had been delayed only by the rumors of the marriage proposals that Abigail was considering. The community was waiting and watching . . . and narrowing her choices.

Guiding Dolly down the road toward the McIntire ranch, Abigail held on to the desperate hope that Jem might come up with an idea. Logically Abigail knew that she had considered every alternative, and none of them was workable; but she wasn't ready to give up on her love for Boyd.

The fact that he was willing to sacrifice everything for her touched the part of her soul that he had already branded. Because if he walked away, he not only gave up their love, he also relinquished his relationship with her son, his position on the ranch and in the community.

Because he would have to leave.

He would drift as he told her his father had done when he had lost his love. The picture that brought to mind tore another hole in her already damaged heart.

Seeing the McIntire ranch up ahead, she gathered her failing courage and hoped that Jem would be somewhere nearby. But no one seemed to be close at hand as she approached another canopy of trees. She spurred Dolly on, anticipating the shade she would find beneath the leaves. In the distance she spotted a rider and wondered if it could be Jem or Reese. From here she couldn't even distinguish the person's gender.

Dolly snorted nervously as they continued down the road. Having to rein in the normally gentle mare, Abigail couldn't understand her sudden willfulness, her reluctance to ride forward. Dolly pulled suddenly to one side, and Abigail nearly slid off. At the same instant shots rang out from the arbor of trees. Horrified, Abigail hung on to Dolly's mane as the shots peppered the road.

Galloping wildly across the field, Abigail felt the air squeezing from her lungs as bullets followed her zigzagging path through the McIntire's grazing land.

When she saw the tall outline of a man on horseback barreling toward her, she didn't know whether to be grateful or to pull Dolly around and try to escape what could be another threat. But Dolly had a mind of her own now as she galloped onward.

Praying that they were headed toward safety instead of danger, Abigail held on as tightly as she could. But when Dolly was faced with the presence of another horse galloping toward her, she reared backward in fright. Abigail had the sudden sickening feeling of losing her grip, then weightlessness as the horse fell from beneath her. She fell to the ground, its rigid, unyielding bulk stunning her.

Her head snapped downward as well, and a curtain of darkness fell over her.

Large, capable arms scooped her up, then placed her in the saddle in front of him, taking her away from the scene of her near murder.

"Who do you think it was?" Jem's voice was low and anxious as she questioned her husband.

Reese sounded equally grim. "I heard the shots and saw Abigail ridin' like hell across the field. A man on horseback rode off as soon as I headed toward her. The way he lit out, I knew he was the one doing the shooting."

"Do you think she'll be okay?" Jem asked as she chafed Abigail's cold hand.

"Just a small bump on her head," Reese confirmed. "I didn't see any rocks on the ground that she might have smashed her head on. A more experienced rider could have hung on. Mostly she just got the wind knocked out of her."

"I hope that's all," Jem responded, seeing how pale and delicate her friend looked. Knowing what Abigail had been through in the past two years, and aware of how much of that had been her fault, Jem fought tears of her own.

Reese's strong hand came down on her shoulder. "Don't do this to yourself, Jem. She'll be okay."

"She looks so defenseless."

"Which is probably why she was a target."

Hearing a noise at the study doors, they both looked up to see a frantic, ragged-looking Boyd. They had sent a rider to tell him about the accident. He must have ridden like the wind to have arrived so quickly.

"How is she?" Boyd asked without preamble, striding to her side, then halting as he gazed at her pale face.

Myriad emotions flitted across his face. Pain, fear, and love. Jem and Reese exchanged a glance.

"She'll be okay," Reese assured him. "Just a nasty fall. Soon as she wakes up, she'll be all right."

"What if she doesn't?" Boyd intoned, his eyes never leaving Abigail.

"Don't talk like that," Jem ordered, feeling his fear, knowing it fueled her own. "I know Abigail Fairchild, and it'll take a hell of a lot more than falling off a horse to do her in."

Boyd met Reese's eyes briefly and saw the reassurance there. "What happened?" he asked his old friend.

Reese briefly outlined what he had witnessed.

"Someone shot at her?" Boyd echoed blankly. "I know the Triple Cross is a powerful lure, but to kill Abby . . ."

Reese and Jem exchanged another knowing look.

"It might have just been a scare tactic," Reese offered.

Boyd pinned him in an intensive stare. "Do you think so?"

Shoving a hand through his tousled hair, Reese met his friend's eyes. "Not really. The shots were too close. If she hadn't veered off the road and torn through the field . . ." He shook his head, not finishing the thought. But it didn't need verbalizing. She could have been killed.

"I should have already left," Boyd said dully. "Then this never would have happened."

"Or you might not be around now to protect her," Reese added sagely. "What if she marries someone and the threats don't stop? Or she chooses the wrong one and is killed because of it?"

"Or what if she chooses someone who was willing to kill her?" Jem's words chased a chill through them all.

Boyd stared at them both. "What's her other choice? Give up the Triple Cross?"

"It doesn't have to come to that," Reese asserted.

"You have a way out?"

"Yes." Reese didn't take his eyes from his friend. "You stand beside her."

"And we'll stand behind you," Jem chimed in.

"You don't know what you're sayin'," Boyd objected, staring between them. "There's more than you know—"

"Between you and Abigail," Jem finished for him. "We know. And this time we won't fail you." Remembered pain and guilt flashed in her eyes. "No matter what it takes."

"You don't have to do this," Boyd protested.

"You saved my life." Reese stood next to his wife, his gaze sober. "That's something I don't forget."

"Me either," Jem agreed. "Besides, I need a second chance to make up for not believing you before."

"Cattle are disappearing again from the Triple Cross," Boyd told them, watching their reactions.

"No doubt by whoever shot at Abigail," Reese guessed.

Boyd hadn't made that connection.

"To get you to leave and have a clear field with Abigail," Jem added, the realization shading her voice. "With you gone, if she didn't decide quickly enough, they could get rid of her."

Boyd's blood ran cold as he glanced back at Abigail's wan face. To his relief, her eyelashes were beginning to flutter. Tactfully Jem moved away, and Boyd took her place at Abigail's side.

"Abby," he said softly, not caring that Jem and Reese could hear. Stroking her cheek with a feather-light touch, he could feel her stirring beneath his hands. Gratitude and anger welled within him. Gratitude that she was awakening and intense anger at whoever had done this.

"Boyd?" Her weak voice was filled with disbelief and gratitude.

"You're going to be all right," he told her, not removing his hand from hers.

She looked around gingerly, her eyes focusing on Jem and Reese as well. But she merely intensified her grip on Boyd's hand as she saw her friends. "Did you see who was shooting?"

Boyd flicked a glance at Reese, who took a step forward. "No, Abigail. He left too quickly."

She started to raise her head, and a flash of pain gripped her.

"Not so soon, Abby. You'll have a pretty good-sized goose egg on your head for a while." Boyd sounded possessive as he continued to hold her hand.

Tentatively she touched the lump on the back of her head, flinching at the contact. "Why would someone want to shoot me?"

"To get the Triple Cross," Reese answered bluntly.

All three heads swung in his direction.

"She needs to know the truth." Reese trained his eyes on Abigail. "You're going to have to watch your back at all times."

Boyd and Abigail's eyes met, both instantly remembering her experience on the trail. Suddenly it didn't seem so farfetched to believe that she had been pushed into the water that had nearly drowned her. With that same memory came ones of John Sims watching her, his eyes always fixed on her.

Abigail clutched Boyd's hand more tightly in hers. "You won't leave?"

It would be easier to carve out his heart and lay it next to her. Protectiveness roared within him. "No, Abby. Whatever happens, we'll see it through together." Until she made her final decision. The one that would take her away forever.

Two tears slid from beneath her eyelashes. Forgetting Jem and Reese, Boyd reached out with his work-worn knuckles and eased the tears from the satin of her skin. He didn't know how they would solve this impossible situation, but he couldn't leave her. Now, or ever.

23

Like wary gladiators, the men rode watch in pairs. Almost half the men from the McIntire ranch had joined the ranks at the Triple Cross. But still the threats came.

Two men were wounded—not seriously—but they were shot while on late watch, making the nighttime especially fearsome. The stars were no longer a comforting blanket layered in the sky, but a disturbing reminder that the darkness hid potential gunmen.

Abigail paced the carpet in the parlor, not caring that she'd countlessly retraced her anxious steps. She had checked on her son a dozen times already, but knew he slept safely upstairs. Miranda had wisely suggested that someone else sleep in the big house besides the women and the baby. This was no time to be concerned with sensibilities and what outsiders would say.

Cameron O'Donnell had offered his protection and took up residence in the upper wing. To offset his presence as the sole male in the household, Abigail had insisted that Boyd take the room next to Cameron's.

She had dismissed his concern, knowing that nothing else could further damage her reputation. They were reduced to a life-and-death situation. Having come to accept that she would probably lose the Triple Cross, she wanted to make sure that there was no loss of life as well.

But Boyd was spending nearly every minute in the saddle, stumbling into the house and into bed for only a few hours each night. It was as though he felt he personally had to watch over every foot of the ranch.

Abigail did not miss the similarities to the days preceding her husband's death. The fear that she would lose Boyd, too, made her wish she could simply give up, turn the ranch over to Peterson, and get on with her life.

She was convinced now that Peterson had instigated the trouble here. He had warned her that he would stop at nothing to get the Triple Cross, and she believed him. At Boyd's insistence, Abigail had stayed in the house, away from the line of danger, but the confinement irritated her.

Now she thought it was time to tell Boyd her concerns about John Sims. She suspected that he was working for Peterson. It made perfect sense. Sims watched her every move, cataloging it in detail for someone who wished either to marry or murder her.

And of course there were others, men who had put their bids in for marriage, a subtle method of staking a claim on the Triple Cross.

Hearing a noise at the front door, Abigail stopped her pacing, her heart beating rapidly. She glanced upstairs, certain that Cameron was already asleep. Retrieving the gun that she had hidden in the side table in the parlor, Abigail inched toward the front door.

When it pushed open suddenly, she jerked the pistol upward, ready to pull the trigger.

But Boyd's weary face greeted her. Too tired even to protest the gun she held, he walked inside and slid into a chair.

Relieved, she lowered the gun to the table and rushed to Boyd's side. "Why are you doing this? Riding all day and all night? Will it do you any good to get yourself killed?"

"Good evenin' to you, too, Abigail."

Regretting the shrewish tone she recognized in her own voice, still she railed out at him. "Would you tell me why you're doing this?"

He leaned forward suddenly, the weariness in his eyes replaced with a burning fire she recognized almost too late. "Because I love you, Abigail Fairchild. God knows why! You're always tearin' into something you shouldn't. Haven't got enough sense to take the easy way out, and now you're greetin' me with a loaded gun!"

"You love me?" she whispered, delight cloaking the words.

One strong hand reached out to cradle her neck, pulling her face next to his. "That I do, Abigail Fairchild. God help me, but I do."

Her lips launched against his, the frenzy of their restraint in the past few weeks bursting through. Unbidden came the memory of his scent, tasting of salt and mystery. It was no longer enough to fulfill those desires with memories.

Her desire reached him, and wordlessly he lifted her into his arms and swept up the stairs. Twining her arms around his neck, she buried her face in his chest as he navigated the hallway and pushed open the door to her bedroom.

Not bothering to light the lamps, instead he relied on the moonlight spearing the night, drifting through the lace curtains that billowed at the window. Fingers of light danced across her face as he lowered her to the bed, illuminating the golden strands of her hair, making them gleam. He picked up a handful of her hair, relishing its texture, like raw silk against his fingers.

The impatience he sensed in her downstairs was replaced with a sudden tenderness as she stroked his jaw and then buried her fingers in his hair.

When he heard the sob that clutched her, he felt any remaining reserve in his heart melt. What would he do without this woman? She had levered him into an impossible situation, yet he wouldn't be anywhere else on earth. If he lost his reputation, even his life, it wouldn't compare with the loss if he couldn't have her.

Tenderly he lowered his lips, asking with the gesture for her reciprocating love. She met them with equal desperation. His tongue danced with hers, tasting her desire, fervently hoping for her love.

With a gentleness he didn't know he possessed, Boyd pushed away her clothing. It didn't matter that he had dreamed of this moment ever since that fateful telegram had arrived, disrupting their lives, putting their passion out of reach.

Instead, all that mattered was the woman who lay beneath him, her skin, all satin and velvet, abrading his with its utter softness. When she lifted her eyes trustingly to his, he wished somehow he could merge their souls at that moment so that she would always remain his.

The movements were gentle, the urgency restrained, yet the passion was matchless. When he took her breast to suckle, he felt her shudder and heard her repressed cry. Then her lips imitated his motion, flowering over his flattened nipple and bringing it to life.

His hands skimmed over the valley of her waist, the bow of her hips, the flatness of her belly. When he would have continued the exploration, her whisper floated to his ears.

"Now please, Boyd. I need to feel you inside of me. All of you."

He complied, entering her gently, but found her slick with anticipation. His thrusts gained momentum, filling her to the length of her womb, wishing he could remain with her like this always. Her movements matched his, the sense of urgency increasing.

Her hands roved over him, seeking what she had been denied.

His mouth devoured hers, answering that need.

Together they rode the stars, their bodies saying what words wouldn't allow. When he spilled his seed, he wished fervently that he had left a permanent mark, one she could never erase.

Her shudders and sudden trembling told him that he might have achieved a portion of that wish.

He didn't withdraw at once, and she savored the sensation of having him fill her. When she felt his fullness subside a bit, still she discouraged him from pulling away. If they could stay joined, she could convince herself that this was forever. That he would always be hers.

Refusing to allow reality to intrude, she stroked his back and gently kissed the tender underside of his chin and throat.

For now this magnificent man was hers. Refusing to think of the future, she grasped the moment and held it with all her might, knowing how easily it could be taken away.

"You're a fool. I'm not paying you to screw up!"

"And you're not payin' me enough to kill her. I never agreed to be part of a murder. I told you that from the beginning. Scare her, yes. But I won't kill her."

"Well, it's too late to back out now. How do you think your friend would like to find out that you've been laying a trap?"

The sucked-in breath was evidence of his reaction. "It'd be pretty hard to expose me without givin' yourself away."

The laugh was sarcastic and almost evil. "You worry too much. Just a little longer, and there'll be plenty to go around."

"You said we'd scare her and she'd run. She's not runnin', and I tell you, I won't be part of killin' her."

A trigger cocked in the darkness. "Would you rather I kill you?"

"You wouldn't!" But there was no conviction in his voice, rather a fear he couldn't disguise.

"It's as easy to kill two as one."

"You mean it." The words were laced with shock.

"Nothing's going to stand between me and that ranch. You can have your share or you can die. The choice is yours."

But there was no choice, and he knew it. Just as he had all along.

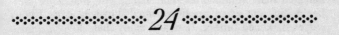

24

Miranda walked quietly into the study, her eyes devouring Cameron's back and shoulders. It was an innocent diversion, one she couldn't indulge in often. Despite their changed relationship, she still felt awkward and uncertain around him.

He turned suddenly, shoving the desk drawer closed, his face shadowed. But she had seen the guilt he tried to hide. Wondering suddenly what he was hiding, she felt a warning bell ringing in her head.

What did she and Abigail know of this man? Despite her feelings for him, she was aware that he was a virtual stranger, one who was privy to the financial heart of the Triple Cross.

"Did you need something, Miranda?"

She nodded her head, searching for an excuse, because suddenly she couldn't bear to share her concerns with him. Not if he could somehow be involved.

She had intended to spill out her worries to him, but now wondered if that was prudent. Despite her attraction to him, she knew her loyalty belonged with her employer. The thought that he could be planning to harm Miz Fairchild touched already frazzled emotions. Because just looking at him still made her heart pound, her soul soar.

"I thought you might be getting hungry," she offered weakly.

"We just had breakfast an hour ago."

"I meant something to drink," she replied, flustered by the steady regard in his unblinking eyes.

He stood suddenly and stepped from behind the desk. "Is that why you sought me out, Miranda?"

Had he always seemed so tall and overpowering? she wondered. Or had her suspicions run rampant along with her desire? She grabbed for an excuse. "I thought perhaps you'd like to share some coffee with me."

A different set of emotions flitted across his eyes. Ebony eyes darkened further. "I would enjoy that."

Relieved, she nearly sighed aloud. "I have some cake, too," she babbled, wondering how to keep up this pretense for long. The strain was already affecting her good sense.

But his hand was suddenly on her arm, staying her motion, effectively stopping her words. "Miranda, you don't need excuses."

Guilt rushed through her, fiery and sudden, accompanied by an equal flash of heat his touch had caused. "I'm not sure what you mean."

His eyes glittered, seemingly fathomless in their dark depths. "I think you do." Still, he reached behind him and pulled up a sheaf of papers, along with a pen and ink. "But we can make today another lesson, if you wish."

Relief, disappointment, and regret pushed their way through her. He had been tutoring her ever since he had discovered she couldn't read. While she was deeply grateful for his tactful help, a time in which they had grown to know each other, part of her wanted him to acknowledge her simply as a woman. Yet, as her initial suspicions stabbed her again, she wondered if that was wise.

He suddenly replaced the papers. He didn't seem to notice that the ink spilled as he pulled her close.

"What is it, Miranda?"

She shook her head, knowing she couldn't voice her suspicions. But then she looked at him and saw the pain crossing his sharp features.

"I've told you all about myself, but I don't really know anything about you."

A different sort of suspicion flashed across his face. "This is rather sudden. What makes you ask?"

The truth stabbed at her and seemed the best course.

"Because I'm not sure about what's between us." She blushed, then paled again. "And I want to know more about you."

"My past, you mean," he replied bluntly. His hands stilled, but he didn't remove them from her hair.

She nodded, almost afraid to move. She needed to know, had to know. But what if she learned something that would take him away from her? True, there was nothing between them but a few kisses that she had cherished. And an awakening that she had never expected. In her most secret fantasies, however, she had dreamed that maybe it would become more. Dreams she scarcely allowed herself to indulge in. But this man was wrapped up in all her hopes, which could shatter with his words.

"It's not a pretty picture," he told her flatly, the scarce light going out of his eyes, leaving them like a dull slate of granite. "You've probably guessed that I used to be more than a bookkeeper."

Again she nodded, afraid almost to breathe.

"I owned my own business—an investment brokerage. It was still growing, and I was putting the majority of the profits back into the business. My wife enjoyed everything my money could buy, but she wanted more. And she found it in one of my clients. He was wealthy, unattached. She left me for him. But she decided to clean out all of my business accounts before she left."

"What did your clients do?" Miranda asked, horrified.

"Most of them were anxious to press charges. All except James Whitaker."

Miranda's brows lifted. "Jem McIntire's father?"

"The same. He covered what had been taken and offered me an accounting position with the bank he partially owned. But I'd lost my reputation. No one was willing to trust me with their money again."

"Except Miz Fairchild," she whispered.

"On Jem McIntire's recommendation."

Their lives were as entwined as the mountains that bisected the territory, guarding, protecting, and blocking them.

"I'm sorry, Cameron. Sorry that she hurt you and stole your reputation."

His eyes softened. "My reputation, not the money?"

"Of course. Money can be replaced. A reputation's harder to get back." Somehow they were close together again, the space between them diminished, his arms secured around her. "But not impossible, Cameron."

He caught up and met her gaze. "Somehow I think with you at my side it could be within reach. I never thought that before."

"Do you miss her?" Miranda asked, hating to, but having to know.

"Not in the way you think. I miss what I'd once wanted from life." He laughed bitterly. "I thought I had everything, a decent business, a wife I loved. I didn't realize her love was wrapped up in something I could never give her. All that was missing for me were children."

"Children?" she echoed, hope blossoming despite all her carefully erected barriers.

"I thought she wanted them, too. But they weren't in her plans. Fool that I was, I kept on hoping."

Miranda laid her hand on his, watching the fine strength of his slender fingers. "It's never foolish to hope . . . to dream . . ."

Their lips met with one accord. Miranda wasn't certain who moved first, and knew it didn't matter. She felt a blaze of passion, of hope, between them. Disregarding the suspicions she had held about him, she melted against him, welcoming his hard warmth. But when they broke apart, regret was etched across his face.

"I have nothing left to give you. I can't ask you to share in my disgrace, an uncertain future."

Knowing this was no time to hide behind her shyness with men, Miranda answered hotly. "Is it better to have a future alone, with no hope of love?" Her voice grew ragged with wanting. "Or babies? Is that better for either of us?"

Uncertainty colored his face for the first time since she had met him. "Would you consider a life with me, Miranda?"

"I would want everything," she replied, knowing it was

time to unveil the entire truth, to shed the remainder of her reserve. "You and children, if that's possible. I won't take just part of that." She knew it was ridiculous at her age to have such notions, but she couldn't give them up without a fight.

His hand reached out to stroke her hair. "A baby with shining red hair and cinnamon eyes," he mused, unexpected excitement and wonder filling his voice.

"I hope not," she answered, holding back a sob of happiness.

"You're beautiful, Miranda Abernathy, and I won't hear otherwise."

She blushed then, a sweeping crimson flood of color. "I'm not!"

But Cameron chuckled, before humor fled and passion took its place. "Yes, Miranda, and I plan to discover every beautiful, delicious inch."

Her gasp was cut off as his mouth covered hers. Suddenly her dreams seemed almost within reach. Her suspicions were waylaid. And the air simmered with the untold tension.

Randy Kreiger unsaddled his horse, and Boyd greeted him with quiet relief.

"Good to have you back."

Randy set aside the saddle. "Like to have never got those cattle sold and onto the train."

"Glad you sent the men back first, though. We needed every one."

"Took a little doin' to convince them that leavin' a town full of women and whiskey was the right thing to do."

Boyd managed a halfhearted grin. "I can see where that could be a mite difficult."

"Got a good price for the herd, though."

"Good," Boyd replied, still distracted.

"Don't get too excited."

Boyd ran a hand over his forehead, weariness and worry marking lines in his face. "Just got a plateful here."

Randy frowned. "Any more trouble lately?"

"Two men shot. An attempt on Miz Fairchild."

"What!" Randy stopped grooming his horse. "Who'd do a thing like that?"

"Someone who wants the Triple Cross."

"That's pretty high stakes."

"High enough to kill for." Boyd stared at the mountains surrounding the ranch, wondering who might be hiding in them, ready to attack.

"Can we get some extra men?" Randy asked.

"Already done. I hired some, and we have half the McIntires' crew."

"Won't that leave them hurting?"

"Reese has put out the word. I imagine he'll have new men hired fairly soon."

"Then you have everything under control."

Boyd's laugh came out more like a caustic bark. "I'm glad you think so. From this end it looks like we're swimmin' underwater and we're about ten miles from shore."

"Any chance Miz Fairchild will marry one of the other owners and put an end to this?"

Boyd felt the fist of pain clutch his heart. "It's probably the only way she'll keep her ranch."

"That's important to her, isn't it?"

"Her and little Michael."

"What about you, Boyd?"

Boyd ran a hand over the horse's flanks. "I'm just an old cowhand. You know that, Randy."

Randy's grin was crooked. "Yeah. I know."

"I'd like you to set up a new watch," Boyd continued. "I need someone I can trust watchin' the weak side leadin' to Peterson's place."

"Why there?"

"He's the one who wants the ranch. And I don't think he'll stop at anything to get it."

"Think he's behind the attacks?"

"He gave the ultimatum while we were gone. If O'Donnell hadn't stepped in, we might have already lost the Triple Cross."

"O'Donnell?" Randy's face was marked with surprise.

"Yeah. Kind of set me back, too. But I think he's got a special interest here."

Randy continued to look puzzled. "You don't think he's vying for Miz Fairchild's hand?"

Boyd shook his hand. "Nope, but she's not the only woman on the ranch."

The possibilities ran through Randy's mind, and shock won out as he stared at Boyd. "You don't mean Miranda?"

"I think so. At any rate, he's willin' to protect the ranch."

"You don't say." Randy drew out the words and then deliberately turned to his horse.

Boyd studied his friend. "What do you know?"

Randy shrugged. "Just talk." Realizing what he had just said, Randy averted his face. "Hell, I know you've got reason to hate badmouthin'. Just forget it."

"No, I want to hear."

Uncomfortably, Randy twisted the currycomb in his hand. Then he met Boyd's eyes. "Word is he's a thief. That's why no one else will hire him."

Shock rocked through Boyd, and he wondered if he could fight treachery from within and without. "Do you know any more?"

"Just that he ran a business handlin' other people's money. One day he said it was all gone. Somebody must've bailed him out 'cause he never went to jail."

Boyd's blood ran cold at the thought. If O'Donnell was working for whoever wanted the Triple Cross, he could strip the finances and leave the ranch at its most vulnerable. Without funds to hire more hands, the ranch would fall to whoever had the most manpower for a land grab.

Maybe it was time to turn his back on his own past and realize that he couldn't always stand up for the underdog. If O'Donnell had been guilty, and he allowed him free access without watching him, it would be his own fault if they lost the Triple Cross.

Boyd met Abigail's eyes across the dinner table. Heat enveloped them both, along with a growing sense of desperation. Miranda served the meal, and she, too, was unusually quiet, seemingly absorbed in something far removed from them. Cameron O'Donnell took his meals as he always did in the study. Boyd had asked the man to join them, but he had declined.

A cry came from the direction of little Michael's room.

Abigail started to rise.

"No, let me get him." Boyd left the table and disappeared up the stairs. A few minutes later he returned with Michael, whose tears had been dried. A smile suffused his plump face.

Abigail watched them, the interplay between the tall, rugged man and her tiny son. Boyd gentled his immense strength for the toddler, as natural with him as if Michael were his own. Knowing how much the child and man meant to each other, she couldn't even bear thinking of wrenching them apart.

Boyd sat down at the table, Michael in his lap. Michael waved his hands toward the plate, diving into the mashed potatoes closest to him. Boyd patiently captured those exuberant hands, wiped them off, and gave the baby a more appropriate piece of bread to occupy him.

Happy now, Michael chattered away in his own specialized language, one only his mother and those closest to him understood. Boyd answered him, keeping his attention occupied, while Michael reached for the chain that held the pocket watch Abigail had given him. Small, chubby fingers grabbed for the "horsie" he saw on the watch, and Boyd patiently showed him the gold carving.

Abigail felt the whole of her heart being squeezed shut. It was horribly unfair to think of separating these two. The love between them was clear. Would any other man care for her child in the same way? She pictured Peterson's cold, calculating stare and Joshua Hodges's pitying attitude toward Michael. Somehow she doubted that either man could ever be considered father material.

But if she didn't choose someone other than Boyd to marry, she would lose her son's legacy. Everything his father had died for.

Her gaze met and caught Boyd's as he dropped a kiss on

Michael's downy head. How could she ever make this decision?

"You're not eating," Boyd pointed out quietly.

"Neither are you."

He stared down at Michael's busy little hands as they tried to destroy his dinner. "I've had plenty."

"Why don't we go into the parlor?" Abigail suggested quietly, wishing desperately for the normality they had been denied.

Boyd agreed, picking up Michael and carrying him into the other room. Trailing behind them, Abigail saw their two heads bent close together, Boyd's so dark, Michael's so fair.

The toddler gurgled and laughed as Boyd nuzzled his cheek and then bounced him in the air. It was a special relationship, one she had been afraid to encourage, one she wouldn't have discouraged for all the world. Now the consequences were tearing her apart.

Boyd set Michael down on the rug that carpeted the middle of the room and then turned to pick up the fragile crystal candlesticks that were on the sidetable, placing them high up in the bookshelf out of harm's way. Then he pushed the table against the wall, leaving a clear space with nothing for Michael to crash into.

The child ran the length of the room, unfettered by restraints, his laugh bouncing off the high ceiling. He and Boyd fell into a game of peekaboo.

Abigail found herself laughing, despite the heavy burden of worry, to see a man far too large for the delicate parlor furniture engaging in a wicked game of peekaboo with her now chortling son.

Still fascinated with her son's growth from baby to child, Abigail watched Michael's plump legs as he toddled toward Boyd, who encouraged him with outstretched arms.

This was the one area of his life in which Boyd had never held back since Abigail had known him. With Michael he gave all.

Protecting himself from other possibly painful involvements, he had never felt that way about her child. Instead he had loosened his heart, giving Michael free rein there.

Tears stung, sending Boyd and Michael into a hazed relief of blurred light as she watched them. Both so precious. Which one could she cheat of what he so richly deserved?

Michael looked up at her then, laughing to include his mother in their game. Wide blue eyes that he had inherited from her fixed on Abigail, crinkling in renewed laughter. Her time was running out as certain as the moon that climbed across the darkened sky to send night into the following day.

Her heart broke even more, knowing a decision had to be made. Regardless of that decision, life would never be the same again for any of them.

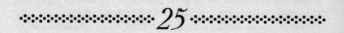

25

More cattle disappeared. It was clear they were being stolen during nighttime raids. Under the cover of darkness, many sins were concealed. Boyd rode the land like a relentless warrior, but still he couldn't prevent the rustling. Each time it was a well-planned attack, almost as though it was an inside job.

Boyd angled his head toward the fallow lay of the land. The thought had struck him more than once. Remembering the suspicions that Abigail had finally voiced about John Sims, he couldn't reconcile the notion of the steady but impressionable young man cold-bloodedly calculating murder attempts and rustling maneuvers.

Still, he couldn't dismiss her concerns. He could hear Abigail's voice even now.

"No matter where I went, I could see him watching me. While I ate, when I was riding. It didn't matter. If I turned around, there he was, as though he was memorizing every move I made. It was creepy, unnerving. Boyd, he scares me. What if he's behind these attempts?"

Indeed, what if he was? Boyd wasn't certain if it would be better to keep the man on the Triple Cross and watch him, or send him packing. The latter might be more preferable, but then they wouldn't be able to keep tabs on his movements.

From his vantage point on top of the ridge, Boyd spotted Randy in the adjacent grazing land and made up his mind. Quickly he galloped over the sloping hills, under the brush of the towering juniper trees. The other man was concentrating on the cattle and didn't see his approach.

"Randy!"

He visibly started and whirled around. "Boyd. Didn't hear you." Rearranging his features into a welcoming smile, he coiled his rope and let it slide between his fingers. "I'm a little jumpy with everything that's been going on."

"Better to be on the jumpy side than have someone catch you off guard." Boyd stared down at him, glad to have the man as his second in command. "We need to talk."

Randy's lips tightened. "Whatever you say."

Boyd swung down from the horse, letting the reins trail in the grass. "It's about the missing cattle."

"Yep?"

"Don't you think it's strange that the rustler seems to know right where to hit each time?"

Randy scratched his head. "Now that you mention it, I guess it is."

"I've been givin' it some thought. Maybe someone on the inside's involved."

"You got any ideas about who?"

"Just a hunch, nothin' solid. But I'd like to keep an eye on John Sims."

"Sims? Why do you think it's him?"

Boyd debated about telling him the whole truth. "Let's just say I have my reasons. Good ones."

Randy shrugged. "All right by me. What do you want me to do?"

"Watch him when you're in the bunkhouse. See if he's actin' strange. Put him on duties close to the ranch so he's not out on the far ranges."

"That'll be easy."

"I just hope it's enough."

Randy looped the rope in his hands. "You worry too much, Boyd."

But Boyd's eyes were sober. "Seems like that's all I do these days."

Randy hesitated. "I'm not quite sure how to put this, but are things all right between you and Miz Fairchild?"

Boyd didn't even react to his words. He realized gossip about them was commonplace. Only her decision regarding her numerous marriage offers had kept the ranch from being blacklisted so far. But he knew that was only a temporary respite.

And if Abigail was blacklisted, then where would she be? None of the drovers would take the larger herds to market. Suppliers would cut them off. Hands would no longer work for them. The Triple Cross would die without a proper burial.

He didn't answer Randy directly. "I'm countin' on you, Randy. We could lose everything."

An array of emotions flitted across the other man's face, but he settled for clapping Boyd on the shoulder. "Hell, it'll all work out, Boyd."

Still Boyd wondered, as he had every minute since Cameron's telegram had signaled an end to their interlude. But he nodded and then angled his horse back around, galloping across the field, the knee-high wild grass parting beneath the horse's hooves.

His suspects were multiplying. After Randy's revelations, Boyd had begun to watch Cameron O'Donnell, noticing that the man seemed quieter than before. Remembering the false accusations he had endured himself, Boyd was reluctant to call the man on his past. Yet he knew he couldn't allow a stranger to cripple the Triple Cross.

And if John Sims was working for Peterson, they would soon find out. Peterson was playing a wait-and-see game so far. Of course, that was provided he wasn't the one orchestrating the rustling or murder attempts. If he was, it was a clever cover-up for his actions.

And then there was Caruthers. Angry enough to spread rumors. And working for one of the men who'd voiced a claim on the Triple Cross. A land that had once offered protection now seemed threatening, dangerous.

Jem McIntire's words rang in Boyd's head. What if by walking away to save the Triple Cross he delivered Abigail into the killer's hands? Not to mention the thought of anyone else's hands on her body. Possessiveness gripped him, strong and hot.

It didn't help that he had to watch a string of suitors nipping at Abigail's heels like eager puppies. Except that these men had quite a bounty to inherit by marrying Abigail.

Muffling a curse, he rode toward the northern boundary. For now, he could protect the ranch and hope it would be enough to protect Abigail.

Abigail stared at Joshua Hodges in growing irritation. Despite his bumbling ways, he was becoming an annoyance she didn't need. He insisted on coming to call nearly every day in spite of her discouragement.

"There's a dance this Saturday night," Joshua told her, his neck and face taking on the unpleasant hue of freshly boiled beets. "At the livery. Most everybody'll be there. I'd be honored if you'd go with me."

She drew a deep breath to summon patience, reminding herself that this man had the grace and subtlety of an adolescent. An adolescent bull, that is. His perspiring body was encased in the stiff, ill-fitting suit he had worn the first time he came to call. He held his hat in equally sweaty hands. "Mr. Hodges—"

"Joshua."

"Joshua. I'm pleased that you thought about me, but I really can't go with you to the dance."

"Why not?"

Her brow puckered into a frown. This was the first time he had pressed for a reason. "That's really not something I want to discuss."

"Your time's running out," he said bluntly, plainspoken despite his red-faced bumbling.

"Maybe so, but my reasons are my own."

"As your prospective husband—"

"Don't say that." She swallowed her gorge of distaste. "I've been honest with you since you first came to call. My feelings for you are as a friend. That's all."

"Then the gossip about you and that foreman of yours is true."

Abigail blanched. Despite her relationship with Boyd, it unnerved her to have the knowledge thrown at her. She realized as her blood stirred that it also angered her to have someone like Joshua Hodges make such a sanctimonious proclamation. "I believe our visit's concluded."

"So you're not even going to bother to deny it?"

She stood up and to her relief saw that Miranda hovered protectively near the doorway. "I've found that people who listen to gossip only wish to believe the worst."

"Maybe that's because it's true," he countered.

"In that case, I wouldn't think you'd want to escort me to the dance," she answered quietly, her dignity still intact.

He glanced up and saw Miranda advance a few feet into the room. "I'll be going now."

"That would be best." Abigail started to escort him to the outer door, but he strode ahead, yanking the door open and leaving.

"Good riddance," Miranda said as the door slammed behind him.

"Another enemy." Abigail's voice held seeds of uneasiness as she turned to her housekeeper. "Just what I needed."

"None of them are goin' to take being turned down too well, Miz Fairchild." Her voice softened as she hesitantly added the next words. "There's a lot ridin' on the outcome."

"No need to dance around the truth, Miranda. I never entertained the idea that they were all enchanted with me."

"Not that they shouldn't be!" Miranda responded loyally.

"Thanks. But holding title to the ranch makes my attributes pale in comparison."

Miranda released a sigh. "Even if you could pick one of them over Boyd, it'd be hard knowing they're lookin' to a ranch instead of you."

"I never thought I'd be in a spot like this. My life has changed so much."

"So have you."

"You think so?" Abigail asked, wondering what the other woman meant.

"It's not something I can put in words." Miranda shrugged as her face screwed into concentrated lines. "It's more than just learnin' how to ride and run a ranch. You're different. You don't just sit aside and wait to see what's going to happen. You make it happen."

Abigail had never stopped to analyze the changes in her life, other than her love for Boyd. Perhaps she had grown stronger, more involved in what was happening. But she sensed it was a change she couldn't have made without Boyd. "Of course, if I hadn't gotten so involved in things and fired Caruthers, we wouldn't be battling the gossip."

Miranda was silent for so long that Abigail had to prompt her to answer. "What is it?"

Shrugging, Miranda ran her hands nervously over the sideboard. "Talk started before then. Not so much about Boyd but about how you went on the trail drive and all."

"Oh?" It occurred to her that if she had listened to Boyd's counsel she might have avoided all this.

"Maybe I shouldn't have said anything."

"No, it's true. I've been stubborn and willful, and all it's gotten me is trouble."

Miranda frowned. "Whatever made you change has been inside of you. If it hadn't come out now, it would have eventually. And maybe then you wouldn't have Boyd."

"I don't have him now." Despite her wish that she could have him forever.

Miranda dropped her eyes. "Sometimes a body has to give up a lot to get love, don't you think?"

"You're the one who reminded me that if I do, I'll be giving up what Michael died for. Remember?"

"I remember all right, Miz Fairchild, but I've had reason to do some more thinkin' about that."

"Would this have something to do with Mr. O'Donnell?" Abigail asked gently.

Miranda jerked her head upward, her cheeks flaming suddenly. "Do you know about that?" she asked in utter mortification.

Abigail smiled softly, having only put the pieces together in the last few days. "Not really. But your voice takes on a special quality when you speak of him. You look different, happier. He's a very nice man, Miranda."

"But I'm havin' the craziest notions," Miranda confided.

"Such as?" Abigail cocked her head, charmed by the soft blush that had settled on Miranda's cheeks. Her housekeeper's transformed appearance was startling, and amazingly Abigail realized that she was a very attractive woman.

Miranda stared at her hands, and Abigail realized with a start that they were trembling. "I want to have a baby," she whispered.

"That's wonderful!" A grin split Abigail's features, but Miranda's eyes were troubled as she raised them.

"At my age?"

"I realize some women start their families at a younger age, but they keep on having babies until they're much older than you."

"Then you don't think I'm crazy?"

"I think you're wise to grab your happiness while you can."

"Sounds like good advice for both of us."

So it did. Abigail stared out the window at the canopy of towering mountains, wishing she could follow her own advice.

A grin split Boyd's face for the first time in weeks, and he pumped Billy Kendall's hand.

"So you're gettin' married. Congratulations, Billy. Who's the unlucky girl?"

Billy blushed and ducked his head. "Elizabeth Danner."

"She's a beauty," Boyd acknowledged. "But what does she want with an ugly thing like you?"

"Dammed if I know, Mr. Harris. But she's gone and said yes." Beaming now, Billy shared a rare moment of camaraderie with his boss.

"Plannin' on a wedding soon?"

"That's what I wanted to talk to you about. Do you think Miz Fairchild will let us live in one of the houses on the ranch for married folks?"

"I don't see why not." Boyd knew that those houses were reserved for men with families who had either enough tenure or qualifications to deserve them. But he also knew the soft spot Abigail had for the young man. "Why don't we ask her?"

"She's done so much for me already," Billy said, glancing down at his leg. It had healed well, and his limp was only barely noticeable. "I hate to ask for a favor, but I'd sure like to marry Elizabeth soon."

Boyd knew it would take Billy a long time to save enough for his own home. It was one of the reasons many of the cowhands remained single. And lonely.

Together they headed toward the house, but spotted Abigail near the corral, standing next to her saddled horse. Boyd frowned. He didn't want Abigail leaving the safety of the immediate area.

"Abigail!" Boyd called out.

She turned, her smile including both Billy and Boyd.

Stumbling through the words, Billy explained about his upcoming nuptials and his request for housing.

"Certainly, Billy," she replied without hesitation.

"Me and Elizabeth are beholden to you. I don't guess she'd have said yes if I'd come home with one leg."

"Don't count on that, Billy." Abigail's glance shifted to include Boyd. "If you love someone enough, you take him for what he is, no matter what the sacrifice."

Despite his youth, Billy's gaze moved between Abigail and Boyd. It was clear that what he had heard was true. But he wasn't shocked or disappointed. They were the two best people he had ever known, and they deserved some happiness.

Then Abigail turned her huge, gentle eyes on him. "Would you like to have the wedding here at the ranch, Billy?"

"Yeah," Boyd chimed in. "Last time we had a party here, it was a stag dance. I'd like to think we could do better than dancin' with some musty old cowhands."

Billy grinned. "I'd like that. But you don't have to go to any trouble."

"No trouble, Billy. We'll have punch and cake, of course.

And a big barbecue for dinner." Abigail's voice lilted as she enlarged the plans. "And music and dancing, of course. Maybe some outside games for the kids."

Boyd rolled his eyes in Billy's direction. "Nope, she won't make a big thing out of this."

"I'd better get started planning. What date did you have in mind?" Abigail asked Billy.

He blushed again. "Soon as possible."

"Two weeks?" Boyd asked, knowing how anxious the young man was.

"But—" Abigail started.

"That'd be right fine!" Billy said with a smile.

"I'm sure Miz Fairchild can get things together by then." It would be a great diversion for her. Between the threats they faced every day and their own desperation, she needed something else to occupy her mind. He worried about the violet smudges shadowing her eyes and the fact that she had grown thin with worry.

"In two weeks?" she wailed, then saw both male faces. Billy's appeared crushed, Boyd's wore a signal, indicating remembered young love. "I'm sure that would be fine."

"Thank you both. Gosh, I never expected the house and a wedding and all. Wait till I tell Elizabeth." Billy was almost leaping for joy as he departed.

"A wedding in two weeks?" Abigail asked skeptically.

Boyd brushed his fingers across her cheek. "You can do whatever you set your mind to, Abby."

Her heart constricted. "You really think so?"

"Yep. I never knew a woman more capable."

Considering her inept behavior on the trail, it amazed her to hear him talk that way. "You don't have to say that."

"I wouldn't if I didn't mean it. You're brave and strong. You take chances." *And I don't know what I'll ever do without you.*

"It's because of you," she admitted. "I didn't used to be this way." *And I'll never be the same without you.*

His hand reached closer, sifting through the silk of her hair. "I just hope we can last two weeks until the wedding."

Her voice grew fierce, both for young Billy and his bride and for themselves. "We will. Somehow we will."

Looking into her eyes, he could almost let himself believe she was right. But a range war was starting, and they were the targets. In two weeks everything could be lost.

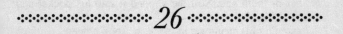

26

The weeks before Billy's wedding passed with trepidation. Everyone waited uneasily to see what would happen next. Abigail and Boyd spent the nights desperately counting the time they had left, praying that a full-fledged war wouldn't start.

Boyd doubled security, yet cattle continued to disappear, and another man was wounded while riding fences. But Peterson still hadn't pulled out everything in his armory, and Boyd knew it. At least Abigail had been temporarily diverted with the wedding preparations.

She had directed the women who cleaned the house mercilessly. Miranda, Lucy, and Rachel polished the furniture and wood floors with fragrant beeswax. Every lace table runner was washed and starched. Food was being cooked and baked around the clock. Only the presence of armed guards marred an otherwise storybook state of affairs.

As the day of the wedding dawned, Boyd wondered if people would stay away to show their disapproval or come to see if the rumors were true. Either way, he knew the wedding that Abigail was painstakingly planning would be an awkward event. Early that morning he had removed his belongings from the big house so that should anyone wander into the bedroom, his clothing wouldn't be discovered. It seemed strange to be back in his own house as he readied for the evening.

After wiping his cleanly shaved face with a fresh towel, he reached for his best shirt, the one Abigail had bought for him. The feel of the fabric against his skin reminded him of Abigail that first time. Her face, her endless giving.

Picking up her other gift to him, the pocket watch, he ran his fingers over the wild stallion on its surface. It seemed ironic that the carving represented freedom—something neither of them had. Still, he slipped it into his pocket and attached the chain.

Fastening his string tie in place, he took a deep breath of fortifying courage. Even though the wedding was being held on safe, friendly ground, Boyd knew he would have to suffer everyone's scrutiny and ultimately their judgment.

The night air was sweet as he covered the distance between his house and the main ranch house. Resenting the feeling of once again being on the outside, he knocked on the door, hearing the scurrying sounds inside. Miranda opened the door with a distracted air and waved him inside.

"Thought you were the preacher," she muttered, leaving him standing in the front hall.

"Not likely," he answered beneath his breath. But she was already in the next room.

The other women scurried about as well. One would almost think it was a normal time. But, thinking of the fine young man who was to wed that night, Boyd was glad they had taken time from their troubles to arrange this special ceremony.

Handpicked wildflowers from the foothills filled the vases, lending their scent to the pungent aroma of lemon and wax, while crystal bowls held equally fragrant dried herbs and flowers. Tapers were lit in the cut-crystal holders and the candelabra, filtering their fingers of light over the highly polished tables. Lace curtains danced gently in the breeze from the huge windows. The house represented Abigail at her best. Gracious, charming, and inviting. Once inside, it was easy to forget for a time the danger that lurked outside.

And then Boyd glanced upward at the curving staircase. Abigail moved—no, floated—downward. His breath caught at her beauty. A white lace and silk dress so delicate it must have been sewn by elves and christened with gold dust revealed her satiny shoulders and hinted at promising cleavage. It was a dress made to tantalize, to incite. One that was designed for the lady of wealth who wore it. He wondered bleakly if any of his Abigail remained.

But then she was at his side, the tempting fragrance of lavender wafting to tease his nostrils. Lifting her eyes to his, he could see them light for him, the passion still smoldering there, the love he desperately needed. She stood on tiptoe to brush his lips lightly with her own. The taste teased him, fortified him.

"You look very handsome." Her voice was husky, like the deepest tones of midnight.

"And you, Abby, are incredible."

She didn't blush; instead the heat in her eyes intensified. "I missed you tonight," she confessed. "I kept turning around and searching for you, but you weren't there." A soft, white hand slipped inside his, the contrast of pale against dark thrilling them both.

He started to remind her that it was something they both had to get used to, that this was the first step in their final separation, but he couldn't bear to spoil her happiness or dim her radiance. She was like a glowing candle, one he couldn't stand to see sputter and then go dark.

"Are you ready for the hordes?" he asked instead.

"I wonder if they'll come." Their minds had run the same course apparently. "I'd hate for Billy and Elizabeth to be disappointed."

"They won't be," he promised, "even if only our friends show up, along with hands it'll make a decent turnout."

She smiled, her lips trembling only a fraction. "You're right, of course. Elizabeth is still upstairs. I should check on her."

Reluctantly he released her hand and watched as she ascended the staircase. As the precious days and minutes ticked to an end, he wondered more and more how he would go on without her.

Upstairs, Abigail walked quickly down the hall and knocked on her bedroom door before entering. Elizabeth turned and then smiled as she recognized Abigail.

"How do I look?" Elizabeth asked anxiously.

"As beautiful as a bride." Abigail rearranged the pearl headdress and smoothed the folds of the exquisite gown.

"I still can't believe you let me wear your wedding gown," Elizabeth said in hushed, awed tones.

"We hardly had time to make one in two weeks," Abigail reminded her, a teasing note entering her voice. "Such anxiousness in young love."

Elizabeth pinkened becomingly. "But, still, it's far more than I ever dreamed of."

"Every girl should have one wonderful day to press into the memory book of her life. Once your children come and life's hardships descend, it's the happy memories that will lighten your load. This shall be the beginning of those wonderful memories."

"Billy will scarcely know me," Elizabeth whispered, staring into the cheval mirror at her reflection.

In his eyes, you no doubt look this beautiful every day."

"You're so wonderful, Miz Fairchild. Billy's told me, and I'm ever so grateful you saved his leg, but this . . . the wedding . . . the dress . . . It's more than I ever dreamed of. I don't know how we'll ever repay you."

Abigail pressed Elizabeth's hand, wishing her own problems were so easily solved. "You both deserve it. Just be happy, and I'll have my reward."

"I can guarantee that. I have the most wonderful man in the world."

Perhaps the second best, Abigail thought as she left Elizabeth to return downstairs. People were filling the hall and spilling into the parlor. So, apparently it was preferable to come and gawk rather than stay away.

The armed men who lined the rooms did not go unnoticed. More than one quizzical or knowing glance landed their way. Jem McIntire made a point of flanking herself next to Abigail while Reese stood solidly next to Boyd.

But soon the whiskey was flowing, and then the piano and fiddles began the wedding march. Elizabeth was a vision as she descended the staircase, and Billy's love shone in his clear eyes as he claimed her hand.

Reverend Filcher, who was deaf as a post, creaked

forward to start the ceremony, his voice booming through the room. Listening to the age-old vows, Boyd and Abigail's eyes met across the press of people.

To love, honor, and cherish, till death do us part. Silently they exchanged their own pledges.

A greater cheer went up as the young couple sealed their vows with a kiss. Turning to the crowd, they were swept into the midst as the music started up again. The rugs had been rolled up and the furniture shoved against the walls, leaving a wide-open space for dancing. The bride and groom waltzed gracefully to the first strains of their dance, before others joined in.

"This was a nice thing you did, Abby." Jem still stood next to her, almost as though daring anyone to approach. "It's so like you."

"They deserved a good start."

"From what I heard, Billy wouldn't be swirling around the room if you hadn't been on the trail drive."

Abigail waved away the words. "We can't be sure of that. I'm just glad he's okay."

"And how about you? Are you okay?"

Abigail's eyes clouded over. "I can't bear thinking that if a range war starts, men might be killed simply because I can't let go of the Triple Cross . . . or Boyd."

"The rumors are getting worse," Jem said bluntly. "You need to know that. Half the people here came 'cause they want to see what's really going on between you and Boyd."

"I can't say that surprises me." Abigail glanced around at her neighbors and wondered how many of them she could still call friends.

"It might be time to get some hired guns," Jem continued. "I know you don't like the idea, but I wish we had before, then maybe . . ."

Abigail knew Jem referred to Michael's death. Her friend had never absolved her guilt about his murder. "None of us could have guessed that Charles was the rustler, that he was so unbalanced that he'd turned into a murderer. You were simply a pawn in his plan. If you'd known, you'd have stopped him. You need to let that guilt go."

"Maybe. But I'll never forget that Boyd saved Reese's life." Jem's voice grew quiet as she met Abigail's eyes. "We've talked about it. Even if it means losing our place, we're standing by you and Boyd."

"Jem! You can't—"

"Yes, we can and we will. When and if a range war starts, we're throwing in with you. I've heard that Peterson, Hodges, and Johnson are all angling for the place. They're probably lining up now, each trying to figure out how to grab the Triple Cross faster than the other."

"Johnson? The man David Caruthers went to work for?"

"Now that you mention it, yes."

Abigail felt a sick pit in her stomach. The man she had fired on the trail, who had come back to spread his vicious gossip. "I could simply give up the Triple Cross," she said slowly. "Then no one would get hurt."

"That's not true, and you know it. Neither you nor Boyd would ever forget that you'd walked away from Michael's legacy. It'd be like a festering wound the rest of your lives."

Abigail battled the tears that threatened. "Oh, Jem. What are we going to do?"

"If Boyd simply owned his own place, any kind of place, you wouldn't have this problem. People might not like that he used to be a foreman, but they'd forget that soon enough. Especially when you reminded them that his family used to be ranch owners."

"I could put his name on the Triple Cross," Abigail suggested, wondering why she hadn't thought of this before.

Jem shook her head. "No. Then you'd still be the lady owner who married her foreman. The consequences would be the same."

"People are so thickheaded," Abigail fumed. "I don't care what others do."

Jem was slow in answering. "I used to think that way, too. After all, Charles was my father's foreman, and I was bent on marrying him. But it's hard to fight a way of life, standards that people set. They might not be right, but they're the code of this land, the foundation of our society." She paused, remembering. "I know now that's why my father never would have let me marry Charles. It's the reason Charles killed him, so he wouldn't stand in the way of getting what he wanted."

"You aren't comparing Charles to Boyd?" Abigail couldn't keep the horror from her voice.

"Of course not. I'm simply saying that it's hard to change the way people think. And I'm not sure you two can. Not unless you can magically transform Boyd into a ranch owner. Hell, I wish I had an answer, Abby. No two people deserve happiness more than you and Boyd."

Abigail glanced up and caught Boyd's gaze fixed on her. His longing and discomfort were both clear. It was difficult being the object of everyone's scrutiny. Even more difficult to remain on opposite sides of the room when they needed each other's support.

"Don't you want to dance with Reese?" Abigail asked her friend.

"Well, sure, but—"

"I'll be fine, Jem. Really. Either these people are my friends or they're not. I think it's time to see."

Reluctantly Jem left her side and approached Reese, who looked equally surprised at her request to dance. It didn't take Abigail long to reach Boyd, who stood waiting, hope and trepidation painted across his features.

"Aren't you going to ask me to dance?" she said as he stared at her hungrily.

"But, Abby—"

"I don't suppose there's a better place to find out just how my neighbors are going to react than in my own home."

She held out her hand, and he took it with a painful mixture of emotions. The music was soft and slow as they danced together over the polished oak floor. Then the music turned lively, and the room filled with the thumping of boots and the *whoosh* of skirts as couples whirled about gaily.

But in less than two turns, the noise faded away. Abigail's men continued to play the fiddle and harmonica, but the couples one by one stopped and moved off to the side of the room. Soon only Jem and Reese McIntire and Billy Kendall and his young bride remained alongside Boyd and Abigail.

Hisses of indrawn breath and muttered disapproval filled the room. As the song ended, Abigail and Boyd bravely turned to meet their neighbors.

And face their censure.

Individually and as a group, they had all withdrawn and locked forces against them.

Jem's housekeeper, Della, wheeled forward, accompanied by her husband, Pete, to join the isolated group. They flanked themselves with Abigail and Boyd. Miranda and Cameron O'Donnell also stepped forward to align themselves. Remarkably nearly all of their hands remained as well. Only a few stepped aside.

And the lines were drawn.

27

Overcoming Abigail's protests, Boyd decided it was time to play tough and hard. He recruited more than a score of mercenary gunmen from Texas to bolster the force of loyal hands that had remained with the Triple Cross.

To protect the boundaries, he ordered rifle pits dug for defense should the area nearest the house be breached. Supplies were ordered and men dispatched to bring them in from the railhead since the merchants in town had cut them off. Those supplies included a hefty number of rifles and ammunition.

Which had already been put to use.

The night after Billy and Elizabeth's wedding, the herd had been fired on. Animals were killed and maimed, the remainder scattered, some run off the cliffs, plunging to their deaths. In the cover of darkness, it had been impossible to identify the culprits.

Wagons of provisions were overturned, sometimes chopped up and then doused with kerosene and burned. Strategic waterholes were poisoned. In addition, other poison was scattered randomly in the grasses of the grazing land, causing steers to buckle over and bloat before the source of contamination was discovered.

The night before, hooded men had jumped the cowhands riding the northwestern boundary, beating them severely and then clubbing the cattle, killing at least fifty animals. One man had only regained consciousness within the last few hours. Both cowhands would be out of commission for a good long while. Yet the assailants remained unidentified.

Boyd chafed at the inability to discover who their
opponents were and confront them directly. Now, as he rode
the land, it seemed as though every ridge, every line of trees,
held possible danger. His back twitched as he realized anyone could be the next target.

And he was the most likely one.

If he was killed, then Abigail would be an easy victim,
with no one to lead the men in her defense. While he had
good men under him, none of them had the same stake in the
outcome as he did. Knowing that, he didn't take any
unnecessary risks. Bravery would have no meaning if he
was killed and Abigail was left without protection.

Riding toward the area that had been attacked last, he
heard an ungodly jangling sound burst through the air,
accompanied by gunfire and the shouts of several men who
remained out of sight. Kicking his horse into a gallop, he
heard the jangling combine with the sudden pounding of
hooves as cattle ran wildly in every direction.

Pulling up over the rise, he could see every man in the
vicinity riding frantically as they tried to stop the sudden
onslaught of wild horses that burst over the hill and into the
herd.

Boyd could scarcely believe his eyes as he watched
nearly a hundred wild mustangs plow through the milling
cattle. And the noise that accompanied them! Pulling out his
rope, he rode alongside one of the horses and lassoed it.

Boyd's horse, trained to stop when its rider had captured
a running steer, halted and held steady as Boyd dismounted.
It didn't take long to find the source of the noise. Cowbells
had been strapped to the horse's neck. In addition, rawhide
had been tied to its tail so that it would whip against the
terrified cattle as the horses galloped through the herd. It
was a mean and dirty trick, not unlike the others so far.

Boyd knew that if he rode over the rise, no one would be
in sight. Very few of the raids had come during daylight, but
this one had been successfully planned so that the culprits
would be far out of sight by the time anyone could ride after
them.

But no men had been wounded this time. Taking a

personal interest in every man, woman, and child on the Triple Cross, Abigail had a difficult time reconciling that injuries or death could be considered necessary in order to win.

Disgusted, Boyd removed the cowbells and rawhide, then released the wild horse. Glancing around, he knew that the sabotage would have done considerable damage. Already the herd was scattering far and fast. And many of the spooked animals would be injured or killed.

One thing was certain. After the herd was rounded up, it was time to confront John Sims. The man would no longer provide inside information to saboteurs.

Boyd's lips thinned into a grim line. No matter what it took, he'd stop him.

Exhausted and angry, Boyd neared the corral. Randy had told him John Sims had been assigned to work there for the day. John had cleverly set up the stampeding maneuver when he would be far enough away to avoid suspicion.

Boyd was half convinced to start the confrontation with fists rather than words. Knowing how shocked Abigail would be at the treachery, Boyd hoped to keep the knowledge contained until the man could be thrown into the territorial jail.

When Boyd reached the corral, John lifted his head, acknowledged his presence, and returned to his work. He was a cool customer, Boyd thought, his anger increasing. Dismounting, Boyd released the horse inside the corral, knowing he would deal with grooming the animal later.

"John."

"Evenin', Mr. Harris." John glanced at the setting sun. "Another nice one."

"I don't think so."

John's smile faltered. "There a problem?"

"You tell me."

But the young man only looked more confused. "No problem I know of."

"What do you call sabotage, treachery, knifing a person in the back?"

John stumbled backward, his Adam's apple bobbing desperately. "I don't know what you're talking about, Mr. Harris."

"Do you deny that you've been watchin' Miz Fairchild?"

John blanched, then turned a dull, ugly red. "What do you mean?"

"Everywhere she goes, your eyes are on her, trackin' every movement so that you can report to whoever's behind the takeover."

"That's not why!" John blurted out.

"What other reason could you have for watchin' her?"

"'Cause . . ." His voice turned into a miserable, embarrassed croak. 'Cause I love her."

"Love her?" Boyd echoed blankly, taken aback. That was the last excuse he had expected to hear, and it took the wind out of him.

But the agony on John's face looked very real. "Ever since I saw her. She's so beautiful and all . . ." His expression glazed over a bit, then turned fervent. "Then she came on the trail drive and fixed up Billy. . . . Hell, Mr. Harris, she's just like a beautiful angel."

Stumped, Boyd just stared. Was the whole of the territory going crazy? He wondered if he should be angry, jealous, or disbelieving. But the genuine misery on John's face precluded the latter.

"So you've just been watchin' her all this time?"

Miserably John nodded. "It's not like I could say nothin' to her, being's I'm just a cowhand."

The irony wasn't lost on Boyd, but he had to be sure. "Have you been approached by any of the other owners?"

John ducked his head, stared at the ground, then reluctantly lifted his eyes. "Hell, we all have, Mr. Harris. Been offered more pay to leave."

Boyd felt his gut sicken. "And?"

John shrugged. "Them that was leavin' are gone. Sometimes you can't put a price on loyalty."

Boyd thought of the scores of men who could certainly use that extra money, yet they had stayed, willing to risk their necks for Abigail Fairchild and the Triple Cross. "We'll match whatever they offered."

"If you want, Mr. Harris. But we'll be stayin' anyway. Least, I know I will."

"I misjudged you, John."

But the younger man only shrugged uncomfortably. "I might've thought the same thing." He paused, the mottled red creeping back up his neck. "You ain't gonna say nothin' to Miz Fairchild, are you?"

"Nope. A man's feelings are his own."

"Thanks, Mr. Harris. 'Cause I don't want to leave here."

"I am goin' to tell her about the pay offer, though. She needs to know so she can match it. But I won't tell her how I know."

John nodded slowly. "I 'spect that would be all right."

Boyd stared one more time at the young man. "I've had my share of being misjudged, and I never wanted to do that to another man."

Clear, young eyes met his. "For a lady like Miz Fairchild, I'd go after the devil himself."

Boyd felt the churning of emotions, appreciation for the loyalty, regret for the accusation, and renewed admiration for the lady who inspired them all. "Why don't you knock off early? I'll take care of my horse and shut up the barn."

The aroma of Henry's dinner wafted through the air. "That fried chicken is smellin' mighty good," John admitted.

"Then go enjoy it."

John didn't need any more convincing. Obviously his confession had been painfully embarrassing, and escape was welcome.

After finishing in the barn, Boyd washed up at the pump and then returned to the big house, knowing he needed to tell Abigail about the pay issue, yet dreading it. She had grown very concerned about the men, involving herself in their lives, to the point that each person meant a great deal to her.

Glancing at the dining room, he saw that the table was set, but no one was seated. Sounds from the kitchen assured him that dinner was being prepared. Going to the sideboard, he uncorked a decanter of whiskey and poured a healthy shot.

A gentle swish of material sounded behind him. Turning, he sucked in his breath. Abigail stood directly behind him, dressed in a silk and satin confection that rivaled the one she had worn to Billy's wedding. Shoulders bared, revealing skin the color of blushed peaches, and a nipped in waist that drew his attention to the curve of her hips, she was a vision.

Boyd cleared his throat, yet his voice remained husky. "Is there a special occasion I didn't know about?"

Her smile was a combination of allure and devastating sweetness. "No, just dinner."

Dressed like an angel, he thought wryly. But then John Sims's words rang in his memory, intruding on the moment, taking him away from the fantasy she was trying to create, back to the reality they both hoped to avoid. "You look beautiful, Abby."

Her eyelids fluttered downward for a moment. "Thank you."

He enjoyed this coy and unexpected side of her. They hadn't had time for a proper courtship, yet he suspected she could give a man a merry chase.

"Can I pour you a sherry?"

She nodded, then accepted the drink.

"I'm not dressed for the occasion," Boyd said after emptying his glass, glancing down at his dusty denims.

"I just thought for one night we could escape all the ugliness."

Sighing, Boyd replaced his glass on the sideboard.

"What is it?"

"I hate to ruin what you've planned. . . ."

"Has something else happened?" she asked, dread lacing the words.

He thought of the ambush of wild horses that had stampeded the herd, but didn't think it was necessary yet to tell her about that since none of the men had been injured. "No one's been hurt," he assured her.

Her sigh of relief chimed in unison with Miranda's as she laid a platter on the table and rearranged the cutlery.

"But I did confront John Sims."

Abigail's eyes widened, worry and fear filling them. "What did you find out?"

"He's not the one we need to be worryin' about. I'm not sayin' that we don't have a traitor workin' from the inside, but it's not him."

"How do you know?"

"Trust me, Abby. It's not John Sims. And, yes, I know he watched you, but that was because he admired what you did for Billy Kendall," he improvised, wanting to assure her, but not willing to reveal John's secret. "Not many women can perform surgery like that."

A gust of air *whooshed* from her. "Oh."

"There's still someone working on the inside, givin' enough information that we're always just one step behind what's happening."

"Who do you think it is?"

Boyd shrugged. "John told me that he had been approached to leave. All the men have. And they've been offered more money to work elsewhere. Anyone needin' a lot of money is ripe for the takin'."

"Then why hasn't he left? Or said something?"

Boyd stared at her steadily. "Loyalty. Pure and simple."

He saw the sheen of tears in her eyes. "I don't deserve this. We're placing their lives in danger, yet they stay."

"I told John that we'd match the pay they were offered."

"Of course," she replied absently. "But it makes me want to ensure that they're out of harm's way. As long as the takeover attempts continue, that won't happen."

He reached inside his heart and closed it to the pain he felt. "Are you ready to call it off?"

"And lose you?" Her voice trembled as her skin paled even further.

Seeing the violet smudges beneath her eyes, Boyd felt a slash of pain at her vulnerability, her oversized heart that was being pulled in far too many directions. "You'll never lose me, Abby. Not until you say so."

He pulled her close, feeling the trembling of her limbs. As he held her in a comforting embrace, Boyd didn't notice the door to the kitchen swinging quietly closed and the figure slipping away.

Miranda didn't bother to knock as she entered the study, turning the lock in place behind her. Cameron lifted his head in surprise before a smile enveloped his features.

"Miranda, I'm glad to see you. If you've finished serving, we can have dinner together." But as she approached, the agitation on her face was clear, and he rose from behind the desk. "What is it?"

Feeling as though her heart would break, Miranda stared at him, this one man who had managed to breach the walls she had kept in place around her all her life. But she couldn't dismiss her suspicion. Even though she had given herself countless reasons for why he had been acting secretively. The yearning for love and a family was almost enough to make her turn her head and ignore what she had seen, what she still suspected.

Almost, but not quite enough.

"Cameron . . ." To her horror, unaccustomed tears pricked her eyelids, thickened her voice.

Instantly he was at her side, gripping her arms. "Tell me, Miranda. Has something happened?"

"I hope not," she whispered. Lifting her gaze to his, she searched the depths of his ebony eyes, seeing that they looked guileless. Fervently she prayed that they would remain so. "Someone has been workin' from inside, givin' enough information so that the Triple Cross can be taken over."

The light in his eyes shifted. "And you think it's me?"

She could see the wounded, haunted expression that replaced his concern. And, more painfully, the resignation.

"When I was in here a few weeks ago, you hid something in your desk. I didn't think much of it at the time, but . . ." She screwed up the remainder of her courage. "You are privy to all the money matters. . . ."

"And I could do more damage than anyone else?"

She lowered her head. "I don't want to believe that. You're a decent, kind man, but I couldn't live with myself if I didn't stand beside Miz Fairchild, too."

His hand reached out to cup her chin. "What do you believe, Miranda?"

"That it's something else, something that has nothin' to do with the ranch. Or that my eyes were playin' tricks on me."

He stared intently at her face. "No, your eyes were working just fine."

Releasing his hold on her, he stepped back behind the desk, unlocked the drawer, and removed a paper that was hidden deep under the ledgers.

Her heart constricting, she watched as he returned to her and offered the paper. Hand shaking, she accepted it. Her skill at reading was still rudimentary, and it took her several minutes to read and absorb what he had written. When she was finished, the tears slid down her face unchecked.

For it was a love poem.

Written to her. Declaring what they had yet to say to each other.

"I never dreamed . . ." Lips trembling, her entire body shaking with repressed emotion, she silently begged him to forgive her.

"I wasn't sure you were ready to hear how I felt about you," he said quietly. "We've talked about a future, but I didn't have the courage to let you know how long I've felt this way."

Her head bowed, she rubbed her fingers tenderly across the finely penned words. "I should have believed in you."

"I'm a man who's subject to suspicion."

"Not from someone who loves you."

Tension filled the sudden silence.

"Would you say that again?"

"I love you. Ever since you came here. So different than any man I'd ever known. My heart leaped into my chest just from havin' you walk into the same room. Until then, I figured I'd grown used to bein' alone. . . ." Bravely her eyes met his. "I don't think I could ever be alone again."

"And I think it's time for some straight talk. I love you, Miranda Abernathy. Every prickly, obstinate thing about you." His black eyes glittered with purpose. "Will you marry me? Have my babies? Share my dubious reputation?"

"Yes, Cameron, I will." The words came out in a sob. And then she was in his arms, the light from the oil lamps flickering over them both.

His voice deepened into a husky drawl. "Did I hear the door lock behind you?" She nodded her head against his chest, and he reached over to blow out the flame in the lamp. "Good. Because I don't think we want to be disturbed."

Her answer was written in the kiss she offered him as the darkness cloaked them both.

28

Jem McIntire rode ruthlessly across the land that separated her ranch from Abigail's, not sparing her horse as she flew toward her destination.

Abigail stood near the corral speaking to Boyd when she spotted her friend barreling in at a breakneck pace. "That looks like Jem."

"She doesn't abuse an animal for sport. Something's wrong."

Leaping from her stallion, Jem didn't pause as her gaze swept to include both Abigail and Boyd. "There's trouble."

"We figured as much," Boyd replied.

"A train's been chartered from Denver," Jem started, looking as though she wished she didn't have to continue. "Loaded with men, horses, ammo, dynamite, and strychnine."

Boyd and Abigail sucked in collective breaths of disbelief. Whoever was behind the attempt meant to pull no punches. Which apparently included blowing them off the land.

"Do you know who it is?" Abigail asked, knowing she needed the information, yet dreading to hear the person named.

But Jem shook her head. "Only reason we heard is a friend of Reese's at the freight yard in Denver got word of the train and where it was headed. He sent us a wire. Figured it might be trouble."

"That's damn straight," Boyd muttered.

"They'll probably try cutting all our fences first," Jem

continued. "Run off the cattle and make it easier to ride through, then have a quick getaway."

Abigail stared hopelessly at Boyd. This was growing far too dangerous. She couldn't risk all their lives.

"We could set traps," Boyd told Jem. "Build bombs so that when the fence is cut, they'll go off."

"But that would take hundreds of bombs!" Jem protested.

"Not if we get the word out that we've covered every fence with them. Then it'd only take a few dozen to do the trick. Purposely set off one or two where someone'll see it happen. That should keep their fence cutters in their pockets."

"What if we do all this and they still get control of the Triple Cross?" Abigail asked.

Boyd turned to her, love and determination burning fiercely in his deep blue eyes. "We don't have a choice now, Abigail. That train will get here either way."

"What if we surrender?"

"To who?" he asked in frustration, wanting to win this battle for her, for them.

"You could wire Reese's friend," Abigail suggested desperately, not wanting to give up her ranch, but unwilling to lose lives over it.

Jem stared between them. "I'll ride to town tomorrow and see what I can find out." Mounting her horse, she stared down at her friend. "But be sure, Abby. 'Cause you won't have a second chance." Whirling the stallion about, Jem kicked the horse into a canter and then rode out of sight.

"Is this what you want?" Boyd asked Abigail, examining the shadows that chased across her face, lingered in her eyes.

"Of course not. I want the ranch for little Michael. I want his father's death to have counted for something." She paused, staring into the huge mountains that towered over them. "And, God help me, I want you. Even though I know that can't be."

He reached out to pull her close, but she held her hands out pleadingly.

"And I don't want our friends and the men who work for

us to die to make that happen. It's simply not right, or fair. . . ."

"When was the last time that life dealt us a fair hand, Abby?" She flinched, but he continued relentlessly. "Was it when your husband was murdered in cold blood? Or when I was too young to protect what was mine and lost it because my father made one mistake? One that cost him his wife, his ranch, and any happiness he had ever hoped for? Was that fair, Abigail? Or right? Was it fair when I got blamed for another man's thieving? And lost my reputation in the process? I don't think so. And I don't believe you do, either. So, what's it going to be? We going to walk away from this? Surrender everything? Or fight for what's ours?"

Her voice was scarcely a whisper against the rising wind. "Fight, Boyd. And I'll stand beside you every step of the way." *Even though there was no hope of winning. Because in the end we can't be together. And there'll be no greater loss.*

The explosion was deafening. The sun had barely risen; milky fingers of white still streaked the sky. Men poured from the bunkhouse, pulling on their revolvers as they ran.

Boyd and Abigail bolted from the kitchen table and ran toward the corral as well. Horses snorted in the confusion as saddles were thrown on them.

"Stay here, Abigail. Line the women in formation like we talked about. Five upstairs, ten down. Put Michael's crib in the hallway. And make sure there's enough ammo in the house before you lock up."

Pulling his head toward her, she kissed him fiercely, hoping desperately that it wouldn't be for the last time. "Be careful, Boyd."

His eyes traveled over her face as though memorizing her features, and she felt her heart constrict. If she lost him . . .

"Don't worry, Abby. I don't want to go and get blown up—I have too much to come home for."

Mounting his horse, he tore off alongside his men. Abigail started to raise her hand in farewell, but couldn't bear to make the gesture, instead lifting her eyes to the house, knowing she had to commandeer the forces inside.

Galloping down the ridge, they could hear the constant spurts of rifles discharging, the pinging sounds of bullets whizzing through the air. Boyd rode low over the horse, trying to contain his fury as he saw flames rising from the supply shed. A blazing hay wagon had been pushed up against the door, igniting the structure.

Boyd knew with dread and sinking certainty that a man was trapped inside. The peppering of returning fire assured him of that fact. The dam that controlled the river running between the Triple Cross and the Peterson spread had been blown to pieces. Water that had to be controlled to sustain the herd through the long, dry months was now flowing recklessly away.

"Hold it!" Boyd hollered as he pulled up his own horse.

Running blind into a volley of bullets wouldn't save the man inside. More likely it was a trap designed so they would do just that, losing a dozen men in the attempt. The men halted, staring at him in surprise as their mounts pawed restlessly at the ground.

"What's wrong?" Randy asked him, pulling at his horse to keep the beast under control.

"We need a plan or we'll all get shot to pieces. Who's in there anyway?"

"Billy Kendall."

Boyd's blood ran cold at the man's reply. If something happened to the young man, Boyd knew all the fight would go out of Abigail. She could lose the ranch, and he most certainly would lose her.

Hearing the pounding hooves of approaching riders, Boyd and his men scattered behind a line of juniper trees that offered scant protection. If reinforcements for their attackers had arrived, they would be hopelessly outnumbered.

But before they could fire, Boyd recognized the man in the lead. Reese McIntire!

"Hold your fire! It's McIntire and his men."

Boyd nudged his horse from behind the tree and into full view.

"We heard the explosion," Reese told him. "Anybody hurt?"

Boyd jerked his head in the direction of the line shack. "Not yet. But they've got Billy Kendall pinned down inside. I think it's time to wire the territorial marshal for help."

Reese shook his head slowly. "Telegraph lines have been cut. Found out when Jem tried to wire and see who chartered the train. There won't be any help from outside. It's just us, Boyd. Against half an army."

"'Bout the same odds we faced in the war, Reese. You still up to it?"

"Being married to Jem keeps me in shape for a battle most every day." Reese grinned, flashing white teeth against his tanned face. "You got a plan?"

"We know the lay of the land better'n these strangers, wouldn't you say?"

Reese nodded his head.

"You know that cave that runs underneath the ridge? Seems like if we used some of our own dynamite, it'd take down anybody sittin' on top of it, tryin' to shoot at Billy."

Reese's grin grew larger. "And it'd be a hell of a sight, wouldn't it?"

Boyd met his friend's eyes. "I hope so, 'cause if I'm wrong, we're liable to blow ourselves up instead."

Abigail paced the confines of the house. Marshaling her own troop of forces hadn't taken long. Thanking the stars for her steady practice with her gun, she was grateful that she had become a competent shot. It surprised her how naturally she had taken charge. With a wry smile she acknowledged that she was certainly a different person than she had been a few months ago.

She glanced out the window at Cameron, armed and decidedly dangerous, patrolling the exterior of the house. Clasping and unclasping her hands, she wondered for the thousandth time if Boyd was safe. Remembering vividly the day her late husband had returned for the last time, laid out in the back of a wagon, she tried to shake away the image. She couldn't bear one more loss.

A single shot rang out, and Abigail pulled herself from her musing and rushed to the window. Pushing aside the lace curtain, she couldn't see anything. Fear clutched her when she realized that included Cameron O'Donnell, who should have been patrolling directly outside.

A knock thundered at the front door, driving the fear through her in relentless waves. Miranda ran from the upstairs hall to the top of the staircase.

"Cameron?" Miranda mouthed, horror distorting her face.

Gripping her gun, Abigail held herself rigid as she neared the front door. Barely able to hold the weapon steady, she raised the barrel as a voice carried through the solid wood structure.

"Open up or O'Donnell's a dead man."

Turning her head to meet Miranda's stricken eyes, Abigail then faced the door and unlatched it. The wooden doors flew open as Cameron O'Donnell was pushed through, a bloody hole in his side evidence of how he had been ambushed.

Miranda started down the stairs, but Cameron's abductor shouted out, "Hold it, or I'll finish the job!" Then his face changed. "Or I might not aim right. Bullet could go up the stairs. No telling who I'll hit."

Cameron wavered unsteadily in front of Abigail, raising his eyes to plead with Miranda to stay put.

And Joshua Hodges watched them all.

Abigail felt a tide of fear far stronger than she had ever imagined. Bumbling, overanxious Joshua Hodges couldn't be the one! Not when Edward Peterson had declared his intentions so clearly. But Joshua wasn't bumbling. Instead he shoved Cameron inside, uncaring as the other man hit the tile floor, the blood flowing in a terrifying fashion.

"I can't believe you're doing this," Abigail whispered.

"Believe it, Abigail. You could have had it the easy way. I offered to marry you, even to keep that brat of yours, but you were too good. Thought I didn't know you were looking down that snooty nose of yours, thinking I wasn't good enough for the likes of you." He snorted, a dangerous feral sound. "You, a woman who spreads her legs for a foreman, thinking you're not good enough for Joshua Hodges. My ranch might not have been as big as yours, but at least I owned mine." He pushed even closer, the spittle near his mouth flying as he forced out the words. "Well, now, missy, I'll own the most land in the territory. 'Cause I'll have the Triple Cross as well."

"You won't get away with this." Abigail tried to bluff, knowing there was no one to defend them. Cameron O'Donnell was their only defense, and he lay horribly still on the floor where Joshua had pushed him.

"But I will. I tried to hold on until you got Cushman's spread as well, but you kept saying no. I ran out of patience."

The sudden sound of approaching horses filled the space behind the open door. It didn't sound like a large group, but it could be help. Or reinforcements for Joshua.

"What the—?" Joshua started to whirl around. But first he grabbed the gun from Abigail's hand before she could react. Tossing the weapon across the hall, it skidded out of sight as he clamped a burly arm around her. "Keep your mouth shut or you'll get the first bullet."

"I don't care," she declared, struggling against his hold, hating the smell of his breath as it grazed near her face.

"You'd better, or I'll shoot the first man of yours I see. If I'm lucky, that'll be Boyd Harris."

Abigail stopped struggling immediately. Her body went slack and dead still. And to her horror, it *was* Boyd who reached the door first, stumbling into the grotesque tableau.

"Hold it, Harris. One wrong move and the lady dies."

Boyd stared between Hodges and Abigail. "You were the one behind all this?"

"You don't believe it, either?" Joshua laughed, a humorless sound. "But then you never were very bright. When you managed the Bar S, I thought sure you'd figure out how the cattle slipped over the boundaries before Charles hid them on the Cushman spread."

"You?" Disbelief filled Boyd's face as he stared at the man who had engineered the ruin of his reputation. "Why?"

"You really are stupid, Harris. I did it for a cut of the profits. Charles had his own strange reasons for wanting the Whitaker spread, but I wanted the money to build my herd and my ranch. Nothing too complicated."

"Or too low to ruin another man's reputation?"

Joshua shrugged, pulling Abigail tighter against him. "If you'd been smart, you'd have left, and the lady would have agreed to marriage, saving her a nasty end."

A noise near the door made all their heads swing in that direction. Randy Kreiger was braced in the open doorway, his gun drawn.

"You were the one who ruined Boyd?" Randy asked, anger lacing his words.

"That's in the past," Joshua spit out. "Get a rope and tie up Harris."

Boyd turned and stared at his friend, disbelief and bone-deep disappointment filling his face, coloring his voice. "Why, Randy?"

"For the land, don't you see? Joshua's gonna give me enough to start my own place."

"After you murder all of us?" Boyd asked. "You think he's going to let you go, knowin' that?"

"No, we're not killin' anybody. Just runnin' you off."

"Is that right, Joshua?" Boyd turned and pinned his stare on the man, never losing sight of the fact that Joshua still held a firm grip on Abigail.

But Joshua directed his words to Randy. "We'll have to get rid of the main troublemakers. But then the rest of them can leave."

Randy's gaze darted between Abigail's stricken face and Boyd's uncompromising stare, then he turned to Joshua. "I told you all along I'd scare 'em, but no killin'. I like to have murdered Miz Fairchild when I pushed her in the river. I didn't know it was risin' so fast. That was bad enough." Randy shook his head. "No, I'm not killin' nobody."

"You'll do as I say, or I shoot you first."

Sunlight glinted on the barrel of Randy's gun as he pointed it in Joshua's direction. Seeing his chance, Boyd lunged at Joshua. His gun went off, the bullet heading for his target. Randy's face went still with surprise and shock before he buckled to the floor.

Boyd thrust Abigail out of Joshua's reach as the men fought for the gun. Bodies rolled over the wooden floor, spurs digging in and hitting the high polish, the men's grunts filling the otherwise shocking silence.

Abigail searched frantically for the gun she had been carrying before Joshua knocked it from her hands. Crawling on her knees, she swept the carpet aside, overturned the table and nearly wept with frustration. Then she spotted it nearly obscured by a planter. The metal was cold as she grasped it.

Feeling the heavy, deadly weight in her palms, she hesitated, then stared at the two men. It was difficult to know who would win, but if Boyd lost . . .

Willing her hands not to shake, Abigail raised the weapon. This was no field target, no stalwart tree, but a human life. Fixing on the grappling bodies, Abigail saw Joshua's hands close on the gun the men fought over. Praying she wouldn't mistakenly hit Boyd, Abigail pulled the trigger.

The deafening roar filled the entry hall. Shaken out of her paralysis, Miranda ran down the stairs. Boyd pushed Joshua's leaden weight off of him, examined the man, and rose to his feet.

"Did . . . did I kill him?" Abigail asked, her voice sounding oddly detached, totally horrified.

"No, the bullet grazed his head. It was enough to knock him out. But he'll live."

Relief made her hands shake as shock set in. In the distance she could hear Michael crying and the sounds of Miranda's terrified words as she examined Cameron. And somewhere she registered the fact that Randy might very well be dead. But Boyd stood strong, tall and alive.

"I love you, Boyd Harris. And nothing will ever keep me from you." Then she collapsed in his arms, sobbing as though she would never stop.

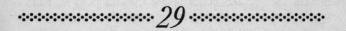

Abigail rode back toward the ranch, humming as she studied the peaceful pale blue sky, the clouds that scuttled by. Even if a storm were to open up and drench the fragrant fields of buffalo grass and wildflowers, it wouldn't dampen her good spirits.

All of Joshua Hodges's hired guns had been shipped back to parts unknown, and the man himself was in the territorial jail awaiting trial. She thought briefly of Randy Kreiger, who had nearly died from Joshua's bullet. His desire to have a place of his own had nearly cost his life, and he would spend a good many years in jail; but she felt he had redeemed himself by refusing to kill them. He had admitted that he was the one shooting at her that day, but that he had purposely missed, hoping to scare her into leaving.

She still didn't believe he was basically a bad man, just one who had been consumed by the need to have something of his own. He'd been tempted by someone who had no compunction in using him to further his schemes.

Turning into the Triple Cross, she trotted up to the barn. She slipped off Dolly's back and led her inside. Billy Kendall accepted the reins, his shoulder still in a sling, but otherwise in good shape from his ambush in the supply shed, thanks to Boyd's quick thinking. They had blown the supports from the ridge and won the advantage. She reached for the saddlebags and unhooked them, draping the soft leather over her arm.

"Do you know where Mr. Harris is?"

A shadow crossed Billy's face. "Up to the big house."

It was an unlikely place to find Boyd in the middle of the day. "Thanks. How's the arm?"

"Fine. It was nothin', ma'am."

Her eyebrows quirked at him. For such a young man, he certainly had undergone quite an indoctrination between his wounded leg and the bullet in his shoulder. But he had escaped the line shack with only a minor wound.

They had much to be grateful for. While Cameron O'Donnell's injuries were more serious, he, too, would mend. And judging from the smiles she had seen him and Miranda exchange, she expected to attend an autumn wedding.

Reaching the main house, she slipped inside and walked quietly up the stairs. Boyd had reclaimed his room in the house the day after Billy and Elizabeth were married. Wandering down the hall, Abigail reached his room and started to knock. The door was partially open, and she saw his things folded neatly on the bed alongside his saddlebags as he emptied a drawer. Quietly she eased the door open wider.

"Are you going somewhere?"

He whirled around. "I thought you were out visiting."

Her voice was dry. "Apparently."

"When I get near you I can't think straight. I make up my mind and next thing I know, I'm doin' what you want."

"Is that so?"

She sidled closer, and he put out his arms to stop her. "Don't do this, Abigail. For once in my life, I've got to do the right thing."

"Is the right thing leaving a child who thinks of you as a father and a woman who loves you?"

"I won't put you through this hell again, Abby." He fisted a hand and reached out to skim his knuckles over the satiny length of her cheek. "I love you too much."

His arm fell to his side, but she took his hand, lacing her fingers through his. "Were you just going to ride away? Without a goodbye?"

A suspicious brightness lit his eyes, and his Adam's apple

worked. "Don't you know I can't ever say goodbye to you? I'd sooner rip out my soul."

"Then stay, Boyd."

He raked a hand through tousled hair, his face twisted. "You're too important to me, Abby."

"But if you could meet me on the same terms, as owner of your own ranch, you'd stay?"

"Don't talk foolish, Abby. You've known that all along. But that's not goin' to happen, and I'm not goin' to lay you open to another attack. So Peterson didn't have a chance to carry through this time. You think he'll hesitate next time? Nope, you and the ranch would be vulnerable, ripe for the pickin'."

Abigail backed away and tossed the saddlebags she held on the bed. "Look inside."

"What—"

"Just look."

She watched as he untied the rawhide string holding the bags closed. A paper rustled as he withdrew it. It was a deed of title. He sank to the bed, and she joined him.

"This is made out to me," he said in awe. "For the entire Cushman spread."

"He's dying," Abigail told Boyd gently. "He has only a few months left. You know he's been a broken man since Charles was caught. His health has gone downhill steadily. Since he had willed his place to me anyway, I simply asked if he could deed it over to you now. I explained that things would remain as they are until he passed on. That he could get to know you and see that you're the best person to leave his ranch to. That you're the kind of man who'll treat his men well."

"And he agreed?"

She nodded. "There was no reason for him not to. He still hasn't recovered from what Charles did. It's hard for a man to accept that his son is a thief and murderer. He wants to do everything he can to make up for what Charles stole from me. He knows he can't bring back little Michael's father, but when I told him that our happiness was tied up with yours, he agreed to deed you his ranch."

Shock settled over Boyd's features as he reverently touched the paper. "My own place. Finally."

"I thought we could wire your father and see if he would like to settle here as well," Abigail suggested, "since he still hasn't found another home."

Boyd dropped the paper and pulled her close, shoving aside the clothing and saddlebags on the bed in one sweep. "What did I ever do to deserve a woman like you?" he asked raggedly, holding her tightly, as though afraid she might disappear.

Her fingers gently eased over his brow and plied through the thick locks of his hair. "I keep thinking that I'm dreaming," she answered instead. "That someone's going to pinch me and tell me that you can't be mine, that I'll have to give up everything." She met his sapphire eyes, a promise searing in her own gaze. "But that would be all right. I'd already decided to do that."

"What?"

"I didn't think of Randolph Cushman until late last night. After you were asleep. I'd already decided to give up the ranch and go with you."

"Abigail!"

"What else could I do? You had my heart, my soul. I couldn't let you leave without the rest of me."

"But the ranch—"

"Is just a piece of property. It all fell into place . . . just came clear to me last night. Michael wouldn't have wanted his son to grow up in the shadow of danger, resented by some man who'd married me and taken him in, just to get control of the Triple Cross. And I truly believe that Michael would have wanted me to be happy as well. And I could never be happy without you."

"I can't believe you were going to give everything up for me."

"You were willing to sacrifice your happiness for mine." Tears pooled in her eyes, then slid down her cheeks. "But without you I would have died inside, and nothing would have ever resurrected me."

His lips closed over hers, greedily at first, then tenderly as he pledged his love with gentle caresses and growing passion. His hands framed her face, and he stared intently at the eyes that always held kindness but could be kindled to flash with sultry allure, smolder with passion. If he was lucky enough to be at her side in fifty years, he knew he would always see her face as it was now. Timeless. Matchless. And, thankfully, shining with love.

She reached up to pull him closer, molding their bodies together as she offered herself to him. His fingers danced over her, worshipping each inch of skin as he peeled away her linen shirt.

Abigail watched his strong hands as they pulled off her boots and then carefully unrolled her stockings, his fingers cupping the sensitive instep, then sliding upward over her legs as he dispatched her breeches. Liquid heat consumed her as he unfastened her camisole and pantalets, tossing them aside.

Happiness filled her as she tugged at his clothing with matching fervor and then reveled in the velvety texture of the skin that abraided her own. Knowing that he was hers for all time flooded her with an intense heat, nearly as great as the one he created with his touch.

Boyd held her reverently, his hands slipping over the satin of her skin, through the raw silk of her golden hair. Like a man recovering from a coma, he savored each sensation, devoured each taste, drowning in the feel of her.

"I won't want to stop for years," he threatened.

"Or centuries," she promised.

His lips dipped to taste the honey of her mouth, as the sweet smell of lavender wafted from her skin. "You are an angel," he whispered, knowing in that instant that he had been granted a very special gift in this woman.

"And you are my shining knight," she replied, her breathing ragged as he nipped at the bud of her hardening nipple.

Tenderness welled up inside him, now that the restraints had been lowered, the barricades removed. Marveling at his good fortune, he felt the final reserve in his heart disappear.

She had offered him everything, and he could do no less for her.

"I love you, Abby."

A sob caught in her throat. "And I love you."

He kissed the tears from her eyes. "Will you marry me, Abigail? And have more brothers and sisters for Michael?"

"Yes, Boyd . . . I never want to let you go."

He buried his face in her throat, thanked the fates for her, and felt Abigail's responding shudder.

The emotion rocked them both.

Sunlight dappled through the lace curtains, embracing their reckless hearts, sealing their love.

"Forever, Abby."

"And always."

The author welcomes mail from her readers. You can write to her: c/o the Publicity Department, The Berkley Publishing Group, 200 Madison Avenue, New York, New York 10016.